Praise for Amy Greene's

LONG MAN

"A story that forces us to examine our relationship with nature, our understanding of community and, significantly, of social class. . . . [Greene] lends this Depression-era story a moral and ethical vibrancy that we should all pay attention to."
—*Pittsburgh Post-Gazette*

"A tense tale of the sacrifices people make in the name of progress."
—*New York Post*

"Exquisite. . . . Greene's prose is as mesmerizing as the story she weaves. Readers will never forget this vividly drawn landscape. . . . [The novel's] breathtaking suspense and images will haunt me forever."
—Jill McCorkle, author of *Life After Life*

"Like Greene's debut, *Bloodroot*, the prevailing tone of *Long Man* is solemn, elegiac. . . . Greene allows the back stories of this small but rich cast of characters to overlap in places, like thin pleats in a skirt."
—*Toronto Star*

"Greene even-handedly renders this lost and mostly forgotten world to perfection."
—*The Free Lance-Star* (Fredericksburg, VA)

"Rich and absorbing. Equal parts mystery, family saga, and backwoods romance, *Long Man* captures the collision of hardscrabble folk with the unstoppable modern world."

—Stewart O'Nan, author of
A Prayer for the Dying and *Emily, Alone*

"*Long Man* reads like a painting—the kind that unravels from a scroll, with a landscape that moves through space and time.... Greene, born and raised in East Tennessee, evokes [beauty] with the simplest strokes."

—*The Greenville News* (Greenville, SC)

"Vibrant.... The novel grapples with real questions about our relationship to nature and the price of progress, even as it delivers a story as touching and timeless as a folk tale."

—*Nashville Scene*

"One of the best young chroniclers of contemporary Appalachia.... *Long Man* dramatizes historical events that are still controversial today and raises issues that will resonate strongly."

—*Mountain Xpress* (Asheville, NC)

"A gem.... *Long Man* is so palpably real that I feel I've spent the last few days actually living in Greene's corner of Depression-era Tennessee. It is a special book—a beautiful piece of work."

—Steve Yarbrough, author of
Prisoners of War and *The Realm of Last Chances*

Amy Greene

LONG MAN

Amy Greene is the author of the national bestseller *Bloodroot*. She was born and raised in the foothills of East Tennessee's Smoky Mountains, where she lives with her husband and two children.

amygreeneauthor.com

Amy Greene is available for select speaking engagements. To inquire about a possible appearance, please contact Penguin Random House Speakers Bureau at speakers@penguinrandomhouse.com or visit www.prhspeakers.com.

ALSO BY AMY GREENE

Bloodroot

LONG MAN

LONG MAN

A NOVEL

Amy Greene

VINTAGE CONTEMPORARIES
VINTAGE BOOKS
A Division of Random House LLC
New York

FIRST VINTAGE CONTEMPORARIES EDITION, MARCH 2015

A portion of this work first appeared in
Appalachian Heritage 41, no. 4 (Fall 2013).

The Library of Congress has cataloged the Knopf edition as follows:
Greene, Amy.
Long Man : A novel / Amy Greene. — First Edition.
pages cm
1. Dams—Tennessee—Fiction.   2. Abduction—Tennessee—Fiction.
3. Missing children—Tennessee—Fiction.   4. Tennessee—Fiction.
I. Title.
PS3607.R45254L66 2013   813'.6—dc23   2013018846

Vintage Books Trade Paperback ISBN: 978-0-307-47687-6
eBook ISBN: 978-0-307-95846-4

Book design by M. Kristen Bearse

www.vintagebooks.com

Printed in the United States of America
10 9 8 7 6 5 4 3 2 1

For my mother and father

LONG MAN

In the summer of 1936 there was one woman left on the mountaintop where the river's headwaters formed in rocks ages old and shining with mica, the sediment washing down to tinge its shoals yellow-brown. Most others with her last name had died or moved on decades ago. Though darkness came to her high place first she could climb to this limestone ridge overlooking the cornfields and see daytime lingering in the valley town below. She would stand shielding her eyes until her legs grew tired. Then she would lower herself to the rocky edge and take off her brogans to rub her sore feet. She would watch with her knees gathered up as the last light mellowed into dusk, falling down the piney bluffs. Before half of the homesteads were razed the lowering sun would stain the tin roofs of houses and barns, deepening the rust to oxblood. Gilding wheat sheaves and tobacco rows, shading red clay furrows. Last summer she might have heard a farmer calling in his cows. She might have heard workers on scaffolds calling to each other over the rumble of cranes and bulldozers, steam shovels gouging the cliffside above the river and dumping out rocks to be crushed for the cement mixer. But now there was only stillness and silence besides the tree frogs singing as twilight drifted toward night. This time next year if she came up here looking for a little more light she would see only miles of endless blue lake.

Long before most of them were run off their land the woman's neighbors in the valley had stopped seeing her, even when she came

down among them. But she kept an eye on them. Looking to the
southeast she could see the dam out near the Whitehall County
line. It stood over two hundred feet high but from up here it seemed
small, wedged between shoulders of limestone with the river wend-
ing downstream through the forested humps of the foothills to its
base. Standing on the riverbank, it was grand enough to steal her
breath. Though the woman's hair was still dark, her face unwrinkled
except at the eye corners, the dam made her feel old. The Methodist
preacher claimed it went against nature but there was nothing he or
anybody else could do to stop it. It took two years to build, billows
of grit from tunneling and excavating bitter in her mouth and dynamite rocking the ground under her feet when she walked to the market. Freight trucks, tractors and the axe men of the clearance crews
blocked the road. Behind the power company's concrete wall, on the
upstream side of the river, the water was rising to form a reservoir
that would drown the town of Yuneetah.

The woman eavesdropped on the talk of her neighbors. They said
it would take a year or longer for the whole town to disappear. But
this spring there had been heavy rainfall and the lake was swelling
faster than expected. Since the dam gates closed on April 30, water
had already moved into the kitchen gardens of the houses nearest
the site, soaking into their foundations, tasting the minerals in the
boulders settlers had hauled with oxen down from the bluffs in 1786.
Soon the growing lake would spread over grassy hillocks dotted with
clover and the chicory edging the roadsides. By the end of the year
lagoons would be made from clefts in the mountains. Fish would
swim in dens once inhabited by foxes. The reservoir would eventually reach sixteen miles wide, spilling across the lowlands the town
had occupied since two brothers put up a lean-to shed along the
riverbank to trade with the Cherokees and a settlement sprang up
around it. The water would keep flooding backward from the base of
the dam over acres of farmland and timber, over the Baptist church

nestled in a copse of pines, over the Methodist church with its neat
white parsonage, over the post office and the druggist's and Gilley's
Hotel, until it reached the marble steps of the courthouse. By August
a hundred families would be evacuated from their dwellings of log,
brick, clapboard and stone. Next summer all of Yuneetah would be
underwater.

But the woman wasn't mourning the loss of the town. She had
done without neighbors for the better part of her forty-four years
and wouldn't miss them. She was thinking of the apple tree. When
the cicadas came each season she remembered it standing in a hayfield old and alone with its fruit. In summer she and her sister used
to follow a winding rut down from the hollow and the white-haired
farmer would give them a bushel basket to fill. Before the leaves
turned this autumn, the tree would be gone. Like her sister. She had
managed to forget the others. Her mother whose plaits unloosed
swept the ground and her father whose Cherokee blood showed in
the glare of the lanterns he carried out hunting. But the memory of
her sister stayed with her. For sixteen years they lived together in a
house hewn from the timber and bedrock of the mountain. A two-
room shack with puncheon floors and a kitchen tacked on the back,
the shake roof buried under honeysuckle in summer and the chimney hung with dead vines in winter. At night they lay in each other's
arms with their dark locks blending together, unable to tell where
one sister ended and the other began, keeping warm in a nest of blankets and each other's hair. Until the day the woman's sister ran off
to live with the white-haired farmer and eat all the apples she could
hold.

Now the woman had the shack to herself. The last to go had been
her grandmother, dead fifteen years. When snakes slithered behind
her walls, even copperheads, she let them be. Long combs of wasp
nest lined the rafters. She welcomed anything but her own kind. It
wasn't that she trusted the copperheads or wasps more than she did

people but animals tended their own business. The woman had chosen her solitude. She liked her house buried in honeysuckle vines that pried into the foundation cracks and wound up the broken windowpanes to make nights sweet in the room where she slept. She liked napping in the heat of the afternoons and making snowshoes for the rambling walks she took when the deep snows came. She had forgotten what hungry meant, growing used to eating no more than it took to keep alive. She had developed a taste for groundhog and muskrat. She had heard about a Depression going on but saw no evidence of it herself. She didn't understand the power company's reasoning. She didn't need electric lights when she could see by the sun and moon. She had the spring and the earth to keep her food from spoiling. She had a washboard for scrubbing clean her dresses. If a person didn't come to depend on material things, it wouldn't hurt to lose them. Not like it hurt to lose a sister.

Most of the woman's kin were buried in the hollow graveyard, but on the farm at the foot of the mountain there lived a three-year-old child with her sister's face. Last summer the woman had gone barefoot through the dry hayfield weeds with a bushel basket for apples, grasshoppers flying before her. She had found the child playing under the tree with a dog, low boughs crooked around them like leafy arms. If the dog hadn't barked the woman might have taken the child's hand and led her to the river where she used to go with her sister. Where the water was broadest a birch leaned over with its roots submerged, touching the surface as if to sip from it. They would scoot along its arched trunk as far as they could to drape themselves over its sturdiest limb, wetting their trailing fingers. Sometimes turtles shared the birch with them, snugged in the algae-bearded forks of its branches, heads tucked in and shells dripping sleek black. In the mornings mist cloaked the river so thick it was hard to see the woods on the opposite bank. If they were still they could watch herons fishing from the rocks. At sundown deer crossed to the other shore, the current rippling out around their velvet brown hides, their white-tipped ears flicked back. The woman had called the child by her sister's name as they stood in the hayfield with fallen blossoms caught in their hair. Her sister was gone. But for the time being, the child was not.

On the last day of April the woman had perched on this overlook and watched most of Yuneetah clear out, some riding on tick mattresses among the heaps of chattel in their wagon or truck beds, the wheels of their mule-drawn carts and packed jalopies stirring the dust of the main road for the last time. The dam site was quiet these days, the dormitories the workers had lived in deserted. Only the child's mother, her sister's daughter, was holding out against the power company. The girl had been fighting to keep her land for two years, but she couldn't hang on to it for much longer. Looking over the hayfield and the lone apple tree, the woman had an urge to rush down the footpath to the farm and beg the girl to take her along when she finally left. The woman had no right to ask. She had kept her distance. But the thought of her last living kin leaving her behind filled her with fear. Soon it would be too late. She had watched the county agents coming and going in their motorcars. They lifted their hats as they passed while she picked wild strawberries along the road, carrying her neighbors off in their backseats to see new farms that might replace the condemned ones. Most of the townspeople had never ridden in automobiles. It must have felt good to rest their feet, after all their lives walking wherever they went. They couldn't resist the change that had come, for better or worse. Nobody could stand alone against the government. The girl would surely give in. Even now a slow black Dodge was weaving its way into town, taking the curves between the bluffs like something with a carapace.

JUNE 30, 1936

Sam Washburn had driven for miles without seeing a house, the gravel road turning to dirt as it snaked around the rugged bluffs. There had been rain in the night and freshets poured off the rock ledges. The nearness of the woods made him nervous. It was midmorning but dark pooled under the lowest boughs of the pines. Shadows fell across the passenger seat and shifted on the arm of his suit coat. Sometimes the sun showed in darts through holes in the leaves, but otherwise the gloom was impenetrable. When he caught a glimpse of movement through the dense trunks, he nearly veered into a ditch. Leaning closer to the windshield he saw a line of wild turkeys, running as if away from something. Washburn lived in Knoxville, in a tall brick building on a street grooved with trolley tracks, above a busy coffeehouse with pigeons roosting in the letters of its sign. He wasn't born in the city, but he had grown used to it. In Knoxville, there had been electricity for over fifty years. Out here, privies leaned under dogwoods. Preserves lined root cellars dug into banks. Jars of milk cooled in springs. He'd been sent to Yuneetah before but not down this twisting back road, little more than a wagon trail, so narrow that branches of laurel and rhododendron scraped the roof and sides of his car. Washburn's stomach was sour. He wasn't looking forward to his task. He had come to talk a dangerous woman into giving up her land.

Washburn had read the reports. Her name was Annie Clyde Dodson. Last fall she'd ordered the appraiser to get off her farm and not come back until he was ready to give her what it was worth. He'd returned several times but she wouldn't be satisfied. She seemed unconcerned about the rising waters, even with a child in the house. Washburn had grown up near the river, on the outskirts of Knoxville. His father raised cattle. Each spring the floods raged through, ripping trees from the banks by the roots and gashing welts in the earth. Many seasons his father's calves were swept away. Once as a ten-year-old boy Washburn was walking back across the pasture from the barn when a storm came up out of nowhere, rain and hail beating down on his head. As he ran he saw the river rushing out of its banks toward him like something seeking vengeance. He fled from it with his arms pumping and his breath screaming in his throat, hail leaving red slashes across his cheeks. One stone had glanced off the bone under his eye and blacked it. He flung the feed bucket he was carrying aside and headed for the only tree he had a prayer of reaching, a tulip poplar with sturdy limbs. He dangled by one of them over the flood for an instant before finding purchase with his feet and lodging himself in the fork of the tree. He stayed there until evening waiting for the churning waters to recede, his house close enough that he could see the oil lamp burning in a front window as the sun lowered. Once the rain stopped his father came out with a lantern to find him. Surely Annie Clyde Dodson knew the river like he did. Washburn couldn't see how anything she owned was worth the risk she was taking.

Her husband was said to be more reasonable, but it seemed he could do nothing with his wife. Before the dam gates closed she'd gone around knocking on doors, asking her neighbors to sign a petition to send their congressman. Most declined to write their names. They were glad to get out of debt and move on. Yuneetah had been drying up for decades. The timber was overcut, the rail beds washed out. After the Great War, crop prices dropped and never recovered. It wasn't the dam that would kill the town. Yuneetah was already dead. Farmers had clung too long to the old ways. Planting on hillsides and letting fields lie fallow through winter, watching spring rains scour the topsoil away until nothing was left but a handful of limestone. As the woods thinned and pastures unrolled on both sides of the road, Washburn saw stretches of once grassy countryside furrowed with gullies of clay. Only as he drove closer to the riverbed did the land turn greener, where the floods had washed down rich settlings. The Dodson woman was the only holdout, a stubborn figure standing by the side of a grave, Washburn thought. He hadn't met his predecessor, the caseworker she ran off with a gun. All Washburn knew of the man was that he'd been born in Yuneetah, but it must have made no difference to her. According to the report, she wouldn't speak with him even on the porch. She kept a Winchester rifle propped within reach by the front door. The last time the other caseworker tried to visit she didn't wait for him to leave his car. She came down the steps with the rifle pointed. She didn't fire at him, but he wrote in his notes that he thought her capable of it. He refused to have any more dealings with her.

All the way down the road from Knoxville, Washburn had tried to think how he might handle Annie Clyde Dodson. What he might do if she pointed a rifle at him. He could picture her, like the other farmwives he'd met during his time in Yuneetah. Their skin toughened by field work, hands raw from the lye soap they made and washed with, hair the color of the dishwater they dumped out their kitchen doors. They had watched with hard eyes as Washburn appealed to the patriotism of their husbands, as he talked about the benefits of flood control and electric power. They had made their disapproval known without speaking it. If they hadn't been taught since childhood to submit to their men, more of them might have taken up guns.

For months he'd sat with these people in their front rooms and drunk coffee at their kitchen tables. He had eaten with them at McCormick's Cafe and smoked with them on the porch of Joe Dixon's store. He was twenty-three and most of these men were younger with

wives and broods of children to feed. He knew how his shaved face
and neat hands must seem to them. His chief had told him to take off
his class ring before his first trip to Yuneetah but there was no use in
trying to hide his softness. No use in pretending he was anything like
them. He still didn't understand them, but he had found they appreciated forthrightness. Most of the time, all it took was respect to win
them over. After a worker was killed by falling rock when the mountain was blasted for an access road, he saw how they looked with
their brows knitted toward the southeast where the dam was going
up. Whatever it was to them, a blessing or a curse, it represented the
unknown. By then they had come to trust Washburn as much as they
could. He was able to reassure them. It was a death. But it was the
kind of death that had to come before a resurrection.

Before the power company hired Washburn, he was studying to
be a social worker at the University of Tennessee. He had missed
the Great War but there were other ways to serve. When he heard
the federal government was recruiting for the Reservoir Family
Removal Section, he went down to their offices in the Old Customs
House on the corner of Clinch Avenue and Market Street. The chief
liked Washburn well enough but had reservations about his age. He
thought the job might be too big for a man straight out of college.
In the end, Washburn was enthusiastic and the chief was shorthanded.
The removal process was breaking down in Yuneetah, he said, and
there were too many families the Relocation Service couldn't help for
one reason or another. With the dam going up faster than expected
they were in danger of floodwaters from the rains. Some families
were dragging their feet. Some were willing but lacked the resources,
and a few were refusing to cooperate. What they needed was personal
attention. Washburn was hired to convince them of the power company's good intentions and to solve any problems that might keep
them from selling. Those who still refused to move would be turned
over to the Legal Division. He would help them find work, make

sure their children were registered in new schools, establish relief cases on the county rolls wherever they ended up. Though Washburn had only two weeks of training before being sent into the field, until this day he'd encountered no real trouble.

Now he saw the lichen-blotched ladder of a board stile on a fence and glanced down to consult a scrap of paper scrawled with directions, knowing he was getting close. Beneath his suit coat, his white dress shirt was plastered to his skin. He was pouring sweat, as much from the prospect of staring down the barrel of the Dodson woman's rifle as from the stifling heat. When he raised his head the house had come into view across rows of corn. Most of the farmers in Yuneetah had harvested what crops they could early and taken them to market before leaving town, but not the ones living here. The place looked as the other caseworker had described in his report, a two-story clapboard with a covered porch and a fieldstone chimney. There was a smokehouse and a corncrib out back, a barn on the verge of a hayfield with one crooked tree. Past the hayfield, pines marched uphill into the mountains. On the other side of the house were more thick woods. He turned off the road onto a track alongside the cornfield dividing the farm from the looming mountainside. Weeds slapped at his car doors and grasshoppers sprang across the hood. His wheels jarred and bumped over shelves of rough limestone, rocking the car on its springs. Once he was past the shade of the cornfield the sun shone bright on the overgrown lot that fronted the house, the piney swelling of the hills dark in contrast. Washburn had still formed no definite plan for facing the Dodson woman. He couldn't concentrate for the chirr of cicadas. The humidity had brought them early. When he stopped the car and got out, the sound hurt his ears.

Washburn started for the porch but paused when he saw her already standing there with a dog at her side, as if she'd been waiting. As if she had watched him come. He didn't know how he had failed to notice her there on his way up the track. She seemed to have materialized. What startled him even more than her waiting presence was how little she resembled the farmwife he'd been picturing. She was around his age, in her early twenties. It was her bearing that struck him most, how straight she stood, unlike most of the women in Yuneetah with their backs curved over their sunken bellies. He shaded his eyes against the sun and looked up at her. She towered over him. His first instinct was to turn and go back to the car. There was no way to do what was asked of him. She would not be moved. He glanced around, hoping her husband was at home. He had read the reports, but nothing prepared him. Something about her fierceness made her beautiful.

It was an effort to cross the neglected grass and approach the porch, its whitewashed posts drifted over with soot. He had already made it farther than the other caseworker without being shot at and forced himself to keep going. Then he saw the gun propped by the front door and his confidence faltered. It took gumption to set his foot on the bottom step. When the dog began to bark the woman laid her hand on its broad reddish head to hush it. Washburn's mouth was dry as he climbed the steps. Standing across from Annie Clyde Dodson, he realized she wasn't as tall as she'd seemed, but she was no less intimidating. She didn't reach for the rifle. She only looked at him. He'd thought her eyes were brown, but now closer up he saw they were hazel. She wore men's shoes and a faded shift. She had dark hair pulled back from her face and high cheekbones. Her skin was the color of coffee with milk. He was about to speak when a sound came from the open window behind her, like a child crying out in its sleep. The woman glanced over her shoulder. When the cry didn't come again, her eyes settled back on Washburn.

"Annie Clyde Dodson?"

"Yes."

He extended his hand. "My name is Sam Washburn. How do you do?"

"I'm tired," she said.

He dropped his hand.

"I know you're just doing your job, but you're not welcome here."

"I came a long way to talk to you."

She studied him, down to his polished shoes. "Well. You wasted a trip."

He hesitated, choosing his words. He decided to be direct with her. "If you're not gone by the third of August, you'll be evicted. I'm asking you to hear me out, before it comes to that."

"You all say the same things," she said. "I don't need to hear it again."

He lifted his hat and scratched beneath it. He didn't know what else to do with himself. "The problem is all the rain we've had. It's dangerous to stay here with the reservoir rising."

"Then I guess you better get on back to Knoxville."

Washburn's cheeks colored. "You know you're going to lose your land, Mrs. Dodson."

"Yes."

"Why are you making this harder on yourself?"

"You're the one I'm making it harder on, Mr. Washburn."

He hesitated again. "I understand your feelings. I grew up on a farm like yours."

"This is not my farm," she said.

Washburn opened his mouth and closed it.

"I have a little girl. It belongs to her."

He cleared his throat. "Yes. Well. Do you want her to see you dragged off in handcuffs?"

The Dodson woman's eyes caught fire. "That's exactly what I want."

"Mrs. Dodson—"

"I want her to see it and never forget it."

"Will you just sit down with me for a minute?"

"I want her to know I fought for what was hers."

They fell silent, facing each other. There was no sound but the chirring cicadas and the panting dog. Washburn wondered if she would reach for the Winchester beside the door but she kept still. He groped for more to say. She had confused him, made him doubt his reason for being there. Then the noise came again from the house, a child's sleepy crying. Some of the fierceness went out of Annie Clyde Dodson. There was a sag in her posture. He stared, unable to help himself at the freckle on her collarbone, the tendril tucked behind her ear. He saw how thin she was, her cheeks hollow and the neck of her shift bagging. He could almost feel the weight of her weariness on his own chest. He took a pace backward and then wavered. After two years he still felt like he was proving himself. He didn't want the chief to doubt his competence. More than that, it was humbling to have his authority undermined by a woman of his own age. But she had the soul of one much older. It was clear that he wouldn't be able to sway her. She was right. He had wasted a trip. When he got to the office he would start the eviction paperwork. The thought made him uncomfortable, as if he had spoken it out loud. He found himself leaving without being told. She didn't have to point her rifle. But as he backed down the steps, the child's cries drifting after him, his eyes played a trick. Somehow the glare of the sun and the shade of the porch made him think he saw water running down the Dodson woman's face. Not pouring on her, but pouring from her. Seeping between the fullness of her lips, spouting from her lids to mat her lashes, flowing from the roots of her hair and soaking her dress. The image lasted only until he blinked, but it stayed with him all the way back to Knoxville. Driving away he was glad to be done with her and the town of Yuneetah. He didn't know then how soon he would see her again.

JULY 31, 1936

Amos followed the river south twenty miles into Yuneetah, from a train yard in Knoxville. Sleeping on sacks in boxcars and under the struts of bridges he had dreamed of this valley, a green trough carved out between two mountain ranges, made of crumbling limestone ridges plunging into steep lowlands. For most of the way he'd kept to the woods, eating berries and making pine needle tea. At ten o'clock on that morning he crossed over the Sevier County line and picked a path down the snaky bluffs to the road. He could tell by the puddles there had been rain in the night. From the looks of the sky there would be more to come. Cloud banks were moving in from the west to blot out the sun, thunder gathering in their bellies. When he saw the first scattered houses on the edge of town, some tucked in the lee of the foothills and some nearer the road, it was already clear how things had changed. No rags flapped on the clotheslines. No plow mules cropped at the fields. Even the plank shack he passed with goats wrestling in its grassless dooryard seemed empty, their bleats startling in the humid stillness. These homes at the rim of the basin would be spared by the reservoir waters as they hadn't been by decades of punishing weather, slumped on their pilings with their porches canted and their shutters unhung.

For the past seven years, hunger had driven families out of Yuneetah looking for work. It was the same all over the country. In California Amos had picked fruit alongside migrants run off their farms by bankers. In the Midwest where they'd come from their crops were buried under veils of windblown soil and their kin were dying of dust pneumonia, choking on gobs of plowed-up earth. Camping under the arch of a viaduct in New Orleans, he had watched one man stab another in the guts over a tin of sardines. The next day he'd returned to take the gabardine suit pants from the stiffening corpse, having learned enough in these lean times to leave nothing useful behind. He had come upon other men lying frozen in culverts and ditches, children trailing cotton sacks into fields at dawn, whole towns abandoned with the smokestacks of their shut-down factories cold outlines against the skies. He'd seen thousands waiting in line outside steel mill gates where two or three jobs were being offered. Those turned away took to the rails so the boxcars he'd once had to himself were now crowded with men. He had huddled among them in hobo jungles, eaten with them from trash bins behind restaurants and been sickened by the rat poison added to the scraps to keep them out. He had seen them arrested by the dozens for burglary, stealing milk off back stoops and crackers from the shelves of general stores. He had witnessed all manner of hardship since 1929. But what disturbed him most was to see, as he descended the steep slope into Yuneetah, what had become of the place he thought of as home.

Sometimes he stayed away for a few months, sometimes a few years. This time it had been five. Under other circumstances he wouldn't have walked through the middle of town before dusk. Out of habit, he pulled down the brim of his hat to shade his face as he moved between the low buildings. The square was deserted, the only sound a metal signpost marking Gilley's Hotel squeaking when the wind freshened. The hotel had been standing on the same patch of sod since the 1800s. Out front a trough that the owner had kept from those days for the townspeople who still got around by horse or mule was filled with rainwater. Brocade curtains still draped the windows, but the glass was dark. Back in spring the bachelors who rented rooms there would have been perched on the steps or slouched against the trunk of the oak at the porch corner, the smoke of their home-rolled cigarettes threading into the leaves. Across the way the courthouse loomed with its shining dome roof. For once Amos didn't hurry past. Before he would have crossed to that side only during the evening, if no lamp was burning in the sheriff's office. Now he went to the opposite sidewalk and stopped to linger on the wide courthouse lawn. After a moment he moved on, past the boarded-up cafe with no mill-workers eating dinner at the counter, past the shuttered post office with the flag missing from its pole, past the shadowed blacksmith's shed set back from the road in a thicket, past the closed gristmill's roof glinting over the pines. Soon anything not torn down would be swamped. He had waited almost too long.

Amos kept moving until the town square was at his back and the hills closed in on both sides. He watched his boots as he walked, their soles coming untacked, making no footprints even in the softened wheel ruts he followed. He had learned to pass without leaving a trace. He was the sort decent men and women turned their heads from. He had a missing eye and his face was scrawled with whiskers. He was tall and gaunt with long black hair, lank on the shoulders of the peacoat he wore even in the heat of summer. On the streets he wandered crowds parted around him. For the most part he was left alone wherever he went, but traveling this familiar road he felt more at ease than anywhere else. He knew before long it would be a lake bottom, minnows darting in the grass up its middle. On the left he saw acres of stumps. Across a gully a tractor was mired in the mud near a stack of nail-spiked boards and a cellar hole filled with rain-water. One winter the widower who lived there had invited Amos in and given him coffee. But that was a decade ago. He stopped and spat on the tractor's caked tires before pushing on.

Another half mile down the road he came to a field of sedge where the foundation of the Methodist church was tumbled in a heap. He imagined the congregation hauling their river rock sanctuary to

higher ground and rebuilding it stone by stone. It would have been
a painstaking task but he had lived among the people of Yuneetah
long enough to know what they clung to in their war against the land
and the floods. They might be willing to leave behind their dried-up
farms but they would take their God with them. Amos hoped at least
one of them had held out against the power company. His throat was
parched and there was a gnawing in his stomach. Even those who
watched him with mistrust from the corners of their eyes used to
offer whatever they had to eat whenever he came around, turnips and
pone bread and dippers of cool water. After another stretch of woods
he came at last to a derelict cabin with a chimney mortared from
hog's hair and mud, the lot choked with milkweed. A guinea hen
flapped up cackling at his approach, small and ring-tailed, but there
was no other sign of life. He paused to hunt out its nest and found a
clutch of eggs that he pocketed to boil when he finally made camp.
He rested for a spell then shouldered his bindle and walked on. Each
farm he passed looked more vacant than the last. The screen door on
the Shelton place was off its hinges and their hounds were gone from
under the porch. The Hubbards had left a hay mower corroding in
their pasture. He wasn't much surprised. He had met few others like
himself, unafraid of the men in suits who ran everything.

The townspeople had always been wary of Amos. Nobody knew
where he came from. He had only fragmented memories himself, of
being cast into the river when he was four or five years old. Opening
his eyes in the silt-swirling murk, gulping its bitterness, being borne
on its current until he fetched up on the roots of a beech tree. He'd
hauled himself onto the bank and staggered into a clearing where
he fell in a heap at the foot of a bluff. Shivering he turned his head
and saw a crack in the earth, half hidden by ground-cover vines. He
discovered a hole leading into a shallow limestone cave and crawled
inside. Then he waited to die in the stagnant gloom, looking up
at the sun through ropes of woodbine, earthworms coiled like wet

strands of flesh between his toes. When he didn't die and emerged at last the worms came out with him, stuck to the backs of his legs. He might have thought he dreamed it all if he hadn't gone searching for the clearing as an older boy. He'd hacked away the ground cover with a machete and found the cave buried under years of growth, littered with detritus the floods had washed in. Whenever he returned to Yuneetah he uncovered that cave again. Each time there was something of use the river had left him. Combs with broken teeth, twists of baling wire, splinters of barn board for kindling his fires. But there were some things washed up in the floods that he didn't claim. Since time out of mind the river had been giving with one hand and taking away with the other. The remains of what had drowned, the bones it spat back out, he left undisturbed.

It was a woman named Beulah Kesterson who took him in when he was a child. She found him one morning while she was out gathering morels. She was not old back then, her braid not yet the ivory it would turn. She looked at him in thoughtful silence, her mouth sunken over her gums. When she leaned down at last to take his hand, the pouch of fortune-telling bones she wore on a string around her neck dangled before his eyes. She led him to her cabin and scrubbed his ears, trimmed his unruly hair, boiled cornmeal mush in a kettle over the fireplace cinders and set the bowl in his hands to warm them. She called him Amos, after a twin brother that died when she was born. Though he looked old enough to talk he wouldn't speak to her. When he finally did a few months later, the first words out of his mouth were a lie. He had stood watching a neighbor's coonhound dig up Beulah's cucumber seedlings and then waited for her to come out to the garden. She leaned on her hoe and said in disgust, "I wish they'd tie that blamed dog." Amos looked up into her face and told her, "I did it." Her eyebrows lifted some at the sound of his voice. When she recovered from the shock of hearing him speak, she asked what for. He couldn't answer. Then she inspected his hands and saw no crumbs of dirt. When she asked why he wanted to lie on himself, he couldn't answer that either. He'd been a liar ever since.

Amos had stayed with Beulah Kesterson for as long as he could stand it. But a roof, even one with holes, was like a coffin lid over him. At night he'd lie awake with his eyes moving over the cabin's fissured logs, its moldy chinking, the rotting beams of the rafters showing bright coins of moon. In the daytime he'd stand in the shadows beside the hearth as Beulah cast her bones over a flowered tablecloth for the townspeople of Yuneetah, divining the paths their futures would take. Most often they were amorous young girls with chewed bottom lips, but once a wife had brought her sick husband in a horse-drawn cart and led him into the cabin leaning on her shoulder. He looked like a walking skeleton and Beulah said with her hand on the woman's back, "You and me both know I got no reason to cast these bones." The woman crumpled to the cabin floor and wept out loud as her husband looked on, his lips cracked and lids leaking viscous fluid. Beulah sent them away with a powder she had ground from herbs. When Amos asked if it would save him, she said, "No, it won't." After that he began roaming to escape Yuneetah's troubles, through blackberry thickets and laurel hells, down cow paths and cliffside trails. By around thirteen he knew every inch of the town to its farthest reaches. He'd explored the clefts of the mountains and the creases of the valley. He had followed the riverbank into Whitehall County. One day he knew it was time to find out whatever there was beyond the hills.

While the townspeople hadn't liked Amos, they'd tolerated him out of respect for Beulah. But when he came back several years later with a puckered web of scar tissue where his right eye used to be, his foreignness was too much for them. Meeting him on the road they might nod in greeting or even stop to ask where he'd been, but they never stood long in the shadow he cast before him, as if his return portended bad weather or death. If anyone had asked what they wanted to know, he would have told them. He had lost his right eye fighting with another man in a boxcar. All day the man had huddled in the corner sleeping or pretending to sleep on a pallet of grain sacks. As the sun lowered and a rind of moon appeared over the hilltops blurring past, Amos had let the rocking train and the smell of the trackside meadows through the open door put him to sleep. The man had crawled out of the dark and set upon him before he had a chance to pull the weapon he'd made from a rag-wrapped bottle shard out of his coat pocket. They had struggled until they both were winded, the man's rancid breath puffing in grunts between the brown stumps of his teeth. If Amos hadn't been caught by surprise, he wouldn't have been overpowered. He would have thrust the glass into the grizzled wattles of the man's neck and felt the man's hot blood pumping over his fingers. Amos never knew what the man was after. Rather than let the man have whatever it was, he'd leapt from the train and tumbled down an embankment into a gully. When he'd lurched to his feet, there was a branch protruding from his eye socket. He wasn't alarmed once he knew he would live. He had no particular attachment to his right eye. But he did have some attachment to Yuneetah, and to its people, whether they knew it or not.

Now Amos had walked a fair distance without seeing a single one of them, or any other living thing, as if even the squirrels and wild turkeys had cleared out. He'd come to Joe Dixon's store ahead on the left, a weathered shack plastered with signs advertising Red Seal lye, Royal Crown cola and Clabber Girl baking powder. On the last Saturday of each month he and Beulah would leave the hollow to trade, pulling the lace she tatted and the medicines she made behind them in a wooden cart. As Amos neared he saw the door propped open and followed a worn footpath to the porch, the leaf-littered steps groaning as he climbed them, the door creaking when he pushed it the rest of the way open. He went in and stood for a while. All the familiar clutter was gone. No straw brooms hanging from the ceiling, no penny candy filling the glass bins of the counter, no shelves lined with sundries. He had never seen the place empty. There was usually someone sitting on a carbide barrel paring his fingernails. Joe Dixon leaning back in a straight chair, his big belly straining at the buttons of his shirt. Joe would sometimes offer Amos a cold drink in hopes of getting rid of him. The wind picked up, scattering leaves over the threshold and across the gritty planks of the floor. Amos glanced around. The cooler was still there against one wall. He approached it and lifted the lid. There was nothing inside but mildew. After a second he closed it back. He shifted his bindle and went out again.

Back on the road nothing stirred but him and the river, its current still rushing as it spread into a lake. Anywhere he went in the town he could hear water running. Beulah had told him Yuneetah was the white man's corruption of an Indian word for the spirit of the river. She said the Cherokees who once lived on its shores had called it Long Man, with his head in the mountains and his feet in the lowlands. The river had surely seen and heard all that had happened in the place it flowed through. It must have noticed too those who had lived for so long on its banks moving off one by one. With the young leaving and the old getting buried, all the river was to them would be forgotten. Even the spirit the Cherokees worshipped had been defeated by the men who built dams, harnessed to run their machinery. Amos had vowed long ago not to give them the sweat of his brow. He wouldn't submit to the ones in charge, who would have his hair shorn and his offending eye socket covered with a patch. He wouldn't become a thing they could use, as they'd figured out how to use the river's power. It sighed hidden behind a bank topped with shade trees, roots snarled like witch's hair in the dampish brown dirt. That bank dirt had looked so good to him when he was a boy that he'd dug out a clot and held it in his mouth. His first impulse had been to spit out the bitterness but as it melted on his tongue other tastes had come, of lichen and peat moss and rain. He had swallowed and carried it around for a while, to see what would happen. Nothing did, he thought at the time. But maybe his insides had formed around it.

As the pines on either side of him turned to acres of farmland, he looked toward the southeast edge of town where the dam would be. He'd heard about it last winter while working alongside another drifter at a tobacco warehouse in North Carolina. Neither of them wore gloves and it had been so cold that when they put down the steel hooks they were using to unload tobacco baskets the hide was ripped from their hands. At the end of a week the other man had said he was moving on. There's a dam going up in Tennessee, he'd said, a place called Yuneetah. Amos's head had risen from his work. His chest had constricted around his heart. He had dropped the steel hook to the warehouse floor and walked out into the spitting snow in search of a newspaper. In the warmth of a brick library outside of Asheville he had read all about the Tennessee Valley Authority and their plans to inundate his hometown while the librarian watched him with fearful eyes from her circulation desk. He had ruminated on this knowledge for a while, days becoming weeks as he moved through alleys and dumps with home on his mind, avoiding whatever light there was, electric or lantern or carbide, not letting even the flames of the barrel he warmed himself over play on his face. He'd decided to wait until most of the town was evacuated before returning. Soon enough he would find the dam. He would stand before it and take its measure.

Amos rounded a bend and the Walker farmhouse appeared as if out of nowhere. Behind the house there was an apple tree that he used to visit as a child. In springtime when the leaves were full he liked to hide under the tree until the farmer caught him, lying on a bed of white blossoms with more drifts floating down on top of him. In late summer he would sit among the fallen apples as yellow jackets bored holes in them, eating until his stomach ached. Now he was heading toward fifty with threads of white in his hair, still craving sour juice down his chin. He was old considering the miles he had wandered for the most part on foot, across the country from one shore to the other. Then up into Canada and down into Mexico. Most of the men he had traveled and labored and grifted with were dead. Shot, stabbed, beaten and hung. One he had known since he hopped his first train was stoned to death in Boston during the trolley strike of 1910. Lately Amos's days felt loaned out to him. He had begun to wonder if he was meant to have lived this long. He'd begun to ask himself what to do with this cheated time, even before he learned about the dam. Yuneetah's passing only made him more certain that his own was coming.

But he predicted the woman who'd raised him would remain in the hollow for many years after he and the town were gone. Beside the farm Beulah's cabin was tucked high in the woods, above the taking line. He could get to her by crossing a weedy track dividing the farm from the mountain. It was a long climb between tall, slender tree trunks to reach her place. When he closed his eye he could see it, having leaned there so long, through the bitter winters with snow piled to its windowsills and the warm months with rainstorms curling back its rusted roof tin. Saplings and bushes had mostly claimed back the gap where it stood, thatches of ironweed trailing up to the door. Amos thought how many times he had come and gone from that place, the ground still bald in patches from his passing feet, even though he hadn't slept there in ages. Some nights he would stand listening to the thump of walnuts falling in the dark outside the circle of shine made by Beulah's oil lamp. When morning came he would collect them for her, lumpy and specked and pale velvet green. He would bring them to her as payment for something he couldn't name.

Beulah would welcome him back with a meal if he climbed up the hollow. She always did whenever he returned to Yuneetah. But behind the split-rail fence marking the boundaries of the Walker farm rows of corn rustled in the hot wind. He put his boot on the bottom rail and looked into the stalks, already tasting roasting ears. It was unfortunate for them that they hadn't got their crop sold before they were relocated, but their loss was his gain. He knew something of the ones who had lived here before the town was evacuated. The last he heard, the daughter of the white-haired farmer who gave him apples had married a Dodson from Whitehall County and they had struggled to live off the rocky soil she inherited. But it looked as though their corn had fared well this season, lush from all the rain. Amos paused as he straddled the fence, thinking he might hear something. Maybe the call of a bobwhite or the yowl of a roving tomcat. He tried to see the farmhouse over the tasseled stalks but only its upper story was visible. After listening a moment more he climbed down into the dappled shade of the rows where it was somewhat cooler, water seeping up from the soaked loam around the edges of his boots. Looking down the row he took off his hat to smooth back his hair, the blades of the stalks drooping over his head. Then he heard another high noise coming from the direction of the house. This time it was unmistakable, the shriek of a child. But in fear or delight, it was hard to tell which.

Amos liked children. He admired their wildness. Even in the low places he kept to they could be found. The sons of junkmen scrambling over humps of refuse and around the hulls of wrecked cars. The daughters of tar-paper shack dwellers dragging naked baby dolls along backwoods railroad tracks. In a Cleveland switchyard he had come upon an old hobo beating a young boy senseless even after he fell limp. Amos had twisted the hobo's fingers out of joint until they could no longer close into fists. The last child Amos had seen was on his way out of Oklahoma. For days all that he'd passed was coated with soot blown off the plains. When he came to the first stretch of green grass the ditch in front of it was lined with dust-streaked jalopies. In the field below the road there had been a caravan in a circle of tents and a rickety carousel, its circus colors turned dusky.

He'd stepped across the ditch and walked down among the migrant families looking for some reminder of happiness. He saw the little girl outside one of the tents holding a sign with a painted white hand, advertising palm readings for twenty-five cents. He went on, lifting anything useful from the tables of wares, but on his way back to the road he came across the seer's tent again. This time he found the little girl spinning a tin top in a patch of dirt. She looked up at him with trusting eyes. Nobody cared enough to be watching.

Now the corn was parting at the end of the row and he waited for whoever was coming. While his hearing was keen, his eyesight was poor. He couldn't make out what rushed toward him from a distance, until it began to bark. It was a redbone hound, young and gangling, drawn to his stench of rotten wool and wind-scoured stone, the dewy earth he slept on. Like every drifter, Amos hated dogs. He retreated backward between the stalks, their leaves brushing his shoulders. The big hound advanced on him growling, hunkered down with its hackles raised. He had nearly reached the rail fence and was prepared to vault over it when a child came running after the dog. She was small, no more than three or four, wearing a flour sack dress with tousled curls in her eyes. Once she saw what her dog had cornered, not a rabbit or a groundhog but a man, she stopped in her tracks. The redbone hound went on growling. Her mouth opened but nothing came out of it. The last child left in Yuneetah. As they studied one another the clouds that had been gathering all forenoon moved over the cornfield. She seemed more curious than afraid, so he took a step forward. Ignoring the dog, Amos reached into his coat. He pulled out the tin top, a starburst of faded kaleidoscope colors radiating from its knob, gold dulled to brass, blue gone grayish, red aged to flesh, and held it out to her. Without much hesitation she crossed the short distance separating them as the dog barked harder to warn her off. Amos passed the top down into her hands as if performing a sacred rite. She accepted it with the same graveness.

But then the sharp voice of a woman called out from somewhere

close. Amos froze and stood listening with his ear tilted. He could
hear someone coming toward them through the field, shaking the
corn. "Gracie!" she shouted, and whatever spell Amos had managed
to cast over the child was broken. She shied away from him, widening
the space between them again, her toes printing the furrowed earth
in her wake. The hound's barking would lead the woman straight
to them. Amos had time to make himself scarce but he decided to
stay and have a look at her. When she finally burst out of the stalks
into the row she was too concerned with the child at first to see him
standing there. "Gracie," she panted. "Don't you scare me like that."
Then she followed the growling dog's gaze, still fixed on Amos, and
snatched the child back by the arm. After she'd taken an instant to
collect herself, her face hardened. She glared at Amos with recogni-
tion. Everyone in Yuneetah had seen him at least once. "What are
you doing out here?" she demanded.

He reached up to break off an ear of corn. "Helping myself to
some dinner."

The woman clutched the child against her legs. "You're trespassing."

He slipped the corn into his pocket and took her in, the thin smock
hanging at her knees, the white feather clinging to her shoulder, the
flour on her hands. She must have been frying chicken. He knew her,
even as long as it had been since he'd seen her. She was the daughter
of the farmer and his second wife, a woman from the hollow that
Amos had played with as a boy. The last time he visited the apple
tree the farmer's daughter was an awkward girl wandering among the
haystacks behind the barn, chewing on straws, letting ladybugs crawl
over her knuckles. He remembered asking her to fetch him a drink
but she had run off and not come back with it. "I believe I knew your
mama," he said. "We used to swim in the river together."

She went on glaring at him. "You didn't know my mama."

"You look like her." He glanced at the child. "You and your little
girl both."

"Get off my property," she said.

He tipped back his hat to see her better. "Why are you still here? The water will be at your doorstep before you know it."

Her face flushed. "You got yourself some dinner. Now go on."

Amos kept still. "If you're waiting on a fair price for your land, you might as well move. They don't have to give you one."

She backed away with the child. "My husband's at the barn. If I holler, he'll come with his gun." Amos could tell that she was lying. Her husband was nowhere around.

"Your land is worthless to them," he went on. "So are you and your little girl."

The woman had begun to tremble, unable to bluff any longer. In that moment he felt kin to both of them, standing close as the storm moved in, their bodies patterned by the same shade. He glanced again at the child, still holding the kaleidoscope top. Thunder rolled, cornstalks bent and shuffled as if waiting to see what would happen. At last Amos stepped forward until he was close enough to count the beats of the young woman's pulse in her neck. When he reached out to pluck the feather from her shoulder, she flinched as if he had struck her. He closed his fingers around it and took up his bindle. That's when the dog lunged snapping at his shins. Amos felt the bite of the hound's teeth but he didn't let on. He backed down the row without a sound, keeping his eye on the woman's face. When he reached the fence he raised himself up on the bottom rail, pausing as if he might change his mind. Then he turned and climbed over into the road, leaving the woman and her child alone, in a field that would soon lie hundreds of feet underwater.

At half past eleven o'clock on that morning, three days before Annie Clyde Dodson was to be forced off her land, she ran through the corn with her daughter on her hip. Gracie clung tight with her legs locked around Annie Clyde's waist, the dog rushing ahead of them toward the house. Above, the sky looked like a bruised skin barely holding back the rain. The wind blew Annie Clyde's dress up and whirled through the trees, shaking the cornstalks like something chasing her. As if Amos had only fooled her into thinking he was gone. She didn't let herself look back until they emerged from the corn. When she saw nothing besides the green field behind her she stopped running but still hurried around the side of the house with Gracie jostling in her arms. Standing at the bottom of the stoop she threw open the kitchen door with a bang, letting in the stormy gloom, and set Gracie inside on the linoleum. "You stand still while I tend to Rusty," she said, smoothing the tangled curls out of her daughter's face. "I'll be right back." She turned around to catch the dog by the scruff of his neck and led him to the elm tree shading the barn lot. She meant to tether him by the chain wrapped around the base of the trunk. She hated to do it, but she would feel better with him tied close to the house in case the drifter came into the yard.

She was fumbling with the chain when the blackbirds flocked down on the hayfield behind the barn. They came in the hundreds, rustling through the weeds and roosting in the apple tree, milling over the winey fruit underneath. It was the wind that brought them. Her father used to say storms bothered birds' ears and made them fly close to the ground. The rain hadn't started, but it soon would. Water stood ankle deep in the grass, mist hanging over the valley and ringing the crests of the mountains. It had been raining all spring and summer. Now she had something else to worry about. As soon as she saw the blackbirds she knew that she couldn't hold Rusty. He was still strung up from what had happened in the corn, hackles raised and tail high. He gave a sudden lurch and Annie Clyde lost her grip on him. She snatched after him but he was too quick. She watched helpless, a hand to her forehead, as he dashed off barking. Then she glanced over her shoulder at the house. There was a plucked chicken in the

basin and apples to be peeled for the last pie she would make Gracie.
The last one from their tree. She'd meant to bring in a few roasting
ears as well before Gracie took off. She was always running away
like that, tagging after the dog. "I swear," Annie Clyde would tell
her. "You'll be the death of me." But at night she smiled to reach in
Gracie's pockets and find the treasures she'd wandered off to collect.
Forked twigs, buttercups, crawdad claws, rocks of all kinds. Annie
Clyde cursed Rusty under her breath. Any other time she would have
let him alone. But her husband James was gone off to Sevierville and
there was no telling when he'd get home. The dog was the only pro-
tector she and Gracie had.

She headed back to the kitchen door, tripping up the stoop. Gracie
was still holding the tin top the drifter had given her. Annie Clyde's
stomach turned at the sight of it, but there was no time to throw it
away. She swung Gracie onto her hip again and went running with
her, out past the elm and the charred trash barrels standing amid
puddles floating with cinders, inside them heaps of ash wetted to
gray lumps from the storms. As she cut through the blowing hayfield weeds the blackbirds lifted off together in a train the way they
had landed. Rusty gave chase, tracking the rash they made across the
overcast sky. By the time Annie Clyde and Gracie reached the apple
tree Rusty had disappeared into the woods at the end of the field.
She put Gracie down among the fallen fruits, pecked and streaked
with droppings. She whistled and Gracie shouted for Rusty but he
wouldn't come, not even to the one he loved most.

Annie Clyde didn't like the thought of taking Gracie back to the
house without the dog around to bark. She couldn't stop seeing
Amos's one dead eye. He used to come into the yard when she was
a girl, asking for water and apples. Over the last decade many had
knocked on their door looking for work or food. When Annie Clyde's
mother was alive she gave what she could spare, even to Amos, but
she had mistrusted him. Annie Clyde didn't trust him either. But she
couldn't deny what he'd said in the cornfield. The power company

didn't care about her or Gracie. Her neighbors didn't understand why she wouldn't move. She wanted to tell them, but she was too used to keeping to herself. The farm was part of her. She knew the lay of its land like her tongue knew the back of her teeth. On the east side of the house was the field her father had planted with alfalfa and the slope at the verge of the hollow where he'd grown tobacco. On the west was another field where he'd sown wheat and beyond that a stand of pine timber. Below the house were several roadside acres of corn and behind it this hayfield at the foot of the mountain with this apple tree rooted in the weeds. As a child she'd walked among the stobs of the tobacco field after the harvest, touching the teepees the bundled stalks made. She'd stood in the shed under curing leaves, hiding in shadows the same brownish color the wrinkled tobacco was turning. She would pry up flat limestone rocks that her father said were made from the beds of evaporated seas, marked with the fossils of ancient mollusks, and bang them together to hear their echoes. Her father was called Clyde and after three stillborn babies, his wife vowed to give the next one his name whether it was a son or not. Losing the farm would be like losing him all over again.

Now her father's forty acres were quiet aside from the wind stirring the ropes of the swing hanging from one of the apple tree's crooked branches. Gracie stood with yellow and green leaves fluttering down around her. She lifted her toe to scratch her ankle and Annie Clyde wondered if she would be able to tell her child someday. About the farm and the swing and how she looked in this moment, wearing the light blue dress with pink rosebuds that Annie Clyde had sewed for her. How she looked out from under her matted eyelashes with her nose running some. She seldom cried and Annie Clyde wondered if she might have bitten her tongue on their way through the hayfield. She knelt and wiped at Gracie's upper lip. "Where does it hurt?" she asked.

After thinking for a second Gracie pointed to her knee. "Right here."

Annie Clyde tried to smile. "That's a scab. You got shook up, is all." She paused to wave the gnats out of Gracie's face, to make sure her voice wouldn't break. "Did that man scare you?"

Gracie brought her thumb toward her mouth and Annie Clyde tugged it away. Gracie raised the top to show it without answering, the tarnished knob glinting. "Look," she said.

"Can I have it?" Annie Clyde asked. When she reached for it, Gracie drew it closer.

They studied each other's faces. "Rusty bit him," Gracie said.

"Yes," Annie Clyde said. "But he's gone now."

"Where did he go?"

Annie Clyde looked away, down at the fruit on the ground. "You want an apple?"

Gracie nodded, eyes wet.

"Let's find you a good one."

Annie Clyde pretended to sort through the fruit but she was rattled. Gracie squatted with her dress hem soaking up puddles, holding the top aloft in one hand. Annie Clyde was still trying to calm herself when she heard a loud crack from the woods at the end of the hayfield. She jumped up and turned in that direction, listening. Her first thought was not of the dog out there stalking blackbirds, but of Amos out there somehow spying on them. Within seconds another crack came, like a lightning strike. She waited with her eyes fixed on the trees for thunder. Then there was a pop and another, a string of them picking up speed. After that came a whoosh and a roaring crash. The treetops shivered, disturbed as though something monstrous had passed among them. In the wake of that sound there was nothing but the buffeting wind, even Gracie awed to silence. As Annie Clyde stared at the woods, she felt Gracie's warm fingers creeping into her own. Annie Clyde looked down into her daughter's upturned face. "We're all right," she said. "It was just another tree falling." Gracie didn't say anything back but Annie Clyde knew. They both needed the dog around to ease their minds. She decided it wouldn't hurt to walk a piece into the woods. Sometimes the sky brooded all day before it opened up on Yuneetah. Sometimes the wind blew like this for hours before the first drops fell like slugs. Her father would have said the dam had disturbed the natural order of things. After listening another moment for thunder Annie Clyde and Gracie started across the hayfield, parting the coarse weeds with their legs.

At the end of the field they entered the shade, Annie Clyde watching the ferny ground for copperheads. In this dampness everything was growing. Liverwort sprouted on wet rocks, jewelweed poked up through brushwood, lichens wreathed south-facing trunks like chains of greenish ears. They called Rusty's name as they went, the blackbirds he had been chasing settled in the branches overhead. Farther in they came to the thicket where Annie Clyde and James chopped wood, the standing rainwater around the stumps swirling with chips of sawdust. The trees there were so tall it made her dizzy to look up at their swaying tips. At the edge of the thicket, where freshets drained down from the ledges making gullies between the bases of the trunks, they discovered what had fallen. There was an old beech lying at the foot of the mountain.

Annie Clyde had seen more than one tree uprooted in all this foul weather. She had heard the rain every way that it fell, hard like drumming fingers, in sheets like a long sigh, in spates like pebbles tossed at the windows. When she crossed the road and went up the bank, she could see water glinting between the tree stumps. The river had already become a lake. As she watched it seemed to lie stagnant, but maybe it was biding its time until dark. Then it would move again. She could almost hear it seeking whatever there was outside its banks, searching fingers moving over gnarled root and scaly stump bark. Leaking between trunks and lapping at grasses, mussels clicking against each other and the scoured rocks of the shoals. She dreamed of it coming for her, black and rippling. She woke afraid it would be pooled around the porch steps, the rains bringing it closer and closer. Since spring a scent had been lingering in the eastern part of town where the woods and pastures were halved by the river. She smelled it in the house sometimes, algae and carp and decayed wood from long-ago boats run aground. When she opened her door it slipped in as if to scout her home before the lake came to fill her chimney flue with the opposite of fire.

It was the biggest trees that fell in all the wind and rain, the oaks and beeches and hickories, because of their shallow roots. It was harder for them to find purchase in Yuneetah's soil, thin clay with limestone caves underneath. She guessed it was over four years ago that James had buried his horse in a deep cave back here and filled in the hole. A Tennessee walker named Ranger. Now the beech trunk lay over the horse's grave as if to mark it. Just when she was about to whistle for the dog again, Annie Clyde heard the snap of a twig beneath the wind. She froze in her tracks, squeezing Gracie's sweaty hand. "Rusty?" she called into the thicket across the fallen tree. There was a thrashing in the underbrush and she shouted again. "Rusty! Here, boy!" When a low shape shot out of the shadows around the beech's root ball Annie Clyde stopped breathing, although she knew it was only the dog minding her at last. Rusty loped to Gracie's side with his tail wagging, snout caked with clay the color of his coat. "Bad dog," Gracie told him as he licked her chin. Annie Clyde remembered Gracie crouched in the dirt of Dale Hankins's barn after his hound had whelped, the pup with a white patch on its chest tottering over to sniff her fingers. From the day Gracie started walking Rusty followed her everywhere, though James was the one who wanted him for a hunting dog and gave him his name. Annie Clyde didn't know how to tell Gracie they'd have to leave him behind for a while if they moved.

Rusty must have lost interest in the blackbirds after the beech tree came crashing down. Annie Clyde could see where he had already dug around its trunk. Ferns crushed in the fall were disarranged, red clay turned. Annie Clyde could see, too, a white bone in the rich humus. Much like the trees, bones were being dislodged across the valley by weather and water, swept along as the lake moved toward the roads. Most of the dead had been exhumed and reinterred elsewhere, their surnames chalked on the lids of pine boxes as they rode in hearses to strange churchyards. But some had been left alone, those whose kin chose not to disturb them or victims whose grave sites were unknown. Those she imagined the overflow released from secret vaults of mud and crag and riverside root. Femurs sailing on eddies, skulls rising toward the surface seeking light after centuries buried, the unleashed river rushing in to fill burrows and trenches like mouths open to drink its alluvial silt. But this bone unearthed by the rain or uprooted by the fallen tree wasn't human. It belonged to James's horse. She used to ride double with her husband on Ranger's back, his arms loose around her waist and holding the reins in her lap. He would rest his chin on her shoulder or she would lean her head against his chest as they ducked under bowers of twilit leaves in the cool of the evenings, forgetting whatever work they'd left undone.

As Annie Clyde approached the horse's grave for a closer look the beech's limbs creaked. Its leaves twitched and shifted. Gracie let go of Annie Clyde's hand to feel the silvered scabs of the bark, the scars and bumps. Annie Clyde opened her mouth to say they'd better get on to the house but the words stuck in her throat. She found that she was shaking. Her legs were weak. This long morning had been too much for her. She had to get her breath. The rain wouldn't harm them if it came. Some hot afternoons they ran out of the house and played in the chilly showers. "Let me see that," she said, reaching for the tin top again. Gracie resisted for only a second this time before giving it over. Annie Clyde slipped it into her dress pocket like something poisonous. Then she tucked her hands under Gracie's arms and lifted her onto the beech's back. As Gracie sat swinging her feet

Annie Clyde rested against the end of the trunk. Rusty sniffed at the root ball, mounded with orange mud and green sod like a thatched roof for the hut the bowing roots made. They looked almost alive, a tortured mass of petrified legs, twined arms and hooked fingers, overhung with a finer layer of filaments like the stringy hair of a woman caught out in the rain.

If they were staying, James would have come with his saw when he got home and cut the fallen beech into logs. Last year he'd worked with the reservoir clearance gangs stripping the banks of timber to make navigation channels for boats and to keep the penstock in the dam from getting clogged with brush. The power company said the people could take home the good logs but most had no means of carrying them so they ended up being burned. For weeks the smoke was everywhere, Gracie's eyes tearing as she played in the yard. James said it would be crazy to turn down any kind of work and she couldn't dispute him. But it had felt like a betrayal to her.

There were many things she and James had done and said to hurt one another since the power company came to town, but the worst for her had been about a month ago. He had walked up to the porch where she was snapping beans and told her, "The Hankinses' back pasture's flooded. That's right across the hill. Gracie's liable to take off and be in that lake before you know it." He was always finding ways to tell her they should leave without saying it outright. Most of the time he was careful with her, perhaps feeling guilty for not standing with his wife against the government, in spite of his own convictions. Not wanting to argue, she'd gone back to her beans. When she didn't respond he'd shaken his head. "I don't know," he'd said. "Sometimes I believe you love this place more than you do me or her either one." She was stunned by how little he understood her. She loved the farm, but that wasn't why she fought the power company. From the time she realized she was expecting, she had dreamed of her child roaming the fields in summer. She knew the trees she wanted her child to climb, the flowers she wanted her child to name, the fruits she wanted her child to taste. But her husband had still been talking, and she'd lifted her eyes to meet his as he told her about the job in Michigan. He'd said their nearest neighbor Dale Hankins's brother was a foreman at a steel mill. He had offered to hire Dale and James both.

Since then she had watched James making plans to settle them up north, too wounded to talk to him about it much. She had let him rent a house in Detroit and take off their furniture without stopping him, not knowing what she wanted herself. She had thought in the beginning she would never give up the farm. She had watched the power company mapping the reservoir area and waited for them to send her one of the field appraisers. When he came in his suit and striped vest, wingtip shoes and a tack gleaming in his tie, she sent him right back to them. The man said he was offering her fair market price but she asked how much more he was going to give her for the appreciation of the land and the trouble it would cause her to move. She told him to figure out how much all of that was worth and come back. The last time he returned, she listened in silence as he explained how things worked. He said his report went before a committee of county agents that knew the value of land in Yuneetah. He hadn't come up with the price and she ought not to blame him if she didn't like it. When she suggested he should tell his committee that she wasn't going anywhere until the water floated her out, he threatened her with condemnation proceedings. After the appraiser left she told James she was going to make them send a marshal with a court order. She was going to appeal her case to the district court and the circuit court of appeals if it came to that. She had seen how fed up her husband was then, how ready to move on, maybe with or without her. James said, "You can't stand against a flood, Annie Clyde." He was right, but she'd wanted at least to put the power company out some.

In the end, she had worn down like the rest of the town. There was a dead tiredness that sometimes a person had to obey and lately it had come over her. She went to bed some nights without washing her feet. She knew the land would be taken. Her labors were useless. She'd seen the homes of her neighbors knocked down and burned. She had seen the burial mounds on the riverbank, made by Indians that had lived in caves along the water longer ago than the Cherokees, destroyed by archeologists from Knoxville and the workers they'd hired to do the digging. The largest had been over thirty feet tall with trees growing up its sides, their hoary branches like a covering of cobwebs in winter. They had found among the tools and pottery shards counters used for a game like checkers. She heard the diggers weren't careful enough and some of the bones were broken, splintered to pieces. Flakes so fine they had returned to dust, particles whirling among the water bugs. Washed away with all those other lost remains.

She guessed part of her hadn't believed August would ever come, but now it was upon her. She couldn't fathom what it would be like in Michigan. She pictured a house on a square of balding grass near a curb, the dirty color of winter slush. James going off in the early mornings to a factory where he would work behind a welder's mask, sucking in and blowing out the suffocating heat of his own breath, leaving her and Gracie alone. She hadn't even told Gracie they were leaving. She didn't know how to explain it to a three-year-old. But these last few days she'd been thinking, wondering if she could make it farming on her own. Forty acres was too much, but ten she might be able to manage. Maybe she should have taken the house in Whitehall County the relocation man had offered to show her, less than twelve miles away. She'd felt it didn't matter how close she lived to her farm. It would still be underwater. James had accused her of being stubborn and selfish but she listened to him more than he thought. He said change was coming whether she wanted it or not. Neither of them had grown up with much, but these past several years were the leanest they'd ever known. He said she ought to be thankful that Gracie might have it easier someday. He said farming killed their parents. But at least the years Mary and Clyde Walker had were spent where they belonged, on their own land. Annie Clyde couldn't bear to think of Gracie not knowing the closeness to God she had found in this valley. For the first time since Gracie's birth, Annie Clyde wasn't sure what was best for her child.

There wasn't much time to decide one way or another. She and Gracie were supposed to go north with James tomorrow. Two weeks ago he had come driving up in a Model A Ford, the radiator hissing steam. He'd sold their mules to buy it. When he stepped off the running board his eyes were lit up. He grabbed Annie Clyde and kissed her. But his excitement had worn off fast. So far the old stake-bed truck had given him nothing but trouble. He was gone now to see a man in Sevier County about fixing the radiator. Annie Clyde would just as soon he took it to the junkyard. He claimed they needed it to haul their belongings but there wasn't much left to move. In the front room there were curtains and a rocking chair. In the kitchen there was the pine table her father made before she was born, before his first wife died of rheumatic fever. Like the maple bed upstairs that he'd built for her mother when they got married. Mary Walker had passed away in February of 1933 from a cancer of the womb. She died in that bed, during a winter so cold Annie Clyde saw her mother's last breath. Nothing else remained but stray wisps of cobweb.

James had wanted to leave Yuneetah long before the dam gave him a way out. Annie Clyde knew how hard the farming had been on him. She knew how much he hated the river after he lost his father to a flood. She knew how reserved she was and that her silence must have been lonesome for him. It was possible she hadn't told him often enough how much she loved him. In the beginning of their marriage, Annie Clyde's need for James would sometimes smother her. She would watch the front window for him to come in from the fields and rush out to meet him. But after she saw that handbill during their first autumn together, things were different for her. It was an advertisement for factory work up north. She was sewing a tear in his shirtsleeve and noticed it in his breast pocket. She thought it was a matchbook but found a square of paper instead. She unfolded and read it as he sat across the fireplace from her, drowsing in his chair. She would rather have found a love letter from a woman. "What's this?" she asked. James opened his eyes and what she saw in them tightened her chest. He looked like he had been caught. "I never asked you to change your plans for me," she said, holding the handbill out to him. "You made your own choice." He swore to her then that it meant nothing, that he wouldn't dream of leaving her to take care of her mother and the farm alone. "I don't even know why I picked that up," he said. But Annie Clyde knew, whether he did or not. She wouldn't let herself watch for James out the window anymore, though her longing was as smothering as ever.

She had seen him for the first time one summer when he worked pulling tobacco for her father. He was eating his dinner under a tree, cutting off pieces of pear and feeding himself with the blade of his knife. He still insisted he saw her first, being baptized in the river. Annie Clyde was raised in the Free Will Baptist Church and James's uncle was a Methodist minister, but sometimes the congregations joined for special services. He claimed to have worshipped her from the minute he laid eyes on her, standing on the bank with her dress molded to her skin and strands of hair plastered to her face like drawings of vines. But they had met a year before the baptism, when she was sixteen and he eighteen. He had a ruddy look about him, like clay. He smelled of it when he came in from the field. She remembered his auburn hair rumpled and his long legs crossed in front of him. Later he came into the yard for a drink and she brought him the dipper. He thanked her and went on. By the time he came looking for her after the baptism, she had forgotten about him. Her thoughts were scattered then. After decades of farming, Clyde Walker was giving out. Most mornings he couldn't get up. Annie Clyde had prayed on her knees at the revival for her father to get better, but he only weakened. After he died the neighbors brought casseroles, cakes and pies. When the food was gone, Annie Clyde's mother sent her to return the dishes. James found her breaking them against a tree with blood running down her fingers. He took her by the shoulders and led her to the river to wash her gashes. "My daddy's dead, too," he said, lowering himself down on the bank beside her. His hands were calming on her shoulders. He left them there until she was ready to stand. Before getting up she looked into his face and finally remembered him sitting under a tree, eating a pear with the blade of his knife.

James had begun to visit once a week. She felt obliged to offer him food they didn't have, to sit with him on the porch and make small talk. When he asked to help with the chores, she was too beaten to protest. Annie Clyde and her mother had struggled to run the farm by themselves. Getting up before dawn to make a fire and heading out with the milk pails. Feeding the chickens, gathering the eggs, weeding the garden. Hauling water in from the springhouse and ashes out from the stove. Hoeing corn, digging potatoes and chopping wood. By then Annie Clyde had dropped out of school to work in the fields. Sometimes she leaned on the plow handles, tears dripping off her face to salt the cracked ground. She learned to be relieved on Saturdays when James came riding to the farm on his horse with his sleeves rolled up. Then one morning James tied Ranger, letting him crop the roadside clover, and loitered at the fence rather than going straight to work. Annie Clyde went down the path to see what he wanted, hair and shoulders dusted with pollen from the bottom weeds she'd spent all morning hacking down. When she reached the fence, James opened his mouth but closed it again, whatever he meant to say forgotten. He stood there by the road in silence, studying her face. Then he asked if she would like to go for a ride with him. She was about

to say she didn't have time to fool around, but found herself looking into his earnest eyes, the delicate blue of bird eggs. He leaned
in close, arms folded on the fence post, and kissed her. It was out
of weariness that she finally surrendered to James. But there was a
sweetness in it. When he pulled back she hadn't wanted him to stop.

Annie Clyde's mother never asked her to marry James, but she
spoke of what a dependable husband he would make. It was plain to
Annie Clyde what her mother wanted. Mary was growing thin, her
flesh stretched like onionskin over her bones. She hardly resembled
the beauty Annie Clyde had seen in pictures, dressed up in gloves and
a hat with her lips painted red, coiffed head lowered against the sun.
Annie Clyde couldn't run the farm on her own, and Mary wanted
someone to take care of her daughter when she was gone. By the
summer of 1932, Annie Clyde knew her mother wouldn't last much
longer. When James proposed one day as she stood over the kitchen
woodstove, using the last of their cornmeal to make a bite to eat
for him, she couldn't resist leaning against his strong arms. A few
months later, on her wedding day, she tried not to show her doubts.
Mary had become too feeble to leave the house. She watched from
the bed as Annie Clyde pinned a pillbox hat to her hair. She offered
to button Annie Clyde's gloves for her at the wrists. Somehow Annie
Clyde had managed to keep her hands steady as she held them out.
But she was helpless to still them when James's uncle the Methodist
minister came to drive her to the church in his black Packard. It was
August and the fields were turning golden, the sky cloudless over
the spire. Across a pasture was the white parsonage where James had
lived with his aunt and uncle after his parents died. Soon they would
both be orphans. It was the one thing they would always have in
common. Standing outside the double doors of the church holding
a bunch of wildflowers, Annie Clyde felt light-headed. Just before
entering the vestibule she looked up to see a grackle on the peak of
the roof and it heartened her some. She took off the pillbox hat and

tossed it into the rhododendrons beside the steps. She shook her hair down and went inside. As the pianist played the wedding march, she fixed her eyes on James at the end of the aisle in an ill-fitting suit, his hair slicked down and combed back. He looked like a little boy. She released a breath and went to him, making up her mind to love him however she could.

Annie Clyde had come to feel closer to her husband. If she found him bent washing his face at the basin and pressed her cheek against the flesh of his back, it seemed that any worry she had would be erased. In their bed at night, under quilts in winter or naked on top of the sheets in summer, he explored even the inside of her mouth with his fingers. She tasted the bitterness of his shaving soap. His caught breath filled the cup of her ear. Once when she was big with Gracie, he pushed her dress up over her thighs and stomach, over the mounds of her breasts. She raised her arms for him to take it off and they looked together, James propped on his elbow. They took in her taut navel, her darkened nipples, her swollen ankles. He placed his hand on the round of her womb and the baby's foot or fist rose to meet it. But Annie Clyde wasn't the only one whose body had changed. During her pregnancy she cared for her mother while James ran the farm alone. He would leave the house before dawn with a bucket of cold dinner and stay gone until suppertime. He butchered the hog, chopped down trees for wood, spent whole days in the corncrib shelling or carrying boxes of kernels to the mill to be ground. While she had gained weight, he had lost some. There were new shadows under his eyes, new skinned places across his knuckles, a spider bite on his forearm from a black widow hiding in the woodpile. She thought how it must have hurt him and tears rolled from her eye corners toward her ears. James asked, "Why are you crying?" She said, "I don't know." He said, "Look at you. How beautiful you are." She had held on to him, unable to tell his warmth from her own, not wanting the night to be over.

Then morning lit the curtains again, and the silence between them came back. It stretched out long at the breakfast table, with the kitchen still and Mary dying upstairs. In the evenings before Annie Clyde put out the lamps to save oil, she'd catch him drowsing again in his chair by the fire as she sewed buttons back on his shirts and feel as separate from him as she did from the dark outside. She'd think of the mountains brooding over the farm, the wind sweeping its forty acres. She wanted to talk to James, but they seldom knew what to say to each other. Annie Clyde saw her fault in it. She had always been one to keep to herself. Even as a baby she had wriggled out of Mary's confining arms. When she started school she had made no friends. At first the girls and boys were drawn to her prettiness. Lined up in the mornings at the schoolhouse door, the boys had pulled her hair and the other girls had given her gifts of ribbons and peppermint. But her sullenness had finally driven them away. Annie Clyde didn't know why she acted like she did. The others were the same as her in their flour sack dresses with nothing but pone bread for their dinner. All of them had toes poking out of holes in their shoes. There were no outcasts among them. Annie Clyde had made an outcast of herself. She would sit on the schoolhouse bench stiff and straight, too conscious of her sleeve touching the arm of another child.

Gracie had changed things when she came along. Annie Clyde couldn't have kept all to herself if she wanted to anymore. Gracie followed her everywhere, always talking and singing and romping with the dog. Always wanting Annie Clyde's attention, showing her buckeyes and seedpods and bugs. Whatever Annie Clyde's neighbors thought of her sullenness, they'd been drawn to Gracie. She never felt like part of the town, but her daughter was somehow. They would stand at their mailboxes and wave as she walked Gracie down the road to Joe Dixon's, where the old men bought her sticks of horehound candy. At church the old women took her onto their laps. Gracie looked like Annie Clyde, but she was more like James on the inside. She had her father's friendliness about her, his kind nature. Last year when Gracie was two they took her to a molasses-making at the Hankins farm across the road. Dale Hankins grew sorghum cane, his back field high with thin stalks, their ends tasseled umber with seeds. Before dark he would feed the stalks into a cane mill between steel rollers, the juice pouring into vats to be boiled. It took ten gallons of cane juice to make one of molasses. All the neighbors for miles gathered to gossip and tell stories, the little ones playing and the teenagers courting, the men leaning under the shade trees with their hats stacked on a post of the hog pen and their overalls still dusted with the work of the day. Once the moon rose and the cane juice was ready for boiling, Dale would bring out his guitar. It was tradition for some of the children to dance on the cane fodder scattering the ground. That night Gracie had thrown off her shoes and whirled barefoot to the strumming, dress flared out like a bell. She'd stomped and shook her curls as the whole town laughed and clapped. Annie Clyde had felt close to her neighbors. But then she'd noticed Beulah Kesterson with the pouch of bones around her neck, wrinkled face lurid in the firelight, watching Gracie without smiling. After that, the night was ruined for Annie Clyde. The old woman gave her an ill feeling.

Now she looked at Gracie sitting on the back of the fallen beech and felt overcome with such loss that she had to shut her eyes. She had managed not to cry for two years and wouldn't let herself break down now. This was like dreams she'd had as a child of her parents dying, without the relief of waking and knowing it wasn't true. The wind rose again, blowing strands of hair across her face and fluttering the sleeves of her dress. She opened her eyes, too aware of a weight in her pocket. It was the tin top the drifter had given Gracie. It seemed to Annie Clyde in that moment like a threat or a curse. On impulse she pulled it out with disgust and tossed it while Gracie wasn't look-ing into the shadows under the beech tree's tortured roots. She felt somewhat better when she couldn't see it anymore. She wiped her palms on the front of her dress then went to lift her daughter off the beech's back, swung her up and held her close. Gracie's slender arms came around Annie Clyde's neck and they studied each other, their noses inches apart. Gracie's eyes were the same as her grandmother Mary's had been, wide brown with an amber shine to them. Gracie took a lock of Annie Clyde's hair and twisted it up in her fingers, like she used to do when she was nursing. "Come on," Annie Clyde said, pushing her nose against Gracie's. "We better get Rusty to the house before he runs off and leaves us again."

Silver Ledford heard the Model A Ford that belonged to James Dodson rounding the bend before she saw it. She knew it was her niece's husband because the only other vehicle left in Yuneetah belonged to the sheriff and he had no purpose out this way. The Dodsons had been on her mind all morning. Now here came the truck that would drive the last of her people off to a city she couldn't picture. Some man taking her niece away, as a man had taken away her sister. She stepped over into the ditch and stood in the marsh of it, tall and rail thin with black hair that had dulled to smoky gray over the forty-four years she'd spent for the most part alone. She kept still as though James wouldn't see her if she didn't move. But he did see her. He slowed the puttering truck and ducked his head to look at her through the cranked-down window. She feared he would offer her a ride because of the wind and the lowering sky. He seemed to consider it, but raised a hand to her instead and went on. She nodded to him once he was past. Then she climbed out of the ditch, the cotton sack strapped to her shoulder getting snagged on pricker bushes. She watched until the Model A swerved out of sight between the banks, high with spires of purple monkshood. For a while she lingered in the middle of the road, giving James time to get home, not wanting to catch up with him no matter how the weather threatened. Silver supposed all the years alone had made her this way. She'd forgotten how to do anything but hide from people.

Last week Annie Clyde had come up the mountain to ask Silver a favor and brought the child with her. They found Silver picking cucumbers in the garden, a long plot out behind her shack crowded with cornstalks and ruffled with tomato vines. She saw their hound first, trotting along ahead of them. She turned her head to watch him go sniffing around the back lot. She liked animals but not the kind that begged for scraps. When she turned back Annie Clyde and Gracie were standing at the edge of the garden holding hands, the ancient firs that grew so towering up where Silver lived dark green behind them. Above them clouds scudded across the blue sky. Silver would remember them that way for as long as she lived. She had marked every detail. The loose threads at the hem of Gracie's dress and the apples bulging its pockets, the residue of flour rubbed into the grain of its sacking. Annie Clyde's hip bones poking at the thin cotton of her grayed shift, the briar scratches scabbing on her shins. By the time those scabs fell off the girl would be in some other place, this one growing more and more distant in her mind. Silver couldn't stop staring at Annie Clyde's legs. She kept her eyes fixed on them as the girl said her piece. It was easier than looking at her face. Though Silver wasn't listening, she knew what her niece was talking about. The time had come. Annie Clyde and Gracie were leaving Yuneetah.

Silver couldn't see much of herself in either of them. Their bones were fine and she was rawboned. Their hair soft and hers bushy, their skin touched with Cherokee blood and hers with the hoarfrost of the winters she had survived up near the mountaintop. It was Mary they both resembled. She had been the town beauty up until she died. Annie Clyde had Mary's same ripe lips and the same freckle on her collarbone. It was clear when Gracie came along that she too would inherit Mary's looks. But there were other ways to be related. Silver hadn't heard her niece's voice until she was nearly grown. She was still unsure about the girl's eye color, hard to tell through lowered lashes. Annie Clyde had stared off into the woods as she talked, at the top of Silver's head or down at her toes digging into the loam. She didn't like asking favors. She didn't like talking at all. Silver could see that it took something out of her. "We're leaving for Michigan next Saturday morning," Annie Clyde had said, glancing in an uncertain way at the dog as he lapped from a puddle. "I was wondering if you'd take Rusty for a while. Just until we get settled. I reckon James's uncle will sell his corn for him. He'll be back down to get his money then." Silver's hands stilled in the cucumber vines. "You don't have to take him now," Annie Clyde rushed on. "You can wait until Saturday, before we head out. Or I'll bring him up here to you." Silver couldn't answer at first, afraid if she opened her mouth her heart might spill out.

Silver knew she had been no kind of aunt to Annie Clyde. She called on the Dodsons only to pick their apples or knock on their kitchen door and offer a jar of the chartered moonshine she made as medicine before winter set in. Most of the time she could put down her head and work through her days. But sometimes the child's voice drifting up from the farm filled her with regret. She wanted to offer the Dodsons more than moonshine. She thought of asking forgiveness for her absence but didn't trust herself to say the words right. She spoke to Annie Clyde no more than a few times a year. Sometimes Annie Clyde came up the mountain out of obligation, knowing if Silver stood on a rickety chair to string peppers and the legs gave out she could strike her head on the hearthstone. She could catch a fever and not recover, or break her leg out hunting and lie unfound until the crows picked her bones clean and the possums dragged them off. But all of those Silver loved most had left her alone in the end. Annie Clyde would be no different. Silver would watch her niece ride off down the road. When the truck was out of sight she'd go back through the hayfield and past the apple tree still laden with fruit, up the mountain moving over the stones and roots and ridges of a path her feet could have followed in the dead of night, back to the shack her grandfather built that she had always lived in. She would sit in front of her cold fireplace while down below the lake crept over the Walker farm until it disappeared.

As Silver pondered these things, Gracie came to kneel beside her in the garden dirt. While Gracie played in the loam, flies buzzing around them, Silver remembered the one time she had held the child. She'd seen Annie Clyde behind the house hanging sheets on the first warm day of spring, the farm smelling of turned earth and mown hay, on her way down the track to the road. Annie Clyde had waved Silver over. Gracie was crying in a basket at Annie Clyde's feet and she asked Silver with pins in her mouth to take the baby for a minute. Silver was trying to recall what Gracie had felt like in her arms when the child lifted a woolly worm on the bridge of her finger and showed it to Silver. Silver tensed but held out her hand to let the worm pass from Gracie's flesh to her own. They looked at each other as Annie Clyde looked down on their heads. Now Silver wanted that moment to be the last one she spent with her kin. She didn't know if she could face the loss ahead of her even without seeing it happen before her eyes. She didn't want to remember them riding off in James Dodson's Model A Ford, its bed piled high with chattel. Their going no different than any of those other departures she had witnessed from her perch on the ridge.

Kneeling there with Gracie in the garden loam last week, Silver had agreed to take the dog. She couldn't refuse. But even as they walked away from her, Annie Clyde leading Gracie by the hand and their coonhound loping after them, she didn't want him. Not for any length of time. The only dogs she'd known were those her grandfather used to keep to guard his moonshine still. The last had been the meanest, a shepherd bitch that bit Silver if she got too close.

She'd left a tin feed pan and some mildewed bedding up at the still for ages, in the shed where the bitch was put when she went into heat. Silver hadn't had the heart to throw them out because they reminded her of her grandfather's affection for dogs. She had none herself, but she owed her niece something. She felt bound to do the favor Annie Clyde had asked of her, as much as she dreaded it. If Silver could write she might have slipped off with the dog in the night and left a note under a rock on the stoop. She wasn't supposed to take him until tomorrow. But if she did it now, she wouldn't have to say good-bye to her people. She wouldn't have to watch them leaving without her.

Silver's mind had been burdened this way since she woke at dawn. She took a long time lighting a fire and boiling her oats. At last she decided to go down the mountain and figure out what to do about her niece's dog later. She had other business to attend to in the valley. She'd been meaning for weeks to gather the last of the trumpet weed growing on the west end of the Hankinses' pasture before it was drowned. She used the long, hollow stems like straws for reaching into the charred oaken barrels she'd buried underground at the beginning of spring. She would draw out the aged whiskey deep inside and swirl it on her tongue. Then she would spit a mouthful onto the mink-scratched clay of the bank to keep from swallowing it. Whiskey was made for selling and not drinking. That's where her grandfather Plummerman Ledford had gone wrong. He drank about as much moonshine as he ran off until it killed him. When he died Silver watched as her grandmother Mildred placed coins on his eyes and washed his face, pitted and scarred under his whiskers. Then Silver went to the still and plucked a pink clover for his breast pocket. There was no funeral but she had said her own prayers. Before Plum died, he'd showed Silver everywhere trumpet weed flourished. In past seasons she'd hurried to beat the browsing deer and not the coming lake to her straws. These days most of the weed was eaten off, but when she was a girl the meadows of Yuneetah had been thick with it in late summer on into fall, the drooping lances of its leaves and the pale lavender umbels of its flowers rising ten feet over the goldenrod and thistles along the fencerows. Back then she and Plum had been in no danger of running out.

Silver's grandfather had taught her everything about bootlegging, starting with how moonshine got its name, made at night so the law wouldn't see the smoke. She had liked being with him up at the still, set into a stream bank high on the mountain since before she was born. The round metal still pot packed in glistening mud beneath the barrel cap. The stack of the furnace, a fifty-five-gallon drum cut in half, jutting out full of kindling. When the still was running flames wrapped around the pot and shot out the flue at the back, vapors collecting in the barrel cap then moving down into the thumper keg and the condenser. Silver would wash out jars in the trickling stream or whatever her grandfather let her help with. He'd taught her to make whiskey without store-bought yeast or sugar or grain, using corn from their garden and home-sprouted malt. They put half a bushel of meal in each barrel, the other half to be heated for mush in the still pot, and left it a couple of days before coming back to stir it with a stick. Then they added a gallon of ground corn malt and one of meal with a cap of rye sprinkled on top to keep the mash warm. A week or so later when the cap fell off and the top was clear, the whiskey was ready to run off. It was only in the years since Plum died that Silver had taken to chartering moonshine, experimenting with the brew she'd been taught to make. Sometimes she mixed in ginger and orange peel for taste. Sometimes herbs and roots to make the medicine she gave to her niece for Gracie, consulting with Beulah Kesterson on what was wisest to use. She'd found that tulip tree bark worked best for fever. She had sold some of her medicine to Beulah before the old woman gave up peddling, but she made it more for pleasure than for anything else. It was the work she needed, the ritual of following the stream upward each morning until the air turned cooler and purer, to where the still was set in the bank beneath a stand of red buckeye trees.

It wasn't long past ten o'clock this morning when Silver had strapped on the cotton sack she used for picking and climbed down the winding trail that came out at the foot of the mountain behind the Walker farm. Though she had put a rope in her sack for the dog just in case, she'd kept her face turned away as she went through the hayfield, past the house and on down the track. At the end of the track she had crossed the road and ducked under the fence into the Hankins pasture. She'd gone downhill to where the reservoir was visible, fingers of water pointing farther landward, watching her feet. The cattle were gone but the dried pucks of their manure had come back to life. Soaking up the rain they looked fresh again, sprouting frail clusters of nodding toadstools. She'd stopped when she reached where the lake spilled over, wavering with strands of foxtail and crabgrass. She was surprised at the foothold the reservoir had gained within a few months, how much it had overtaken. Most of the trees and barn sides the power company had slashed with paint to mark how far the water would come had already been wetted. Gulls and herons had already begun to nest. After another night of rain, some of the roads would surely be washed out. Like the rest of the town, Silver was used to the floods and their damage. It was the lake's stealthiness that bothered her. She had felt it behind her as she sawed at the hollow stems with her corn knife until her arm grew tired, gathering as much this one last time as she could carry home.

Now it was past noon and Silver had remained in the middle of the road for too long looking after James Dodson's truck, the cotton sack full but light on her shoulder. Even with the day overcast she could feel August breathing on her. It had another look, its own kind of heat. On the way out of the pasture she'd seen the first henbit stalks tipped with clusters of the seed that would spread them. The end of summer was near and then autumn. But this season the stinkbugs and crickets wouldn't come into the houses for warmth. No leaves would blow down the road on the fall winds, no apples would harden under the frost. Pawpaws would go to ruin at the bottom of the lake with nobody around to taste the sweet mash of their middles. Silver used to think she wanted nothing more than to be left alone like this. Nothing more than room to breathe. Until she was twelve, six Ledfords had lived in the shack near the mountaintop. Silver and her sister Mary. Her parents, Esther and Jeremiah. Her grandparents Plum and Mildred. Before Plum moved his family to Tennessee from Kentucky he and Mildred had eight boys, but Silver never knew her uncles. The Ledford sons had taken off as soon as they came of age. Only Silver's father returned home with his fortune unfound. He'd brought Silver's mother with him, already big with Mary.

As close as the Ledfords had lived in their shack, they'd seldom touched. Silver wasn't beaten or cared for either one. She learned not to seek attention after she woke with the croup and tried to climb onto her hateful grandmother's lap, slopping the old woman's coffee over the rim of her cup. Mildred had called Silver a clumsy ox with more contempt in her voice than any grandchild deserved. Not long after that Silver had lost a front tooth and tried to show her father while he was skinning a squirrel. She held out her palm wanting him to take it or at least to look at it, a piece of her fallen off, but without glancing up he just told her to get along. So she closed her fingers into a fist and ran into the woods to throw the tooth down, kicking pine duff over it. Her father had been silent and morose and she'd been somewhat afraid of him. But she'd liked peeking out at him through the front window as he came back from hunting in the dark. His skin polished by the lantern shine, black hair running over his shoulders. Plum used to say Jeremiah took after his Cherokee grand-mother that had lived on the reservation in North Carolina. Mildred had called Jeremiah trifling because he would sit in the tree stand with his rifle for hours letting deer pass beneath him, staring off at the distant hills. Silver was too young then to understand her father's discontent, but now she felt for him. Even though he'd seemed to feel nothing for her.

Silver didn't miss her father much when he was gone. Not like her mother. Her best memory was of sitting beside Esther Ledford on the edge of the doorsill looking up at the sky, Esther reaching into her pocket and giving Silver a chunk of fool's gold. "It might be good luck," she said, pressing it into Silver's palm. From what Silver recalled her mother was slim with straw-colored braids wound at her nape. She kept a valise brought from wherever Silver's father had found her, full of fancy dresses. Sometimes Esther put them on, though she had nowhere to wear them. She'd strap her heeled shoes onto Silver's feet and laugh as her daughter stumbled around in them. Back then Silver believed what her mother told her when they went seining in the river at night, dragging the fishing net along between them as they waded out toward the deeper reaches. "Look at that reflection the moon makes on the water. Prettiest thing I ever seen, until you was born. That's how come I named you Silver. You was the most precious thing in the world to me."

But Silver's worst memory was of her mother as well, Esther drinking down a cup of pennyroyal tea with Mildred standing by to make sure she took every drop. At the time Silver didn't know what Mildred meant when she said, "We don't need no more mouths to feed around here." That afternoon Silver had found her mother lying abed and clutching her belly. When Silver asked what was wrong Esther wept in pain, tears soaking her dress collar. Knowing now what pennyroyal tea was for, Silver guessed she and Mary would have had more siblings if Mildred had allowed them to live. A few months after drinking down that cup Esther woke Silver and Mary with the brush of her lips on their foreheads. "Me and your daddy's got to go away," she told them. "See about a job of work. We'll be back after you soon as we can." But they never came back to Yuneetah, or wrote to say where they went. Silver knew it was Mildred they were leaving behind, but neither she nor Mary had been reason enough for her parents to stay.

Once Silver's mother was gone, she clung to her sister. Silver was younger by two years and followed Mary everywhere. They played together from morning until evening, chasing each other through the woods, scuffing up leaves to hear the brittle stir of them. They spent whole days on the riverbank, hiding from each other in the rushes and skipping stones, making cane poles to fish with. They walked the dirt road to the schoolhouse holding hands in the cool of the mornings, a strip of grass up its middle like the brush of a mane. The other children looked sidelong at Silver's burlap sack dresses, the snags of hair down her back. They would play with Mary but not with her. She quit after the third grade, but Mary went on until the eighth. Silver couldn't say when she and Mary first turned over and slept with their backs to each other. They grew farther apart as their legs grew longer. Then when Mary turned fifteen she went to work for Clyde Walker. His wife had died in the winter from rheumatic fever and he needed a girl to help with the household chores. Silver noticed how much time her sister was spending on the Walker farm, not coming home until after dark, but she didn't want to believe it when Mary announced she was getting married. She asked Mary what she wanted with a man thirty years her senior and Mary said there was nobody kinder alive than Clyde Walker. Once Mary left the mountain she didn't come back, even to visit. Just like their parents. Mildred claimed she had got above her raising, thought she was too good for them. But Mary hadn't got above. She had got away.

After Plum passed on and Mary took up with Clyde Walker, Silver was alone with her grandmother. She couldn't see how her light-hearted grandfather had ended up married to such a shrewish woman. Before Plum died Mildred was always harping on him about the farm the Ledfords had in Kentucky before he went to jail for bootlegging, a two-story house with a stocked pond and strawberry fields. Silver figured that farm was what Mildred had wanted with Plum in the first place, but when he was caught by the revenuers he'd mortgaged it to pay his legal bills. After he was convicted he lost his land. Mildred claimed she would have left him then if not for the baby she was carrying. She hadn't uttered a kind word to him within Silver's hearing, but he'd always seemed more amused by her than anything. Silver vowed that she wouldn't be cowed by the old woman either. They went weeks without speaking, Silver spending most of her time making moonshine. When the still was frozen into the stream bed under clumps of snow-drifted laurel she ignored Mildred as best she could. She stared into the fire until shadows crept across the floor and up the room corners, drafts sending dervishes of dust like whisking tails across the floorboards. She'd watch the flames dwindle to glowing coals until the sound of her own clacking teeth brought her around. Then she'd get up with blued toes and gather enough wood to burn through the night. Those winters Silver slept under buckskins, the only covering that held in her heat once the fire died. It seemed the memories of deer transferred into her dreams as she moved through the woods with no voice in them, as she swam across the river at sunset parting the water with herself. She slept and dreamed the hours away, waiting for the thaw when she could go back up to the still. Until finally one spring the old woman died and Silver buried her in the hollow graveyard where the ground was darkened by the maples pushing against the fence. She stood under the leaves tossing dirt on her grandmother's casket until someone took the shovel from her. Then she went back to making moonshine and had been at it ever since. Her business hadn't waned until the dam gates closed. Customers kept coming to her back door, trading hanks of salt pork, cured hides and strings of squirrel for something to make their heads feel lighter. But even if nobody bought her moonshine, Silver would go on making it.

She would have stood there longer with her thoughts if the wind hadn't picked up and pushed her from behind, blowing her hair in knots and fetters before her, shuffling the trumpet weed in her sack. She glanced up at the skies and got moving, following the grooves James Dodson's truck had made in the road, her feet marring the rankled print of his tires. Still deciding what to do when she reached the Walker farm, she almost walked into the back of the Model A Ford pulled over to the shoulder. When she saw it parked there she stopped short. Then she took a hesitant step forward, trying to see through the back window into the boxy cab. She had never been this close to the vehicle that would take her people away. The rusted hubcaps and running boards, the arched fenders and the round headlamps on either side of the grille. Through the stakes she could see there was nothing inside. But she pictured it loaded with furniture that once belonged to her sister. It crossed her mind that if she raised the hood and yanked out a cable the Dodsons would be going nowhere tomorrow. She might have done it if she hadn't been distracted by a bustling behind the barbwire fence. She thought at first it must be James coming back to the truck, though she couldn't think why he'd be in the Hankins pasture. Then a blackbird burst out of the hedge and disappeared in the trees above. The roadside bank was astir with them, foraging for seed, grub and cricket before the rain. She could sense the beads of their eyes watching her, as if they knew what she'd considered. She bowed her face and hurried to the other side of the road, dragging her sack through puddles floating with canoes of willow leaf.

Silver didn't slow down until she came to her niece's split-rail fence. There she paused and looked into the cornstalks, the shucks holding the roasting ears swaddled. After decades the Walker farm still reminded Silver of how her sister chose a man and his land over her own flesh and blood. But as far as they'd drifted from one another, Silver had felt like she was dying herself when she learned Mary had a cancer of the womb. On the winter night Mary died

Annie Clyde sent James up the mountain to fetch Silver. He knocked on her door holding a lantern. She followed him back down with a quilt bundled around her shoulders. Mary was talking out of her head by the time Silver got there. Silver sat all night with Annie Clyde in Mary's freezing bedroom shivering as the fire burned out. But she left before it was over, refusing to watch Mary take her last breath. She didn't attend the funeral at the Free Will Baptist church either. She went back up the mountain and stayed indoors the rest of that winter, skitters of ice ticking at the windowpanes. She spent those months grieving and trying to keep warm. She forgot her own birthday that year because Mary would grow no older. Now standing this close to where Mary died was like reliving it all. She couldn't fathom going up to the house and knocking on the door.

She was lingering at the fence, putting off the long walk up the track, when something dropped from above and landed at her feet. Her first confused thought was of the blackbirds. She half expected to find a pile of feathers in the damp grass. But when she crouched with the cotton sack trailing and her dress around her thighs what she discovered was an ear of sweet corn. Gnawed down to a few yellow-white kernels, fat to bursting and shining like pearls in the dimness. Silver rose and whirled around. When she saw the man across the road her backbone straightened. He was hunkered on one knee atop the bank overlooking the cornfield picking his teeth with a matchstick, staring across the tassels at the roof of Annie Clyde's house. After a second he pitched the matchstick and shifted his stare onto Silver. She was overcome with a feeling like spiders crawling up her arms. He stood then, trampling wildflowers underneath his boots, the wind lifting the heavy tail of his peacoat. At the same time, some heaviness lifted from Silver. She hadn't thought of Amos in years, but a part of her must have been waiting for him all along. She stayed put as he strode down the bank and stopped before her, his bindle on his shoulder. Up close, he smelled like moss and fungus. "How are you making it, Silver?" he asked.

She opened her mouth but could find no fitting answer. She studied him in silence, too moved to speak. She realized she'd given him up for dead years ago. It was a feat that he had managed to live this long. But she shouldn't have doubted him. Amos was the only one who always came back. He was a force as sure and dangerous as the river. She took him in, her eyes starting at his worn boot toes, moving up the ragged legs of his gabardine trousers, resting at last on his lean face. Something came over Silver then. Maybe it was the day she'd spent out of sorts. Or the months spent feeling alone like never before. She reached out to lay her palm against his black-whiskered cheek. "You still look like yourself," she told him. With her thumb she grazed over the scarring of his eye socket, a pocket of fever-hot flesh. "How come you don't change?"

Amos didn't flinch, but his fingers raised between them and closed around her wrist. He guided her hand back to her side and it hung there, burning. "I never saw the use in change."

Silver swallowed a catch in her throat. "I guess you saw things are different around here."

"But not you." His attention turned to the cotton sack strapped on her shoulder, the wooden handle of her corn knife poking out among the trumpet weed umbels. "Still an outlaw."

Silver felt herself smiling, her dry lips splitting in places. She touched the cuts as if to take her smile back, but Amos returned it. She glanced down again at the cuffs of his trousers, laden with muck from the ditch. He must have eaten his dinner in the gully, as she had hidden herself less than an hour earlier. But Amos was probably avoiding the sheriff and not James Dodson. She could have told him Ellard Moody was occupied with the power company, but she figured it would be better not to mention the sheriff's name given her history with both men. "We got the place to ourselves now," she said. "Ain't that what we wanted when we was little?"

Amos's smile vanished. "Seems so. They couldn't get rid of us so they left it to us."

Silver didn't like the shadow that crossed his brow, the gleam that had come into his eye. She decided to change the subject. "Beulah's still around, though. You headed up the holler?"

"And your niece," Amos said, ignoring her question. "She's still here."

She thought of him up on the bank, staring across the corn. "You've seen Annie Clyde?"

"Not much of her," he said. "She ran me off."

"What are you doing out here, Amos?"

"Wondering if I can beat the rain up to Beulah's."

"I doubt it. You better find someplace to get in."

"You better, too."

"I don't mind the rain," she said.

"No," he said, his one eye meeting hers. "You never did."

Silver felt the burn in her palm spreading. "You can come up the mountain with me."

He looked over his shoulder, toward the weedy bank. "I ought to be getting along."

"Will you come directly? I got a lard can full of blackberries going to waste up yonder."

Amos paused, gazing at her in a way that would later trouble her dreams. "I don't know this time, Silver," he said. Then he tipped his hat and walked off. She watched him go with loose-limbed grace up the bank, his lithe back moving away from her. Once he was out of sight she turned and braced herself on the fence rail. Since childhood Amos had had a way of shaking Silver up, muddling her senses. She suspected he had the same effect on other women in the far-off places he passed through, at least those unafraid to look at him for long. Silver had never feared Amos as most others did. From the time he was a foundling the townspeople of Yuneetah had turned their heads when Beulah Kesterson brought him along on her peddling rounds. He wasn't an ugly boy. His face was almost too perfect. Like a mask, white and smooth as porcelain. Unlike the rest of Yuneetah, Silver couldn't get her fill of Amos's looks, even after his eye was lost. When they were children playing in the hollow he used to smile at her like they had a secret, as though she was complicit in his mischief. Ellard Moody was a sweeter boy, braiding willow crowns for Silver's head and giving her his best marbles. But she had wanted Amos.

When Mary started leaving Silver behind, Amos was her friend. He sought her company, tossing chips of shale at her window to call her out. She would go with him collecting rocks and periwinkles along the river, standing still together when fawns came out of the bluff oaks to drink. One night during a meteor shower they climbed to the mountaintop, stars streaking close enough to catch them on fire. He showed her all of the town's hiding places. The caves where men escaped from the Home Guard during the Civil War. The foundation stones of a burned-down tavern where there had been a battle with many soldiers killed inside. One summer he led her across the Whitehall County line to an abandoned iron mine up in the hills. They went several miles down a cart trail used by mules to pull the ore then followed an old railbed until the woods thinned enough for them to see the tipple. They stood inside the shaft's lower entrance, fifty feet high with chalked arrows marking the ore veins. Outside the upper shaft they watched the cool air of the mine turn to steam as it met the heat outside. They ventured a long way down the deep tunnels, curving out of sight into nothingness. They peered into the broken windows of the superintendent's house, once painted white with cheerful blue trim, and Silver had wished to live there with Amos until she died. Never to go back to Yuneetah and her hateful grandmother.

As much as Silver loved her sister she felt kin to Amos in a way that went deeper than blood. Every few years since he left on a train he had come back to visit her. She might get home from picking blackberries and find him leaning against her door with his hat brim shading his eye socket. He would greet her as though days and not years had passed. Then he'd ask for a bite to eat and she'd bring him whatever she had. When he was full he would get up without a word to see what needed fixing around her place. In winter he chopped firewood. In summer he hacked down the honeysuckle burying the side of her shack. When the work was done he might camp for a night in her woods. He would build his fire and she'd sit with him awhile. She would look at him through the rolling smoke and he would look back, mouth corners lifting. She'd remember other fires they built together as children in the caves where they hunted for mica, feldspar and quartz. Where they drew in the ash with their fingers and wrote their names on the craggy walls. She would meet his eye as she seldom did anyone else's and a heat that had nothing to do with the fire would rise up from her belly. She tried to contain such feelings. It was hard on her, though. With his hat off and his hair black as oil tucked behind his ears he looked naked. She always went to him first, sometimes crawling, getting her hands and knees sooty. He wouldn't touch her otherwise. She'd slip her dress off her shoulders, reach for his hand and put it where she wanted it. Then he would lay her down so close to the flames that cinders lit on her forehead, that the ends of her hair were singed. She might feel ashamed of herself once he was gone, and even more unwanted, but for some reason she had no pride when it came to Amos.

Though Silver had a kind of love for Amos she'd seen the other side of him. He hadn't turned his cruelty on her, but she'd been witness to it. There was a thoughtful anger he harbored, patient like all else about him. The summer before he first left Yuneetah, Buck Shelton had accused him of stopping up his well with rocks. Shelton was a gambler and a drunkard with more than one enemy, but somehow he was convinced that Amos was the culprit. He probably figured he could thrash a young boy easier than he could a grown man. When Shelton came up the mountain to buy whiskey Silver had heard him

cussing Amos, swearing to Plum that he was going to stripe the boy
with a switch. After he sobered up he'd gone to the sheriff, but Beulah had slipped Amos out the side door when they came up the hollow looking for him. Silver had forgotten all about the incident until
twenty-five years later, when Shelton's back field caught fire. She
had watched it burn from her ridge near the mountaintop, able to
see miles of the valley when the trees were bare in autumn. As she
stood there on the cool limestone ledge Amos appeared beside her,
the only creature that could sneak up on her. She hadn't seen him in
months but he made no greeting. Just lingered at her side smoking a
cigarette. "I never stopped up any well," he said at last. He was a liar
but Silver believed he was mostly honest with her. She looked at the
ember of his cigarette tip and then back at the other smoke below,
knowing without having to ask that he'd used the blazing sedge like
a match as he walked out of the field.

Silver had taught herself not to think of Amos while he was away
but when she was younger she used to wonder as she drifted to sleep
what other fires he had set elsewhere. What other, worse trouble
he might have caused. She supposed he should have been locked up
long ago. But she couldn't imagine him caged. Now she looked into
the corn tossing behind the split-rail fence, unable to see the house
with Annie Clyde and Gracie alone inside. She had known Amos for
almost forty years but that didn't mean she fully trusted him. This
would be the time for him to settle any business left unfinished in
Yuneetah. She couldn't think of anything he might hold against the
Dodsons but she wasn't fool enough to believe he would leave her
family alone on her account either. She rubbed a knuckle across her
split lips, tasting blood and dirt. Then she heard the racket of James
Dodson's truck coming again and felt far more burdened than she
had started out this morning. Before James appeared around the
curve Silver hoisted herself over the fence into the field, pulling
the sack across the top rail behind her. She receded into the corn

as the Model A Ford approached, the plants shaking in the wind and the blackbirds scolding each other in the fencerow. She didn't want to ever come out. She might stand there among the living stalks until she became one of them. Until the lake came at last to drown her with them.

Near one o'clock James Dodson had parked his truck alongside the road, less than a mile from home. He had set out early to Sevierville and been gone for hours. His back ached and his head pounded. What stopped him was the absence of Dale Hankins's house from the field where it had stood for at least a century. As Dale told it, the Hankins patriarch had built the house himself. He dragged from the river on a sledge the same kind of rocks that could be found in cemeteries all over the valley marking graves of men, women and children the floods had swept away. Each time James ate Sunday dinner there it seemed he could smell brackish water in the walls. It wasn't unusual to come upon houses torn down in Yuneetah these days, but Dale's wasn't being demolished. James thought he was seeing things. He rubbed his eyes and got out of the truck, knowing that he risked never getting it started again. He climbed stiff-legged up the bank and paused at the fence, seeing in his mind what used to be there. Dale's homeplace standing alone in the flat pasture looking stranded, cattle grazing near the porch with nothing to keep them out of the yard. Dale had farmed this plot since he was a boy, a hundred acres of bottomland on the river. Now the livestock had gone to slaughter and the house had disappeared.

James ducked between the barbed strands of the fence and swished through the weeds, knee high without cows to crop them. He hadn't gone far when he saw it. A rugged gash at least sixty feet wide and almost as deep cleaved the pasture in two. A chasm had opened up in Dale's field. It must have swallowed the house whole. James stood still. He could almost hear the groan as he pictured it listing and then heaving into the abyss, joists splitting and floorboards popping, sending up a column of sand. He guessed the ground had sunk under the weight of standing rainwater. All over Yuneetah the land was eroding, groundwater causing depressions like bowls, soil over cavernous bedrock collapsing. The same caves underlay the Walker farm. James had noticed some of the fence posts slumping. They were lucky to be getting out of town unscathed. Everybody else was already gone. James hadn't passed a soul on the way in, save for Annie Clyde's aunt with a sack full of trumpet weed along the ditch, and Silver lived above the taking line. They were cutting it too close for James's comfort, leaving just before the August 3 deadline the power company had given them, but he was thankful they were finally going. He moved as near to the edge as he dared and looked into the red clay pit piled with rubble. On top of the busted rock, warped tin collected rain. Glass shards reflected the sun behind a knot of clouds. At least Dale and his family were safe in Detroit. They had left Yuneetah months ago.

James had known since he was a child that the valley belonged to the river and the weather, no matter what a man did to tame it. Dale had once confided to James that he felt the same way. It could beat a man down, trying to farm land not fit for row crops, each season losing some of what little he was able to grow to the floods. "I'm ready to get out of here," Dale told James when the TVA came to town. "Everybody's squalling, but I ain't sorry. I'll take what I can get and run. All I care about is my people. That's all that's worth anything, when it comes down to it." They both knew that working in a steel mill would be no easier than farming. They would trade hot sun for a furnace, cracked earth for molten metal, a cloud of grit for a film of black soot. Neither of them knew exactly what to expect, moving off to live in a northern city. But at least there would be a paycheck at the end of each week. Now finally Dale had escaped Yuneetah and tomorrow James would follow him out. They would be neighbors again in Michigan.

Dale and James were often mistaken for brothers, with their same reddish hair, but they hadn't met until James married Annie Clyde. Dale was the kind of man who offered his help before a neighbor had to ask for it. Like after what happened to James's horse. His uncle Wallace had given him Ranger, already old, a Tennessee walker with a sorrel coat. In the months after James's father died and he went to live at the parsonage beside the Methodist church, being with the horse had eased his mind as nothing else could. A tap of his booted heels would send Ranger trotting across creeks and pastureland, wind lifting James's sweaty hair from his forehead. Some nights he slept in the barn under a blanket matted with hairs, lulled by the sound of the horse and the two plow mules snorting and pawing at their stalls. He'd dreamed back then of moving to Texas and working on a ranch breaking wild mustangs. He imagined how it would be to stand in a corral among their jostling necks, their muscled flanks, their high tails, the plumes of dust they kicked up settling over him. But as he grew into a man he saw how that couldn't happen.

After James and Annie Clyde got married Ranger was the only thing he brought with him to her farm, the only thing worth having from his former life. When they were courting, each Saturday he'd ridden over the hills and down the back roads to visit her. One morning he galloped to the garden as she drudged in the loam on her knees. He dismounted and stood over her. She looked up but didn't smile, as if he was bothering her in the middle of something important. He saw the lines around her hazel eyes that hours of toil in the sun had already hatched. "Get up," he ordered and she frowned. "Come on, just for a little while." She came to him at last, seeming doubtful even as he took hold of her hips and hoisted her up into the saddle. He climbed on behind her and walked Ranger up the hill where tobacco used to grow, past the pond yellowed with pollen and dimpled by the mouths of walleyed bass. They rode into the pines where there was only the clop of the horse's hooves, the salty tang of Annie Clyde's sweat. When she said, "I ought to be getting back," James dug his heels into Ranger's sides, urging him into a gallop again. Annie Clyde laughed then, carefree in a way that James seldom saw her.

Not long after Annie Clyde and James were married, Ranger stumbled in the rocky furrows of the farm's lower field and broke his leg. On the morning it happened, Dale had come driving up to the fence to see if James and Annie Clyde wanted a ride to the market in Knoxville. He found James kneeling with his back to the field, unable to look at the horse. Ranger lay where he'd gone down, bloodshot eyes rolling. Dale asked what was wrong and James was ashamed to tell him. Dale looked toward the field, eyes squinted. He squirted tobacco juice between his teeth and said, "I lost mine the same way. The horse doctor put him down for me. I couldn't do it myself." He glanced at James. "I got my rifle in the truck." James nodded once then dropped his eyes. When the shot came, he jumped as if the bullet had hit him instead. They hitched Ranger to Dale's team and dragged him into the trees across the hayfield to a cave something like the sinkhole gaping now in Dale's pasture, fifteen feet deep with roots coiling down its walls. James and Dale heaved the corpse into the hole then filled it up with a load of dirt. Afterward they drove the mules out of the woods and had a snort of moonshine. Ever since, they'd felt like kin.

It was the mutter of thunder that roused James to attention. If it started raining the truck might get stuck. He backed away from the edge of the sinkhole and headed for the road again, keeping an eye on the clouds as he crossed the pasture. The weeks of foul weather had unsettled him. It felt like Yuneetah's last attempt to hold him back, to swallow him up as it had Dale's house. But it might suit his wife, if it meant they could put off leaving. He dreaded now the coldness waiting at home. Sometimes he wished he hadn't seen Annie Clyde being baptized that morning down at the river. He would have left Yuneetah before they met but obligation had kept him bound. He worked to support his sister Dora until she eloped and moved across the mountain, walking each morning to the rayon plant in Whitehall County, working twelve hours a day operating a spinning machine and coming home at dark reeking of the chemicals used to make the fiber. By then he was old compared to the boys he grew up with who settled down before they had whiskers. He didn't intend to be tied down himself. Then he laid eyes on Annie Clyde Walker.

It wasn't her looks. He'd seen prettier girls. His first love was a beauty with wheat-colored hair hanging to her waist, bottle green eyes and freckles sprinkling her tanned skin. He'd met her picking strawberries for a farmer near the river. They had kissed each other in a potting shed rich with the smell of river bottom soil. When she pulled him close her hair was sun-warm and dusty like the fur of barn kittens he'd nuzzled. Sometimes he thought he would have been better off marrying her. Annie Clyde was nothing like that guile- less strawberry-picking girl. That's why he'd wanted her. She had a mysteriousness that made him need to unravel her. He admired her smarts and her toughness. But he hated how weak she could make him. His uncle Wallace had tried to warn him before he proposed to Annie Clyde. "It's hard to live with a quiet woman, James," he had said. That was all, but they both knew what he meant. James's aunt Verna had devoted most of her time to keeping a hushed and unclut- tered household. She was a handsome woman who never raised her voice and laughed behind her hand. She wasn't unkind but the silence of the parsonage became unnerving. James had kept busy outdoors, bringing in coal and digging potatoes, cutting the churchyard grass. Wallace wasn't much of a talker himself. He'd seldom spoken to James or Dora, patting their heads once in a while and telling them they were fine children before going back to his theology books. Dora was too much younger than James to make a good companion, so he'd spent most of his boyhood craving conversation. Maybe it hadn't been the wisest choice to pursue Annie Clyde, but wisdom had nothing to do with it. He had taken one look at her and known in his gut she was what he wanted.

The day James asked Annie Clyde to marry him, he had found her splitting wood behind the farmhouse. She lodged the axe in a stump and asked if she could fix him a cup of coffee. He sat in the front room waiting as she went into the kitchen to make it. Her mother was already sick by then, asleep in the upstairs bedroom, and the house was too still. It was taking Annie Clyde a long time and when he went into the kitchen to check on her, she was standing in the middle of the floor wringing her hands. "I thought we had coffee," she said, her cheeks on fire with embarrassment. James went to the larder and saw little there besides a few shriveled potatoes and a sack of meal. "If you can wait a minute," she said, reaching past him for the sack, "I'll make you a bite to eat." There were worms in the cornmeal but she picked them out and stood at the woodstove frying mush. He understood how it would have shamed her to offer him nothing.

For a while he watched her cook, mustering his courage. "I've been wanting to ask you something a long time," he said, his voice loud in the still house. She didn't turn around, bent over the iron skillet, but he saw her back stiffen. "I think you and me ought to get married."

His heart didn't beat until she spoke.

"Why is that?" she asked.

"Why is what?"

"Why should we get married?"

James thought for a second. "Well," he said, "because I love you."

Annie Clyde kept her eyes on the skillet. "I guess me and Mama are in a bind."

James crossed the kitchen and took her around the waist. He felt the strength of her, the firmness under her dress from months of wielding the axe and driving the plow and working the hoe. Her hands were rough, flecked with splinters, her face windburned and chapped by the sun, but she was still the loveliest thing in the world to him. He thought with sorrow how much living she had done at eighteen. Girls got married her age and younger, but in spite of the sheath of field muscle she'd put on like armor he could tell that she was afraid. She didn't know if she was ready to be his wife. "That's got nothing to do with it," he said, putting his face in the back of her hair. "I've been crazy about you ever since I seen you. I can't get along without you no more."

Annie Clyde softened some against him. "You don't need us to take care of."

"I can do it. We could go up north. We'll make out better up there."

"You know I can't leave Mama."

"She can come with us."

"She's sick. And even if she wasn't, she'd never leave here and neither would I."

"Then we'll make it farming, like our daddies did. But you'll have to marry me."

"You'll hate me for keeping you here," she said.

"Never," he said. "I'd hate myself for letting you go."

She turned around to look in his eyes, still seeming unsure. In the pause before she gave her answer, James's breath came short. Sweat broke on his brow. "All right then," she said at last.

Most things were disappointing when a man got them after wanting them for a long time, but Annie Clyde had not been. When he saw her nakedness on the day they were married by his uncle at the Methodist church, she was more perfect than he had ever pictured in his mind. She pulled off her powder blue dress in the daylight of their bedroom and stood before him in her slip. The window was open so that he could hear the chickens fussing in the barn lot, but the sound was distant enough not to matter. He took her in, hair piled in dark curls on her shoulders, the shape of her breasts under the thin satin fabric of her slip. Something happened to him then, a feeling of deliriousness sitting there on the end of the bed, like he was rising up out of his body. He had never loved anything as he did Annie Clyde. He had made his choice and tried to remember that when he imagined hacking his way through the endless corn to the road leading out of Yuneetah. He swallowed the gall that rose in his throat, choked down the rocks that broke his plow tines. He looked at his wife whose grace had once knocked the wind out of him on the riverbank and told himself he had no regrets. He thought back to the spring days when Gracie was newborn, going down at dawn to hear Annie Clyde humming over the squeak of the rocker, making a fire while she opened the curtains. She would stand swaying with Gracie at the window, talking about how the ground was thawing for the plow, how the shoots were pushing up through the winter bracken. That season out working James would look toward the house and see Annie Clyde watching him from the porch with Gracie in her arms. He was still desperate to have and keep her. Even with the tension between them since the power company came to town.

Annie Clyde was against the dam from the start. Not long after the first meeting the TVA held at Hardin Bluff School, a few locals were sent around with surveys. The man who knocked on the door said he had to know each family's needs in order to prepare for relocating them. James looked at the questions, about where they got water and what their source of heat was, whether they had a phonograph or a sewing machine. The man was Annie Clyde's old schoolteacher and when she came out he said how nice it was to see her. She snatched the papers from James's hands and ordered the man off her porch. His ears turned red and he hurried away, too confounded to say anything back. After that, James knew she didn't want him attending the town meetings the power company held, but somehow he couldn't stay at home. He hadn't felt that kind of hope since his father died. At the first meeting, a man in a necktie stood before the crowd gathered in the schoolroom to explain how electricity would bring the valley into modern times. He talked about how newspapers were a day late by the time they got to Yuneetah and their radios were battery-powered and most of them had no education past the eighth grade. He insulted the people and they left the schoolhouse angry. But James wasn't deterred. He saw the opportunities. Electric power might attract factories to compete with the low-paying mills, and there would be plenty of work in Yuneetah once the dam building got under way.

Later, when there was a meeting at the Methodist church about moving the dead, he went without telling his wife. The man who spoke was a mechanical engineer from the college in Knoxville. There were hundreds of graves in churchyards and family cemeteries, some over a century old. He said they would need to identify the graves of their loved ones and sign removal permits, unless they wanted to leave them where they were undisturbed. The remains would be reburied at a place of the next of kin's choosing. He and his men would have to supervise, but someone from the family could witness the removal unless there was risk of infection from contagious diseases. The undertaker, a man who had been a friend of James's uncle, volunteered to preside over removals and graveside ceremonies for those who wanted him. After the meeting, James pulled him aside and offered to assist any way that he could. He remembered his father helping dig graves in the fall of 1918, when James was five and the influenza epidemic had reached the valley. James's mother, who was expecting then the stillborn child that would kill her, had fretted that he would bring the sickness back to his family. But James's father had told her, "I can't stand to set here on my hands, Grace." She had let him go, as scared as she was of the influenza. James only wished that Annie Clyde could understand him the same way. That she would consider what the dam must mean to him, especially after how he had lost his father.

Annie Clyde didn't seem to care what it was like for James being so near the river, rising out of its banks across the road each time it rained. As hard as he had labored to wrest a living from the ground of Yuneetah, there had been an enmity between him and the river since he was twelve years old. In flooding season, people watched their homes rush away from the tops of the trees they had climbed to survive. When the water receded they went along the banks hunting up their dead. Sometimes it seemed James could hear his drowned father's voice in the water, as if it had kept Earl Dodson's spirit. He had never told Annie Clyde as much, but she held his hand tighter whenever there was a baptizing or a church picnic on the shore. He'd thought that his wife knew him better than anybody. After centuries of houses, livestock and bodies swept off in the floods, there had been a wall built to end them. James couldn't be against such a thing, not even for her sake. Annie Clyde of all people should have understood how it was to lose family.

He had tried to make her see. Staying in the valley to farm would take years off their lives, and probably Gracie's. People lived longer up north, where the workdays were shorter and the pay was better, where there were hospitals minutes and not hours away. Gracie could go to school and become a nurse herself if she chose. Annie Clyde might get homesick but it would be worth the adjustment. Even with the dam, there were fewer opportunities here than there were in the cities. He and Annie Clyde were still young. In Detroit they could figure out what path they wanted to take. In Tennessee, every path led to the graveyard. But he guessed he'd been losing his wife before the power company ever came along and opened up the rift that was already between them. Annie Clyde still had some notion that he resented her. James couldn't seem to convince her otherwise. All because of a handbill advertising factory work. He would have given anything to go back to the beginning of their marriage and leave it tacked to the post office wall. Annie Clyde was distant by nature but he had been winning her over until she found that paper. He had picked it up without thinking, so used to planning his escape before he saw her. He had tucked it into his pocket and forgotten about it. No matter what she believed, he wouldn't have abandoned her. He had only hoped she could be persuaded to leave Tennessee after her mother died. Then she saw the handbill and a distance crept back into her eyes that had widened in the last two years. James didn't want to lose Annie Clyde like his parents, like the sister he hadn't seen in ages. He worried that he had already, even if he got his way and she left for Michigan with him tomorrow. But more than anything, he worried that she might not come with him at all.

As he worked to spark the truck's engine, stomping the starter and pulling the choke until it finally sputtered to life, he thought of the way she looked at him lately without much feeling. But he remembered being loved by her. How in hot weather she would carry water out to him in an earthen jug. He'd stop plowing long enough to drink, runnels trickling into his dusty shirt collar. Once during a drought the earth was so dry that it boiled up to cover him, clogging his throat and blinding his eyes. She led him by the hand to a redbud tree and as he lay stretched out in the shade beside her she took his bandana from the bib of his overalls. She dipped it in the jug to bathe away the dirt then tied it dripping around his sunburnt neck. As she pressed her lips against his she took his face into her hands, holding him still as if there was anything he would rather be doing than kissing her. He was counting on her to remember that day. He was praying that when the time came to go in the morning she would love him enough to choose him.

Steering the Ford past the cornfield and up the track, he felt lonelier than he'd ever been. Not even Rusty greeted him when he pulled up to the house. He heard the dog barking, tied out by the barn. He went up the porch steps and leaned against the door to pull off his muddy boots, resting with his eyes closed before turning the knob. When he stepped into the dim front room it was so quiet that he thought for a second Annie Clyde was gone. She had taken Gracie and left him. Then he heard Gracie's chirping voice in the kitchen and followed the sound to the table. "We meant to wait on you but she got too hungry," Annie Clyde said, glancing up from her plate. Her food looked untouched. Corn bread and soup beans, sliced tomato, fried chicken.

Gracie climbed out of her chair and ran to James. He lifted and turned her upside down to make her laugh. "You're getting heavy," he teased as he set her feet back on the floor. Then he went to Annie Clyde and touched her shoulder. He noticed how she tensed but he was grateful when she covered his hand with her own. "What about the truck?" she asked, not looking at him.

He pulled out a chair across from her. "It's running, that's about all I can say for it."

"Sit down and let me fix you a plate," she said, getting up and going to the stove where the beans still simmered. She brought back his dinner and slid an apple pie onto the tabletop. Gracie sat on her knees and poked at the steaming crust, licking off the stickiness. James thought of the day she was born. He was so struck by the blood on the sheets, in the shape of a bird with widespread wings, that he didn't look at the baby. But once he was sure Annie Clyde was all right, he went to see what she held in her arms. The room was filled with light. Like that day he saw Annie Clyde standing there, a new creature on the riverbank. Gracie had a dark head of hair and little fists curled under her chin. She seemed at first like another part of Annie Clyde, but later he saw that she was her own self. She had a temper and was too stubborn to cry even when she got hurt. She liked being carried and rode everywhere on his hip. When James forked hay, mice would fall down from the bundles and scurry off, making her laugh and clap her hands. In summer she hunkered down in the loam to look for sow bugs under the rocks while James weeded the garden and Annie Clyde picked beans squatted on her haunches, deft fingers shaking the leaves and sweat making patches of damp on her summer dress. In autumn when they burned brush Gracie watched the glowing embers shoot up, the heat lulling her still long enough for James to see how much she resembled Annie Clyde. He tried to picture her in Detroit. In the tract house he had rented with one naked lightbulb in the center of the front room. Instead of mountains she would see tall buildings there. Instead of burning brush she would smell hot tar. "This is some good corn bread," he said, to ward off his sadness.

"Gracie stirred the batter," Annie Clyde told him.

"Did you? What else did you do?"

"I got some apples," she said.

He pointed his fork at her pie. "Ain't you going to share?"

She shook her head, eyes shining.

"Give your daddy a bite," Annie Clyde said.

Gracie scooped up a sticky clump and held it out for James to gobble off her fingers.

"I swear, it's like having two younguns," Annie Clyde said, but she was smiling. "If you're done playing with that, Gracie, go wash your hands. Your face, too, while you're at it."

Gracie climbed down from her chair and went out. James listened as she padded to the end of the hall where the washstand stood and scraped back the wooden stool she used to reach the enamel bowl. He felt a sinking. Without her the kitchen was closer and darker. After a spell of silence Annie Clyde got up and headed for the door to rake her scraps to the dog. James tried to go on eating but found that his appetite was gone. He couldn't bear the strain anymore. He made up his mind to have it out with Annie Clyde at last. To say all that had gone unsaid for the past two years. They had to if they meant to start over in Michigan. But when Annie Clyde came inside and cleared the dishes from the table, he couldn't bring himself to say anything at all. He stared at her, bent over the basin. He wished Gracie would come back but she had quit splashing at the washstand and gone off most likely to play with her dolls. James was alone with his wife. When the dishes were done he would have to say something. He watched her taking time with each cup and utensil, washing some of them twice. Scrubbing the bread pan after it was clean. Drying the plates one by one until they squeaked, putting him off. She seemed to know what was coming. He glanced up at the wall clock. It was almost three. His tailbone was sore on the cane seat. Finally she turned around with the dishrag in her fist, pale and drawn. James blinked. Nothing he'd planned to say came out. What did was the truth he guessed he had known.

"Annie Clyde," he said. "You don't mean to come with me. Do you?"

She didn't answer, but her face told him enough.

His shoulders sagged. "I was wrong the other night."

"James," she said.

"You love Gracie better than life."

"Please hush."

"Why don't you love me, though?"

She looked pained. "I do."

"Where do you aim to go?"

"I'm staying here."

"There ain't no staying here."

"We'll live in Whitehall County."

"And do what?"

"I could farm a few acres."

"By yourself?"

"Yes. We'll be all right."

His hands clenched on the table. "You and Gracie."

She looked at him again without speaking.

"You can't have my little girl, Annie Clyde."

She shook her head. "No. That's not what I meant."

"She's as much mine as she is yours."

Annie Clyde paused, twisting the dishrag. "Then stay with us."

James fell silent. He rubbed his forehead. "You know I'd do anything for you and Gracie. But I can't—" Before he could go on the storm that had been brewing all day broke loose, barraging the tin roof with rain. They both looked up, startled. Annie Clyde had dropped the dishrag. As she stooped to grab it her eyes settled on a fallen lump of Gracie's apple pie.

"Just come with me," James was saying. "I ain't never begged you for nothing before."

Annie Clyde glanced around the kitchen, not seeming to see him anymore. She started for the doorway but James blocked her path. "What are you doing?" he asked. "Don't ignore me, Annie Clyde. I've had enough of that." He saw the color rising in her cheeks. She pushed past him and he followed her into the hall. She looked toward the washstand, at the spilled water on the floor before it. She turned and went to the front room, rivulets pouring down the windows.

"Where's Gracie?" she asked, almost to herself, lifting the curtains that Gracie liked to hide behind sometimes. She stood in the middle of the shadowed room, seeming to forget James was there. She went to the bottom of the stairs and called Gracie's name, her voice ringing in the emptiness. When she started up James took her arm. She whirled on him. "Let me go," she said.

He went up to the bedroom close on her heels. "I ain't done talking to you," he said. She knelt to look under the maple bed as if she hadn't heard him, tossing the hem of their quilt out of her way. He had thought he knew what she was doing, avoiding the argument they should have had a long time ago. But then she raised up and looked him in the eye. Stormy light from the window shone on her face and the cabbage roses of the wallpaper. She was white, now, with fear.

"Lord, Annie Clyde," James said. "What's got into you?" She pushed past him again and stumbled down the stairs. "Slow down," he hollered after her. "Before you break your neck. She can't be too far." But he felt the first inkling of worry himself. If Gracie had gone outside, she was caught in the storm. He followed Annie Clyde back through the front room and out the door. He paused on the porch to shove his feet into his boots, not bothering to tie them, then hurried to catch up with her. Together they moved through the yard, through the sheeting rain that was plastering their hair to their skulls, running into their mouths and filling their ears. When there was no sign of Gracie they ran around the side of the house, puddles splashing up their legs. As they reached the elm shading the barn lot Annie Clyde staggered to a stop. The chain was still wrapped around the base of the trunk but Rusty was gone. She turned to James with wide eyes. He knew what she was thinking. Someone had let the dog loose. Gracie couldn't unfasten the hasp on the chain by herself. They ran on to the barn where Gracie liked to play sometimes and stood panting in the opening, water pouring from the eaves. James was certain she would be there. There had been moments of panic before when she was only hiding from them in the box wagon or the corncrib. But there was nothing in the barn besides the smell of old saddle leather.

After that, without even having to speak, Annie Clyde and James split up. She headed across the hayfield while he went back around the side of the house. He whistled for Rusty under the porch, checked the privy and the hog pen. Everywhere he looked, he expected to find Gracie. He couldn't grasp what was happening. Only minutes ago he had been in the kitchen pleading with his wife. He was thinking how foolish he would feel later, after Gracie came out of her hiding place, when Annie Clyde called his name. It was a strangled scream, loud enough to be heard over the downpour. James ran out to the hayfield, his breath coming in wheezing huffs. Through the weeds he saw the dark top of Annie Clyde's hair. She was on her knees under the apple tree. He was sure then that Gracie had fallen out of the swing and hit her head. He was sure that he would find Annie Clyde kneeling over their little girl. He was prepared to gather Gracie into his arms and run with her to the truck, praying the road to the doctor's

office in Whitehall County would be passable. But when he reached
the tree Annie Clyde hovered over nothing it seemed, on her hands
and knees among the puddles under the lowest boughs, where there
wasn't enough light for grass to grow. "What?" James shouted at her.
"What is it?" She turned her face up to him, drenched hair in strings,
shuddering in the cold rain. "Amos," she said. "What are you talking
about?" he asked, sinking down beside her. Then he saw it. There
in the mud, surrounded by leaves and filled with water, was a single
long footprint.

At four o'clock on the afternoon Gracie Dodson went missing, Beulah Kesterson was eating a biscuit smeared with apple butter, whit-
ish light falling across the flowered tablecloth under the window.
She dreaded getting up to wash her dinner dishes. There had been
enough rain that toadstools sprouted between the floorboards. The
dampness pained her joints. In recent years her fingers had grown
too crooked to tat the lace she used to sell. Few bought the medicines
she made either, since the druggist had come to town and a doctor
had set up an office right across the county line. With no neighbors
left she didn't have the offerings they brought her in return for read-
ing the bones. She was growing too feeble to hunt and trap, even to
gather morels. The savings once pinned to the lining of her night-
gown had dwindled to nothing. She didn't know how she was going
to survive whatever days she had left, especially if she lived to see
another winter. This high in the mountains she was snowbound for
months at a time, icicles hanging from the eaves like prison bars.
Her days seemed endless then in the one room of her cabin, walls
papered with pages of newsprint to keep out the cold. Often her fingers would travel to the bones hung around her neck and trace their
familiar shapes inside the soft brown pouch, worn thin but somehow
not worn through. They called on her to convene with them, to hear
out the sorrows they had to tell.

Beulah had come to depend on the weight of the bones, in spite of the bothersome things they showed her. Worse than what formed in them was what she had seen with her first sight and not her second. The stillborn babies she had caught, the dead and dying she had been begged to save. One winter after the banks closed in 1929 a woman had brought her child bowlegged and bloat-bellied seeking some elixir to cure him. She was the wife of a tenant farmer and had seven more children in similar shape but the youngest was the worst off, too listless to play anymore. Beulah told the woman that the only cure for the child was food. She gave him a cup of goat's milk and gave the woman some of her savings to see about buying a shoat. After the first thaw she went down to the woman's tar-paper shack in the valley. The woman showed her the child's grave under a chokecherry tree, the only thing growing green on their plot of rented land.

It had been given to Beulah to know and she had done her duty. When she died, she wanted the Lord to say well done. But she hoped for a little more time. As many burdensome things as she had witnessed, there had been many more things of beauty. She would like to sit again in her yard watching the leaves turn colors. She would like to raise a few more goats. She would like to eat more apple butter. She would like to see another Easter flower pushing up from the early springtime ground. She would like to wipe the afterbirth from one more living baby.

It was the rain and lack of sleep that turned her thoughts woeful. When her aching joints wouldn't let her lie still she sometimes went wandering in the dark. Last night she'd walked under the dripping limbs of the hollow woods all the way to Hardin Bluff School, moldering now with its benches overturned, its blackboard coming unanchored from the wall. The schoolhouse was built high out of reach after the first one washed down the river in the flood of 1904. Before it was closed, students came up from their houses in the valley or walked from the narrow hillsides their fathers farmed until they got tired of hauling their corn down the ridges to market and moved off

to work at the rayon plant in Whitehall County. Some who gradu-
ated from Hardin Bluff School had left town and gone on to make
names for themselves. In Nashville there was a state senator growing old in a mansion grander than anything he must have imagined
while staring out the schoolhouse window. There was a well-known
baseball player who was said to have carved his initials into one of
the schoolroom benches. Most of the rest settled in Yuneetah but
others died in wars and bar fights and logging accidents. Since this
past spring when the last class was dismissed, the schoolhouse had
stood empty. Much like seven years ago, when half the town headed
north. Back then Beulah could have walked down the road and seen
near as many deserted homesteads as she did today. But when the
factories started closing up there they came back, and the land had
deteriorated even more after those who couldn't make it in the cities
returned to their hillsides to farm again. Yuneetah had been declining
for a long time. These days Beulah wondered what would finish it off
first, the power company or the weather.

According to Beulah's mother, Yuneetah had gone downhill farther back. She claimed this part of the country never recovered from
the Civil War. The men of these mountains were as likely to fight
on the Union side as the Confederate since they couldn't afford to
own slaves. When the war was over they were even poorer. She said
that's why there were so many believers around here. God was all
they had left in the end. But before the Civil War, a clan of Beulah's
kin descended from those who came across the ocean had lodged
between the wooded ridges of the mountains surrounding the farmland below, a wedge-shaped notch barely flat enough to build on,
isolated from the rest of Yuneetah by two sheer rock walls. The
bottomland had been claimed by the English, leaving the latecomers
and the poor to settle the highlands. They trapped for hides and shot
deer for venison and raised cabins smelling of raw timber. Sometimes
when Beulah sat in her yard it seemed she could scent the smoke of
their hearth fires, could hear the notes of their ballads about lovers

left on distant shores. After the war, the first of them had gone down to the valley as a child bride and married a farmer. Soon others had moved closer to the road, a dirt trail weaving its way between the hills. Over the decades their abandoned barns and shacks had fallen in and lay decomposing under piles of mossy shingles. Beulah often came upon the ruins on her walks, the creeper-hung chimneys of their forgotten homesteads. They had gone and built sturdier houses below, living as close to the road as they could get. Before they blamed all their hardship on the mountain's rockiness, until they came down to the valley and saw the floods. That's when they first started moving out of town, into the big cities and up into the north.

By the time Beulah was born, most of her kin were gone from the hollow, besides a handful of distant cousins. Beulah and her mother had lived alone in the cabin. Her mother was a midwife and Beulah's first memory was of being strapped to her back on the way to a birthing, rocked to sleep by the gait of their white jenny mule. After the mule died of old age Beulah and her mother walked everywhere. They had the blacksmith to build them a cart for peddling the medicines they made. When Beulah's feet got sore, she rode in the cart. Sometimes they slept in open fields under the moon. When they got tired of traveling they put the cart away for a while and took up lace tatting, connecting knots and loops into doilies, dress collars and curtains. Beulah still had her mother's shuttle, an oval piece of ivory with a hook on one end. They spent many peaceful years together gardening, canning and doing the wash. Then one morning without warning, Beulah found her mother lying under the sassafras tree near the cabin. She must have been gathering the bark and leaves she used to soothe laboring women. Her eyes were not closed but Beulah could tell they saw nothing, at least in this world. She knelt to touch the tasseled end of her mother's long braid to her lips. Then she bent to kiss her mother's toes, remembering them sunk in garden soil and spread in riverbank silt as she cast her seining net.

Now Beulah was alone in the hollow besides Silver Ledford who seldom came down from her shack near the mountaintop and Sheriff Ellard Moody who sometimes came back home to sleep in the loft of the frame house where he grew up. As the town emptied little by little, she had seen more and more of the power company men. Last summer she had walked down the hollow to bring the Willets a bottle of the liniment she made for arthritis and met one of the men headed back to his car dressed in a pin-striped suit. His eyes had passed over Beulah like she was nothing. When she got to the porch the Willets had been sitting there crying. She'd asked what was wrong and Bud couldn't talk, looking bewildered with his swollen hands hanging between his knees. "I tried to tell him we can't go yet," Fay had said. "I keep dreaming about crossing the river, Beulah. You know as well as I do what that means. If one of us is fixing to pass on, I want it to be in our own house." Fay had dabbed at her eyes, struggling to get the rest of it out. "He said that ain't nothing but superstition. Said it's unchristian." Beulah had been holding her temper, but when she heard that word she tried to catch up with the power company man. She had gone halfway down the track waving her walking stick. She'd wanted to ask him who he thought he was, talking to the Willets that way. She'd wanted to ask him what he knew about the state of their souls. He had a job to do but passing judgment wasn't part of his business in Yuneetah. Unchristian was the worst thing he could have called Bud and Fay. "I'll guarantee they know the Lord a whole lot better than you do, feller!" she had shouted toward the road, even though the man was gone.

Beulah had tried to be tolerant of these outsiders, reasoning that they had different ideas about religion in the cities some of them came from. They didn't understand what faith meant in Yuneetah. Without something bigger than themselves to lean on, the people might not survive their losses. Bud and Fay Willet turned to the land rather than books to decipher the Lord's plans for them. They couldn't read the Bible but they could read signs and omens. They knew how to take the burn out of fire and plant by the phases of the moon. They ate black-eyed peas on New Year's Eve and carried buckeyes in their pockets to ward off evil. Their ancestors had brought such teachings across the water alongside the Scriptures. It was how they were raised and they'd never been called on to defend themselves or their ways before the dam was built. If Beulah was fifty years younger she might have tried to comfort Bud and Fay, but being their age she knew there was nothing she could say. It was the old she felt for most. The river had formed them, as sure as it had the land. The young might be able to take other shapes but not her or the Willets. They were already mapped and carved out. There was no more give to them, worn stiff as hanks of rawhide. It might be hard to love a place that had used them up, but it was what they knew. They set even greater store by signs and omens with everything familiar to them falling away.

Beulah figured the power company man would have called her the same thing as he did the Willets. But she considered her gift of discernment divine and herself as Christian as anybody else, although she was born at a time when Yuneetah was still mostly unchurched. The first to settle here wanted nothing more to do with formal rites or cathedrals. They adhered to the Gospel but worshipped on the bank with their feet steeped in the river. When the Free Will Baptists put up a church house it was small and plain besides an oaken pulpit that had come across from Ireland on a boat, ornately carved with scrolls and garlands. Most Sundays the congregants kept the church doors propped open with rocks and the windows propped open with branches fallen from the close trees. The pianist played by ear and they knew the hymns by rote. Wasps would drift in sometimes. Butterflies would flutter through the sanctuary, mourning doves would coo in the rafters. The church was near enough to the river that Beulah could hear it flowing underneath the preacher's sermon. She sat on the back row for years with the sun warming her face. Then the congregation decided they needed a roomier place to meet with a spire and stained-glass windows. Beulah knew that times and people changed, even in Yuneetah. She didn't protest but she hated to see the old building torn down. She wished they had saved at least a few relics, like the pulpit she used to admire during preaching, thinking about the hands that had carved it and the land it had come from. But anything scarred and worm-eaten the congregation cast out.

Once the grander church was built Beulah kept at home on Sundays. It was too suffocating without the doors and windows open. Stained glass couldn't be raised to let in butterflies. Beulah had a fine time talking to Jesus standing in front of her cabin looking into the woods anyway. She didn't have to sit in a hot church house to be a Christian, and she could read enough to interpret the Scriptures for herself. Not that she was against the churches. They brought people together, gave them somewhere to go for fellowship on Sunday mornings away from the fields and factories. The people of Yuneetah were losing more than their property. They relied on each other. If a house was taken by a flood they rebuilt it. If a man got sick they worked his crops. If he died they rang the death bell and the whole town came to see what needed doing. It hurt them to part not knowing when or if they'd meet again. But grieved as they were, most had no bitterness about leaving. They believed they were doing it for their country, the same reason they signed up to fight in wars. It pained Beulah to see them going but she understood. She was eighty-five years old. Through the generations she had witnessed it again and again. What remained in the end was the rocks and the trees, the water running its course. To watch from her lonesome cabin made an ache in her chest, but there was just as much hope in it. Yuneetah might be dying out but those leaving on the road would surely take some of it along to the new places they settled. Even the river would go with them in the jars of water they took to pour in their radiators and dampen their parched throats. All the electric lights in the world couldn't blind them enough to forget what they brought out and passed along to the babies she wouldn't birth. Wherever they ended up, they'd still hear Long Man rushing in their sleep.

Beulah realized she'd been dozing only when she started awake again. She decided to allow herself a nap before clearing the dishes. Last night when she returned from her walk, her rest had been uneasy. She had dreamed all night of crossing the river. She hoped Fay Willet was wrong about what such dreaming meant. She hoped too as she got up from the table that the weather and her full stomach would lull her into an easier sleep this afternoon. But she halted halfway out of her chair. As much as she wanted to go to bed, she found herself unable to rise. That's how it came over her sometimes, the knowing her mother claimed she was born with. It might be nothing more than a feeling that she shouldn't lie down. Somehow she knew to be still and wait. She sat for several minutes looking at the door, half drowsing. When the sound came at last it was so faint that she wouldn't have heard it if she hadn't been listening. There were voices approaching the cabin and her fingers went to the pouch of bones around her neck. She tilted her head as the cries came closer and closer, trying to make out whose name they were calling. When a hammering finally came at the door her urge was to pretend she wasn't home. She wanted nothing more than to climb into her bed and burrow under the blanket, but she brushed the biscuit crumbs from her dress front and went to open it. Annie Clyde Dodson was standing on the steps. Her hair was plastered to her cheeks and forehead, her face blanched white. Her husband James stood behind her looking shell-shocked, both of them huddled under the eave.

"Where is he?" Annie Clyde blurted out, her eyes glowing lamps in their sockets.

Beulah blinked behind her glasses. "Who do you mean?"

"Your boy, Amos," James answered for his wife.

Beulah gaped at them, trying to think. She should have invited them to come inside but somehow she was afraid for them to cross her threshold, bringing the smell of the rain with them, tracking in leaves, slopping their trouble on her floor. She looked down at Annie Clyde's mucky feet on the limestone slabs of the steps and felt ashamed of herself, but she still didn't open the door wide enough for them to pass through. "Well, he's not here—" she began.

Annie Clyde cut her off. "He was in my cornfield this morning."

Beulah's fingers went to the bones again. "What's happened?"

For a moment she thought Annie Clyde might faint, leaning ashen against the doorframe. "He took her," she said, and Beulah felt the color draining from her own face.

James put a hand on his wife's shoulder. "We can't find Gracie. Have you seen her?"

"Where's Amos?" Annie Clyde shouted over him, moving as if to push her way inside.

Beulah licked her lips. They were numb, but her words came out even. "I ain't seen her, Annie Clyde. And Amos ain't here." She paused. "I know he ain't been up to nothing, though. He's been with me. He came straight up the holler from your place. Brought me some corn."

James let out a breath. He seemed relieved, but Annie Clyde was still trying to see around Beulah into the cabin. "He's been here with you?"

"Yes," Beulah said. "About all day, but you know how Amos comes and goes. He took off again an hour or so ago." She glanced away. "I might not see him for another five years."

"You sure you ain't seen Gracie?" James asked.

"No, honey," Beulah told him, still watching his wife. "But I'll keep my eyes open."

"He's here," Annie Clyde said, looking at Beulah hard enough to make her fidget.

"Let's go," James said, taking his wife by the elbow. "We're wasting time."

Then they were gone from her steps as quick as they'd come. Beulah went to the front window and peeled back the lace curtain. She watched through the blurring rain as they searched the clearing. When they disappeared around the cabin she went to the window over the table and peered out but couldn't see them anymore. She went back to her chair, lowering herself with a grunt, letting out the breath she'd held while they were at her door. She stared at the soiled dishes on the tabletop, her old heart laboring. If Annie Clyde had come in she might have noticed one plate, one cup. Beulah hadn't seen Amos in five years. But she still loved him like a son.

Her mind went to Gracie Dodson and the day the little girl was born. She remembered it well because she had woke feeling puny. She used to be a stout woman but that morning she'd noticed herself shrinking. She had outlived the age at which her mother died but she wasn't ready yet to lie down under the sassafras tree. She still feared death like a child. She supposed it was foolish to be so old and want so much to keep on living, but that's how it was. So she'd rolled out of bed like it was any other day and carried on, wiping her handkerchief across her clammy brow again and again as she went about her chores. Around dinnertime she went behind the cabin to pick greens, all she could think of eating. The best place to find them in early March was along the spring, its edges brittle with ice left over from winter. She was looking on the bank when she came upon a crack in the ground. As she watched a nest of granddaddy longlegs boiled up from it, thousands upon thousands, and her own legs nearly gave out. She stumbled away without picking any greens, sure she'd seen an ill omen. On her way back to the cabin snow began to flurry in whorls, whitening the grass. Coming into the yard she could make out the shape of a man sitting on the steps and her dread deepened. But once she got closer she saw that it was James Dodson. He was a different man then than the one she had seen minutes ago, with clear blue eyes and high color in his cheeks, dots of snow in his auburn hair. She smiled because she knew what he wanted. Annie Clyde's time had come. Just the sight of James perked Beulah up. If the child hadn't been born on that particular day, she might have laid down and died like her mother. In a way, birthing Gracie Dodson had given her new life.

Beulah had been the first to look upon Gracie's face, red and crumpled. She had been the one to sever the cord binding mother and child. She couldn't bear to think of Gracie harmed. But wherever Gracie was, Amos had nothing to do with her absence. She was sure of that. It was true that he was a hard man to figure out. All the years he lived with Beulah there was a sort of fog rising off him, swirling up his legs and around his shoulders, issuing from his mouth. She didn't lie to herself about Amos. She only tried not to think about the wrong he was doing out in the world. She didn't want to know of his other sins. But he wouldn't take an innocent child. He'd been one himself. Beulah couldn't forget the condition he was in when she found him. There was a clearing by the river that only Yuneetah's elders knew about. Any habitable dwelling ever built there was crept over with thornbushes and ground-cover vines, a shaggy overgrowth that draped down a bluff into a shaded glade. Beulah doubted even Dale Hankins knew of the spot and it was on his property. She hadn't told anyone in town about it either. Mushroom hunters like her kept their secrets. Morels grew from early April to the beginning of May, and they usually didn't come up in the same places each year. But in that clearing on Hankins's land there was a dead chestnut tree with fat clusters of the spongy cones always sprouting from its base. It was hidden behind a laurel thicket but Beulah knew another way to get there. When she was more nimble, she used to climb down the bluff using tough strands of woodbine and creeper like rope. The day she found Amos, she was on her knees at the base of the chestnut with a burlap sack when she heard a sound that raised the hairs on her arms. It was a kind of keening, so mournful that she thought it was coming from a spirit. She followed the sound to a hole at the foot of the bluff and when she pulled back the vines there was a small boy in a cave, lying in a gruel of stagnant water. He turned his face to look up at her, his eyes wide blanks, his mouth open and that high-pitched noise coming out as if some other boy trapped inside him was making it. Beulah was frightened before her vision cleared and she saw him for what he was, an abandoned child.

She told the sheriff at the time about finding Amos but nobody claimed him. She was thankful because as strange as he was, he already felt like her son. He was as close to a child of her own as she'd ever have and she loved him like a mother would, even after he started vexing her. The tidiness of the house she kept seemed to provoke him somehow. The crockery stacked on the sideboard, the ladle hanging on a nail within reach of her hand, the preserves put away in the pie safe. Often he would take a jar of apple butter and dash it against the limestone slabs up to the cabin door, would hide her skinning knife or her iron skillet. At first she had encouraged Amos to play with the other children in the hollow, figuring a little boy like him shouldn't spend all of his time with an old woman. She had hoped too that he might learn how to act from them. But often Ellard Moody or Mary Ledford would come running to tell on Amos for tossing their marbles into the weeds or kicking down the forts they built. As he grew up the neighbors began to complain that he slept in their barns, plundered their gardens or left the remains of his campfires smoldering in their fields. Rambling through town he would stomp down the tulips farmwives planted near the road. Beulah hadn't known what to do about him.

She would turn to the bones, trying to understand. But on the subject of Amos the bones were silent. It took much thinking on her part, and much watching. It was the boy's lies that baffled Beulah most. Every man, woman and child alive had lied at some time or another. Most lied because they wished to be something else than what they were, or because they had something to gain. Amos's reasoning didn't make sense to Beulah. More than once he owned up to something he couldn't have done. Like the time Lee Hubbard came up the hollow looking for the muddy work boots he'd left on his stoop, swearing Amos stole them. Beulah said Amos was helping her in the garden and hadn't left her side long enough to steal anything. But Amos stepped forward and said, "I took them. I took them and threw them off the bluff." Beulah stared at her boy flabbergasted. Then she saw Lee Hubbard's face turning plum, spittle gathering in his mouth corners. She had to stave Lee off with a hoe to keep him from whipping Amos. Once Lee Hubbard lost his wits, Amos got the upper hand. He took charge for a minute or two of the world he passed through nearly invisible. The people of Yuneetah noticed Amos only when he lied or got into meanness. They looked at him directly instead of turning their heads from his unsettling face, his glittering eyes that seldom blinked. It seemed to Beulah a child like Amos, left for dead by his mother and treated like a cur dog by his neighbors, might want to make a mark just to prove that he was alive. She almost couldn't blame him. Beulah didn't deny that Amos was a troublemaker. But she believed there was more goodness in him than ire.

There had been many times with Amos that rewarded her belief, peaceful days that reminded her of those spent with her mother. Even as a small boy he would rather work than play. He couldn't stand to be idle and Beulah was the same way. When they ran out of chores they made up more for themselves. They kept busy stacking cordwood in the winter months, shucking corn and breaking beans in the summers, canning and making jam in the fall. At night he helped her darn stockings, patch their clothes and tat lace to trade at the general store. They kept bees and Beulah sold the honey to their neighbors, floating with pieces of comb. She and Amos had built the hives together one year out of scrap wood. Amos robbed the bees as if he belonged among them. They stung Beulah but never him, crawling sluggish over his face and arms. He had the steadiest hands she'd ever seen. She didn't have to rely on the smithy to fix her tools or her cart when a wheel came off. Once during a chestnut blight Amos sawed down the diseased trees in danger of falling on her roof and then mixed batches of homemade dynamite to blast the rotten stumps. He wouldn't say how he learned to make it, pouring nitric acid and glycerin in a bowl of oats to soak up the liquid. Only one as still and patient as he was could have kept from losing a finger. Beulah knew there would be trouble when she saw how Amos took to the dynamite, how his usually blank eyes kindled up with sparks when he handled it.

One night not long before Amos left on a boxcar Beulah noticed that he was gone from his pallet on the floor. She wasn't alarmed because he had taken to sleeping outdoors. Even in winter he lay in the woods under a strand of hanging chimney smoke, covered with a mound of frost-etched leaves. When she called him to breakfast in the mornings he would bolt upright, the makings of his bed fluttering around him and catching in his hair. She got into her own bed that night and about the time her eyes slipped shut there came a bang that clattered her dishes. She sat up fast in the dark. At that hour sound carried for miles. When she went out the cabin door she could hear dogs barking all over Yuneetah. She turned and saw smoke above the treetops, but not from her chimney. She knew it was Amos. She only prayed that he hadn't hurt himself or anybody else. She followed the smoke up the hollow, half certain she would find her son in pieces. The closer she got to the source of the smoke the stronger the night smelled of blasted earth. She walked under the scorched trees, over the showered-down bark, to a clearing where branches were burnt away. By the moon she saw a patch of seared ground. She knew that part of the woods, where one of the old homesteaders had left behind a root cellar dug into the mountainside, stacked limestone with a plank door. In its place was a mound of rubble, splintered boards still smoking. She stood at a distance and called Amos's name, convinced he was buried under the pile. After a pause she heard a rustle in the thicket. He stepped out from behind a sapling to show himself. Beulah understood then why others were disturbed by the mask of his face. His eyes made her feel as if he knew her better than she did herself. Nobody had been harmed. For once she turned away like the rest of the town and went back down the hollow.

Now, as they often did in times of trouble, Beulah's fingers crept to the pouch her mother had given her. An inheritance passed down through generations of the women in her family, come across the ocean with the first of them to settle in the hollow. Her mother had given her the bones when she started dreaming. Before each flood she would dream of a fish, the same middling-sized bass, washed up and gasping for air. She would wet the bed she shared with her mother and they would get up to change both their nightgowns. They would sit by the lamp together and wait for the rain to start, wait to see how many would drown. It was around the same time that Beulah began to bleed. The night the blood came her mother showed her how to catch it in rags pinned to her bloomers. Then she reached under the bed, the same one Beulah still slept in, and pulled out a tarnished snuff tin. She opened the tin and took from it the brown pouch. Everything they had was old, tattered and frayed, but the pouch was older. Beulah's mother stroked her unbound hair as she told Beulah how it was with Kesterson women. There was something in their makeup, or something ordained by God, that they would have daughters. If a son was born, like the twin that had come with Beulah, he seldom drew breath. Once in a while one of these daughters saw things most others couldn't. She led Beulah back then to this same table but with a different cloth and told her what to do. For the first time Beulah upended the pouch and spilled out the bones. When she could make nothing of them she was abashed, for herself and for her mother who might have felt like a fool. She said,

"I can't see anything." Her mother said, "You will." Beulah asked, "How do you know?" Her mother said, "I just do." Not because she had second sight herself, but because a mother has faith in her child.

Beulah guessed there was no use in repenting what she'd done for Amos. She had lied for him, as her mother would have for her, as Annie Clyde would for Gracie. She meant to stand behind him. She was afraid for him and the little girl both. She didn't like what she'd seen in Annie Clyde's eyes. The cabin was dim and she raised up to light the wick of the lamp, casting her shadow across the table and the ceiling. Then she lifted the pouch from her bosom, loosened the neck and spilled what was inside. The bones were stained with age and worn shiny from handling, their scattering muffled by the flowered cloth. It was hard to tell what kind of living thing they'd come from. If Beulah's mother knew, she never said. Beulah moved her fingers across them. After puzzling over the pattern they made, she grew discouraged. For a while she saw nothing, like that first time. But after staring longer it seemed they had knitted themselves into a ring. As she studied the circle, a shining bead formed in the center on the tablecloth. Then another and another, drops drawing together. She thought it was blood, like that long-ago blossom on the dingy cotton of her underclothes. It had been ages since she bled that way, at least thirty years, but she remembered what it looked like. It took only a second to realize that she was wrong. It was water. More and more of it. Clear and gleaming, the faded tablecloth flowers magnified under the beads before they soaked in. For a choking instant Beulah's mouth and nose filled with its mineral coldness. Then the water was gone and she could breathe. She stared until her eyes blurred out of focus. When she blinked the bones went back to being scattered, the tablecloth dry again. She gathered them into the pouch and went to her bed in the corner. She lay on her side listening to the rain, looking at the gray light pressing against the window glass and falling on the floor, at the showers driven by the wind under the door. Annie Clyde and James were out searching in this storm and she hadn't asked them inside. Sometimes she felt like in eighty-five years she had learned nothing. Had grown no wiser than that child who bled and was given the bones. She was tireder than ever, but no sleep came to her.

At dusk of the same day Sheriff Ellard Moody drove toward the ink-stained sky glimpsed between rashes of wet leaves. He gripped the wheel and leaned close to the windshield, squinting through the flood down the glass, the weak shine of the headlamps doing little to light the curves ahead. So far he had been able to skirt the sloughs in the road winding deeper into Yuneetah but he didn't know how much longer he could. From the corner of his eye he watched the man huddled against the car door, his face a pallid smear above the collar of the slicker Ellard had given him back at the courthouse. James Dodson's truck had gotten stuck somewhere along the ditch. After he gave up trying to push it out of the mire he'd walked the rest of the way to the town square. When he came banging on the locked courthouse doors, Ellard had taken one look at him and seen the direness of the situation. James had refused at first to come inside but his teeth were chattering so that Ellard couldn't understand a word he was saying until he'd warmed up some by the coal grate. Once Ellard heard a child was missing he'd got on the shortwave and roused the constable over in Whitehall County. Before this evening he'd been glad that most of Yuneetah had moved on without giving him trouble, but now he wished for the townspeople back. He would have to count on outside help to round up a search party, if they could make it across the county line at all in such foul weather without becoming mired as James had done.

Now as they were on their way to the Walker farm, James seemed unwilling or unable to speak anymore. Ellard was acquainted with

him through Dale Hankins. They had once spent a winter night in
Dale's barn with their breath smoking, helping him turn a calf. After
hours of labor, it had come out of the heifer steaming and fallen in a
bundle on the hay with sealed-shut eyes and the umbilicus stringing
from its underside. James was the kind of young man others respected,
friendly and hardworking, raised right by his aunt and uncle. Ellard
used to watch James walking down the road with Annie Clyde on
their way to church, riding the little girl on his shoulders. Whatever
struggles the Dodsons had farming, come Sunday it didn't show on
their faces. He hated to see that same smiling man in such miserable
shape tonight. Ellard left James alone for the moment. There would
be time for questioning later, after he took a look around.

More than anything, Ellard dreaded seeing Annie Clyde Dodson.
He figured she would be even worse off than her husband. As a child
he'd roamed the hollow with her aunt and her mother. He'd watched
Annie Clyde grow up and had a fondness for her, though their relations had been complicated of late with her holding out against the
power company. She had treated Ellard with reserve as the deadline for her removal drew closer, not knowing she would have been
evicted weeks ago if he hadn't held up the process. He'd done everything he could to keep the government from taking action, determined to avoid driving out to the farm with handcuffs in his back
pocket. When the eviction paperwork came to him, he claimed it was
shoddy and sent it back to the offices in Knoxville. He told the ones
in charge that he couldn't enforce evictions in good conscience until
they proved their documents were in proper and legal order. Ellard
had made enemies for Annie Clyde's sake, but in his experience those
with power often abused it.

When the first men in dark suits and late-model sedans showed up
in Yuneetah, Ellard had vowed to keep a close eye on how the Tennessee Valley Authority conducted their business. He was on Annie
Clyde's side. He still thought of her as a bashful child with her head

down and her eyes on the ground. She had always been different than her mother, Mary Ledford Walker, a well-liked and outspoken woman. Annie Clyde was unsociable in a way that put her neighbors off. She was polite to them but nothing more. Ellard heard some of them wondering out loud where Annie Clyde came from, as cordial as both her parents had been. They weren't thinking, as Ellard often did, about her aunt Silver Ledford who lived like a hermit on top of the mountain, coming down so seldom that he caught sight of her only once or twice a year. He knew what Annie Clyde's neighbors would say about her now if they were around. She was warned about the water getting up. If she'd moved months ago she wouldn't be in this fix. But Ellard was sorry for Annie Clyde, whether or not she'd brought this on herself. He was sorry for the whole town.

On his last birthday Ellard had turned forty-six but he looked older. His face was carved with furrows. His eyelids drooped, his hair was powdered with ash. For twenty years he had kept his vigil over Yuneetah. In 1929 he'd heard of men jumping off the tall buildings in New York City and seen things come to pass here at home that he would rather not have. Women pawned their wedding bands for a few dollars and men turned in their shoes for the price of a meal, until the pawnshop business dried up when there was nothing left to trade. Some had even begun to steal watermelons from gardens, laundry from clotheslines, eggs from henhouses. One night sitting in his apartment at the back of the courthouse Ellard had heard President Roosevelt talking on the radio about a social experiment involving the future lives and welfare of millions. Talking about an uneducated man living on a mountainside with his ten children, making twenty-five dollars in cash a year, who had been forgotten by the American people. Roosevelt spoke of giving that man a chance on better land, bringing him schools and industries and electric lights, stopping erosion and growing trees. But as an incident to all of that, he said, it was necessary to build some dams. It seemed to Ellard the president

sounded too far away to know what he was talking about, but he
hoped it was true. The people of Yuneetah needed help beyond what
Ellard could give them.

For the most part Ellard believed he had done right by his hometown. Outsiders might have judged him for looking the other way
when the moonshine runners came through from Kentucky and
packed whiskey out by the carloads, but the next day he would see
the bootleggers paying their druggist bills and settling up with Joe
Dixon. Ellard had always put the well-being of his neighbors above
any stranger's idea of morality or justice. When the TVA showed
up he decided it might be better for the town if he worked with
the federal government rather than against them, regardless of his
disdain. He only hoped the losses his people suffered were in their
best interests, as Roosevelt had claimed on the radio. But whoever
was responsible for the dam, God or the devil, it was out of Ellard's
hands. He meant to keep his badge on until the last soul was gone
from Yuneetah. Then he would unpin it and head back up to his
childhood house in the hollow. He would stand under the shade trees
until it felt like he'd never left. He would clear away the leaves drifted
against the door. He would sit on the unswept floorboards letting
home sink back into him, listening to the crows cawing in the locusts
and the bleat of Beulah Kesterson's goats carried downhill. He would
go squirrel hunting. He would see if he could make corn bread to
taste like his mother's or at least somewhat close, as hers was the
best he'd ever put in his mouth. He would try to remember what he
must have known once, what he guessed all of Yuneetah had forgot.
How a fresh crewelwork of snow dressed even the dustiest of their
farmyards. How leaves shaped like the hands of their babies sailed
and turned on the eddies of the river. How an open meadow sounded
when they stood still. How ripe plums tasted when they closed their
eyes. How cucumbers smelled like summer. How lightning bugs
made lanterns of their cupped palms. How it felt to come in from the

cold to where a fire was built. These things they hadn't lost. But, like Ellard, they had grown too weary to see them anymore.

Now the little Dodson girl was missing and there would be no rest for him after all, at least not tonight. He tried to remember when he last saw her. It must have been back in March, at Joe Dixon's. It was chilly but warm enough for the door to be propped open. She was standing against it, her head not high as the handle, leaning there under a sign advertising the Hadacol Goodwill show. She was wearing a sweater buttoned over her belly and a gingham dress that showed her dimpled knees, grubby socks rolled down and scuffed shoes chalky from the gravel outside. Somebody had given her a bottle of orange drink and as she waited for her mother to pay at the counter she kept her mouth on the rim of it, looking at Ellard from under her lashes as if he might try to steal it from her, staring at his tall lankiness and his long mustache and the silver star on his lapel. "Hey, Fred," he had teased, trying to look stern. After a while she had smiled at him around the soda pop bottle. "Is your name Fred?" he had asked, and she had shaken her mop of messy curls from side to side. When they left he watched them go down the steps, Annie Clyde carrying a parcel in one hand and Gracie swinging the other back and forth, prattling on about something only her mother could have understood. Just like Ellard, everybody in town got a kick out of Gracie Dodson. He thought of her at that last molasses making, dancing in the firelight. Nobody could take their eyes off her because she was hope right there in the middle of them. It was probably the last night they'd spend together in one place, but if they could believe it was all for her sake, they could bear it. If they could think about it like that. They were leaving behind their homes so things might be easier on Gracie someday than they had ever been on them. It was more than amusement that made them whoop and clap their hands. She was making everything all right, at least for the time being. They might have to start packing up their things in the morning, but in that moment they felt like it would all work out for the best.

Ellard intended to look for Gracie alive, but if she didn't turn up by first light he could assume what had happened. She'd wandered off and drowned in the spreading lake, less than half a mile from the front door of her house and growing closer with each passing minute. He didn't like to draw such a conclusion before he'd even reached the Walker farm or spoken to Annie Clyde, but it was where his mind went after the bleak decade he had lived through. After all he had seen. Just three months ago he'd gone out to talk with a man named Clabe Randall who was slow about moving. Clabe was a widower and lived in a brick house on a hill with musket balls embedded in its walls from the Revolutionary War. After his wife died he had stopped growing tobacco and sold off several acres of the pine timber on his farm. The timber had fetched a fair price and he was able to retire. Ellard had spent many afternoons listening to Clabe's stories, sitting under the shade of the red oak in his yard. Clabe had spoken at length of his great-great-grandfather who built the house and of his grandmother who shot several Yankees to defend it. One afternoon Clabe had looked up at the red oak's limbs and told Ellard, "This is a fine old tree. I had a swing here when I was a boy." On the first of May, Ellard had parked at the road and gone up the hill into the clearing where Clabe's brick house stood in the shade of the red oak. When he entered the lot he saw the grass cut and the flower beds tended, as if Clabe didn't plan on going anywhere. The house was silent but he figured Clabe was tinkering in the barn. Then the breeze picked up and shivered the leaves and the hollyhocks in the garden. Ellard heard the creak of the rope before he saw Clabe Randall hanging from one of the red oak's limbs. Perhaps the same one he'd swung from as a boy. Ellard approached and stood for a spell looking up at the swaying body before cutting it down, at the dried earth of Clabe's land edging his boot heels. Ellard had seen the dead before. But he had never felt such sorrow as he did right then, not only for his friend but for the graveyard all of Yuneetah was soon to become.

Before the TVA came along, flooding caused Ellard's neighbors

as much or more grief as being run off their land by the government
would. He couldn't help thinking back to the flood of 1925 on his
way out to the Walker farm to search for Gracie Dodson, especially
since James's father Earl Dodson had been among the many lost that
season. It was the worst flood Yuneetah had ever seen, the whole valley devastated. He heard when it was over there was a steamboat in
the middle of the street in Chattanooga. After the waters receded he
went out in rubber waders to see what he could do for the town and
came upon Wayne Deering stumbling around with one brogan on,
the other sucked off by the sump. Not much remained of Wayne's
hog farm by the river. His two eldest sons were with him but his wife
and three other children were missing, swept away when the porch
they stood on was rent from the house. It didn't take Ellard long to
find the body of Wayne's daughter slathered in clay on the riverbank.
Farther down shore he spotted a mattress lodged in the branches of
a sweet gum. He waded out and shinnied up the tree high enough to
look down on the mattress, soaked and matted with vines. Lying in
the middle was the smallest Deering, a baby in a nightshirt waving its
arms and legs, its jaw trembling and its lips blue. As Ellard shifted his
weight shavings of bark fell into its eyes. When it turned red in the
face and began to wail, Ellard knew that it would live. He clung to
the sweet gum branches for longer than he should have, too stunned
to reach for the baby. Wayne's wife washed up dead the next morning with the wreckage on a raft of barn board. But the third Deering
child had seemed to vanish. No body was ever found. Ten years later
Ellard was still looking for him, beating the bushes for his bones.
Not finding him numbered among the regrets he counted alone in
his apartment at night. Ellard had been a younger and more hopeful
man back in 1925. Now, after twenty years as sheriff, he thought a
second missing child might be more than he could stand.

With his mind wandering, Ellard was startled when James's Model A
Ford loomed out of the rain ahead. By then they were within sight

of the Walker farm, which meant James had walked over five miles to town. Ellard guessed without looking at his pocket watch that it was sometime around eight o'clock. He guided the car through the slough and around the truck as well as he could, his wheels spinning but not getting stuck. James didn't look at the mired Ford as they passed. He kept his eyes on the rills streaming down the window until Ellard turned beside the cornfield, headlamps cutting through the downpour and sweeping the stalks. But partway up the track Ellard slammed on his brakes. Something else had appeared like a ghost in the glow of his headlamps. It took an instant for him to recognize Annie Clyde Dodson. He'd come close to running her down. She came around to his side of the car and took his arm as soon as he stepped out, her fingers biting in deep. "Come," she panted, water dripping off her chin.

Ellard stood in the rain trying to light the lantern he'd brought. "Hold up, Annie Clyde—"

"That old woman's lying," she said.

"If you'll just be still for a minute—"

"Beulah Kesterson claims he was with her."

Ellard's eyes flicked to James. "Can you fetch us another lantern?" he asked. After James disappeared in the dark he turned back to Annie Clyde. "I need you to talk sense."

"What did James tell you?"

"That your little one slipped off from the house."

Annie Clyde shook her head. "No."

"Well, what did happen then?"

"Somebody took her."

"You seen somebody take her?"

"I saw him with her."

"Who did you see?"

"Amos."

Ellard covered her hand with his own. "Amos was here?"

"He was down there in the corn."

"Are you sure about that?"

"Come on," she repeated. "We don't have time."

"Wait, now," Ellard said. "Let's figure this out."

She snatched her hand away. "I'm trying to tell you. There's a footprint."

"All right," he said, stepping back some. "Here comes your husband with the light."

When James reached them, the lantern he carried haloed in mist, the three of them headed out to the hayfield together. Ellard's thoughts were racing. There were few people he disliked, but Amos was one of them. Ellard's father had been kind to Amos because he was an orphan. He had taught Ellard and Amos both to shoot. Ellard thought back to the night that, for the first time, his father allowed the boys to carry rifles. They were around ten years old. It was November and cold on the mountainside where they turned loose the hounds. While they trudged over the crackling leaves Amos's eyes were fixed on Ellard and not the path before them. As Ellard's father went on with the neighbors in their mackinaws and caps, Ellard lagged behind. Amos matched his stride, holding back even though he was nimble enough to move faster. Then the dogs took off baying and the men ran after them. Ellard hustled to keep up, but their lanterns grew farther off. Soon the high yelping of the dogs faded and the men were out of sight over a ridge. There was silence except for the sound of his feet on the trail. He could barely make out the faint glow of light through the woods ahead. Clumsy in the oversized boots he was wearing, Ellard tripped forward and lay in the powdery snow. He was about to get up when he heard the cock of a rifle. He turned himself over on the frozen ground and saw Amos standing above him with the gun pointed at his heart. He gaped up at the other boy's soulless face, unable to breathe. At the age of ten, Ellard already had a sense of his fate being decided. He covered his eyes. There was nothing but the cold and the yelping dogs. In his mind he saw the hounds gathered around the tree, leaping over each other to get at the coon as it clung to the tip of a branch. He waited for the gunshot, but nothing happened. "Blam," Amos said. Ellard uncovered his face. Amos lowered the rifle. "What's wrong with you?" he asked. "I was just funning you."

There was no way of knowing why Amos did such things or when he would do them. He was unpredictable. Ellard had learned back then to stay away from him. He had felt from the time they were children together in the hollow that darkness seeping out of Amos. In later years he'd had clearer reasons, but as a boy Ellard couldn't have explained his loathing. It seemed they were born enemies. Of course, it was hard to tell if Amos had enough human feeling in his breast to love or hate Ellard either one. At the least, he was a troublemaker. As sheriff, Ellard had kept the town as ordered as his rooms at the courthouse. He had seen himself to Yuneetah's upkeep, appointing crews to repair any storm damage done to the roofs each spring and to dig drainage ditches along the roads. The town was for the most part peaceful, until Amos would arrive. He always brought disorder. There were more fights for Ellard to break up, more farming accidents. There seemed even to be more deaths of natural causes when Amos passed through. He never left Yuneetah without making some manner of mess, if it was only a shattered storefront window. One autumn he had failed to smother a campfire he'd lit in Buck Shelton's back field and burned down the pole barn. Ellard was sure Amos had left that fire going on purpose.

But to accuse Amos of taking a child, that was something else. Amos hadn't done serious harm in Yuneetah that Ellard knew of, although he got a feeling the man might be capable of murder just from the deadness in his one eye. Amos was dangerous aside from any threat he posed to the Dodsons. It had been so long since Ellard last saw Amos he'd begun to hope the drifter had finally landed himself in the penitentiary somewhere. There must be a reason he was in Yuneetah during its last days that had nothing to do with Gracie Dodson, but Amos being seen hours before she disappeared seemed like too much of a coincidence. Whether she'd drowned or not, he might well have had a hand in whatever happened to her.

If Ellard had known before leaving the courthouse that Amos was around he could have radioed the other counties to be on the lookout for the drifter as well as for Gracie. He wished James had said more about the situation up front. Amos was a worse menace than the lake. He moved faster and with more cunning. He would be hard to track and Ellard needed backup if he meant to catch him, maybe more than the boys from Whitehall County. He would have to get the state police involved if Gracie didn't turn up by morning. Now he moved around the house behind Annie Clyde with rain pouring off his hat brim. Nearly half an hour had passed from the time he turned up the track by the cornfield until they stopped at the elm beside the barn. "We can't find the dog either," James spoke up, his voice hoarse. "He was tied here. Gracie must have turned him loose." Ellard bent with his lantern, drops falling from the leaves onto his back. He plucked the chain out of the bog at the base of the trunk. The links and hasp were unbroken. The slurry was marred with prints from both feet and paws, too mottled to tell Ellard anything useful. He stood and held the lantern aloft, lighting the tree's skinned bark and the ropy twist of its roots. His brow knitted. Every second evidence was washing away and there was nothing he could do to prevent it. When he was ready to go on, they crossed the hayfield under the starless sky. Weeds whisked over Ellard's slicker, water bounced off his shoulders. It had become nighttime. Looking up he saw that the clouds were dark shapes against a darker backdrop. The weather was dulling his senses, muffling his hearing, blurring his vision. It seemed to Ellard that everything was working against him and the Dodsons. The hour, the empty town, nature.

When they reached the second tree it shook like something alive, pelted leaves whirling, apples thudding. Ellard lowered himself to one knee and inspected the ground where Annie Clyde pointed. What might have been a footprint was now a misshapen trough. "It was there," Annie Clyde said, begging with her eyes for him to believe her. He got to his feet and she took his arm again, jogging the lantern. "We ought to be out finding Amos," she said. He looked at James standing hatless beside his wife, as if he didn't feel the rain down the planes of his face. Their eyes met long enough for Ellard to see that what little hope James had had in the first place was waning. When Ellard plunged back into the weeds they followed like lost children themselves.

For another half hour they canvassed the farm. Ellard walked through the cornrows but Amos had left no trace behind. In the barn, the smokehouse, the corncrib, Ellard cast his light into corners looking for tracks in the dirt, blood drips on the plank walls, strands of hair or cloth snagged on nails. After the three of them had inspected the outbuildings they went back through the slapping hayfield weeds to where the trees started, the storm and the deep shade making the woods pitch black. Even with their lanterns it was near impossible to see under the dense canopy of leaves, fog seeping between the close trunks. Ellard could hardly hear himself shouting for Gracie over the storm. They climbed a ways up the mountain, calling to the child and whistling for the dog. But if she was calling back they couldn't hear it. Or if Amos was in the trees laughing at them. All Ellard could do was keep his eyes open for signs of movement. Finally he led them out of the woods to convene in the hayfield. "I've done radioed Whitehall County," he said. "They'll be along anytime. We can talk back at the house until they get here."

"We need our own people to look," Annie Clyde rasped. "But everybody's gone now."

"There's still some around," Ellard said.

Annie Clyde leaned against James. "Where are your men? They're taking too long."

"Me and James'll go on if they don't make it before much longer," Ellard said. "Best thing for you to do is stay and light the lamps so she can see to get home if she's out here lost."

"No. I'm going with you."

James looked down. "Gracie can't come back to an empty house."

Ellard nodded. "I'd say she'll be wanting her mama."

It got quiet besides the rain tapping on the slickers of the men. Annie Clyde looked from James to Ellard, as if trying to believe it was possible that Gracie might come home on her own. Then she wilted, her shoulders caving. When her knees weakened James put his arm around her waist and helped her back across the field behind Ellard. They went in the kitchen door. James led Annie Clyde to the pine table where she sat staring at the stove as he made a fire in it. Ellard took a seat across from her while James lit the lamps. He removed his hat and set it aside on the table, hung his slicker from the back of the chair. He wondered if Annie Clyde or James wanted to change their clothes but they only waited for him to go on. He brought a notebook from his breast pocket and asked them to talk him through the details of the day. James began with coming home from Sevierville. Annie Clyde began with Gracie chasing the dog into the corn. Their voices flat, their eyes glazed. When they had both fallen silent he replaced the notebook in his pocket. "All right then," he said. "You all sit and rest yourselves while I take a look around."

Ellard stood and shrugged back into his slicker. Annie Clyde asked, as if out of nowhere, "Will you get my aunt Silver? I didn't make it that far up the mountain. She don't know yet."

At the mention of Silver Ledford's name Ellard felt his mouth corner twitching. He didn't know if he could take her on top of everything else. She was a nerve-racking woman, and as far as Ellard knew not much of a doting aunt either. But he supposed Annie Clyde needed her mother right now and Silver was the closest thing she had. "I'll send somebody up yonder to get your aunt before me and James leave," he said. "You ought not to be here by yourself."

Annie Clyde dropped her head, her hands lying limp in her lap. Ellard put on his hat and left her at the table with James to investigate the rest of the house, his shadow moving on the wallpaper. There was nothing out of place, no print they hadn't tracked in themselves.

He thought as he climbed the stairs about what came next, once the Whitehall County constable made it to the farm. Beulah Kesterson would have to be questioned, but Ellard didn't know how far he would get with her, in spite of the soft spot she had for him. Beulah had been something like a grandmother to Ellard growing up in the hollow. He'd spent many afternoons shooting marbles under the shade trees around her cabin. In the summers after Amos hopped a train he'd helped Beulah tend her goats and her bees. But he didn't doubt where her loyalties lay. It might be better to send the constable up to see her, considering she knew Ellard and Amos to be enemies. She might be more willing to give Amos up to somebody else. Ellard needed to put most of his efforts tonight into rounding up a search party. Standing alone in the Dodsons' bedroom, his lantern casting a shine on Gracie's empty crib in the corner, he feared it would be a difficult task. He was relieved when he heard at last the sound of slamming vehicle doors and the faint but clear voices of men in the yard below. Ellard hoped for a competent tracker in the bunch, or that someone had brought along a dog. Though as far as Ellard knew there was one man in these parts that raised bloodhounds and he was in Clinchfield, an hour out of reach.

When Ellard went back downstairs James was waiting for him at the front door. "Let's go," he said. Ellard didn't have to ask where he meant. But before they left Annie Clyde spoke up from behind them, her voice a husk. "James." They turned around and she was standing there in her still-soaked dress. In one hand she held James's hat, in the other a Winchester rifle. James took the hat and put it on his head. He hesitated before reaching for the gun. Annie Clyde thrust it into his hands. "If he's got her, I want you to kill him." Ellard studied Annie Clyde's haggard face. Without a word James took the rifle and went out the door. Ellard followed, boots thumping across the porch planks and down the steps toward whatever waited.

AUGUST 1, 1936

When the sun was barely up and Amos felt confident any workman or watchman left in the bunkhouse was asleep or just rising, he went out on the dam spanning the gorge where the river valley narrowed. There was a road running across the top of the mammoth structure, a two-lane highway with double yellow lines. Looking west he could see the road crooking out of sight around the humped mountainsides, blasted by the power company. When it was open it would connect this part of the valley to US 25 and Knoxville. Along the deserted highway there ran a pedestrian sidewalk. Amos trailed his fingers down its metal railing, overlaid in places with a sticky netting of cobwebs. He paused when he came to the middle of the dam where a concrete tower loomed over his head with two flags hanging limp from a pole, one American and the other blue with a white TVA emblem. Inside the tower an elevator shaft led down to the powerhouse, its locked steel door scratched and grimed with dirt. From two hundred feet high Amos could see, far in the distance, the rain-pocked water curving away between the forested hills. Leaning over with both hands on the railing he could look straight down the slant of the algae-stained spillway and see the dam doing its work, white water sluicing into the river below. He could see the tile roof of the powerhouse and its reflection rippling on the outflow, the framework of the transformer pad like a cage of prison bars on the bank. He supposed the design of the dam and the buildings was meant to be modern but they reminded him of a penitentiary.

Amos had watched the dam site all night, camped in the trees at the edge of the cliff on the west side. Up there the limestone was so sheer and wet that he had to crouch on an incline clinging to saplings. He was perched there for so long that his leaking boots had given him trench foot and his fingers had shriveled like those of the dead. A salamander had shinnied up his arm and hung by its spatulate toes to his coat shoulder. Rainwater had run off his brow to pool in the curve of his eye socket. For now the site was as vacant as the town but at dusk yesterday a watchman in a slicker had patrolled the perimeter of the chain-link fence surrounding the transformer pad and the paved path along the bank up to the powerhouse. After midnight when Amos was certain the watchman was gone he had scrambled down, showering pebbles before him, to look up close at the waters in the dark. On the downstream side of the dam there was no shore to stand on, nothing but an edging of bleached rocks crowded with poplar, cottonwood and elderberry trees. On the res- ervoir side peninsulas of red sand peeked from beneath the skirts of thick evergreens. The lake was much deeper and bluer than the river, rilled with waves. Looking out across the water from the bluff Amos had seen two rowboats lined up for use by the workers, painted orange with numbers stenciled on their sides, anchored by tie-off pins to a small dock.

Now that there was more light, Amos turned and walked through the misty rain down the double yellow lines of the highway. He went back across the dam and through the fog over to the east side where he stood atop a rolling hill among a sparse copse of hardwoods with power wires strung between them. From this vantage point he had a side view of the transformer pad and beyond it the low powerhouse set on the riverbed with its rows of reflective windows, its great gen- erators connected to the turbine inside the dam. He followed the slope downward along the east abutment wall where the concrete met the grass, tar hardened in patches and rivets bleeding rust down its slanted face. At the bottom of the slope he hunkered for a while behind a crop of milkweed, studying the transformers through the chain-link fence, the chalky white metal of the framework bars. Then Amos went around the transformer pad and picked his way over the rock rubble of the shore until the river entered his boots. He craned his neck to see the dam's tower from below, a castle turret with its drooping flags. He left his bindle and waded out, icy water riding up his legs, toward the bluff where he'd spent the night. He went farther across the foggy river, drawing closer to the dam, battling the outflow until his toes bumped the cement edge of the spillway. He stepped up onto it, the thunderous spray cascading over his boots, and inched forward to where the west abutment wall joined the cliffside. The seam was drifted with trailing scarves of scattered leaves, almost hidden by vines. Amos probed among them, parting the strands enough to see several snaking chinks. Settling like this wouldn't affect the structure but he figured the TVA was worried about leaks anyway, wondering if their unproven dam would hold as fast as the reservoir was backing up. Whatever their concerns they'd keep them quiet. They wouldn't draw unwelcome attention to their business in Yuneetah. In this same spot on the other side the structure would be most vulnerable, where it clung to the weak limestone. This was a gravity dam. It would have to be struck at the base to cause a breach near the bottom. Then the pressure of the water the wall held back would sweep it away, releasing the surging lake.

Amos knew as much because he understood explosives. If he had been born for anything, it was to handle dynamite. He had the steady hands it took. Once he'd worked as a powder monkey at a gravel quarry, the first job he found after leaving Yuneetah. His duty was to bring tools and explosives to the other men. Eventually they saw how fearless he was in spite of his young age and let him insert the fuses in the dynamite, punching holes in the cylindrical sticks with crimpers. Then for a time after the Federal-Aid Highway Act of 1925 was passed, bringing with it rest areas and filling stations and eyesore bridges of steel, Amos had blasted tunnels in mountainsides to make room for the roads. He'd watched as motorcars caught on and blacktop reached deeper into the backwoods, cutting down whatever was in the way, sickened by what he saw. It used to be that he could walk a trail with deer grazing in open fields on both sides of him, plovers leading chicks through the bracken. These days traffic was running the plovers off and killing the deer. The bird nests Amos used to plunder gone. The gullies he once slept in fouled with roadkill. But however much he hated road building he sought the work out wherever he could find it. If he put himself in the right situations, sometimes an opportunity arose to hinder the government's progress. It was then a matter of deciding whether or not to take it.

Yesterday before sunset after his camp was made, his guinea hen eggs boiled and eaten, the dog bite on his shin cleaned and wrapped with a strip torn from his shirt, Amos walked southeast until he saw a gap in the trees near the Whitehall County line where he knew the dam would be. Because there was still some daylight he avoided the site itself and ventured down an access road to the dormitories where the workmen used to be housed. He climbed the embankment alongside the dam into the woods where he discovered a stone wall marking the boundaries of the watershed. He followed the wall to a cinder-block hut with a padlocked door and stood contemplating it. When he pried a heavy rock from the mud and tried to smash the pendulous lock, the rock broke to pieces in his hands. But there were other ways to open it. There might be nothing inside but he was willing to wager there had been dynamite left after blasting the dam's foundation. He wasn't impatient to find out. He had learned to wait and see. He made decisions when the time came and not before, his actions dictated by what his instincts told him in the moment. If he discovered a shed full of explosives behind the door he might turn and walk away from them. But standing there he felt the opposition that had been inside him since his first memories of consciousness, thrusting like a fist under his breastbone, to all forms of government and hierarchy and authority. His resistance to all those who tried to keep him out with their locks.

In the Midwest where Amos had spent most of the last five years he could buy cheap plastic explosives with fuses and blasting caps at hardware stores. The farmers out there used them to clear their land of trees and stumps for pasture. He had carried a length of detonating cord across the country rolled in his bindle. Anyone who found it among his possessions would take it for a spool of rope. Amos had spent a longer time in Nebraska than he did in most places. He had a woman there. He'd seen her son first, bringing in water from a well. He remembered that day with fondness, moving between seas of pale witchgrass on an old wagon road underneath a wide blue sky. A hawk had swooped down to snatch up a blacksnake stretched basking across the road not a yard ahead of him. He had watched it rise and soar out of sight with the snake dangling from its clutches, the only witness. The only human being for miles, he'd assumed. A little farther on he'd come to a stretch where a path was mown through the grasses out to an oak tree. Beneath its shade, aged stones marked what Amos had supposed to be graves. He'd lowered himself down and sat looking ahead at the cloud shadows on the swells of the cedar hills at the end of the plains for most of an afternoon, until he saw the boy's towhead moving above the high weeds and got up to follow. He had hung back unnoticed watching the boy lug the bucket home, sloshing water onto his legs, until he came at last into the yard of a run-down farmhouse. The woman had been on her knees bent over a washtub. She'd looked up startled when Amos asked for a drink. He'd thought then she must have been comely as a child. Her hair was something like her son's but dulled by years of field work. She'd stared at Amos with fevered brown eyes as he drained the dipper. Then she'd asked if he wanted to come in where it was cooler. There was only her and the boy. Her husband had abandoned them and the land had gone to seed. She grew a garden and took in washing to feed her son. She made no demands of Amos. It was enough to have him sometimes in her bed. She was the one who told him about the man from the county Farmers' Holiday Association. He had knocked on her door and invited her to a meeting.

Later that week Amos went down the old wagon road to a library basement in the nearest town where the meeting was held. He had read of the national association in the newspapers. They had formed to protest their land being auctioned off by the government. They had named themselves after the nationwide bank holiday, saying if bankers could take time off to reorder their business then farmers could do the same. Farm prices were so low they were dumping milk and burning corn for fuel. They thought if they reduced the supply by cutting off delivery of their goods the demand and the prices would rise. They had been blockading roads and highways to cut off milk deliveries, picketing cheese factories and creameries. Amos thought they were going about it wrong. Their protests had done nothing so far, their petitions had fallen on deaf ears. Thousands had marched on the capitol building in Lincoln demanding a moratorium on farm foreclosures. Chanting, "We'll eat our wheat and ham and eggs, and let them eat their gold." The legislature had halted foreclosure sales but still let district judges decide how long a foreclosure could be postponed. They could still order the proceedings to go forward anyway if they chose.

Over the year that Amos stayed with the woman and her son he made himself a presence among the farmers until they got used to him. He began speaking up, not during their meetings but before them, as they milled around with coffee gossiping and complaining. He told them it wasn't reform they were after, not gradual change. It would take a revolt to see relief in their lifetimes and they were too hungry to wait. He whispered into their ears that they had to fight in defense of their homes and families. He made suggestions in such a subtle way that they thought his ideas were their own. In Bedford they dragged a judge out of his courtroom and put a noose around his neck, threatening to hang him if he didn't stop approving farm foreclosures. In Brainard they burned down a milk bottling plant. In Falls City they rigged explosives on a switch track to go off when a boxcar hauling livestock crossed the state line. But the charge didn't explode, as cheap dynamite bought over hardware store counters was harder to detonate. Then things took a turn when they tried to storm a butter creamery in Madison County. The gatekeeper called the sheriff and when he came the strikers pelted him and his deputies with rocks. A brawl broke out, blackjacks made from bars of soap in stockings knocking men down at Amos's feet. He crossed the road and stood on a knoll in a wildflower meadow as a mob rocked the sheriff's car until it turned over. One deputy hit a striker with his pistol butt. The sheriff sent off a tear gas canister. Most of the gas went into the crowd but some blew back on the deputies. In the confusion they started firing. Amos took up his bindle and headed east. The satisfaction he felt as he walked away had nothing to do with the farmers he'd spent the past year among. He had no real ideology. He had no set convictions. He had only his loathing for the men who ran everything. He left Nebraska without seeing the woman and her towheaded son again. But he thought about them often, and still carried in his inner coat pocket one of the boy's toy soldiers.

Amos had brought that soldier out of the Midwest along with the length of detonating cord, reaching in sometimes to rub it with the ball of his thumb like a charm against the images that followed him. Children wearing masks to school in towns so covered with dust that he spat brown clots for days after passing through. Starving jackrabbits coming down from the hills in multitudes, fathers and their young sons herding the animals into pens and clubbing them to death. On a country road in Iowa he came upon a man changing a flat on his DeSoto. As he approached the jack slipped and the weight of the car came down on the man, whose face Amos never saw. Amos pried at the front fender but in the end he could only stand in the road and watch the man die, legs jerking as the DeSoto crushed the life out of him. When the man's legs were still, Amos moved on. Not long after that he passed through Kansas as a dust storm was coming. It had seemed like the end of everything, a wall of swarming cloud stretched across the horizon, blotting out the sun. Amos stood still at first, rooted in place. Then the wind began to stir the roadside trees and an oppressive silence descended, every other living soul in hiding. When the first of the grit pelted his face he took off running until he came at last to an outhouse, the only shelter he could find, and shut himself in with the stink as the blackness drew down.

Now as he stood on the dam's spillway before its chinked seam, there was not enough light to burn off the fog so it lingered. Amos thought it would be safe to head for Beulah's cabin if he kept to the trees. He waded back across the river, took his bindle and went up the slope again, following the hillside deeper into the hardwoods until he came at last to a roadside bluff. He descended the stepped ledges then crossed the road and climbed another bank. The going was slick with waterfalls trickling down from the mountains. After gaining the top of the bank he disappeared into the hollow, copper needles muting his footfalls. It was in those woods away from the roar of the dam that he began to hear voices. At first he pushed on, thinking it might be the rush of the outflow down the spillway impressed on his eardrums. But when he grew certain that he wasn't imagining things he stopped on the crest of a rise, the edge ragged with hanging roots, overlooking the leafy ground where it dropped off below. Amos listened. There were a number of them. They must have come from other counties, or some of the townspeople must have returned. It was plain to Amos that they were searching for someone. If they had been making less noise he would have assumed they were looking

for him. It was hard to tell what direction the voices were coming
from but the searchers sounded far enough away that he wouldn't
encounter them. He stood still awhile longer in the mist among the
alder trunks, soaked sleek and tall like one of them. He tilted his ear
until at last he made out the name they were calling. It was Gracie,
the same name he had heard in the cornfield yesterday morning.

Considering the distance of the voices Amos was caught off guard
when someone came weaving through the trees below him, shoes
sliding through the leaf litter. A moment after the rustle of feet she
came into sight, her head rising and falling with the uneven terrain.
He knew before she got close enough for him to see her profile that
it was Annie Clyde Dodson. She paused almost directly beneath him
to rest against a poplar trunk. This time Amos didn't make himself
known to her as he had in the corn, though he could have knelt down
and reached out to touch her shoulder. He wasn't surprised to see her
searching apart from the others. She was more like her aunt Silver
than like her mother. Even among the people of this forgotten town,
Annie Clyde Dodson and Amos were outsiders. They were not as
different as she would want to believe. But she couldn't see herself
as he did now. Laid bare with her sodden dress showing the starved
slats of her ribs, no more than a film on her tawny skin. It was common knowledge the Ledfords were Cherokees, the first to be run off
this land. Maybe that loss, and not her father's farm, was Annie Clyde
Dodson's inheritance. As Amos observed her from the thicket she
lifted her chin. Though she hadn't spotted him, he could see the rain
beaded on her lips and on the fine hairs of her arms. He waited for
her to sense his presence, to call him out or charge up to meet him,
but she didn't feel how close they were. "Gracie?" she shouted into
the trees above her head. "Gracie!" Amos didn't move, his breathing
even. Then Annie Clyde's eyes shifted. She turned back toward the
way she'd come, hearing something. It was the other searchers, making a commotion somewhere near the river. Annie Clyde took off in

that direction. Amos figured she would slow down once she realized she might not want to see what they had found in the water.

Amos had seen the drowned himself and chose not to picture Gracie Dodson that way. He thought of how she had looked in the cornfield instead, standing between the rows with seedpods in her curls like those he shook from his own hair after sleeping on the ground. If they found her alive they would likely take her up north, where no corn was growing. Many of the displaced were heading to the cities. Amos hated the smog, the heat shimmering off the streets. He hated the neighborhoods with neat bungalows lining the gaslit curbs, yapping dogs snapping at him through the pickets and gates of fenced yards. He liked knowing whether those inside did or not that he was trespassing where he wasn't wanted. Sometimes he waited for them to part their window curtains and see him standing on their flagstone walks. He always left something behind for them to find in the morning, a cigarette butt floating in a birdbath or a heel print at the edge of a flower bed. He didn't want to think of the little girl from the cornfield growing up somewhere like that. If they had her back they would just make her over in their own image, raise her up in their ways and marry her off to a man who gave orders from behind a desk. Amos thought it might be for the best if they never found her. Best if she was returned to the earth.

Amos knew there were ways to use this distraction to his advantage. It was bound to cause problems for the power company. But he put the notion aside for the time being. Annie Clyde Dodson was looking for her daughter. He was looking for something to break a lock. His mind turned back to the dam and the task at hand. He pushed on deeper into the hollow until he reached the clearing where Beulah's cabin stood, approaching from the back of the lot. He would have followed the path his boots had worn to her door over the years and asked for a bite of breakfast, but he didn't want to cause the old woman any trouble. Maybe there would be time to pay her a visit later. For now, he only needed to visit her shed. Hurrying for cover, he went past the ordered rows of the garden and the bagging wire of the goat pen. When he got to the shed he found the plank door open a crack and forced it the rest of the way. He stood in the weak light falling through the door and searched the shadows, cloying with mold and corroding tin. He and Beulah had built the shed for storing tools, seeds and grain. Over the years it had grown full and junk had accumulated out behind the cabin. Somewhere Beulah had a bolt cropper. He knew because he'd used it himself for cutting wire mesh when they built the henhouse. His eye scanned the boards of the wall where Beulah had hung her gardening shears, her mule bridles, her rusty machete. When he spied the long bolt cropper hanging from a tenpenny nail he slipped it down at his side. Then he stopped cold, still facing the wall. He could feel someone standing behind him. With sudden speed, he snatched the machete off the wall with his other hand and turned around. Beulah was there just inside the shed door, a head scarf tied under her chin against the weather. They regarded each other for a moment. She looked the same as ever, hair in a yellowed braid over her shoulder and the pouch on a string around her neck. After a while, she took off her pointed glasses to wipe the raindrops from the lenses. "Hidee, Amos," she said.

"Hello, Beulah," he said back.

"What are you looking for?"

Amos held up the machete. "Bluff's too wet. I'll have to cut through the thicket."

Beulah put her glasses back on. "Your place might be flooded. You think of that?"

Amos smiled. "What are you doing out here?"

"Fixing to check my traps."

He noticed the burlap sack she was holding. At first she'd seemed unchanged, but looking closer he saw a difference. Her hand was shaking, her eyes dull, her dress stained. It wasn't just Yuneetah that had seen its last days. "Don't look like you been catching anything," he said.

She took a step closer, sizing him up. "You're one to talk."

Amos smiled again. "I've been eating."

"What, pine needles? You can't live on that. A man needs meat."

"I get some every once in a while."

"Well. I wish I could offer you some breakfast."

"I know," he said. "Another time."

Beulah nodded. "You better clear out."

"I will tomorrow."

"Why not today?"

He didn't answer.

"What do you need with them bolt croppers anyhow?"

After a pause he said, "I better not tell you."

"Amos," she said. "I got an awful feeling."

He smirked. "Bones been talking to you?"

"I ain't kidding. I believe there's fixing to be bloodshed. I just don't want it to be yourn."

"I'll risk it."

"Huh. You wouldn't risk your own hide for nothing."

"Things change," he said.

"Yes," she said. "Nothing wrong with change."

"But there's something wrong with those that have taking away from those that don't."

"Well. There's the right way to stand against something and the wrong way."

"Who gets to decide what the right way is, Beulah?"

Her mouth folded over her gums. "I never could tell you nothing."

He turned the machete over, inspecting the blade. "You believe in gods."

"I believe in one God."

"All right. What if God took that child they're looking for as a punishment?"

Beulah's brow creased. "Who, Gracie? That innocent little girl?"

"For messing with Him."

"It don't work that way. The Lord won't take a child away from her mama over a dam."

Amos looked up. "Yeah, well. Maybe He'll give her back if the dam goes away."

Beulah shook her head. They studied each other.

"If I make it out of here I won't be back," he said.

"Why in the world not?" she asked. "This place is your home."

"If the government has their way, this place is about to be gone."

"Even if it's covered up, it'll still be here."

He gestured with the machete. "Look around. Nothing left here but hard times."

"Amos," Beulah said. "It don't matter what's built or tore down by a man's hands. The Lord's in charge. Sure as the river keeps on running, good times will come back around."

Amos grinned. "Maybe you ought to ask your bones if you've got it right or not."

She smiled back a little. "You better watch that smart lip."

"I better get out of sight," he said. "Fog's burning off."

She held out the burlap sack, bloodied by the rabbits, coons and groundhogs she had snared and carried home to the cabin. "Here," she said. "See if there's some meat for your breakfast." He tucked the bolt cropper under his arm and took the sack. Their fingers touched and he felt a pang of sorrow or love for this old woman he might never lay his one eye on again. He didn't know why she had always been kind to him. They never spoke of it. She stepped aside and let him pass through the door on his way to the clearing at the foot of the viny bluff.

At a quarter to eight, Sheriff Ellard Moody sat parked at the curb in front of the former Customs House on the corner of Clinch and

Market, across from the Tennessee Theatre. He tapped his fingers on the steering wheel as he waited for the caseworker assigned to Yuneetah, Sam Washburn. In the other hand he pinched a cigarette, smoke curling out the window. He peered up through the windshield at the light poles, the power lines crossing over the rooftops. Much had changed since the first time Ellard came into the city with his father, gawping at the tall buildings and the motorcars lining the brick-paved streets, watching the fashionable ladies pass with their hair cut short and marcelled into waves. The Customs House still had the same facade as it did back then, gray marble with cast-iron columns, but it had changed in other ways since the power company took it over for their headquarters. Until 1933 the old building had housed the federal court, the excise offices and the post office. Now it held only the TVA offices. Ellard had made this trip too often in the last couple of years. When the townspeople complained of how they were treated he came here and demanded to see somebody in charge, determined not to let the big government machine forget they were dealing with individuals in Yuneetah. Most of the time he was put off or sent away dissatisfied. This morning at least he was seeing an official, the chief of the Reservoir Family Removal Section.

In Knoxville the morning was fair and bright, the car already heating up. The city had always seemed like a different world to Ellard. Now it had its own weather, not thirty miles north of his drowning town. Earlier when it was still darkish he had come through the fog that blanketed Yuneetah, watching as the clouds massed over the wooded hills receded in his rearview mirror, his tires slinging orange clay as they turned off the dirt byways onto blacktop. The sun had risen higher as Ellard passed under the arched girders of the steel bridge on the way into the city, crossing over a different river than what he knew, this one floating barges and steamboats on to Chattanooga. Leaving behind the pickup trucks and mule-drawn carts of the countryside and joining the faster traffic of the highway, the smells through his open window changing from wet farmland and rich manure to factory smoke and gasoline. Part of Ellard was relieved to be escaping, but he was ill with worry over what was happening in his absence.

As Ellard sat waiting for Washburn his head swam with all that had passed the night before. He and James had gone first across the road into the Hankins pasture, down to the uneven shoreline of the reservoir. They had split up, James heading left with a group of Whitehall County men toward where the field was bordered by a stand of loblolly pines. Ellard had gone to the opposite end where a dense thicket crowded against the barbwire. Before climbing over the fence he'd held his lantern across and seen light reflected on water. It was hard to say how deep it would be in some places. If Gracie had ventured in too far, the ground might have dropped from beneath her. But he would rather the lake have taken the child than Amos. Ellard had crossed the fence and spent close to an hour crashing through the overgrowth in the dark, burrs catching in his cuffs and shale wedging in his boot treads. He had pushed into the hemlocks as far as the water reached, shining his light into spidery tree holes and beating at drifts of forage with a branch, plunging his fingers into root tangles groping for the touch of hair or flesh or bone. Looking for Amos and Gracie Dodson both, his hand going to his revolver each time the brush crackled.

When the search in the pasture yielded nothing James had gone with the men from Whitehall County to round up as many as they could from the coves and hollows above the taking line while Ellard stayed at the courthouse on the shortwave, calling for assistance. So far only a handful had showed up from surrounding counties and the state police were dragging their feet. He couldn't help thinking a missing child from somewhere else might warrant more attention. Yuneetah had never been of much concern to outsiders, even before it was evacuated. Most anything Ellard asked of the higher-ups was years in coming, if it came at all. He had learned to make do with his piddling salary, his rooms at the courthouse and the use of this car, a humped-trunk Ford sedan with a black top and gold stars painted on the doors. But now Ellard cursed his lack of resources. He guessed he should be thankful anybody had come at all. He'd feared the townspeople wouldn't return if they believed Gracie Dodson was dead, having watched enough of what they loved disappear. He had been relieved to see at least a few of his old neighbors among the other searchers gathered at the courthouse around midnight, standing in the lamplit entrance hall as Ellard gave them instructions. James Dodson had been there looking addled with his eyes roving over the pressed-tin ceiling, the fly-specked plaster walls, the high windows darted and dashed with raindrops. Ellard had told the searchers to sweep in lines through meadows and woods, to enter each vacant building and house. He'd advised them to spread out, to be slow and deliberate.

Around dawn there had still been no trace of Gracie or Amos found, but there was a commotion on the riverbank. Ellard was organizing a group of fishermen with musseling boats to drag the lake when he heard the shouting. By the time he reached the other men upriver the ruckus had settled down. He came upon them bent over something at the edge of the lapping water, a hilly form lying on its side and drifted around with debris. At first sight he thought of Gracie's coonhound. It was about the size of a large dog and resembled Rusty from a distance. James had told Ellard last night as they searched along the reservoir that his daughter would have followed that dog anywhere. If this was the hound that had gone missing with the child, she wouldn't be far behind. But moving closer he saw that it had golden fur and a long tail, outstretched forelegs ending in big paws. It was a panther, with one marble eye shut and one open, its tongue hanging between ivoried teeth. Even in death, it had a sinuous beauty. Ellard toed its haunches. He knelt to look for buckshot, musk rising from

its soggy hide into his nose, but the panther was unmarked. He had
come across all manner of drowned animal. Moles, possums, groundhogs. But nothing like this. It troubled his mind.

Then Annie Clyde Dodson came stumbling along the river as he
was rolling the panther in a tarp. Ellard froze, watching as she ran
down the slick bank. It was only when she fell that he and the other
men rushed to her side. They tried to help her up but she shook
them off, her dress front heavy with mud. She went to the tarp and
dropped on her knees, pulling a flap back. She stared down for a long
time. When one of the men made as if to cover the stinking corpse
Ellard stopped him. They allowed Annie Clyde to look until she was
satisfied, the babbling river filling their silence. When she stirred at
last they all scrambled again to help her to her feet. Ellard asked if
he could take her home but she turned and went off on unsteady legs
into the trees without him. He started after her but didn't know in
the end what she might do if he interfered. He'd told the constable
before heading for Knoxville to keep an eye on her.

Now he felt like he had been away from Yuneetah too long. He
began to regret his decision to come this far from home. He pulled
out his pocket watch and shoved it back in his coat. He was considering going inside without Washburn when he heard the rap of knuckles against the glass at his ear. He dropped the stub of his cigarette
into his lap and then flicked it out the window crack. Washburn stood
back waiting as Ellard brushed the ash from his trousers and opened
the door to get out. He was a handsome but solemn young man
with startling blue eyes and dark blond hair slicked under a fedora.
Their paths had crossed more than once in their effort to relocate
the people of Yuneetah. In two years, Ellard hadn't seen Washburn's
tie crooked or his shoes unpolished. He always smelled of pomade
and aftershave, though he didn't look old enough to grow whiskers.
When Washburn offered his hand, their last meeting came back to
Ellard. A month ago they had spoken in Ellard's office about Annie

Clyde Dodson. Ellard supposed they had known then it could come to something like this.

"Are you ready to go in?" Washburn asked.

"As I'll ever be," Ellard said.

He followed Washburn up the steps under the columned portico and into the lobby, their heels ringing as they passed a crowd of potential hires waiting outside the employment office. They rode up in the elevator to the third floor and went down a hallway, clacking typewriters behind the closed doors. At the end of the hall they were ushered by a secretary into the office of a man named Clarence Harville. The room had a low ceiling and one window with a half-pulled shade, showing a glimpse of the Tennessee Theatre sign across the street. Under the window there was an oak desk and beside it a row of filing cabinets. Against another wall were shelves stacked with ledgers and boxes of supplies. Ellard's eyes moved over these things without seeing them. He and Washburn sat in silence as Harville spoke to someone outside the office door, wavy shapes behind patterned glass. When he came in at last, a dour old man in a tailored suit and round spectacles, Washburn and Ellard stood. "I've already kept you gentlemen too long," Harville said, taking a seat behind his desk. "So I'll get to the point. You both know as well as I do this could have been prevented."

Ellard held his hat in his lap. "I don't see that it matters now. There's a child missing."

Harville nodded. "I'm sorry to hear it. I've been concerned something like this would happen." He looked at Washburn. "I want you to work with Sheriff Moody however you can."

"Of course," Washburn said. "I've made some calls about getting dogs out there—"

"Let's leave that to state law enforcement," Harville interrupted.

Washburn shrugged in his stiff-looking suit coat. "So far the state police have been slow to get involved. They might be more inclined to act if we put some pressure on them."

"I'd rather not step on any toes, if we can avoid it," Harville said.

"With respect, sir," Washburn said. "We can't worry about that."

"I want to hear from the sheriff. What's the quickest way to solve this?"

Ellard stared at the desktop, sun from the window lighting the objects there, a wire basket, an ashtray, a stamper, a mercury glass paperweight shaped like a globe. Anything to keep from looking at Harville's smug face. "If the water was drained, we could cover more ground."

Harville regarded Ellard overtop his spectacles. "I'm not sure what you're getting at."

"We're going to need a drawdown. That's all there is to it."

Harville's bushy eyebrows lifted. "A drawdown? We can't do that."

"I don't see why not."

"It would take a week to drain the lake. They've got to be out in two days."

"Two days?" Washburn broke in. "You still mean to enforce the deadline?"

"I hope it won't take a week to find her," Ellard said. "But I have to plan on it."

"I don't have the authority to order a drawdown anyway," Harville told him.

Ellard put on his hat. "Well then, I need to see somebody that does."

"Wait a minute," Washburn said. "Let's talk about what we can do, not what we can't."

Harville turned from Ellard to Washburn. "You can go down and be with the family."

Washburn shifted in his chair. "I'm heading out to Yuneetah as soon as we're finished here. I'll talk to the public relations staff first. We should get the child's picture in the *Sentinel*—"

"Public relations is not your area either," Harville spoke up, cutting the boy off again.

"Public relations," Ellard said, his blood heating and his voice rising. "What in the hell are we talking about?" He rounded on Washburn. "What's wrong with you, son? I might as well have come here by myself. You're supposed to be an advocate for these people. You know them. This man don't. You ought to be ashamed of yourself, letting him run over you this way."

"There's no reason to get loud," Harville said. "We're all on the same page."

"But not on the newspaper page," Ellard said. "Ain't that right?"

Harville pursed his lips. "Why don't you tell me exactly what I can do for you?"

"I done told you," Ellard said. "I need a drawdown. I need the state police. I need the word out in the newspapers. I need bloodhounds. And I need you to put yourself in James Dodson's shoes. He's looking for his daughter while we're sitting here talking about what all you can't do. Washburn don't have any children, but I'd say you've got some. Grandchildren, too."

Harville slouched behind the desk, as if wearied by the turn things had taken. "Yes."

"Then you ought to understand. Unless you think your babies are worth more than ours."

Harville flushed. "I won't sit here and listen to this."

Ellard got up with balled fists. "You ain't hearing me noway," he said. Washburn sat forward, knees knocking against the desk. Ellard made himself pause. He lowered his voice. "That's all right, Harville. I see how it is. It's my problem and you people don't give a damn."

"I'll do whatever I can to help you," Harville said. "But there won't be any drawdown."

Ellard went to the door and turned back. He drew breath to speak but couldn't think what he wanted to say. Finally he opened the door and shut it behind him. By the time he got to the elevator he'd run out of steam. He walked out of the building into the street with his head down.

When Washburn called Ellard's name he didn't turn around. "Sheriff!" he called again. Ellard stopped at the car and saw Washburn coming down the wide steps toward him, past others on their way inside. "You can't just leave," the boy said, out of breath as he reached the curb.

Standing between the bleak buildings, the sun glaring off the vehicles motoring by, Ellard felt cornered. He had to look way up to see the sky. "No use wasting more time going over it."

"Clarence Harville's a decent person," Washburn said, not sounding convinced himself.

"Right now I ain't too worried about Clarence Harville one way or the other."

"Will you come back in with me?"

"I told you, I'm done wasting time. He don't care if that child's alive or dead."

"Well, I care," Washburn said. "I mean to help you find her."

Ellard looked Washburn in the face. "What if we don't find her? Are you going to help me cuff Annie Clyde Dodson and drag her off of her farm? Like that man in there wants?"

Washburn averted his eyes. "I don't know."

"That's right. You don't know nothing. What do you think will happen down yonder?"

"I think we're going to find the child and give her back to her mother."

"Maybe. But she might be tied up dead in a barbwire fence. Or tangled up in a brush pile."

Washburn paled but he didn't respond.

"I've found them with their eyes eat out by the catfish, and I've found them without a mark on them, like they're just asleep. That might be the worst. Are you ready to see that?"

"No," Washburn said softly. "But I've seen a lot of good things done in Yuneetah over these last two years. If you'll work with me, we might get one more good thing done."

The boy sounded so young and chastened then that Ellard felt sorry for him. "I don't want to argue with you, son," he said. "We ought to get along if we mean to help the Dodsons."

Washburn nodded. "If Harville won't see reason, I'll go over his head."

Ellard opened the car door. "I got to get on back."

"I'm behind you," Washburn said.

Ellard didn't know if the boy meant on the way to Yuneetah or something else. He felt alone either way as he got into his car. He dreaded the long trip back home. He had too much time to wonder what was waiting for him. Too much time to think about his exchange with Washburn. He already regretted what he'd said about Gracie. He didn't know what had come over him. Ellard supposed he wanted to knock the boy down a peg, standing there on the curb in his polished shoes, looking so hopeful and sure of himself. Washburn was an idealist. He believed progress was the answer to everything. Ellard wished he saw it like Washburn did, but in his experience the state was motivated less by altruism and more by their own selfish pursuit of power. The boy needed to believe that Harville was a decent man, that the Tennessee Valley Authority was trying to save the people of Yuneetah. But Ellard had come to the conclusion after twenty years that there was no saving his people. Sometimes he thought they didn't want to be saved. He'd had many rows with his neighbors on the porch of Joe Dixon's. For all their common sense they'd rather starve than take what they called handouts. They voted Republican or Democrat according to what side their grandfathers had picked before they were born. They said there had always been a Depression going on around here. It was hard to get much poorer than they had been. But to Ellard it seemed foolish for any but the wealthy to back a man like Herbert Hoover, giving aid to banks and railroads and corporations instead of workingmen with families.

Regardless of what Washburn wanted Ellard to believe, Harville

was no better than the politicians in Washington claiming it wasn't
their place to provide relief, passing the responsibility off to chari-
ties and churches. Ellard thought the government that got them into
this mess ought to get them out of it. But he'd do what he could for
the Dodsons, as he had done what he could for his own kin when the
banks began to take their farms. His mother was from a place called
Caney Fork, right outside of Whitehall County, and he had a first
cousin there named Bill Harrell. A few years ago he'd stopped to
see Bill on his way back from Clinchfield and found an auction sign
at the end of the road up to his place. Before supper was over Ellard
had decided to stay and see what he could do to help Bill keep his
fifteen acres. They'd gone to the neighboring farmers, worried they
might lose their own property. It wasn't hard to talk them into organizing. Come the day of the auction men from all over Caney Fork
converged on Bill's land. Ellard watched from the chaff-floating
shade of the barn with his revolver showing on his hip and a noose
hanging from a nail over his head, letting strangers know they were
unwelcome. The auctioneer stood on a wagon bed pouring sweat
under the morning sun. But when he called for bids and the other
Caney Fork farmers piped up with their offers, his face flamed from
more than the heat. Every starting bid was a penny, for tracts of hard-
wood timber and tools alike. The bidding commenced at one cent
for the house and closed at a quarter. Bill's neighbors refused to bid
over a nickel for anything, until the auctioneer gave up in disgust.
By the end of the day Bill had bought back all that he owned for five
dollars. Ellard knew a child was not a farm but the principle was the
same. The ones that loved her would have to be the ones to try and
save her.

Ellard had vowed long ago to treat the people of Yuneetah the same
as he would his first cousin. They all felt like kin to him, especially
Annie Clyde Dodson, since he'd grown up with her mother and her
aunt. Now driving farther into the foothills he hoped he hadn't made
things worse for her by turning Clarence Harville against him. Once

he was across the steel bridge the first splatters of rain hit Ellard's windshield. By the time he reached Yuneetah it was falling in curtains across the hood. His tires spun on the way down the slope into town, churning in the ruts made by other vehicles passing or getting stuck that way while he was gone. As he drove through the square he saw two uniformed men standing on the courthouse steps, one lighting a cigarette behind his cupped palm. Deputies from Sevier County, not state police. He nodded to them but didn't slow down. He meant to put off dealing with any more outsiders as long as he could. Aside from them the town square was empty of lawmen and searchers. They were likely using the Walker farm as their base of operations. Ellard headed that way, listening to the distant cries of the men and women spread out through the pines bordering the fields along the road before cranking up his window against the weather. He would see about the Dodsons, but Amos was his priority. He didn't need the state police. Ellard knew the drifter and his habits better than they did anyway.

He had almost reached the farm when he saw Silver Ledford at the side of the road. She was coming down the bank across from the cornfield, her pale ankle flashing in the chicory as she stepped across the gully. Silver was unmistakable as anybody else. She possessed her own wild beauty, like bark and quartz rocks and flowering weeds. As she hurried ahead of the car Ellard sped up to pull alongside her. She glanced his way but kept walking in her liver-colored dress. He cranked the window back down, chill droplets splashing in on him. "Silver Ledford," he called. She tucked her chin, pretending not to hear. He blasted the siren mounted on his front fender once and she stopped where she was, glowering as if he had slapped her. He reached across the seat and pushed open the passenger door for her. "Get in. I won't keep you long." She looked at him for another second before climbing inside. He turned off the engine, the down-pour battering the roof. He closed up the window, the cornfield and the weedy bank blurring out of focus. "Why didn't you go to Annie Clyde last night?" he asked. "I sent somebody after you."

Silver huddled against the door, leaning her head on the misted window. Water had already begun to spread on the upholstery under her legs. "I'm on my way to see her now."

"What about Amos? You ain't seen him, have you?"

She turned farther away. "I been looking for him myself."

"I got every lawman that would come here tracking him, but I bet you'd beat them all."

"Amos don't leave no tracks," Silver muttered. "Not even for me to find him."

"Amos is a human being, Silver. He can be caught. He's just quicker and quieter than the average individual. Except maybe for you. I thought you might know the best place to look."

Silver hugged herself, shivering. "I don't know him as well as you think I do, Ellard."

"You two seem awful close to me."

"Anyhow I'd say Amos is long gone."

"I figure you've seen him, though."

"What if he ain't done nothing wrong?"

"He never does no wrong, according to you and Beulah Kesterson."

"I ain't like the rest of you," she said. "Blaming everything on him." Even with her expression hidden behind her hair, Ellard could see the set of her jaw. "You been looking for an excuse to hang Amos going on forty years. All you been waiting for is a good enough reason."

"That's your sister's grandbaby," Ellard said. "You ought to be handing me the rope."

Silver whipped her head around. "Don't talk to me about my people."

"I'd like to give you the benefit of the doubt," he went on. "Far back as we go. But if you ain't telling me something, I'll throw you and Amos both in jail. See how you like him then."

She turned back to the window. "Amos is a lot of things, but he don't bother children."

"How do you know that?"

She didn't answer.

"He's up to something, or he wouldn't be here. He needs to be put away."

"I wouldn't want to keep nothing from you that might help you find Gracie," Silver said finally. "But I wouldn't want to get Amos hung for something he didn't do either."

Ellard sighed. "It's as bad to let a guilty man go as it is to hang an innocent one."

She bowed her face, hiding it again. "I ain't saying I'd let him go. I'd just have to look him in the eye before I made up my mind if he did anything wrong. Yours is done made up."

Ellard studied the blurry windshield. "Surely you wouldn't protect him over your kin."

Silver shut her mouth tight, no sound but rain. Then Ellard was shocked when she opened the door and sprang from the car. He lunged across the empty seat where she had been. "Hold it."

"I'm going to see Annie Clyde," she shouted without looking back.

"I ain't done with you," he called after her. "Don't stray too far."

Ellard knew he shouldn't let Silver get away but his temples were throbbing. He needed to collect himself. He shut the passenger door and leaned back in the seat, her woodsy smell still in the car with him. Most of the time he was careful not to think about Silver. About that day he'd found her under the shade trees along the river without her dress on, painted from head to toe in mud, hair plastered down with it. She'd seemed like part of the bank, as if she was growing up out of it. Back then she wasn't a liar but Amos might have turned her into one. He had some kind of hold over her. She saw some appeal to him that nobody else in Yuneetah did. When Ellard, Silver and Mary had played together as children they would turn around and find Amos spying on them from the thicket. Or they might be catching minnows and tadpoles in a coffee can when Amos would come out of nowhere and kneel on the bank beside them. He would splash his hands in the water to scare away the fish and pull the claws off the crawdads they had been baiting with worms. After a while his eyes would meet Silver's and she would walk off into the trees with him, leaving Ellard and Mary alone. It gnawed at Ellard how they seemed to belong together, both tall and lanky with hair the color of the shadows they passed through. Ellard would have liked to bloody Amos's nose, to fight him as he sometimes did other boys in the school yard, but Amos had never raised his fists first. It wasn't in Ellard's nature to start a fight, so he stood back and watched as Amos stole Silver away from him again and again.

Both Ledford sisters were lovely to look at, but Silver was the loveliest to Ellard. In those days most girls wore their hair in plaits, but Silver kept hers unbound. It poured like mountain water down her back, into her eyes, over her shoulders. She was hard to catch when they played tag, hard to find when they played hide-and-seek. She could fit herself into any crevice or hole. Once she'd hidden from Ellard in a junked stovepipe. She didn't talk much and when she did her words were gruff, but he recognized her bluster for what it was. She might have fooled Amos and Mary but Ellard saw tender skin underneath the shell she had grown over years of mistreatment. Sometimes he heard Silver mimicking the birds, blowing through her thumbs to answer a bobwhite. He had come upon her peeping in at a praying mantis she'd caught in the trap of her fingers. Sometimes she hummed or whistled if she thought nobody was paying attention.

It was only after Mary got married that Ellard had Silver to himself. Amos had been gone for three years by then. Silver seemed lost without her sister, wandering around with bewildered eyes. At that time her grandfather had already drunk himself to death and she lived alone with her grandmother. Ellard didn't care what made Silver turn to him. For one summer when he was seventeen and she was fifteen they walked the back roads and ridges of Yuneetah alone. Crossing meadows on the way to the river with their cane poles he would pluck the frilled petals off a daisy and give her the yolk at the center. He would find red cardinal feathers in the grass and tuck them behind her ears. He wanted her to have the color she was missing in her drab shack on the mountaintop. Whatever was bright in a landscape of putty gray, faded green, smoky blue.

One hazy afternoon at the end of June, Ellard left his chores and went up the mountain to see if Silver wanted to go swimming. When he found that she wasn't at home he headed to the shoals alone, undressing on his way to a part of the river where the water was broad and the current was tame, where willows bowed shedding yellowy leaves. Entering the deep shade naked he saw a flash of motion before he reached the edge of the shore. Silver was hunkered on the bank several feet downriver, camouflaged by the silt she had slathered on against the mosquitoes and the burning sun. She looked at him, eyes glittering coals in her smeared face. When she rose up Ellard couldn't keep from rushing to her. He took in her clotted hair, her pointed breasts, the fork of her legs. As she stood on the bank bare as the day she was born Ellard saw the last plates of her shell fall away. Nothing could have stopped him then from pulling her slippery into his arms, kissing her so hard that their teeth clashed together. He was trembling as he lifted her up, as her thighs closed around his hips. Though Ellard felt everything it was almost like watching himself.

Once they'd turned themselves loose, they couldn't get enough of each other. Silver would find Ellard in the henhouse gathering eggs and they'd lie down in the patterns the chickens had scratched. They would roll in spruce needles under the trees until their sweating flesh was pasted with them, motes dancing around Silver's head as the sun sank behind the mountains. But that whole summer, some part of Ellard was miserable waiting for it to end. Looking back he

understood. All those warm months he felt like he'd just been bor-
rowing Silver. When Amos showed up that September, back for the
first time in three years, it was almost like Ellard had been expecting him. He'd been nailing down a piece of roof tin that had come
loose in a storm for his mother when he spotted a figure heading up
the hollow footpath with a bedroll under one arm, bending to drink
from the trickling spring. He had grown taller, his hair longer, but
he moved with the same stealth. When he lifted his face dripping
from the spring Ellard could tell there was something altered about
it, could see the void where his hat shaded an empty eye socket. But
Ellard never doubted it was Amos. He didn't come down the ladder. He watched Amos disappear up the path, his own eyes watering.
Maybe Ellard wouldn't have wanted Silver as much if she hadn't preferred his enemy. Maybe his hatred for Amos had made his love for
her burn hotter. Whatever the reason, the fire took ages to go out.
It was years before Ellard could think of Silver without longing and
only as something that had once happened to him.

Now Ellard wondered if Amos still had a hold over Silver. He
looked at the damp she'd left on the seat, the same shape her hair
used to make when she lay on the ground underneath him. He put
his hand on the upholstery and pressed but nothing seeped up. She
knew something she wasn't saying. He would talk to her again if he
hadn't found Gracie or Amos by this afternoon. The constable had
gone to see Beulah Kesterson last night and gotten nowhere with
her either. It was time for Ellard to pay Beulah a visit himself. He
pulled his revolver from its holster, popped out the cylinder, emptied
the bullets into his hand then reloaded them. As he sat behind the
wheel of the sheriff's car the lake broadened and deepened across the
bank in the Hankins pasture, overtaking the tasseled weeds in uneven
ponds, touching the lowest wires of the fence still tufted with hanks
of bovine hair. Rising over any scrap of sacking snagged from a child's
home-sewn dress hem. Swirling up any pattered bead of red. Drifting

off any wisp of hair. Washing away every remaining shred of anyone's child, not just the one he was searching for. Erasing the footprints of those living along with those dead, those moved on to inhabit other towns along with those lost forever. Too soon no sign would remain of any child ever torn from its mother.

That midmorning Annie Clyde Dodson wound up back in the cornfield where she'd started, as if she might find Gracie and Rusty waiting again at the end of a row. She didn't know what hour it was but when she looked up the sun was higher behind rafts of cloud. After all night without sleep she felt lost on her own land. As she wandered between the stalks calling her daughter's name she dreamed on her feet, remembering how she'd sat yesterday on the bottom porch step plucking chicken feathers and looking out at this field, corn swaying in the uneasiness before the windstorm. Earlier going into the musty gloom of the coop, singing to soothe the rooster. He had perched on an empty nesting box, manure hardened on the rotting straw, waiting for her. Once the rooster was plucked she had meant to ride Gracie among these rows in the wheelbarrow, collecting roasting ears for their dinner. She had told Gracie to stay on the porch, left the front door propped open with an iron long enough to put the carcass in the basin and get the flour. From the kitchen she had heard Rusty barking and gone through the dim hall toward the lit doorway. She had watched the dog running into the field with Gracie behind him. Then the corn had swallowed Gracie up and she couldn't see her anymore. That was where everything had gone wrong. Now she slapped aside the stalks spraying drops, shouting for her daughter. There was no answer. Not even Rusty barking to say there was someone in the field who didn't belong. This time there was only water standing at the end of the row. Instead of Gracie, a formless puddle.

But Annie Clyde felt in her bones that Gracie was somewhere close. The reservoir was filling, the floodwaters spreading. If they didn't

find her quick she might be drowned with the rest of the town. Annie
Clyde couldn't stop imagining Gracie wrapped in algae, sinking into
a darkness with no bottom. Last night after James left with the sheriff
she had waited in the house until she could take it no longer. She had
gone back out and searched the roadside pines alone while the others were down at the water. She'd known even as she ran to the river
at dawn when she heard clamoring voices that it wasn't Gracie. No
matter what the men believed, or what her husband believed. It made
her wonder how much James loved Gracie if he could give up on her.
Then she thought of the day Gracie was born, when he bent over the
swaddled bundle of her to kiss the tips of her matchstick fingers. She
thought of him carrying Gracie on his shoulders to church, handsome in suspenders and a hat with a striped band. But a man's love,
a father's love, must be different than a mother's. She'd seen his eyes
before he went to the water last night. He was mourning already. She
remembered the remark he made weeks ago about Gracie running
off into the lake. She'd wanted to kill him when he said that. Now
she wanted to kill herself. She might have done it already, if she didn't
believe Gracie was still alive.

It seemed James couldn't admit that Gracie may have been taken
by Amos. It seemed he would rather accept that anything else had
happened to her. Amos had been passing in and out of town since
before Annie Clyde was born. It was frightening to find Gracie in the
cornfield with him, but she didn't believe he was a child murderer,
however certain she felt that he was keeping her daughter from her.
Whatever Amos did to Gracie, as long as Annie Clyde got her back
alive, it could be fixed. Annie Clyde could wash away any mark he
left. As long as Gracie was found and returned with life still in her
body, the one Annie Clyde knew every inch of as well as or better
than she did her own, they'd be all right. Annie Clyde could love
her child back from anything but death. If James was here beside
her now she would have reminded him there was no coming out of
that lake. Whatever it spread over was gone. Whatever the water

took, it kept. But she could make Amos give Gracie back to them. All she had to do was get to him before the law did. Thus far she had managed to remain in motion, even with guilt crushing the breath out of her. It was her fault for not watching Gracie. There was no one else to blame. If she hadn't been planning to leave her husband, she wouldn't have been distracted. She had to be the one to make it right.

Annie Clyde was trying to get her bearings in the field when she heard a vehicle fishtailing down the track to the road, another band of men going off to look for her daughter. Around sunup a truckload had left with the only picture of Gracie she owned, taken last summer by a man who traveled around the countryside with his camera making family portraits. Annie Clyde had used money set aside for coffee and salt to pay him with, but it was worth the sacrifice. She hadn't wanted to forget what Gracie looked like at two years old. Now she wanted her picture back. Her instincts told her it was as useless looking outside of Yuneetah as it was looking into the lake. It was the same waste of time. She thrashed her way between the rows and out of the field to see more cars and trucks parked in the knee-high grass of the lot fronting the house. One belonged to James's uncle, the Packard she rode in on her wedding day. Wallace and his wife Verna had come from Sevier County, where the Methodist church was relocated. They'd been there after James lost his father in the flood of 1925 and now they were back to see their nephew through again. Annie Clyde didn't know how they got word, or any of the others. She'd returned home sometime in the night to find Verna with the wives of men who came down from the mountains and from other counties making coffee in her kitchen. Her mouth grew dry thinking about it. She needed to have a drink of water and a bite of bread in her stomach. Maybe to sit and warm herself beside the stove for a minute, change into a clean dress and put on a hat. She had to get her head on straight if she meant to outwit the drifter and find his hiding place.

Emerging from the corn to cross the yard she nearly slipped again as she had at the riverside, the ground a leaching mouth that sucked at her shoes, patterned by treads from all those that had come and gone. There were footprints under the elm and the apple tree of every shape and size, the whole farm tracked over. If the one print she believed had belonged to the drifter remained it was mixed up among the rest. Walking with her eyes lowered to watch her own feet, she didn't see the government man standing on the porch until she started up the steps. Right away she recognized him, from a month ago when their positions were reversed. He stood above her now under the pouring eave, his umbrella propped beside the front door instead of James's gun. As if he had already taken possession of the place. He looked wrong with the unpainted door and the peeling clapboard of the house behind him. He seemed untouched by the weather, the slicker he wore over his charcoal suit the only evidence he'd come through it. He took off his fedora to reveal a head of dark golden hair. They looked at each other, his eyes very blue. "How long have you been here?" she asked, glancing over to see his black Dodge coupe near the end of the track as if he'd made it no farther, its wheels sunk into the marshy grass.

"Not long. I hoped you'd be back."

"Who sent you?"

"Pardon?"

"Who made you come?"

"Oh. My chief sent me."

"Why didn't he come himself?"

"Well," Washburn said, fidgeting with his shirt collar. "I volunteered. I was sorry to hear about your daughter. I came out here to see what I could do for you and your husband."

"No, you didn't," Annie Clyde said.

Washburn stared at her. "I'm afraid I don't understand."

"You came out here to run me off. Same as you did before."

"Not at all, Mrs. Dodson. That's not so. I came out here to let you know we're doing everything we can to aid the law in finding your daughter. You can rest assured of that."

"So I ought to go on and leave it up to you. Is that it?"

"No, ma'am. I didn't say that."

Annie Clyde forgot her chilled and aching bones, her shaky legs. She came up the steps onto the porch until they stood toe-to-toe. "I'm not going anywhere without my child. I don't care if I have to row out of here in a boat. If Ellard tries to arrest me, I'll shoot him. He's a nice man, but I'm not above it. You go back and tell the bastards that sent you the same thing."

"Please, Mrs. Dodson," Washburn said. A lock of hair had fallen out of place on his forehead. He held his hat between them and she felt its crown against her belly. He seemed more human then, too much like her husband. She wished that he didn't. "I want to be of service."

"You mean to help me look for my little girl?"

"Yes," he said. "I intend to help with the search."

"You might as well not."

He gaped at her dumbfounded.

"If you're looking for a dead body floating in the water, you're not going to find one. I'm telling you, she didn't wander off and drown. She was taken. But nobody will listen to me."

"I'll listen to you. I'm on your side."

"What do you think you can do for me?"

"I've spoken to Sheriff Moody. I'll make sure he has whatever resources he needs at his disposal, and I'll do what I can to get your little girl's picture in the Knoxville newspapers."

"You haven't said her name. Do you even know it?"

Washburn glanced down at his fedora, sullied by her dress front. "Yes. I know it."

"We named her Mary Grace, after both of our mothers. We call her Gracie."

"I know her name—"

"What if her last name was Lindbergh?"

He blinked at her, speechless again.

"What would you do for her then?"

"Mrs. Dodson—"

"We read the newspapers. They come to us late, but we get them. Even way out here, we've heard about that Lindbergh baby. You think the Lindberghs have heard of Gracie?"

Washburn was losing his composure. "I sympathize with your situation, Mrs. Dodson. I'm asking you to cooperate with me, for your daughter's sake. You need my help."

"You're not helping me," Annie Clyde said. "You're holding me up."

"Please," he said, and moved as if to touch her. She shrank from his hand, backing out of his reach. She felt weak. One finger laid on her shoulder might break her down. She stepped around him and made for the door. When she yanked it open she could smell coffee and bread. Her stomach seized with hunger. She was about to shut the door in the government man's face when she saw the Winchester leaned against the wallpaper in the shadows at the foot of the stairs. James must have figured he wouldn't be using it. Without hesitation she reached out to grab it, all thought of food and rest driven from her mind. Holding on to the rifle, she felt renewed somewhat. She felt like she could walk a piece farther. She took up the lightweight gun and turned to face Washburn again. "Gracie's not dead," she told him. "I'm going to find her."

"All right," he said. "I'll go with you."

"You'll go home, Mr. Washburn. If your vehicle's stuck somebody will push you out."

"If you'll just give me a chance—"

"If you don't get out of my way," she said, "I'll have to point my husband's gun at you."

Washburn held her gaze as long as he could. "I'll be here when you get back," he said.

"Get out of my way," she ordered, and he stepped aside. She felt his blue eyes on her as she went down the steps and out of the yard, across the track toward the slope leading into the hollow. He called after her as she climbed over the split-rail fence marking the boundary of her property and she almost turned around. If she went back he would come with her and she wouldn't be alone in this, even if he was only pretending to believe her. At least she wouldn't be heading off to shoot a man and bring Gracie home by herself. At the last second though she came to her senses, pulled herself upright and squared her shoulders so Washburn could see her resolve. She kept moving ahead with only her husband's Winchester rifle for company.

Halfway up the hillside weariness overtook her. She panted as she tripped on roots and rocks, skinning her knees and palms. By the time she reached the graveyard, a shady plot of grass bordered with white pickets, she was winded and had to lean on the gate. The cemetery was within a hair of the taking line. A few weeks ago James had offered to help move these graves for the power company. He would have dug her parents up and had them shipped by train to Michigan, but Annie Clyde was leaving her people to lie in peace. From where she stood she could see her father's headstone. Sometimes she came to sit against it, comforted by the granite at her back, as firm and rough as his hands had been. It was easier there to remember how she took off her shoes to walk behind him as he plowed. To remember the rattle of the harness as he drove the mules, his soft voice urging them. Annie Clyde's mother had saved for months to pay a stonecutter to carve Clyde Walker's name on his marker. Now Mary's grave was there beside her husband's, too meager a headstone to cover the person she'd been. Annie Clyde would have given anything to talk to her parents. But they were gone and she was on her own.

She thought then for the first time that day of her aunt Silver.

From the hollow there was a shortcut to Silver's house, a path twisting around and along the ridges. She still felt a need to see her
aunt, the only blood kin she had left besides Gracie. She pictured
Silver's hands, the part that resembled her mother most. If Annie
Clyde could see them, the delicate fingers with chapped knuckles,
she might breathe easier. But Silver hadn't come and Annie Clyde
didn't know if she could make it much farther on her wobbling legs.
It was a long climb. Silver used to visit the farm on occasion but Mary
never went to her sister's high shack. She told Annie Clyde it was
lonesome up there, and scary at night. In the winter if Clyde took
a sled up the mountain to haul in firewood Mary would ask him to
see about Silver. "She's liable to freeze to death and we'd never know
it," she'd say. Annie Clyde had gathered that Mary and Silver were
close as children, strange as it was to think of her aunt being close
to anyone. Silver would stay away from the farm for months then
reappear out of nowhere to help Mary with the chores, both silent as
they scrubbed laundry or did the canning or made lye soap. When
Mary died Silver hadn't attended the funeral at the Free Will Baptist
church, but Annie Clyde understood. Silver didn't seem to belong
there among the townspeople. She belonged on the mountaintop by
herself. Annie Clyde wasn't offended by Silver's absence now either.
She empathized with her aunt in a way that others couldn't. If she got
a second wind she'd head up the mountain later. She knew Silver and
Amos once played together in the hollow. But Annie Clyde couldn't
dwell on that. She concentrated on making it to Beulah Kesterson's
first. There was a chance it would all end there.

Annie Clyde pushed herself away from the cemetery gate and continued up the slope with weeds brushing her shins, the rifle on her
shoulder. She would have come this way last night if the Whitehall
County constable hadn't been roaming around. She had wanted to
see Beulah alone, and now these woods were empty. The ground
roughened the higher she climbed, shale hidden in the thinning

grasses. It made her feel sick to follow the same footpath she and James had taken yesterday afternoon looking for Gracie but she kept going. When Beulah's place came into view she paused once more at the edge of the lot to rest against a locust tree. She was struck by the cabin's stillness. In fair weather the old woman usually sat outside in a lattice chair, the bareness around it splotched with the snuff she dipped. Annie Clyde's mother used to send her after medicine. Mary and Beulah were friends. Some winters when Annie Clyde was a child Beulah helped the Walkers butcher hogs in exchange for meat. Clyde would shoot the sow and stick its throat. Mary and Beulah would tie ropes around its legs and drag it to the scalding boards. They would take turns scraping its hide then hang the carcass up, warm blood seeping into the frozen ground as snow dusted their mackinaws. They would work into the night, packing hams and shoulders in salt in the smokehouse. Then Mary and Beulah would cook a late supper of pork. Annie Clyde liked the meal but for days afterward she had nightmares about the slaughter. Someway she associated that bloodletting with Beulah and the pouch around her neck.

To this day, Annie Clyde was afraid of the old woman's fortune-telling bones. She'd seen them once, when she was eleven and went up the hollow after a poultice for hornet stings. She had knocked down the hornets' nest under the barn eave with a rock and stirred them up. Her whole face had been swollen tight and red when the wasps were through with her. On that sunny morning the plank door of Beulah's cabin was propped open and Annie Clyde had mounted the rock steps to rap on it. When there was no answer she'd peered inside and discovered Beulah stooped over a table studying the aged bones scattered across it, stained and configured into odd shapes. Beulah had looked up, startled by Annie Clyde's knocking. Whatever she had seen in the bones must have been harrowing because her face was the color of parchment. Her eyes were wide, the pupils dilated behind her pointed glasses. Annie Clyde had turned and run off. When Mary asked why she was back without a poultice for her stings, she had refused to speak of what happened.

Annie Clyde hadn't wanted Beulah to birth Gracie. She would have sent James after the doctor in Whitehall County if not for her mother. Not long before Mary breathed her last, she'd put a hand on Annie Clyde's rounded belly and said, "Go to Miss Beulah when your time comes. If it wasn't for her, you wouldn't be in this world." It was only then that Mary told Annie Clyde how before she was born there had been three other babies lost. Beulah had seen how Mary was suffering and come down the hollow one morning with a tea made from partridgeberry to strengthen her womb. Within a few weeks Mary was expecting, and for the first time the baby had thrived. She had trusted Beulah over any doctor ever since, and even gone to the old woman first when the cancer began to make her ill. But Beulah had said to Mary with sorrowful eyes, "Honey, there ain't much I can do for you this time." After her mother's burial Annie Clyde had explored the graveyard to see if she could find her older siblings. There were no names carved on the markers Clyde had fashioned from rocks turned up by the tines of his plow. She pictured him coming with a spade and the babies wrapped in rags or tiny enough to fit in shoe boxes, digging in the shadiest corner where the flowering arms of a dogwood tree shed its blooms. Annie Clyde had brushed the leaves from the flat limestone tablets and lowered herself to sit among them, heavy with Gracie by then. She'd thought how if not for Beulah Kesterson her tiny bones might be under another rock next to theirs. She had known then she would honor her mother's wish.

On the day Gracie was born, she was sitting up in bed when James rose at first light. She told him the baby was coming but when he started after Beulah she put out a hand to stop him. "It's not time. I'll let you know." A little after noon when the pains got closer together she gave in and went to the chicken coop where he was checking nesting boxes, as much as she dreaded seeing the old woman. While he was gone she waited at the window watching the whirling March snow flurries, lacy skeins blowing across the yard. When she heard the front door open and steps groaning up the stairs, she hopped into bed as if she'd been caught at something. James came in with Beulah behind him. He took Annie Clyde's hand as Beulah unwound her shawl. Then she went to the window and cracked it enough to let in the crisp air. She turned to James and said, "Go fix you some coffee. This is woman's business." When James kissed Annie Clyde and headed for the door she reached for his sleeve, afraid to be alone with Beulah. By the time Gracie was ready to be born it was dark. Beulah scrubbed her hands and examined Annie Clyde under the lamp, moths circling up its glass chimney, the night so hushed Annie Clyde believed she could hear the papery rub of their wings. She was careful to look away from the pouch around the old woman's neck, into the unlit corners of the room. As Gracie came she stared into the lamp so hard the flame made a stamp on her vision, giving birth in the same bed her mother died in. It wasn't a difficult labor. The pains were distant. When she looked at her newborn for the first time, she felt grief over anything. She should have been happy but she couldn't help missing her mother, left alone to share the birth of her baby with somebody she'd always feared.

Now as she stood at the edge of the clearing leaning on the rifle like a crutch, looking at Beulah's dilapidated cabin, she supposed among all the other reasons Beulah made a foul taste in her mouth there had always been Amos. For as long as she could remember she had known about the one-eyed man, whose marred face she saw up close for the first time in the hayfield during early autumn. Her father and the neighbors were out that morning with the hay baler, the valley flooded not with water but with mist the bluish gray tint her newborn daughter's eyes would be ten years later. Wandering among the haystacks she stopped to pull out a straw to chew on. When she looked up, Amos was under the apple tree watching her as if he had never not been there, dew glimmering on his shoulders. Annie Clyde felt like they were the last ones alive, the sound of the baler and the voices of the farmhands far away. Then Amos asked if she'd fetch him a drink and her paralysis broke. She ran through the door into the kitchen where her mother was cooking and panted that Amos was out in the field. Mary didn't look up from the biscuit dough she was rolling but told Annie Clyde through tight lips, "You keep to the house. He can get his own water." Annie Clyde understood then there was more wrong with Amos than a missing eye. That night in her bed she imagined him standing in front of this cabin looking down on the farm, thinking of her. It was possible he was hiding here now but she doubted him being that careless. Beulah probably had a notion where he was, though. If the old woman was keeping a secret, Annie Clyde intended to make her tell it. She wouldn't let herself think of Beulah stooped over those odd-shaped fortune-telling bones. She wouldn't ask if there was such a thing as second sight.

She drew in a shuddering breath and started across the lot to the cabin, wind clashing through the leaves. She braced herself before mounting the steps and knocking on the door as she had just yesterday. When there was no response she pounded harder, until she heard the shuffle of footsteps inside. At long last Beulah opened up with a broom in her hands. She looked as tired as Annie Clyde felt. Her puckered face browned with age, the folds of her neck grimed it seemed with years of soil, wearing a shawl over her checkered dress in spite of the season. As soon as Annie Clyde saw her time seemed to stop and the words tumbled out. "I know you lied."

Beulah studied Annie Clyde, her rheumy eyes gleaming out of wrinkled pits. "I didn't know where he was, though," the old woman said. "That was the truth. And he ain't here now."

"But you know where he could be."

"If I did, I wouldn't tell it. Look at you. You might shoot him."

"I'd shoot anybody over Gracie."

"Well. I'd take a bullet over Amos."

Beulah pressed her mouth into a line, her chin jutting. The sun came out some. Annie Clyde felt the light on her back. "He's my son," Beulah said, as if that was explanation enough.

Annie Clyde saw herself reflected in the old woman's glasses, a gaunt shadow holding a gun. She lowered the rifle from her shoulder, overcome with sudden regret. She looked down at the rain blowing in on Beulah's feet. "Would you let your son take my daughter away from me?"

"If I believed for a minute Amos had that baby girl," Beulah said, "I'd put the law on him myself. I'd take a bullet for him, but that don't mean I'd let him get away with nothing like that."

There was another silence. Annie Clyde opened her mouth but her voice cracked.

"Lord, youngun," Beulah said. "You're plumb peaked. Get yourself in here."

Annie Clyde sighed through her nose as she stepped across the threshold. Beulah put aside her broom and took the gun from Annie Clyde's hands. She leaned it against the pie safe in the corner. She steered Annie Clyde to the table at the back of the room and pulled out a chair. It was straight and hard but Annie Clyde was glad to be off her feet. Beulah must have heard the click of her throat. She poured Annie Clyde a cup of water from an aluminum pitcher and sat down across from her. Annie Clyde drank deep, tasting the bitter minerals of the spring. There was no sound in the gloom of the cabin besides a clock ticking somewhere. Then Beulah asked, "Why don't we get down to it, honey?" There was such compassion in her voice that Annie Clyde felt like crying. But she wouldn't let herself. If the tears came out, she might be unable to stop them.

"I don't believe in fortune-telling," Annie Clyde said.

Beulah smiled. "That's all right."

"Seems like if anybody could see where Gracie is, it ought to be me."

Beulah reached across the table to touch her hand. "It's a mystery why certain ones have the sight. I never know if I'll be showed anything. A lot of times it ain't what I want to see."

Annie Clyde flinched away. "I shouldn't have come in here. I just needed to know if there's a chance you could help me someway." She swallowed hard. "Have you tried to look?"

"For your little one?"

Annie Clyde nodded.

"I been looking ever since you left here yesterday."

"Have you seen anything?"

Beulah's eyes were sad behind the scratched lenses of her glasses. "No," she said. "I ain't seen a thing." She lifted the pouch from around her neck. "But if you want me to, I'll try again."

Annie Clyde's pulse quickened. She put down the cup. It was what she wanted, but she recoiled at the thought of the bones. Beulah got up and stood at the head of the table. After a moment, Annie Clyde rose from her chair at the opposite end. Beulah loosened the neck of the pouch, her face lit by the drizzly window between them. She looked into Annie Clyde's eyes. "Now, you be sure about this," she said. Annie Clyde wiped her lips and nodded again.

Beulah turned the pouch up and spilled its contents. They bent over and studied them together, heads nearly touching. Annie Clyde wanted to see something herself, maybe Gracie's face, but she couldn't discern any pattern in the bones. After an agonizing minute or so she lost patience with Beulah's silent concentration. "What is it?" she asked. "Do you see Gracie?"

Beulah raised her head like somebody waking up. "Yes," she said, but with seeming reluctance. Her voice was far off and troubled. "Not where she's at. Just that she's alive."

Annie Clyde released the breath she'd been holding and sat back down in the chair, almost knocking it over. The tears came then. There was no holding them in. It was a deliverance to hear someone say it, whether or not it was true. The sobs tore from her throat and wrenched her shoulders. "Hush now," Beulah said. When she came around the table Annie Clyde could smell her oldness, like snuff and drying lavender and mellowing fruit. After a while, Beulah got slowly to her knees in front of Annie Clyde's chair and took off the brogans she was wearing. She began to rub and knead Annie Clyde's sore feet in her hands. "You're wore out. Why don't you come over here and close your eyes for a minute?" She led Annie Clyde to a bed in the corner and helped her onto the sagging mattress, drawing a blanket over her legs.

Annie Clyde meant to lie still just long enough to catch one breath. When she opened her puffed lids again she thought she'd slept a few seconds. But once her eyes adjusted she could tell by the slant of light across the bed and the dryness of her dress that it had been much longer. She got up quickly and began hunting her shoes. Beulah was standing at the fireplace making hoecakes, the smell filling the cabin. When she saw Annie Clyde awake she went to the table and took the brogans from under it. "Thank you," Annie Clyde said as Beulah handed them to her. "You can thank me by having a bite of dinner," Beulah said. "I get tired of eating by myself." Annie Clyde paused and then put down the shoes. They sat at the table together and ate in silence. The hoecakes were sweet in Annie Clyde's mouth. She shoveled them in, washing each bite down with more water from the spring. When she was finished at last she got up from the table without a word and went to the pie safe where James's rifle was propped. She took the gun up and turned toward Beulah, clenching the stock tight enough to blanch her fingers. They looked into each other's faces. Unlike Washburn's, Beulah's gaze didn't waver. "Come back anytime," she said. Annie Clyde was the first to drop her eyes. The heat from the cook fire made the room hard to breathe in. The gun was light enough to hold in one hand. She picked up both brogans in the other, gripping them by the heels. Tying the laces would take too long. She felt an urgent need to be away from Beulah and the stifling cabin. She would stop to put her shoes on once she'd put some distance between herself and the old woman's fortune-telling bones.

She lowered her head and rushed out the door. With a full stomach she descended the steps into the showering rain, afternoon sun shining through it. She thought as she hurried across the clearing toward the woods that there was no telling what had happened at the house while she was gone. She even allowed herself a flicker of hope that Gracie would be there when she got back. The deluge had washed a rut down the steepness of the lot and she skirted around it, through the locust trees at the edge of Beulah's property, seeking what shelter they afforded. Before she'd made it far from the cabin there came a stabbing in her foot, so sharp that she cried out. She dropped the rifle and sat down on the watery ground. She lifted the foot and found in its sole the biggest locust thorn she'd ever seen. Her feet bottoms were leathered from more than twenty summers spent barefoot, but not tough enough it seemed. She bit her lip, steeling herself to pull the thorn out. But when she did, its point stayed behind, broken off inside her. She considered trying to dig it out, but it was in too deep and she'd already been at Beulah's longer than she planned. She would have to leave it there embedded. She'd have to carry it home with her.

At noon James Dodson was back in the Hankins pasture. The sun was struggling to come out and in this poor light the lake looked like a slab of soapstone. He'd ended up here again after searching through the night with the others, some he had worked shoulder to shoulder with tending crops, raising barns and digging drainage ditches along the roads. They had come upon Long Man everywhere it was spread. They'd sloshed into abandoned houses where the river stood knee deep, washed into front rooms papered with newsprint, over fireplace hearths blacked by decades of cooking. Then James had followed the other men back to the fields along the former riverbed. He had gone with them over the bleached stones of the shore calling for Gracie, his old neighbors righting him whenever he stumbled, giving him sups from their canteens. When the canteens were dry they made their way to the reservoir to refill them, James crouched on a boulder staring into the pitchy water. It had come to him as he knelt there that with each passing hour his chances lessened of finding Gracie alive. He'd realized then that he couldn't bear to be the one who found Gracie dead. He used to think farming had broken him, but he was wrong. This was what broken felt like, and there was no coming out of it whole.

Now James didn't know how long he'd been standing here at the edge of this water. After a decade of avoiding the river, despising and cursing it, he couldn't bring himself to leave the shore. He listened close for his father's voice in the flood as he used to think he could hear it, but whatever had once spoken to him was gone. There were no answers for him in this part of the pasture where the reservoir had come far enough to cover the Hankins family graveyard, not even the top of a headstone visible. Two months ago he had helped with the removal of Dale's kin, a hearse parked in the pasture to take away pine boxes filled with generations of Hankinses. He'd found beneath an unmarked stone the skeleton of an infant wrapped in a blanket turned to rags after long years in the ground, its bones delicate as periwinkles. The undertaker and the pastor of the Baptist church had been there, sober in dark suits with both hands clasped before them. James had stood there gripping a spade handle, the markers of opened graves littered around him, earthen walls writhing with grubs and tunneling beetles, not knowing how soon the remains of his own child would be on his mind.

His uncle Wallace had tried at some point to talk him away, had taken him by the shoulders and begged him to get some rest. Looking back into Wallace's wearied eyes, James saw that his mother's brother had grown old. His hair snowy under a rain hood, his hands twisted with rheumatism. It was plain that Wallace needed to rest himself. But James couldn't go back to the farm with his uncle. He wanted to lie down and close his eyes but he couldn't enter that house without his daughter inside. It seemed that Gracie had called him to the lake. If he heard any voice in the water now it was hers saying, "Daddy." He had sent his uncle away alone. Though Wallace had raised James from a young age, he had never been James's father. Once Earl Dodson died James had felt on his own. He took paying work wherever he could find it, pulling tobacco and threshing wheat, chopping sugarcane and plowing gardens for ten cents an hour. One summer he worked with the iceman, riding in his Model T to the plant in Whitehall County early each morning, helping him load the truck, covering the ice with canvas to slow its melting. He had stayed at the parsonage with his sister Dora when all he wanted was to forget Tennessee. Like he would stay now at the water's edge, where he felt as though Gracie had led him.

The only one James needed with him besides his daughter was Annie Clyde. He looked down the shore like she might be coming to him. He was used to seeing her from far off, doing chores. Beating rugs, airing out feather beds, scouring windows with newspaper. Even when they worked together she stood apart from him, digging potatoes or hoeing corn at the other end of the field. From a distance he appreciated her most, naked under the few dresses she owned. The red gingham with a tiny hole at the armpit, the flowered one with a bit of tattered lace at the collar, the blue one she wore to their wedding. If the sun was shining right he could see her skin through them. He needed her to lean on, like the time he twisted his ankle in a snake hole and she shored him up all the way to the house with her bone-thin but solid self. They should have been together. Though she was around somewhere he hadn't seen her all night. She felt as lost to him as Gracie.

James knew why his wife was staying away from him and the lake.

She was convinced the drifter was to blame for Gracie's disappearance. Riding away from the courthouse after midnight in the backseat of some volunteer's Studebaker James had heard the man behind the wheel talking about Amos, saying the sheriff had instructed the searchers to keep their eyes open for him. James had spoken up although his voice by that time was no more than a croak and told those in the car that the only one they needed to keep an eye open for was Gracie. He didn't want their attention divided. James had been seeing Amos since he was a boy. Once when he was riding to town in the wagon bed on a pile of logs he and his father meant to sell, Amos stood in the ditch to let them pass. James couldn't take his eyes off the drifter's ruined face. When he turned around to stare Amos tipped his hat. Back when James's mother was alive she complained if Amos cut through their cotton on his way to somewhere else. But Earl would say, "Why, he ain't bothering nothing." James didn't hold the drifter's strangeness against him any more than his father had. As a child he was curious but once he was grown he didn't look twice if he saw Amos on the road. The last time they crossed paths, he and Annie Clyde were just married. James was about to dump the ash bucket over the fence and nearly ran into Amos, found himself looking into the pit of an eye socket. Amos tipped his hat again and said good morning. Then he climbed over the fence and walked up the slope into the hollow. James hadn't liked seeing Amos on the farm that day. But if the searchers came across the drifter's camp somewhere in Yuneetah, he didn't expect they would find Gracie there.

On this morning it wasn't Amos that James couldn't take his eyes off. It was the boats floating out on the water, there on the horizon since sunrise. They were musseling boats and James had been seeing them since he was a child growing up on the river, the same as he had always seen the drifter. Homemade skiffs with boards at bow and stern on each side, notched at the tops to hold iron bars with strings of dangling scrap nails for hooks. Fishermen would drop the bars into the water and drag them across the mussel bed, then draw them in with shells hanging from the strings. As the sheriff organized the boats James couldn't comprehend why the men would be out musseling. It was several minutes before it dawned on him that they weren't dragging the lake for mussels. They were dragging the lake for his daughter. When he understood the wind rushed out of him as if he'd been hit. He had wanted to shout at them, to swim out and tell them they were wrong. But he knew that they weren't. James couldn't stop believing the river had taken Gracie, like it took his father away from him when he was twelve years old.

The Knoxville newspaper had called the flood that claimed Earl Dodson the May Tide. James's aunt Verna had saved the clipping for him. The house the Dodsons rented was set so close to the river that when it was high James and Dora could lean out the rear window and trail their fingers in it. That night when the water came up to their doorstep they felt more awe than fear, until it began to leak inside. Earl gathered Dora onto his hip and hoisted James up under the arms. They sloshed through the rising water in the front room and out the door, plunging into the flood. As far as James could see the land was covered with roaring water. He could feel the current trying to sweep him away. He could hear his father grunting as he battled toward the higher ground of the ridge alongside the house. When Earl had made it through the rapids with both children still in his grasp he pushed them uphill ahead of him. At the top he paused, looking down on the flood and the hog lot. James knew what his father was thinking. He'd been counting on that sow to feed them through winter. Earl ordered James and Dora not to move. Then he lowered himself back down the ridge. James stood under the sycamore watching Earl wade into the flood, his head a black spot. Earl had almost made it to the hog pen before he lost his footing, the blot of his hair disappearing underwater. James kept on looking, straining to see through the lashing rain, but his father never resurfaced.

After what must have been hours he sank down under the sycamore and took Dora into his arms. When the May Tide was over nine other lives had been lost and the body of Wayne Deering's son was never found. It was a chilly spring. All that night James and Dora huddled shaking on the ridge, too shocked to speak. They watched straw stacks and barn doors rush down the river until their landlord found them.

Not long before he married Annie Clyde, James saw again that riverside shack where he and Dora had lived on the cotton farm. He'd found himself in the vicinity, helping one of the church deacons round up beeves for the stock barn. The house was wide open and caked with clay, the doors and windows missing. It looked like a corpse with a gaping mouth and sightless eyes. James stood outside staring into the rooms, unable to cross the threshold, grateful for having been spared. Now he thought he might have been better off if he had drowned with his father that night. He was still looking at the musseling boats floating over the stones of the Hankins family graveyard, at the men leaned over the sides with their grappling hooks, when he felt a firm hand on his shoulder. He thought it would be his uncle again. When he turned he was startled to see Ellard Moody. He tried to gauge the sheriff's hangdog face but it was long and mournful as usual. There was no telling what kind of news Ellard had brought. James opened his mouth, feeling outside of himself, trying to work up the courage to ask. He hadn't spoken in hours. When the words came they were almost too rough to discern. "Did you find anything?"

"No," Ellard said. "But I been to Beulah Kesterson's." James noticed that Ellard held something in each hand. At first he thought the sheriff had brought his useless rifle back, the one he'd sent to the house with Wallace, tired of lugging it around. Then he blinked his blurry eyes and realized that what the sheriff had brought him was an axe. "I sent the constable to see her last night but she wouldn't tell him nothing," Ellard continued. "So I decided to go back and try her myself. Looks like Beulah's had a change of heart. She's done told me where Amos is at."

"How come?" James asked, still out of sorts.

"On account of your wife."

"What's Annie Clyde got to do with it?"

"I reckon Annie Clyde went up there and scared some sense into Beulah. She wants me to find him before your wife does, is what she told me. She thinks he might be safer locked up." Ellard paused, squinting out at the bobbing skiffs on the lake. "I ain't seen him yet, though."

"Why not?"

"This may not be the smartest thing I ever done, James, but I think you've got a right to come with me. If you want to, that is. I believe you can keep your head or I wouldn't offer."

James closed his eyes for a second. "We better stop at the house and tell Annie Clyde."

"I don't know about that." Ellard paused again. "She ain't home nohow."

"You mean Annie Clyde?"

Ellard nodded. "I seen her sleeping up at Beulah's."

"Sleeping?"

"Listen, we ought to move before Amos does."

James rubbed his grizzled face. "All right," he said. "Let's go find him."

Ellard inclined his head toward the other end of the pasture, where the thick woods steamed with mist. He held up the axes, their blades whetted. "Beulah claimed he makes his camp over yonder. Said you go about half a mile through the thicket and come to a clearing."

"Across the fence? That ain't nothing but a laurel hell. Can't nobody camp over there."

Ellard looked at James without saying what they both knew. If anybody could, it was Amos. James had seen some of the deputies from elsewhere poking around the thicket but he doubted they had ventured far into it, with the poison ivy and copperheads. James and Dale hadn't even tried to penetrate the laurel whenever they went hunting on the other side of the fence. Only rabbits and squirrels and songbirds lived in it, nothing worth shooting at. He and Dale had preferred bigger game. Pheasants, deer, wild turkeys. Dale had talked over the years about having the laurel cleared but never got around to it before the TVA came to town.

"You sure you want to come with me?" Ellard asked.

"I know I don't want to stand around here no more," James said.

Ellard passed James an axe. "If he ain't lit out by now, we'll give him a surprise."

"People say he can't be tracked," James said, hefting the handle. "Like he's a spook."

"Well, he ain't a spook. Otherwise he'd have two eyes instead of one. It might be tricky keeping quiet in them briars but we can slip up on him. Pay no mind to the nonsense."

"You don't have to tell me that," James said. "Come on, if we're going."

James and Ellard set out across the field, ragweed soaking their pant legs to the knees. When they reached the other end they straddled the fence, the mesh of the tree canopy shielding them like an umbrella. A fecund odor rose up from the swamp between the close trunks. The deeper in they walked, the wilder the growth became. Soon they were traipsing through the nettles foot by foot, tearing the bushes aside with their hands. They had the axes but neither of them was prepared for the laurel hell when they came to it, their way blocked by a dense tract of shrubbery stretching what looked like miles in every direction, crowded branches twelve feet high blocking out what little sun there was shining. Hunters and trappers had been known to get lost trying to hack through lesser laurel hells than this one. Though James was sure they were wasting their time he started chopping anyway because his wife would have wanted him to, rooting out a tunnel for himself as Gracie used to do in the snowball bushes on the farm.

He and Ellard labored for what seemed all day to make a yard or two of progress, cutting into the leafy darkness until their shoulders ached. After a while James became so intent on his work that he stopped feeling anything. It was dim enough that he forgot about Ellard being there with him. He chopped on with single-minded purpose, blisters breaking open on his palms, locked in battle with the land he'd come to hate long before this day. He should have already been a hundred miles closer to Michigan. He and Annie Clyde and Gracie would have already stopped along the road to eat their dinner, biscuits and salt pork that Annie Clyde had wrapped in a dish towel. A brown bag of apples for Gracie. He should have already been shed of this godforsaken place. By the time he and Ellard had forged a half mile through the thicket he could hardly move his arms. At first he doubted his sight when he detected a shaft of light ahead, sun filtering into the claustrophobic shade. As he forced a path toward a gap in the laurel, he couldn't help feeling hopeful. If Amos did have Gracie, if she was on the other side of this thicket, it would be over. When he reached the gap he slung the axe into the bushes and shouldered his way through, ripping aside branches until he stumbled out of the shrubbery.

James remembered Ellard only when the sheriff emerged from the laurel himself. He stepped in front of James, a scratch on his forehead. He brought a grim finger to his lips and James nodded. Dazed and out of breath, James followed Ellard on through a copse of poplars until he saw up ahead the clearing Beulah Kesterson had told Ellard about. He noticed Ellard's hand hovering over the holster at his hip and wished for his own weapon. If he had been thinking straight he would have kept the axe. With each step closer to the clearing his daughter seemed more within his reach. He fought to bring his breathing under control, to walk with the same steadiness as the sheriff. Ellard searched the ground as they went for fresh-turned earth or perhaps footprints smaller than a man's. After proceeding for several yards they entered what appeared to be a makeshift camp near the foot of a bluff draped in vines. There was a lantern hanging from a low bough, a lean-to fashioned from birch limbs and a tarp. James's boots stuttered. Under the lean-to Amos was sitting on a milk crate, bent over a kettle and a smoldering cook fire. He lifted his face, looking up with bland expectation. He seemed unalarmed to have been discovered. James's first urge was to run and take him by the throat but he saw lying not far from the kettle a rusted machete. He had to think. One mistake could cost him Gracie.

"Hello, Ellard," Amos said, stirring the swill in his pot with a ladle. "I see you got here the hard way. But you wouldn't have made it down the bluff in this rain. I nearly fell myself."

"Hidee, Amos. I was hoping I wouldn't be seeing you again."

Amos smiled. "I didn't mean for you to."

"What are you doing out here?" Ellard asked.

"Nothing much," Amos said.

"You know this place is fixing to be flooded?"

"That's why I came back. I wanted to see it one more time before it's gone."

Ellard spat into the drifter's fire. "You're awful brave," he said. "Or dumb."

Amos blinked at Ellard in the dripping green shade. There was an almost preternatural stillness about him. "I appreciate it, but don't concern yourself. I won't let the water get me."

"Somebody's liable to get you for trespassing," Ellard said.

Amos went back to tending his pot. "This land belongs to nobody now."

"I guess the power company would disagree with you about that."

Amos turned his attention to James. "Who did you bring with you?"

"This here's James Dodson."

"Do we know each other?" Amos asked.

James took the drifter in, his forearms where his shirtsleeves were rolled up crosshatched with cuts. Thin lashes, scabbing but fresh. "I'd say we know of each other," he said.

Amos considered. "That's a good way to put it. We all know of each other around here, don't we?" He sipped from the battered ladle, sampling his dinner. "Are you men hungry?"

Ellard's jaw tightened. "I didn't come out here to eat."

Amos stopped stirring. "What can I do for you then?"

"I came to have a talk with you. But I figure you won't care if I take a look around first." Ellard kept his eyes on Amos as he neared the fire and picked up a blown-down branch. He poked with the stick at the charred stones around the kettle, probably looking for signs of bone or tooth. The thought knotted James's guts. When Ellard seemed satisfied there was nothing to be gleaned from the ashes he ducked under the plinking lean-to eave. After a moment James saw him prodding at a bundle tucked in one corner of the shelter with his foot, something wrapped in a piece of canvas. James held his breath. Ellard knelt and James heard the sheriff's knees popping over the rain. He unwound the covering and let its contents fall out. It was the drifter's bedroll, tied with a piece of twine. Ellard pulled the string to unbind it. Rolled inside were the implements a drifter carried. A tin plate, a cook pot, a frying pan. Ellard studied these provisions for a time then got up and walked back to the front of the lean-to with his hands on his hips.

Amos sat back on the milk crate. "What is it you want to talk about, Ellard?"

"James's little girl is missing."

Amos looked at James. "I heard something about that. I'm sorry for you and your wife."

"You scared Annie Clyde yesterday," James said.

Amos put down the ladle. "That wasn't my intention."

"Annie Clyde thinks you know where Gracie's at," Ellard interrupted, as Amos went on gazing at James without response. "You ain't seen any missing children, have you?"

Amos seemed to mull it over. Then his one eye settled back on James. "Yes," he said.

"You've seen one?"

"Yes."

"A lost child?"

"A dead child."

James gaped at him, stricken. For a second Ellard didn't move or speak either. Rain tapped at the tarp roof of the shelter. "You saying you found a body?" Ellard asked at last.

"Yes."

Ellard moved toward Amos. "Why didn't you tell me that before?"

"I generally try to avoid the law," Amos said.

Sweat sprang out in beads on James's brow. "Where is it?"

"I'd have to take you to it."

"Then take me to it," James said, his voice unfamiliar to his own ears.

"Wait a minute, James," Ellard said. "I don't trust him as far as I can throw him."

James's hands tensed into fists. "I'm done waiting."

Ellard cursed under his breath, touching his holster. "Watch your step," he warned Amos.

The drifter took his hat from beside the milk crate and put it on his head. He stood up and regarded James as if to make sure of something. Then he nodded and glided past James on almost silent feet. James followed him numb and mindless across the clearing toward the bluff. Ellard came behind them, revolver drawn, but James ignored both of the other men. As he walked, he conjured Gracie's face to hold before him in place of whatever he was about to see. He pictured her sleeping in her crib with her fingers curled under her chin, lips suckling as if she nursed in a dream. He didn't know if a human being was made to withstand a thing like this. It seemed possible he wouldn't survive. They walked a few yards to the rocky ledges, lush with a fall of white-flowered woodbine. At the bottom of the bluff it appeared as though Amos had hacked through the greenery with the rusted machete. He pulled the vines aside and looked up at James with his impassive face, waiting. Ellard stepped between them. "Let me do this," he said.

James shook his head. "No. She's mine." But he stopped and bent over, gulping.

"Don't you want to see?" Amos asked.

"Shut your mouth," Ellard shouted at Amos.

It took every ounce of James's will to look down. There was a fissure at the foot of the bluff, something he took at first for an animal burrow. On closer inspection, he saw that it was a shallow limestone cave, the kind that honeycombed the valley floor. He let out a chuff of breath and lowered himself to his hands and knees. From that position he realized he would have to stretch flat on his belly to see what was inside. That close to the spongy topsoil the smell of it choked him. Bugs crawled into his collar, tickling his neck. He braced himself and turned his head to peer in the hole. For an instant in the grainy light he saw not the corpse he dreaded but Gracie as he remembered her, asleep on the floor of the cave as she would have been in her crib. But when his vision cleared what he saw was the skeleton of a child. Blackened leaves had sifted down through the shroud of woodbine to drift all around it, rotting in a scum of stagnant water. Some of the ribs were missing, carried off by animals. Milk teeth were gone from the jawbone. The small, tea-stained skull was broken, bashed in on one side. James scrambled backward in the litter of chopped-away vines and pushed himself up onto his knees. He retched but nothing came out. "That's not Gracie," he heard himself saying, but in his heart he felt that it was.

———

Not long after two o'clock, Beulah Kesterson went to the washstand
and splashed her face. She ran a comb through her long ivory hair
and braided it. She put on her best smock, the one she wore to funer-
als, then strained to bend and tie her shoes. After covering her braid
with a head scarf, she crossed to the door with Annie Clyde Dodson still on her mind. The girl seemed to have aged a decade since
yesterday. Her eyes had been like holes, her hair snarled, her dress
soiled. In the past when Beulah couldn't help those who came to
have the bones read she sent them away without false hope. But she'd
never been asked to look for a missing child. Others had disappeared
after the floods but they were found, besides the Deering boy. Beulah
imagined it would be even worse left wondering like this than knowing Gracie was dead. She felt she had to do something for Annie
Clyde but she hadn't meant to lie to her again. The words came out
of her mouth before she could stop them. She claimed to have seen
the little girl alive, when in truth the bones had showed her nothing.
Beulah told Annie Clyde what she wanted to hear because she had
witnessed too much suffering. She couldn't take any more of it. But
maybe one last lie made no difference. Maybe there was nothing else
Annie Clyde Dodson would have believed.

Then Ellard Moody had pecked on the door while Annie Clyde
was still sleeping in Beulah's bed. She couldn't remember the last
time she'd had more than one visitor in the same day. Under other
circumstances her spirits would have lifted to see Ellard. His parents had been good neighbors and he was always a respectful boy.
He'd spent many afternoons playing under the shade trees around
her cabin. Sometimes in the winters after Amos left, Beulah would
pay Ellard a dime to bust kindling for her. She had watched him
grow into a fine man over the years. When she opened the door she
was troubled to see him looking nearly as bad off as Annie Clyde,
standing on her steps slump-shouldered in the pouring rain. Each
line of his face was a crack under iron-colored stubble, his drooping

eyes red-rimmed. She knew what he came for and what she had to do, as much as it pained her. She told Ellard about Amos's hiding place in the clearing only to protect him. She had seen a desperation close to madness in Annie Clyde Dodson. She wouldn't have betrayed her son for any other reason than to save him. Not just from Annie Clyde, but from himself. After talking with Amos in the shed yesterday morning she'd come away certain of what he was planning. Something he might not live through. What troubled Beulah most was that Amos didn't seem to care whether he got out of Yuneetah in one piece or not. She needed to make sure he understood her reasoning. She was headed out to tell him herself.

Beulah stepped into the storm, the sun still trying to break through the clouds. The rain was slackening but not over. She'd seen it pour weeks at a time on the valley. If it didn't let up the search would be impossible to continue. Soon the lake would reach the main road. There would be no getting in or out. It wasn't just the child slipping farther away every minute. It was all of Yuneetah. She hurried down the hollow, past the graveyard and the Walker farm. At the end of the track she turned north, catching winks of water between the roadside trees. She used to go to the shoals on the first of March each season to see the river unthawing, a ritual that meant winter was over. In the cold months she dreamed of its damp slate smell, its eroding banks studded with oval rocks washed smooth as glass. Like the Cherokees, Beulah thought the river might be speaking to her. She wondered if the bones passed down to her had come from some strange fish caught in its waters. If it wasn't Long Man whispering to her about the people that lived along its shores, communicating in some way much older than hers, from before language. As close as the people of Yuneetah had lived to it, having fished from and drunk of and swam through its waters, maybe they too could have heard the truths it told if they'd listened closer.

But the river as Beulah knew it was gone. She moved on from

what it was becoming, a flood seeping into her shoes and wetting her rolled-down stockings. About two miles from the Walker farm she came to a truck mired along the shoulder to its running boards. She recognized James Dodson's Model A Ford and stopped to see if he was close by. She listened for the searchers she'd heard calling through the night but their voices had abated. A little farther down the road she met a party of men walking and they tipped their hats at her. She could read the defeat in their postures. She knew how much they wanted to find the child alive, especially the townspeople who had returned from other counties. She understood what it would have meant to them. Now the search had become one last disappointment. She'd seen the same thing in Ellard's long face. He had given up on finding Gracie, maybe even before he started looking for her. At least Beulah had helped him in some small way, though she doubted he would get much satisfaction from Amos. She ducked her head as she rushed past the Hankins property and the thorny wood where her son would be arrested, if he wasn't already locked up in the courthouse basement. He had been content camping there, close enough to the river that when it left its banks all manner of useful junk washed up and got snared in the vines at the foot of the bluff. Amos might have hidden there comfortably until the lake flooded him out if not for Beulah.

She kept her eyes on the road as she passed the demolished and burned-down houses of Yuneetah. Seeing the destruction she felt the souls of those who built the town from its foundation and died within its boundaries. The settlers who wasted away from starvation and disease, the Rebel and Union soldiers, the farmers who dropped in the boiling heat of cotton fields and tobacco rows, the mothers who died in the sweat of childbed fever, the elders who went in their sleep at the end of long lives with loved ones holding their hands. It was the last time she'd travel this way, her last trip to town. But Amos mattered more to her than anything else right now. She was out of breath before she made it to the square, her legs and back aching. When she reached the courthouse and saw that the sheriff wasn't parked out front she went up the broad steps and heaved herself down to wait under the portico. The sidewalk was deserted besides a car and two trucks alongside the curb, bathed shiny with the overcast sun lighting their beaded cabs. Beulah could remember when the town had no sidewalks. When the square was made of dirt, a rain like this had turned it into a hoof-printed sump, the horses people rode then wearing crusty mud boots. She hadn't been here since spring, before everybody cleared out. She'd gone into McCormick's to see some of her neighbors off, having birthed them and their babies. She sat at the counter and with a nickel of her dwindling savings ordered a piece of cherry pie. Now the café's plate-glass window was broken. She looked out at the neat buildings lined up in a row, red brick with white-painted moldings, awnings darkening their boarded facades. Sitting there in her funeral dress, saddened by the emptiness of the main street, she began to fear something had gone wrong. She prayed she'd done the right thing by turning Amos in.

When Beulah saw Ellard's car coming at last, a red light revolving on its roof, she got to her feet. As he pulled up to the steps and switched the motor off she noticed through the blurred windshield someone sitting beside him in the front seat. Ellard got out and went around the car to open a rear door. At the same time the man on the passenger side almost tripped onto the sidewalk. It was James Dodson. She knew her fears had been founded. Something had gone wrong, but she couldn't understand exactly what. Then she saw that Ellard was pulling her boy out of the backseat by the arm and her fingers went to her pouch of bones. She stood there clutching the pouch as Ellard led Amos up the courthouse steps with his hands cuffed behind him. When they reached the top Amos lifted his chin, hatless with his hair wetted sleek. Beulah sucked in a breath. His face was beaten misshapen. His lips mashed against his teeth, his nose bent, his eyebrow gashed, blood caked at his hairline. And yet he seemed unruffled as ever. Ellard was the one who looked shaken. James Dodson shambled up the steps behind them with his skinned fists hanging at his sides like he had taken the beating. When Beulah found the voice to ask Ellard what happened he turned to her and said, "He's lucky I didn't blow his head off."

She didn't follow them right away into the courthouse. She watched them disappear behind the double doors, afraid to find out what damage she had caused. It took a moment to collect herself and walk in through the entrance hall, past the mahogany staircase and the bulletin boards tacked with old notices, her shoes squeaking on the checkerboard tiles. She stopped and stood in the middle of the confusion with nobody paying attention to her. The constable that had questioned Beulah last night shuffled Amos to a desk in the corner scattered with papers beneath a map of the county. James Dodson sat on a bench against the wall holding his head in his hands, the curve of his back rouged by the stained-glass fanlights above the windows. Ellard walked over to a high counter where uniformed men from other police departments were operating a shortwave radio. Beulah tried to make sense of what he was telling these lawmen about bones in a cave, saying they needed to get somebody down to the Hankins woods to collect the remains. She thought at first he was talking about Gracie, but then one of the others mentioned contacting someone from the college in Knoxville to determine the age of the bones. She stood there for some unknown amount of time. Her eyes found the wall clock but it had run down. The calendar above the file cabinets hadn't been changed since April either, as if the town had ceased to exist when the dam gates closed. Unable to stay on her blistered feet any longer, Beulah went to the bench and sat beside James. She touched his back through his coat but he didn't lift his head.

Then she noticed the constable rising from behind the desk in the corner, steering Amos still handcuffed toward the stairwell leading down to the basement. She got up as quick as she could and hurried after them, too old to keep up. They went down two flights of stairs and a hall lined with shelves of moldering volumes labeled CRIMI-NAL MINUTES, their aged bindings unraveling and strings trailing from their broken spines, on past the door to a vault that held county records she supposed would be thrown away for all they mattered to the power company. At the end of the hall they came to the only cell. It looked hardly wide enough to turn around in, with a concrete floor and cinder-block walls, a bunk with a thin woolen blanket folded on top. The constable glared at Beulah as he opened the door. She knew he wasn't fond of her since she'd refused to talk to him about Amos. After it clanged shut Amos backed up to the bars to have the hand-cuffs removed. When they were left alone he took a seat on the bunk and turned his beaten face to Beulah. She couldn't keep from crying. "How come them to hurt you this way?"

"They didn't give me a reason," he said.

Beulah fished a handkerchief from her pocket. "What are they so wrought up over?"

Amos blinked at her between the bars. "They found some bones."

"A child's bones?"

"Yes."

"A skeleton?"

He nodded.

"Where at?"

"Same place you found me."

"How did they know where to look?"

"I showed them."

Beulah mopped at her eyes. "How did you know where to look, then?"

Amos winced as he leaned against the cinder-block wall. "It's been in there ten years or longer. Every time I get back a few more bones are carried off. But I've left it alone."

"How do you reckon it got in there?"

"I would say the floods washed it in. Or the child crawled in, like I did."

After a silence it struck her. "The little Deering boy. He's the only one never found."

"I guess he's found now."

Beulah stared down at the handkerchief crumpled in her hand, unable to look anymore at Amos's swelling face, his bloody eye socket. "That still don't tell me why James hurt you."

There was a drawn-out pause. Beulah could hear rumbling voices and a flurry of movement upstairs. "He might have thought it was his daughter," Amos said.

Beulah looked up. "Why would he think that?"

Amos touched his split eyebrow and studied his fingers without answering.

"You told him you found Gracie in that cave?"

"No," he said. "That's what he believed."

Beulah felt light-headed. "Why would you do him that way?"

"I was just giving him what he wanted."

"What in the devil does that mean?"

"He wanted to see a dead child and I showed him one."

"That's crazy talk. He didn't want no such thing."

"He wanted it over one way or another. If it was me, I wouldn't have given up."

"Lord, Amos. What have you done this time?"

He tried to smile. "Ellard was going to arrest me anyway."

Beulah sighed. "You're fixing to get yourself killed, son. You've nearly done it already."

"Leave it alone," he said, and she heard the pain in his voice.

She moved to the bars of the cell, wrapped her knotty fingers around them with the handkerchief balled in her palm. "They ought to let me clean you up. Where's that constable?"

Amos closed his eye. "He won't let you in here."

"He will, too," she said.

Amos rested against the wall and she loitered a moment more watching him. It felt like she was seeing his true face for the first time under that veil of bruises. It was something she'd needed to see before she died. She turned away from the cell with purpose, replacing the handkerchief in her pocket. She went down the hall the same way they'd come. She had started up the stairs when an echoing bang resounded down the stairwell. She paused. It sounded like the courthouse doors thrown open. Her first incoherent thought was that the wind had blown them in. Then she heard raised voices, one of them a woman's. There was a pounding of feet overhead. Something toppled and crashed. As Beulah stood with her eyes fixed on the carpet rising out of sight around the bend leading to another flight of stairs, there was a second blast that could only have come from a gun. Annie Clyde had finally done it. Somebody was lying dead up there. Beulah should have rushed upstairs to see if she could help, but she didn't want to know who it was. Ellard or James or some out-of-county lawman. Listening harder, she heard frantic scuffling. She looked over her shoulder toward Amos's cell. "Don't go up there," he called down the hall.

"How did she find out where you are?" Beulah called back.

"Evidently word still gets around fast in Yuneetah," he said. Then they both hushed and Beulah stood listening again. After several minutes passed the muffled voices upstairs seemed to calm somewhat. Beulah began to hope there was nobody shot. She was about to climb the stairs when she heard approaching feet and backed away from the bottom step. She kept her eyes on the bend in the staircase. It was Annie Clyde she saw first, the girl's face wan and frail as a china cup. Her arms looked just as breakable, encircled by men's hands. She was flanked by Ellard on one side and on the other by somebody Beulah didn't know but whose kind she recognized. Her glance went to his wingtip shoes and back to his bewildered expression. He was surely wondering how he had gotten himself into this. He was younger than most of the caseworkers and county agents she'd seen sniffing around Yuneetah the last two years but he was one of them. His white shirt clean beside Annie Clyde's dirtiness, his golden hair combed neat. Descending the stairs behind them was the constable, keeping an eye on James Dodson. But James didn't need guarding. It looked to Beulah like he didn't know where he was, still drunk with shock. She was relieved to see they all appeared unwounded as they brushed by her. None of them acknowledged Beulah as they passed. There was only the shuffle and screech of their footfalls down the dim hallway. As Beulah watched them go, it began to dawn on her what they were doing. "What's wrong with you, letting her come down here?" she hollered after Ellard.

Ellard didn't look back. "I should have let her shoot him, after what he done."

"He's in bad shape, Ellard. He ought to be in the hospital."

"He's right where he ought to be, and you know it," Ellard said. "He's got trouble on his mind one way or another. It's the best thing for him and everybody else if he stays locked up."

"Well, I believe you've lost your mind," Beulah said, out of breath as she shoved past him and the others to stand in front of the cell. Her eyes fell on the young power company man, holding Annie Clyde's arm. As though he had some claim on her, some authority over any of them. "What are you doing," she demanded of him, "poking your nose where it don't belong?"

He seemed startled to be addressed. "Mrs. Dodson needed a ride and I offered her one."

"Get out of the way, Miss Beulah," Ellard ordered. "I told her she could talk to him."

"Let her talk, then," Amos spoke up, and a quiet fell over the rest of them. They stood still, gathered close in the grayish light from the window near the ceiling. Annie Clyde stared at Amos, her breath rapid. Beulah saw the rise and fall of her chest. If she wanted free from the men they might not be able to hold her. But Beulah did as Ellard said. She got out of the way.

Annie Clyde came forward and Amos rose from the bunk. Ellard's other hand went to the butt of his revolver. Beulah looked from one to another of them. Amos shadowed in the recess of the cell. Annie Clyde lit by the window. The men holding her away from the bars with their backs almost against the wall. James Dodson standing there with the constable like someone dreaming. "What do you want to know?" Amos asked, any trace of pain gone from his voice.

"Where's Gracie?"

"That I can't tell you."

"What did you do to her?"

"Nothing."

"You took her."

"What makes you think so?"

"You were down at the house."

"That doesn't mean anything."

"Have you got her?"

"No," he said. "I don't have her."

"Did you hurt my baby?"

"I wouldn't hurt her. She's all that's worth saving in this place."

"You tell me the truth," Annie Clyde said through her teeth.

"All right," Amos said back. "Here's the truth. I'm not the one you ought to be worried about." His gaze flicked to the young power company man standing near Annie Clyde's elbow. "That's your enemy right there. He's the one fooling you, acting like he's going to help you. But he'll be at your door with a court order in the morning."

"Shut up," Annie Clyde said. "You. You took Gracie."

Amos favored her with his one swollen eye. "I didn't take her," he said. "You lost her."

There was a moment of stunned silence. Then Annie Clyde moved like a blur. She yanked her arms up and brought them downward, wrenching free in an instant. It was the power company man who acted first, lurching in front of Annie Clyde as if to take a bullet for her. At almost the same time Amos's arm shot between the bars and snaked around the man's neck, pulling him into a choke hold. Beulah saw dully that there was something in Amos's hand. A hunting knife. Somehow he had kept it concealed from Ellard and the other lawmen in all the uproar. But he hadn't pulled the knife on James Dodson, even to defend himself. Beulah searched out James in the tumult and saw him snatching Annie Clyde against his chest. Amos was holding the power company man close enough to whisper in his ear, their cheeks smashed together between the bars, the knife tip dimpling the flesh under his chin. The man struggled, his wingtip shoes scuffing the floor, until Amos's hold tightened enough to cut off his wind. Then he went limp. Ellard pulled his revolver and leveled it at Amos. "Drop what you're holding there."

"Just a minute," Amos said. "I want to ask him something." He pressed the knife tip into the power company man's flesh, drawing a line of blood in its pale smoothness. Beulah remembered one of the man's coworkers walking away from Bud and Fay Willet in a pin-striped suit, leaving them weeping on their porch. As young as he looked, she had no sympathy for him.

"Let him go," Ellard said.

"What are you here for?" Amos asked.

The power company man stared straight ahead unable to answer, walleyed with fear.

"You're here to run people off their land," Amos answered for him.

"No—" the man protested, cringing away from the knife.

"Don't you work for the TVA?"

The man raised a feeble hand to pry at Amos's forearm, a ring with a topaz stone glinting on one of his fingers. Beulah doubted he even knew what he was saying. "Yes, but—"

"What department?"

"Family Removal Section," he gasped out.

"Removal Section. That's a choice. Who else is running people off, if not you?"

"Not me," he insisted, his face turning bluish. "They give the orders—"

"There is no 'they,'" Amos said, pressing the point of the knife deeper into the man's throat. "Like your head. It's one part of your body, but you wouldn't be much use without it."

"That's about enough," Ellard shouted, pulling the hammer back on his gun.

The power company man's eyes rolled around as if to seek help, his blood mixing pink with the sweat soaking his once clean white shirt collar. "What would happen," Amos asked into the man's ear, "if I cut off one of this dam builder's parts? Would it make any difference?"

"No," the man begged.

Ellard stared at Amos's battered face over the barrel of the revolver. Amos looked back at him steadily. "I've been itching to kill you going on forty years," Ellard said. "I'll do it, Amos."

"I know you pretty well after that long," Amos said. "You're all talk."

"What about me?" James broke in, letting go of Annie Clyde. "You reckon I'm all talk?" He stepped forward, his auburn hair and ruddy skin bright in the dreary cinder-block basement. He was a head taller and twenty years younger than Ellard or the constable. Beulah didn't see what either one of them could do if he rushed the jail cell bars and got his hands on Amos again.

Amos's eye stayed on Ellard and the gun. "No," he said. "But I think you're beat."

Splotches bloomed in James's cheeks. "You just keep on thinking that way."

Beulah felt panic overtaking her. Threatening the power company

man wouldn't stop James Dodson from finishing what he'd started
in the Hankins woods. She doubted James would care much if Amos
cut off the power company man's fine blond head. But Amos was
ignoring the danger. "I've been shot at before," he told Ellard. "As
long as I can remember, people have been trying to get rid of me.
You won't be the one to do it." Then he shifted his shining eye back
to Annie Clyde. "Go ahead and put the blame on me, if it makes you
feel better."

"Please, son," Beulah pleaded. "Turn him loose." There was a
charged pause. She could hear the breathing of those around her.
The power company man's eyes darted about in search of rescue but
nobody moved. Then without warning Amos let go, giving the man a
shove. He took in a whoop of air and staggered out of Amos's reach,
falling then scuttling to his feet. Even in that moment Beulah knew
Amos hadn't released the man because she told him to do it. He did
nothing unless it suited him. He let the power company man go for
the same reason he would never have hurt Gracie Dodson. Amos was
not a murderer, no matter what they thought of him.

As dark settled over the valley Silver Ledford plodded down the
winding mountainside. She carried no light through the trees but
over the years she had learned not to need one, feeling her way along
the ridges. She was headed to Beulah Kesterson's cabin after having spent an hour in the woods a mile above her shack. She'd meant
to make sure no lawman or searcher had stumbled across the still,
though it would have been nigh impossible. Plum had taught her
that trails led the law to a man's whiskey so she never took the same
path twice in a row. She'd approached from downstream, the water
rushing engorged. She knelt to inspect the concealing laurel she'd
piled and it seemed undisturbed. There were no footprints in the
clay of the bank save those of minks and raccoons. She moved the

bushy limbs, drops spraying from the leaves, and found the still pot unmolested. After a while she got up again and looked into the foggy woods to the right of the stream. Over there she could see the out-line of the shed leaning under a chinquapin tree, leaves and spiked burrs littering its tin roof. Like her grandfather before her, she stored sugar, sweet oil and mash barrels inside. But now the shed held more than that. She had wanted to move toward it but her feet were rooted for a long time. Her eyes wouldn't blink. They filled with rain. For most of her life Silver had kept her own counsel. But as she stood there immobile, Beulah had come to her mind. She knew she had to see the old woman, if she couldn't see Amos.

When it was still early morning Silver had gone into the cane-brakes other searchers avoided, the briar thickets that tore scarlet lines in their arms. Disturbing nests of copperheads heaped over with leaves, probing with her fingers into the slick nooks of the riverbank on the other side of the dam and drawing them out catfish-bitten. She had scouted the Hankins pasture and the bracken across the fence, knowing Amos made his camp somewhere close. She'd tried to crawl into the laurel, twigs snagging her hair, but not even a child Gracie's size could have forced her way in. Then at around eleven o'clock, coming down the bank in front of the Walker farm, she was stopped by Ellard Moody. While she was trapped in a car with him the old loss had threatened to surface. If she drew pictures, she could have sketched his boyhood face from memory. It was once that dear to her, freckled and serious with sad brown eyes. His body lean with muscle, his head full of cowlicks the color of maple sap. Decades had passed since her summer with Ellard but she could still feel his lips forming her name against her ear. Sometimes she would go to the river and remember lying there with him, the sun lighting his smooth brow above her, minnows swimming over and between their skins. When the wind mimicked the wail of a baby she looked around as if she might have had some other life with Ellard that she'd somehow forgotten. Theirs would have been a girl with eyes like flakes of moon. If she fretted, Silver would have held her. If she got cold, Silver would have stoked the fire. If food was scarce, Silver would have given her portion. If colored leaves were ankle deep, Silver would have swished through them with her.

Ellard had treated Silver like something precious. But when Amos came back to Yuneetah at the end of that summer, three years after he left for the first time on a northbound boxcar, Silver was drawn right back to him. She had tried not to think about Amos when she closed her eyes, but she tossed and turned all night in her bed. Knowing he was down the hollow at Beulah's she burned herself lighting the fire at breakfast. At dinnertime she scorched the beans. She cared for Ellard but she didn't belong with him. She had thought while she was caught up in his arms that she might always be with him, that she might even marry him. Then Amos came back tossing shale at her window and the pull she felt toward him was stronger than ever. She found herself choosing to go off with Amos when she had agreed to wait for Ellard down at the river with her fishing pole. Amos would come to her with a bucket for blackberry picking and she would follow him into the canes to sit on the trunk of a fallen chestnut, to gorge together until their bellies swelled. Silver spoke her mind more to Amos than to anybody. But that late September she didn't tell him about the illness she'd begun to feel in the mornings.

Silver should have been more careful during her time with Ellard. It didn't occur to her until she grew sick how foolish they had been. Though she told herself the blood would come any day, she was worried. She tried to keep even farther away from her grandmother during those months but one evening as she sat with Mildred at the kitchen table not eating her supper, she felt the old woman's eyes on her. She got up and rushed outside for some air, trying to settle her stomach. When she came back inside with an armload of kindling, the coals were glowing under the kettle. Mildred pulled out a chair for her to sit. She took the kettle off the fire and poured its scalding contents into a cup. "You think I don't know what you've been doing?" she spat, thrusting the cup into Silver's hand. "Just like your mama." Silver stared into the swirling pennyroyal dregs. She knew it would make her trouble go away, but in that moment she hated her grandmother more than ever. Even as she drained the cup in one searing gulp.

For almost three decades Silver had kept that secret from Ellard Moody. Now she was keeping another one. But she hadn't lied to him about where she was headed when she got out of his car this morning. She'd gone straight across the road to the Walker farm and up to the porch where a group of men in slickers were drinking coffee. She recognized one of them without remembering his name. Someone she had gone to third grade with until she quit, one of the boys that had chucked rocks at her in the school yard. He told her that Annie Clyde wasn't home, his mean eyes calling her all the names his mouth used to thirty-five years ago. Silver wanted to wait for her niece but not with the man's eyes on her. Not inside with the women either. She knew what they thought of her. She went around to the barn where she could rest within earshot of the house, lying on her side in the scattered hay of a stall. Sometime later she heard tires churning and realized she'd been asleep. She scrambled up shedding straw and went to the side of the house. A group of men were pushing a pickup truck out of the bog of the yard. The farm had emptied over the course of the afternoon. When the truck was gone only the Packard remained. Silver knocked on the kitchen door and James's aunt opened it. Her face was severe, strands escaping the knot at her nape. Silver asked for Annie Clyde and the woman said, "She's down at the jail. I reckon they got Amos." Without hesitation Silver turned and fled for town.

She had arrived at the courthouse near dusk, the sky whorled with orange clouds. The rain had tapered enough for swifts to return to the clock tower, wheeling and swooping around the dome roof. Silver paused at the flagpole to catch her breath. She'd expected to see curious or perhaps angry searchers but the lawn was deserted, only a few vehicles at the curb. She'd thought they were leaving the farm to come to the courthouse but maybe Ellard had already run them off. He would probably send Silver away as well, but she meant to try. She was about to make for the courthouse doors when they burst open. A young fair-headed man came down the steps. Rushing across the lawn to the street he slid and pitched forward, skidding on his face. He lay there without getting up, his mouth plugged with the earth and grass and water of Yuneetah as if he was drowning in it. Silver was too astonished to go to him. Finally the young man picked himself up, coughing and wiping his face, then limped on to the curb and drove away. Silver wanted to run into the building and demand to know what had happened. But she forced herself to take care up the cobbled walk, treacherous with leaves. As she reached for the door a lawman with a badge pinned to his shirt was coming out of the building. "Nobody's getting in here tonight," he said. "You'll have to come back in the morning." Then he went down the steps to a car like Ellard's, a gold star on its side. Silver paced back and forth for a while under the portico wringing her hands, thinking of begging Ellard to let her see Amos but knowing better.

Now she continued down the footpath winding around the side of the mountain until she saw a glow through the limbs clustered over the trail she was following, the only light visible for miles. The cabin in the clearing looked like a haven when she came upon it, sheltered by walnut trees and wild chokecherry bushes, a curl of chimney smoke hanging over the shakes of the roof. Silver tramped up the steps and pounded on the plank door. "It's Silver Ledford," she cried out. There was a long lapse although Silver knew Beulah was in there. When the old woman answered she sounded reluctant, like she would rather have hidden from her company.

"Come on in," Beulah allowed.

Silver pushed open the door then poked her head inside, the blustery draft she brought with her riffling the calendar pages tacked over Beulah's bed in the corner and swaying the bundled herbs in the rafters. Her eyes moved over the split-log walls, the fireplace with a heap of cinders spilled onto the hearth. She smelled cooking. When she turned her head the old woman was taking a jar from a pie safe. She crossed the threshold, her shoes tracking the floor. It had been years since she entered a home not her own. "I hate to bother you late like this," she said.

"It ain't no bother. I been gone all day. I'm just now getting done with supper."

"I won't stay long."

"I got squirrel. Tastes pretty good if you ain't had meat in a while."

"Nothing wrong with squirrel," Silver said. She looked down at herself, still wearing the liver-colored dress, her legs streaked with silt. But Beulah didn't seem to mind her state.

"Here's some apple butter, too." She opened the jar she held in her hand, popping the seal. "This is the last of it, but I can't think of no reason to save it."

"Neither can I," Silver said.

Beulah took down crockery from a shelf and a pan of biscuits from the sideboard. She dished what was left of her supper onto a plate and Silver's mouth filled with water. She hadn't eaten. Beulah pulled out a chair but Silver hunkered before the waning cook fire with her food as she did at home. Beulah sighed and took the seat herself. "I never saw such a day. Did you?"

Silver took a bite of the stringy meat. "Not that I remember."

"I never dreamed I'd see you at my door neither."

"It's a strange time," Silver said.

Beulah shook her head. "It surely is." She watched as Silver gnawed the squirrel bones clean and tossed them one by one into the fireplace. "I reckon we're the only ones left up here now. I've thought about coming to see you sometime. But you don't seem to like visitors."

Silver went on chewing, not saying what came into her mind. Amos was about the only visitor she ever had. She looked around the shadowy cabin and thought it was no wonder he had left. He couldn't have stayed here. The room was too smothering and close. She pictured him in a jail cell and lost some of her appetite. She supposed the reason she hadn't asked Beulah about Amos yet was that she wasn't sure how much she wanted to know anymore. Then Beulah put her out of her misery. "Go ahead. You got such a cloud over you, it's liable to rain in here."

Silver choked down a last bite. "They wouldn't let me in to see Amos."

Beulah studied her lap. "Well. I seen him."

"Is he all right?"

"He's alive, but I won't say he's all right."

"I knew it," Silver said. "Ellard would just as soon kill him as look at him."

Beulah pulled a handkerchief from her apron. Her eyes when she took off her pointed glasses to dab them were small and naked. "I'm the one that turned him in."

Silver's mouth dropped open. "What? Why?"

"I been trying to keep him from hurting hisself or anybody else."

Silver's hands trembled as she put aside her cleaned plate. She stared back into the dying fire with her knees gathered up. "There's no telling what they'll do to him tonight, much less if this goes to court. They'll find a way to hang him. Mark my words. Even if Gracie ain't found."

Beulah sniffed and put her handkerchief away. "All we can do is wait and see."

"I need you to tell me, Beulah," Silver said. "Tell me he wouldn't hurt a child."

Beulah shook her head. "I can't do that. I'm tired of telling."

"If you don't believe him," Silver said, "he ain't got nobody."

"I didn't say I don't believe him," Beulah said. "I'm just wore out."

Silver covered her mouth as if to wipe it. Then she said through her greasy fingers, "If Amos has done something to Gracie, on purpose or not, how am I supposed to live with that?"

When Beulah didn't answer, Silver raised her head. The old woman was still there, bathed in firelight. She got up heavily from her chair, hands on her back. "Laws, I'll be glad for this day to end," she said, eyes wandering to the pile of squirrel bones in the ashes. After another moment Beulah's crooked fingers went to the pouch around her neck. She opened the drawstring and dumped the bones from it into the fire. They were quickly blackened by the guttering flames.

Silver looked up at her in shock. "Why did you do that?" she asked.

"There ain't no more future I want to see," Beulah said.

Silver felt sick to her stomach, like that long-ago evening at supper with her hateful grandmother. She got abruptly to her feet and left the cabin, not even thanking Beulah for the meal. She inhaled the fresh air as she went through the rain, across the lot and back into the trees. Before she lost her nerve she headed down the hollow, past the house where Ellard Moody once lived with his parents and the graveyard where Mary was buried, on to the Walker homestead. Gilded clouds hung over the roof, the moon a smudge behind them. One lamp burned in a front window and Silver made for the lit porch. There were no vehicles parked now at the end of the track. Even the Packard was missing. Silver mounted the porch steps and opened the door without knocking. It couldn't wait any longer. If Annie Clyde was asleep she would wake her.

But when the door swung in on the front room, its darkened walls papered with vines, Silver couldn't go in. She hadn't been here since Mary died. She leaned on the doorjamb, looking into the shine of the oil lamp perched on the fireplace mantel. Aside from the lamp the mantel was bare, cleared of the china figurines that had belonged to her sister. There was an oval of paler wallpaper where a tinted portrait of Mary and Clyde used to hang. The house was silent, not even settling. Then Silver heard a whispery sound. A ragged intake of breath. With a start she turned her head. There was someone sitting on the shadowed bottom stair. For one disoriented instant she thought it was Gracie. But stepping through the doorway she realized that it was her niece instead. "Annie Clyde?" Silver asked, kneeling before her. What she saw sped up her heart. The lamp was running low on oil but she could tell anyhow that the girl was in trouble. Annie Clyde's eyes were glazed over. There was heat coming off her in waves. "Where is everybody?"

"Gone," Annie Clyde said, her voice a scratch. "They have babies of their own."

"Come on. Let's get you in the bed."

Annie Clyde shook her head. "I can't get up."

"You're all right," Silver said, willing it to be true.

"No," Annie Clyde said. "It's my foot."

"What's wrong with it?"

"I stepped on a locust thorn."

"When?"

"I don't know."

Silver took hold of Annie Clyde's foot. It was wrapped in a discolored bandage, stained with seepage. She untied the wrapping and saw that the foot was bloated, red and hot to the touch with streaks of infection climbing up the ankle. "Oh," she breathed. "I believe you've got blood poisoning, Annie Clyde. We can't fool around with that. As run-down as you are, it's hit you hard. I better go to the road and see if I can find somebody that'll take you to the doctor."

Annie Clyde shook her head again. "I have to be here when Gracie gets back."

"You need medicine," Silver insisted. "Just let me go down to the road."

Annie Clyde reached out and clutched Silver's wrist. "Don't leave me."

Silver stared down at her niece's burning fingers. "Then let's cool you off some."

"I can't walk," Annie Clyde said.

Silver looked around as if for some kind of help but she and Annie Clyde were alone in the stillness of the house. Being taller and sturdier than Annie Clyde, Silver stooped and picked her niece up without much effort, like the girl child she might have had. Annie Clyde was light on the way up the stairs, a bundle of rags. Silver remembered the way to Mary's upper bedroom but she watched her step with only the sallow shine from the front room to guide her. After lowering Annie Clyde to the feather mattress she ripped off a length of the sheet to make a fresh bandage, working almost in the dark. She went to the washstand in the corner, a cloth draped on the side of its flowered porcelain bowl. Annie Clyde closed her eyes as Silver swabbed her face, her throat, her wrists. Silver thought her niece was dozing, hair spread out and arms limp at her sides. Then Annie Clyde said with her eyes still shut, "I told her she'd be the death of me."

Silver dropped the washcloth back into the flowered bowl. "You ain't dying," she said, too loudly in the quiet room. "All you need is medicine. I'll see if I can find something here."

"No," Annie Clyde said. "Stay with me."

Silver felt the prick of tears. She felt all the years she had lived alone, every stick of wood she had chopped and pail of water she had toted, every winter she had lasted through, every night with the woods pressing in around the weak flicker of her light. "Close your eyes," she said.

When Annie Clyde obeyed Silver hurried down the stairs, taking the lamp with her into the kitchen. In there the walls were sooty from the woodstove, the mildewed curtains hanging limp. She found nothing much in the larder besides a sack of meal and a stack of newspapers for lighting cook fires. She flung open the cupboard doors, loose on their rusty hinges. Finally she yanked back the skirt under the sink basin and found what she had been rummaging for. An old bootleg jar of her own chartered whiskey, half gone from many seasons of treating croups and fevers. She remembered this batch by the beryl-colored glass. Dandelion, horsetail, nettle and birch leaves. She went back upstairs with the lamp in one hand and the medicine in the other, the risers groaning under her shoes. She paused in the doorway watching Annie Clyde breathe. She was reminded too much of the night Mary died, when she came into this same room with her teeth rattling in the February cold. Only now it was too hot. She put down the lamp on the bedside table and opened the window. Then she went to the bed and sat on the edge. "Here," she said, propping the back of Annie Clyde's head to let her drink. "Take you a few sups of this."

Annie Clyde grimaced but didn't protest, although the whiskey was strong. At Silver's urging, she took several long gulps before falling back on the pillows. As Annie Clyde rested Silver listened to the weather outside. Studying her own distorted reflection in the windowpanes she began to talk, not knowing at first what would come out. "I won't ask you to forgive me," she said. "For none of this." She stole a glance at Annie Clyde. The girl's eyes were open but they seemed unfocused. "I hope you're listening to me. Because I don't believe I can tell it twice."

Annie Clyde moistened her parched lips but didn't speak.

"I seen Amos out here yesterday, not much after dinnertime. I didn't say nothing to you or Ellard because I didn't think Amos took Gracie. I still don't think so. I ain't saying I trust him all the way, but I don't believe he would bother a child." Silver hesitated. "He's been a friend to me. I was frightened of what might happen to him if I said he was hanging around your house."

Annie Clyde's brow furrowed. "You saw Amos?" she asked, her speech whiskey-thick.

"Yes. But that ain't the worst of it." Silver tried to swallow down a thickness in her own throat. "I saw Gracie, too. I guess I was the last one to see her." Silver shut her mouth but the words were already out. "I reckon it was about two o'clock. I decided to go ahead and take the dog, so I didn't have to be around when you left." She tried to remember it right. She'd walked out of the cornfield flustered after her run-in with Amos, knowing she didn't have the will to come back down the mountain tomorrow and see the Dodsons off. She'd passed James's Model A Ford at the end of the track and pressed on to the front door. She'd rapped on the wood but the wind had carried her knock away. When nobody came she'd gone around to the side. Her hair had been whipping as she stood on the stoop but she could still hear raised voices from the kitchen. "I meant to tell you I was taking the dog but it sounded like you was fussing with your husband," Silver said. "I wanted no part of that. You never asked me a favor before and I wanted to do it, but my nerves was all to pieces. I went back down the steps not hardly knowing if I was coming or going. I was fixing to give up and head home, until I seen her." Gracie. Standing under the elm where the dog was tied, reaching up to catch the blowing leaves, chattering to him like he was another child. Silver would have gone on up the mountain, no matter how much it hurt to come back the next morning as they loaded their truck, if Gracie hadn't been there looking so much like Mary. She thought it might kill her to see her sister's granddaughter leaving Yuneetah.

"I should have figured you wouldn't let her out by herself," Silver stammered on. "I don't know nothing about children." She hesitated again, shaking her head. "Gracie didn't want me to take him. Said Rusty was her dog. I knew I shouldn't take him without telling you, but I thought I had to get it over with." It had felt too late somehow to abandon her course, so she'd turned her back to Gracie and unchained the dog. Once the rope was around his neck she'd set out pulling him across the field, wind rippling the weeds. When she'd looked over her shoulder Gracie was behind her, watching with a somber face. "She followed me as far as the apple tree. I stopped and told her to get to the house but she wouldn't." Silver paused once more, gathering herself to finish. "I looked back when I got to the woods and she was still there. I figured she'd be all right in her own yard. I never dreamed anything would happen to her." What Silver didn't tell Annie Clyde was how she had waved to the child with her left hand as she stood at the verge of the pines, grappling with the rope in her right. How she had said good-bye to Gracie knowing it was the last time she would ever see her, but not that it might be the last time anybody ever saw her again.

"You have Rusty?" Annie Clyde asked. Her forehead was clammy. Her fever had broken.

Silver blew out a breath. "If I gave him back to you yesterday I would have had to tell on myself and Amos both. Just because he was hanging around don't mean he's to blame. Gracie wouldn't have wandered off if I'd knocked on the door. Or made sure she went back to the house before I took the dog home with me. I put him in the shed, up at the still where Granddaddy used to keep his watchdogs. It was nighttime before anybody came and told me Gracie was gone."

"Gracie," Annie Clyde whispered, tears dropping from her reddened lids.

Silver reached to thumb the wetness from her niece's cheek. "I don't believe I'll ever be able to look you in the face again after this, Annie Clyde," she said. "As much as I care for you. I'll turn your dog loose, but I won't be bringing him back. I know that dog can find his way."

Annie Clyde tried to push up on her elbows and they gave out. "But where's Gracie?"

"No," Silver said. "I don't know where Gracie's at. You're mixed up, Annie Clyde." She was selfishly glad for the medicine muddling her niece's head. She didn't want to hear what the girl might say if she had her faculties. She captured Annie Clyde's hand, the delicate fingers so much like her sister's. So much like her own. Then she heard a creak and leapt up like she'd been caught stealing. She turned to see James Dodson leaning against the wall, the room filled with a reek of moonshine but not from the jar by the bed. His hair was mussed, his clothes disheveled.

"What's going on?" he asked.

Silver was startled by her own anger. "Your wife's sick. How come you had to leave her?"

"I didn't leave her," James said. "I was in the barn."

"Where's your aunt and uncle?"

James squinted down at Annie Clyde. "I asked you what's going on."

"She's got blood poisoning," Silver snapped. "She stepped on a locust thorn. Her fever's broke, but if it comes back don't you wait until morning to get her to the doctor. That medicine is bitter, but make her drink some more if she wakes up hurting. And don't let her get out of the bed, either." When Silver stopped her mouth was dry, having talked more on this night than she had in a decade. A weariness came over her. She couldn't tell it again, what she had told Annie Clyde. Not to this man who had sought to take what remained of her sister away from her again. They stood across from each other in the lamplight, James blinking at her with bloodshot eyes. Then she pushed past him, the whiskey fumes enough to sting her nose, and ran down the stairs.

She escaped out the wide-open door into the endless rain and went around the side of the house, splashing up darts of water. Thistles lashed her legs as she cut through the hayfield, as she tripped over what had blown down on her way to the foot of the mountain. Once again she followed the familiar ridges up to the still. She was shaking as she approached the shed and paused under its eave, burrs falling from the chinquapin onto the roof. She reached to touch the splintery boards, drew close to press her ear against the side of the building. After a second there came a whimpering. Then scratching where the warped boards met the packed dirt. She closed her eyes and rested her forehead on the rough wood. There was nothing left to do but let him go.

AUGUST 2, 1936

By the first light of morning the rain had stopped. When the sun rose it twinkled on the surface of the water standing everywhere like thousands of eyes coming open. It was dawn of the third day, but Rusty had come down the mountain when it was still dark. For a long time he had been pent up, lying shivering on the packed earth. Nosing at blankets that still held the scent of other dogs, faint but present enough to vex him. He had been left a pone of burnt bread but he wouldn't eat or drink. Whenever he heard movement he had barked to be let out. He had paced and scratched but nobody came. When the shed door opened at last he wasted no time. As lonely as he'd been he didn't greet the one who turned him loose. He ran down the ridges on his way back home. But when he came to the woods behind the Walker farm he slowed down. He could tell Gracie had been there. So had others with blood like hers, left in flecks on the ferns and briars. He was sidetracked by the blackbirds that had reemerged after the storm to forage, rustling in multitudes as if the dark lake had already come to fill the woods. After he flushed them away he went on looking for Gracie with his nose to the ground. He missed her. She fed him biscuits and clover and sometimes sticks. She let him lick her eyes and mouth. She rolled with him on the ground. She tried to ride on his back. They knew each other's smells and tastes and sounds.

In the night his keen ears had heard, apart from the rain, a distant crying. It might have been the gobble of wild turkeys or the chitter of weasels but it might have been otherwise. He went on through the pines with his broad head lowered, moving toward the source of the sound.

In a dream she heard Rusty whining and digging, crumbs of red clay sifting down on her eyes. She couldn't open them anymore. There were pictures in her hurting head of the dog and the woman going into the pines where she couldn't see them. She had waited near the apple tree, hanging back because she knew she shouldn't follow. She thought the woman might scold her. But she wanted to see what they were doing in the woods. Spore caps of moss sprouted on rotten log backs with dotted tips like swarms of green gnats. Pokeberry shed its poisonous seeds like polished black beads. She looked up and tried to make out the high tops of the trees shifting in the wind, their slender trunks and leafy branches moving in a circular motion like dancing. They were too tall, swaying back and forth, creaking in a secretive way that almost scared her. They made her feel like she was up there clinging to their tips. One of the trees had fallen near the foot of the mountain. She had seen it with her mama. She wanted to climb on it like before but she couldn't without help. She squatted and picked at the bark, skinned in places to reveal the lighter meat of the beech's insides. Some of the tree's limbs had broken in the fall, making splinters. There were crumbled chunks of shale and limestone washed white from the rain scattered all around. Gracie picked some up and dropped them in the pockets sewn onto her flour sack dress.

Then she wandered to the end of the trunk where the root ball arched above her head, thatched with sod ripped from the forest floor. It looked to her like an umbrella made of twisted roots. Some were braided pigtails and some coiled bedsprings, some claw fingers laced together. She squatted once again in the leaves plastering the ground and peered into the shadows between where the bowed roots parted. But she might never have crawled inside if not for a glimmer in the darkness. Just enough light penetrating the gloom under the umbrella to bounce off something shiny. Enough to make her curious. She found where the hanging roots were raised a little off the ground and got down on her belly. She reached for the shiny thing but her arm wasn't that long. She gave up and tried wriggling underneath. Her dress rucked up as she slid on the orange mud into someplace her mama or daddy wouldn't fit. Later they would search around the fallen beech, would even shine their lanterns on the tangled root ball, without ever knowing.

Gracie's face brightened when saw what was glinting. It was the present the man gave her in the cornfield. She'd forgotten him and the toy both until that moment. Because she was three she didn't wonder how or why the tin top had ended up under a tree. She couldn't have known that her mama tossed it there a few hours ago. She scooted in farther, as she often burrowed into snowball bushes. She tried to get up on her knees but the arched roof of the root cavern was too low. She was reaching to pick up the toy when the mud began to shift beneath her weight.

Before she had time to fear a hole opened up. The ground collapsed and swallowed her. Either the fallen tree had created the hole or the weakened cave ceiling had caused the tree to fall. It didn't matter. Gracie dropped four feet. It wasn't too far. It was more how she landed, hitting her head and biting her tongue almost in two, mounds of clay piling on top of her. From below the hole was a source of pearly light that limned the moss dusting the limestone walls, narrow like a chimney stack. If Gracie had been able to move farther in, she would have found a blocked passage to another deeper and wider cave, one her daddy had used as a grave for his horse. On the first day and night Gracie didn't wake at all. On the second day she cried and tried to call for her mama but her tongue was too big. Her head hurt too much. There was just enough space for her to lie in a knot with her knees drawn up to her chin. When rainwater ran down the narrow chimney stack of the mossy cave walls there was no

room to get away. By the third morning she was lying in a puddle.
She was cold and dreamed the stove had gone out. She was hungry
and dreamed her mama was boiling oats. She wanted to go home and
dreamed of the farm between the hills, cloud shadows passing over
the fields. She dreamed of waving a stick with Rusty chasing her. She
dreamed of other animals she had seen. Going across the road with
her daddy where there was a ruddy calf in a pen with a leaky, pale
pink nose. Going with her mama into the moldy shade of the springhouse and finding a mink curved around the butter crock. Stalking
blackbirds that descended on the field like a funeral train. Running
after them when they lifted off all together, the apples in her dress
pockets bouncing against her knees.

More than anything she wanted her mama and daddy. It was them
she dreamed of most. Riding on her daddy's shoulders to church
in her blue dress with tiny pink rosebuds. Him lifting her onto the
wagon seat and showing her a garter snake he had found in the
weeds. Walking out to the field with her mama to take him his dinner in a basket. Taking him water in hot weather, the cool smell of
the earthen jug as she carried it across the baking furrows making her
wish she was small enough to crawl inside. Lying in her crib pulled
up close to her mama's side of the bed, falling asleep with their hands
clasped through the wooden slats. Getting an earache and nestling
into the feather mattress between them, her mama pouring warm
sweet oil into her ears. Sometimes she woke first and lay listening to
them breathe. When it thundered she would seek out one of them to
be rocked. When she got sick or stung, got a splinter or a tick, they
held and kissed her. There had been no time before this when she
cried and wasn't comforted.

For two days Gracie had been by herself in the cave, buried under
an avalanche of mud that dried to thick scales then cracked and
fell off when she stirred. Her eyes were gummed shut by the matted blood from her scalp. When she finally struggled them open,

she came out of a twilight state into a near darkness. Sometimes she turned her face to sip the water collecting in the craters of the cave floor, the same rain that filled the reservoir keeping her alive, but the effort hurt her bitten tongue. She had stopped crying for her mama, too, because her own voice ached her head. When light fell into the hole at dawn of that third day she rolled over in her sleep, trying to get warm. But she couldn't wake up, even when Rusty barked. When he failed to force his shoulders through the roots he dug around the trunk, nosing deep enough to unearth some of the horse's bones, already excavated and strewn about by other animals over the years. But as hard as Rusty tried he couldn't get to Gracie. He scrambled among the roots and clods and rocks whimpering, too far from the house to be heard. By then it was Sunday and almost all of the searchers had gone home to church. Tomorrow they would go back to their jobs in factories and knitting mills, tobacco fields and logging camps. Yuneetah was empty again. Lying unfound, Gracie stopped moving. As the hours passed she opened her eyes less and less to look for her mama and daddy. She felt less and less like rolling over into the light filtering through the hole. She had lost the will to suck at the lukewarm water that came from the sky. She was too weak to cry anymore. Even one day was too long for a child to lie buried in the ground, given up for dead.

James Dodson opened his eyes at seven o'clock, having heard a sound in his sleep. His mouth was furred and foul-tasting. His hands were so swollen from the beating he'd given Amos that he could hardly open his fingers. His throbbing head was almost too weighted to lift. For an unclear moment after waking he thought he was taking a nap with his wife and child, like they did sometimes after Sunday dinner. It was good to sleep up there on summer afternoons, the bedroom shaded by the close trees. They could hear branches creaking if the window was open, a breeze puffing in the ruffled white curtains. When he blinked the blurriness from his eyes the first thing he saw was light reflected on the watermarked ceiling, low and slanted under the eave. Not as it looked grayed through storm clouds, but the golden yellow cast it had on fair mornings. Without the sound of rain, beating on the tin and ringing off the leaves, tapping his hat and his coat shoulders, James felt deaf. It took some amount of time for his eyes to readjust to the sun. He looked around the room at the wallpaper, faded green with paler roses. He looked at Gracie's crib, whitewashed by Annie Clyde when she was still expecting, on the same day that she took a notion to paint all of the doors and windowsills and moldings in the house. He remembered her standing barefoot on sheets of newsprint, belly round beneath her apron. Seeing the crib brought the truth back. It was Sunday, but there had been no nap after church with his wife and child.

James remembered little of the night before. He'd insisted that Wallace and Verna go home and rest. Wallace had to get back to his congregation. He had a sermon to prepare. James meant to lie down and sleep with Annie Clyde. He had sworn to his aunt and uncle that he and Annie Clyde would be fine on their own until morning. But after they left James was overcome. He went out to the barn where he'd stashed a jar of Silver Ledford's moonshine in the loft. Mary and Clyde Walker had been hard-shell Baptists who wouldn't have a drop of liquor in their house. Out of respect to them Annie Clyde didn't keep any herself, other than for medicine. James wasn't much of a drinker, aside from taking a swig or two with Dale some evenings when their work was done. But last night he had drunk himself blind. James had a faint recollection of Annie Clyde's aunt being here when he came back inside. The next thing he remembered was taking off his boots, unbuttoning his shirt and dropping it to the floor. Climbing into bed and curving himself around his wife, making a cocoon for her body. Now he lay with his arms around her waist,

listening to the absence of drumming on the roof. "Annie Clyde,"
he said into her hair, "it ain't raining." But she didn't stir. He became
aware of her heat under the cover, like an ember from the fireplace.
It brought back what Silver had told him. That Annie Clyde had
blood poisoning. James sat up with sudden alarm. He had slept with
her, woke holding her, but someway he'd been too deep in his own
misery to notice how bad off she was. James took his wife by the
shoulder. "Annie Clyde," he repeated over the thud of his heart. "Are
you awake?"

"I think so," she mumbled, without opening her eyes.

"Get up. It's time to go to the doctor."

She drew the sheet around her. "No. Somebody might come about
Gracie."

"Dammit, Annie Clyde," James said.

"Why don't you go get him? Bring him back here."

"Sit up," James ordered. "Take some of this medicine."

"No," she said again, sounding near tears. "It don't help me."

"You drink this and then we're leaving."

"Go on," she said. "I just need to sleep."

James thought then of his truck, still mired to the running boards.
There was no way Annie Clyde could walk that far down the road.
She was too ill even to be carried. He would have to push the truck
out and go by himself. "At least let me change that dressing first," he
said.

He got out of bed and went to the washstand feeling warm himself,
not with fever but with shame. After what happened in the courthouse he should have been more worried about Annie Clyde. Bust-
ing in wild-eyed with his rifle. James hadn't even moved when they
wrestled it away from her. Hadn't flinched when she fired a shot into
the wall, plaster showering down. He ripped another strip from the
sheet for a clean bandage. He washed and wrapped his wife's foot as
well as he could. Then he knelt at her bedside. Her flushed face was

turned aside, her hair dark against her neck. He might have thought her at peace if not for the line between her brows, if not for her thinness. She hadn't been eating much, not just for the last two days but for the last two years. Each evening he watched her rake some of her supper onto Gracie's plate. But as she lay there in the sunlight her beauty still moved him. He didn't want to leave her. He wanted to put his aching head back down and sleep with her. He lifted her clammy hand and pressed it to his cheek. "Whatever you want when this is over, I'll do it," he said. "I'll live wherever you tell me."

"I'm not going tomorrow, if they try to make us," she murmured, drifting off deeper into sleep. "I can't leave Gracie. If she's alive or if she's dead, I'm taking her with me."

James smoothed her hair. "I'll stand behind you this time," he said, but she didn't hear.

Buttoning his shirt on the way downstairs, his other bruised hand stiff on the banister, James felt like he was choking. He didn't want to but he was already thinking of the people he'd have to tell that Gracie was gone for good. Dale Hankins. His sister across the mountain, the one he still pictured as a toddler chewing on a stalk of sugarcane. Her white-blond hair so much like the soft-blossomed tufts of cotton they plucked with sacks strapped to their small shoulders, the dried bristles at the ends of the plants making stinging cuts on their fingers. Dora was there the last time the river took somebody away from him. Dora stood with him at their mother's bedside after she died giving birth to a stillborn baby, staring down at the mattress soaked with more blood than it seemed a woman's body could hold. But this time James was alone. Disbelief washed over him, that any of this was happening. Last summer he and Annie Clyde were hoeing in the garden with Gracie at their feet, at dusk with the first stars out and a ghost of moon hovering. Their life on the farm had been for the most part happy. He could see that now. When it was all over. There was seldom more than a few cents in James's pocket and their clothes were washed thin, but they hadn't missed what they didn't have. They'd always managed to keep Gracie's belly full, even if it was with beans and pone bread instead of meat. When there were only vegetables from the garden, Annie Clyde fixed a meal of cabbage, peppers and tomatoes. They were poor but Gracie didn't know it. Now she was lost and Annie Clyde was burning alive.

When he went outside the glare of the sun blinded him. The sky looked bluer, the corn down at the road greener than he remembered. He could hear running water but the spring was too far away, at the verge of the hollow. In the night the lake must have crossed the last hillock of the Hankins pasture, spilling off the edge of the bank into the roadside gully. Whether the road was washed out or not, he wouldn't be going anywhere if he couldn't find somebody to help him push his Model A out of the slough. He should have had it towed out with a tractor before the other men went home but he didn't think of that. The truck was the last thing on his mind yesterday. He lowered himself to the top step to put on his muddy boots. Out of habit he had left them on the porch last night to keep from tracking dirt through the house. He was about to get up when he heard a thump from beneath him. He frowned and peered between the cracks in the steps. As he bent over, something dashed out from under the porch. He jumped up, catching himself on the railing. When he saw it, he didn't understand at first. There was a red dog with a white patch on its chest standing in the yard where the snowball bushes drooped. Its tail wagged as it looked at James, waiting for him to move. When James came down the steps with leaden feet the dog ran to him, dancing a circle around his boots. James sank to his knees, thinking it couldn't be Rusty. It must be some other coonhound that looked the same. But once James pinned the dog down and held it still, he felt like the wind had been knocked out of him again.

For too long James knelt in the grass unable to get up. Rusty went on lapping at his face, lunging and twisting in his arms, soiling his shirtfront. He fumbled his stiff fingers over Rusty's coat, scabbed with burrs and beggar's-lice, searching for clues to where the dog had been. He tried to shout for Annie Clyde but his voice was gone. He couldn't think what it meant that Gracie's dog was not dead, not drowned in the lake. He was about to take the dog around the house and call his wife's name under the bedroom window when he spotted something stark against the grass. Something he realized Rusty must have dragged from under the porch and through the yard. It appeared to be a bone, but after all James had seen his eyes might be playing tricks. He crawled across the ground for a closer look, water seeping into his trouser knees. It was long and balled like a fist at one end. He had been right. It was a bone. But not a human one.

James picked the bone up in both hands to inspect it, hefty with thick orange mud caking its porous marrow. Then he dropped it as though it had seared his palms.

He got to his feet and ran in a lurch around the house toward the barn. Somewhere inside there was a mattock with a dull chopping blade and a split ash handle, so worn he wouldn't have taken it to Detroit. Just like on the day that Gracie went missing, he paused and stood panting in the barn opening, the eave plinking above his head. His eyes skated over the near emptiness, knowing he had seen it but not sure where. The feed buckets still hung from the brassy wall planks, sun streaming between them. The rafters were still lined with swallow nests, abandoned and crumbling. He went into the first stall, heaving a dusty crate out of his path, the dog shying from the racket. The mattock was propped in the stall corner, the digging end of its head buried in chaff. He grabbed it by the handle, flashing back to yesterday when he'd chopped through the laurel with Ellard's axe, the blisters bursting to raw flesh again. He tore out of the barn and into the field with Rusty loping in front of him. He could hear the dog's barking and his own tortured breathing, his boots stomping up rainwater. But that was all far away. The hayfield seemed a mile long stretching out before him, the mountain swelling high and shady at the other end, the beaded weeds clashing as Rusty dove through them, his red tail waving over the purpled tips.

When James finally reached the woods it seemed the hour had changed from morning to gloaming. Bugs swarmed in shafts of golden light, mosquitoes hovered over marshes lying flat and still between the trunks. The peepers and cicadas had come back out, snake doctors buzzing in darts and swoops. James didn't feel the gnats in his eye corners. He didn't bother to blink them out, or slap at the sweat bees teasing his ears. Near certain that he was running toward his daughter's death, for as long as she had been missing, he barreled forward anyway. By the time he heard freshets trickling down the mountain his breath was sobbing, his legs giving out. When he reached the place where his horse Ranger was buried he came to a halt, the mattock hanging at his side. He must have seen the beech across the grave, must have clambered over it as he looked for Gracie. But this whole time, from the second he held the horse bone in his palms, as he crashed through the thicket, he was picturing the cave as he and Dale had left it after they filled it in. A slick pit that Gracie could have slipped into and gotten stuck. Drowning not in the lake but in the wagonload of dirt he had dumped himself. James had been this way more than once with the other searchers, shouting Gracie's name over the rain until they lost their voices, and never once considered the ground could have swallowed her up like it did Dale's house.

Catching his breath with his hands on his knees, James noticed that Rusty had been digging around the beech trunk. Ferns were disturbed, white horse bones scattered. But the truth didn't dawn on him until the dog raced to the end of the trunk and began to burrow again, spraying dirt with his hindquarters raised and his nose hidden under the scaly roots. James straightened and took off after Rusty to where the root ball bowed scraping the softened ground. Thinking his little girl's name but too winded to call it, he dropped to his knees and shoved the dog aside. There was no way a grown man could shoulder through the tangle. Rusty had made progress, but the trough he'd dug wasn't deep enough for James. His first instinct was to make a trench for himself using the shovel end of the mattock. He worked for what felt like too long before attempting to wriggle under the roots, his face printing the mud and his nostrils plugging with it. But James couldn't force his way in. He backed out and groped for the mattock, raised it high and began to hack at the sod-thatched root ball. Chopping with the pick end, guttural breaths wrenching from his throat, pulp flying into his mouth, the cuts Amos's teeth had made on his knuckles bleeding. He cleaved and severed until slivers were lying everywhere, the mangled roots flayed back. Then Rusty rushed into the cavern the roots had once made and stood in the rubble, barking so hard that foam flew from his jaws. With the morning sun penetrating the leaves overhead, James saw the same thing the dog did. There was an opening in the packed earth. Something like the groundhog holes he found along the fencerows bordering the farm. Too much like the last hole he had looked in. He dropped the mattock and stretched out flat once more, bars of light striping his filthy shirt. He slid forward until he was near enough to peer inside. But this time he didn't see a child's skull on the floor of a cave. He saw nothing, blinded by tears and sweat. When he rubbed his eyes he still couldn't see. There wasn't enough light.

Though he feared widening the hole with his hands might send more mud collapsing in, he had no choice but to furrow back the loamy earth with his fingers. He kept shoveling handfuls until there was enough room for him to lean inside, until there was enough light to make out a hump at the bottom of the burrow. It looked like a mound of clay. But as more sun filtered into the well of the cave, more of his child was revealed to him. Like the day she was born, pulling back the blanket to discover one part of her at a time so as not to make all of her cold. He rubbed his eyes to clear them again. Gracie was down there. Lying in a knot on her side. Knees drawn up and chin tucked. Under the mud he saw her dirty dress. Her dark curls. Her feet, small and creased. Not much bigger now than when he kissed them for the first time. But unlike that first time, her toes were blue instead of pink. A near-crippling dread came over James. He thrust his arm inside the cave to the shoulder, grasping with desperation. He could feel how chilly it was down there where his daughter had lain for two days and nights without him. She was too still. She should have been shivering. He couldn't let her lie there any longer unmoving. If he could just snag the hem of her dress. If he could graze one curl of her hair. If he could touch her anywhere. He pushed in deeper, arm swiping, holding his breath until it burst out in frustration as his fingers skimmed nothing besides the dank air. But when he backed out of the hole some he found that his shoulders had forged its mouth wider, flooding the cave with more light.

Now James could see the side of Gracie's face, blotched with dried red blooms. He could see the gash on her forehead clotting beneath the matted clumps of her hair. She looked like a doll carved from wax. Nothing like the child he last saw eating apple pie with her hands in the kitchen. Gracie wasn't far below him. But he didn't know if she was really there in the cave with him at all, or in some other place where he could never reach her. As lost to him as she had been when he opened his eyes this morning. James's will failed him. The strength ran out of his arm. It dangled there useless. That's when Annie Clyde's words came back to him as though she spoke into his ear. No matter what, alive or dead, James had to give Gracie back to her mother. "Please Jesus," he whispered, his tendons stretching taut. His whole self strained toward his child. He needed to widen the hole, to dig and shovel more with the mattock, but getting up would be too much like leaving her. He couldn't let her out of his sight. Rusty barked and paced somewhere behind him, treading over and over his outstretched legs, his scrabbling boots. Dirt crumbs sifted and water trickled down the crags of the narrow cave walls. But to James everything had stopped. He was so close. When his fingertips made contact at last, just a brush against the sole of her foot, sparks rocketed up his arm. "Gracie," he said, but she didn't respond. "Gracie," he crooned to her as he used to when she slept in her crib, when he tickled the bottoms of her feet to rouse her. "Gracie," he pleaded, beginning to weep. "Wake up." And down there in the pit, struggling against the blood that crusted it shut, his daughter's eye fluttered open.

Annie Clyde Dodson had been asleep for what might have been minutes or days. By the light in the room she guessed it to be around nine but the clock she'd always kept near the bed was packed away in a crate. She had been dreaming that James was gone out to harvest the corn before the water took it. Standing in the box wagon holding the reins, opening the shucks with his peg, scooping corn into the crib with the neighbors that helped him each season. But then the dream of James merged into another one, of Rusty ranging the hills, poking his nose into burrows and dens to sniff the musk other animals had left behind, exploring thickets and caverns and shadowed breaches between plunging rock faces where his barking echoed off the cool walls. The sound had seemed to come from outside of Annie Clyde's sleep. It seemed to have been the thing that woke her. She pushed herself up on her elbows and listened, then rested back on the pillows. She had vague memories of Silver sitting on the edge of the bed. Some of what her aunt said came back to her. But Annie Clyde couldn't be sure that she hadn't dreamed Silver and Rusty both. There was nobody in the room with her now. When she sat up the walls spun. She held her sweaty head until her dizziness passed. Then she lowered herself off the bed, crying out from the pain in her foot. She steeled herself before limping to the window to see the elm where the dog had been tethered. He still wasn't there, but the barking had been so real.

Annie Clyde left the window and went out of the bedroom, descended the stairs with her head still swimming and her bad foot lifted, the sheeting bandage already stained through. On her way down, the shine through the crevices of the front door hurt her eyes. The rain was over. The lake would stop rising. She could find Gracie if the power company left her alone. All she needed was time. She stopped to breathe, leaning against the banister, before hobbling on to the kitchen. Crossing the linoleum was enough to sap what remained of Annie Clyde's strength, but she was determined. She didn't bother looking for her shoes. The damage was done. Her foot was too swollen. It throbbed with her pulse as she concentrated on moving forward. The closer she got to the door, the more convinced she became that the dog's barking hadn't been a dream. Finally she pushed the door open, shielding her eyes from the glaring sun, and hopped down the stoop.

If Annie Clyde had gone out the front door she would have seen paw prints around the porch steps. She would have discovered the horse bone where her husband dropped it. But in the side yard, where it seemed the barking came from, there was no evidence of Rusty. She turned her head toward the barn her father had repainted red not long before he died, now a dulled maroon, and took some uncertain steps out into the grass. She wanted to whistle but didn't have the breath. The farm was silent besides the cicadas and bullfrogs, farther off the running water. Then she heard a bang from behind her. A car door slamming. She pivoted around, wincing at the pain shooting through her foot. The Dodge coupe she had come to recognize was parked at the end of the track. It must have been there all along. She waited as Washburn came through the sweet clover to reach her. From a distance he looked more composed than the last time she saw him, in a clean suit and tie with his dark blond hair combed neat again, a feather in the band of his fedora. When he got close she saw the cut under his chin. She remembered blood running down his neck into his collar. She felt none of her former anger, seeing the government man back again. She was almost too distracted to acknowledge him at all. "I thought nobody was home," Washburn said. Then he paused to scrutinize her face. "You're unwell, Mrs. Dodson."

"My husband went after the doctor."

"Shouldn't you be in bed?"

"I heard barking out here."

Washburn glanced around the yard, then over her head toward the hayfield. "I got ahold of a man in Clinchfield with bloodhounds. I wasn't expecting him until this afternoon, though."

"Shh," she said. "Listen."

"How long has your husband been gone?"

"Do you hear that? That's Rusty's bark."

"I believe you need to sit down, Mrs. Dodson."

"Silver told me last night. I thought I was dreaming."

Washburn looked to the kitchen door and the cement steps Annie Clyde's father had poured when she was a child, the neglected geraniums of her mother's flower beds growing up against them. His arm came around her waist but she wouldn't let him lead her to the stoop. She'd heard again what she had been listening for since she made it outside. It was the sound from her dream. A high yelping that echoed across the emptiness of Yuneetah. It was how Rusty sounded when he saw a snake or cornered a muskrat at the spring. When he found a drifter in the cornfield. The way he warned her that something was wrong. "I know you heard it that time," she said to Washburn. He opened his mouth to answer but she raised a hand to hush him again. When another string of barks drifted across the field she grabbed his arm for leverage to turn around, both of them staring in that direction. Then Annie Clyde took off, bad foot forgotten.

As she dodged past the barn and thrashed into the hayfield, Washburn hurried to match her stride, his arm around her waist again. "Rusty!" She had made it as far as the apple tree when she saw the dog emerging from the pines. From fifty yards away Annie Clyde still recognized him. He rushed toward her through the long grasses, tongue flopping. If not for the press of Washburn's fingers holding her up by the ribs she might have believed she was dreaming again.

Washburn's voice broke her stupor, sharp as a slap. "Who is that?" he asked. She followed his eyes, staring across the weed tips. Her throat clenched shut, cutting off her breath.

Even as she watched him coming behind the dog, his auburn hair a blaze against the pines, she thought she might be seeing things. It was her husband. It was James. Then he was saying her name. "Annie Clyde!" His voice was as real as Rusty's barking had been. He was carrying their daughter, bringing Gracie out of the woods. She lolled in his arms as he tried to run with her. Legs dangling like when he used to scoop her sleeping from a nest of hay at the end of a summer evening spent working in the barn. Annie Clyde was paralyzed at first. Washburn had to yank her forward, wading out to James and Gracie with her foot bandage unraveling.

When the four of them came together in the middle of the field Annie Clyde reached for her child. "Give her to me!" she demanded, but James kept on running like she wasn't there.

"Where was she?" Washburn asked. "Is she breathing?"

"Why isn't she moving?" Annie Clyde shouted. "James!"

"I ain't got the truck," James panted as they ran.

"We can take my car," Washburn flung back over his shoulder, racing on ahead, trampling a path through the sedge. Annie Clyde stumbled, trying to keep up. She didn't want to hinder them, but she didn't know how she'd survive if they drove off without her.

She caught up as Washburn was opening a back door for James and Gracie. Washburn waited for her with his arm outstretched. She climbed in after James, bumping her head without feeling it. Washburn slammed the door behind her, catching her dress tail. She tore it loose and moved to take her child, cold and painted with orange mud. For the first time since Gracie was born, Annie Clyde didn't want to look at her. The fear was too much. But she made herself study Gracie under the clay and blood as if it had been two years and not two days. She lifted her daughter, careful of her wounded head, and pressed an ear to her frail chest. She gathered up Gracie's limp arms, buried her face in Gracie's curls. Washburn swiveled to pass his suit coat across the seat, warm from his skin, and she used it to swaddle Gracie tight. She promised as Washburn reversed down the track to make Gracie an apple pie, to build her a rabbit hutch, to let her hold the baby chicks. Promising anything if she would only wake up. "Please, hurry," Annie Clyde begged Washburn. She could feel Gracie's spirit leaving her body faster than the car was moving.

Annie Clyde didn't look back as Yuneetah receded. At the steep rising mountains or the ponded cow pastures or the river glinting between the shade trees. At Joe Dixon's store or Hardin Bluff School or the tumbled-down foundation stones of the churches. The thought of this day had once broken her heart. Now the death of the town seemed like nothing compared to the waning life she held in her arms. Let the lake have it. She had all that counted. She closed her eyes and inhaled the farmland smell of Whitehall County blowing through the car, replacing the graveyard stench of dirt, limestone and moss. Buffeting her hair and flapping the sleeves of Washburn's suit coat. She clutched the bundle of Gracie to her chest and pretended they were somewhere else to keep from losing her mind. They were riding to the market in the bed of Dale Hankins's pickup. She was leaning against the cab holding Gracie between her knees, loose straw flying all around them. Or they were on a hayride tucked in a musky horse blanket, the wagon bumping down the road under the harvest moon, passing the frosted fields with James's arms around her and Gracie both, the scent of autumn crisp and smoky on their skins. She remembered her husband then. She cracked her fevered lids to see him slumped beside her on the seat. His hair tousled, his shirt torn ragged. Mud and bark caking his fingernails. Soaked to the hip from the tall weeds he'd parted to bring Gracie home. "James," Annie Clyde rasped, and his eyes rolled toward her. She was overcome with love for him, even in the midst of all this. The one who gave her daughter back to her. At last she understood what he'd meant when he said he had worshipped her from the moment he saw her standing on the riverbank. "She won't wake up," Annie Clyde whispered, shaking Gracie a little, tears leaking down her face. James forced himself to smile. For her sake, like so much of what he had done. "She will," he said, and Annie Clyde tried to believe him.

Around noon Ellard Moody found himself alone with the Deering child's bones. The remains from the cave in the clearing had been brought to the courtroom where the light would be best. Despite the power company's deadline, there were still pews behind the railing. Flags still flanked the judge's bench. Chairs remained on the witness stand and the raised jury platform as if there might be a trial tomorrow. Not that many trials had taken place in Yuneetah. There hadn't been enough crime to warrant building a courthouse until 1830. Before then the sheriff made do with a stockade on the riverbank. Many times Ellard had stood at the back of this room with his hands clasped in front of him and his revolver on his hip as men were sentenced for public drunkenness or disturbing the peace. He had broken up only one fight in the courtroom himself, a scuffle between the owner of Gilley's Hotel and a bachelor who owed him rent. Only once had there been a gunshot fired in the courthouse during his tenure, and that was yesterday afternoon. Ellard supposed there wasn't much history worth preserving here, but he hoped before the water flooded in that somebody would take away the old furnishings and the old portraits of white-headed circuit court judges lining the walls. It could all be used elsewhere, in a church or in some other county's court. If not, at least one of the lawyer's tables was serving a final purpose. It had been cleared of the water pitcher and the stacks of law books to make room for the Deering boy's skeleton, arranged now in the pattern of a child on its scarred walnut top.

Most of the morning Ellard had been there with a professor of anthropology from the college in Knoxville and a serious young man that appeared to be his student. For hours Ellard had looked over their shoulders at the broken skull and the brittle rib fragments, listening as they pieced together a story he could have told them. Judging by the pelvis, the professor said, this was a male. No more than five years old given the length of the femur. In his brief lifetime he had suffered from rickets. Then his head had been dashed on the rocks of the riverbed. For at least a decade after that his bones had lain in a shallow limestone cave being gnawed at by animals and eroded by weather. But the professor didn't say what a shame it was that this child had suffered and died. That somebody had lost a son. Ellard wished they'd seen Wayne Deering slogging through the floodwaters with one boot on, out of his mind with grief. He hated to hear them talking about this child's life and death in the same offhand way they'd remarked on the condition of the roads in from Knoxville, but he was unwilling to leave one of his own alone in the hands of these strangers. From the time the professor and his student had arrived in town this morning, Ellard had been out of temper. He couldn't summon much friendliness toward them.

They had come as far as the courthouse then Ellard drove them down to the Hankins woods. He would have liked a preacher or at least an undertaker present to speak over the remains before they were disturbed but neither could be reached, so he had done the best he could by himself. He had stood at the foot of the bluff holding his hat in his hands, looking down at the leftover signs of a struggle. Furrows made in the spongy earth by feet digging and sliding as Ellard tried to grapple James off of Amos. Vines littered around the mouth of the cave. He had shut his eyes and bowed his head against the memory of the day before. Not just what had taken place between Amos and James Dodson, but the sight of the drifter sitting there unfazed beneath his shelter when Ellard and James found the camp, as if he was expecting them. It had taken all of Ellard's will-power to match Amos's maddening calm. Even when he was standing over the Deering child's bones in the cave Ellard's blood had begun to heat again, remembering the glint of mockery in Amos's eye. After fumbling through the Lord's Prayer he had turned his back and walked off.

While the college men huddled over the hole at the foot of the bluff with their sleeves rolled up, a tarp spread to receive the bones, Ellard went about his own business. In the cut-back laurel he found the axes, James's thrown and his set aside forgotten. He had surveyed the drifter's camp again, collapsing lumps of cook fire ash with his boot toe, crouching to examine the print of his own heel still marking the topsoil. He had knelt to retrieve the drifter's belongings, untying the bindle and sorting through the chattel, finding nothing much besides pots and pans. A thick spool of rope. Matches kept dry in a corked glass bottle. A bolt cropper, surely used for thieving. A ball-peen hammer and some railroad spikes, Ellard supposed for building his shelters. His hat with the wilted brim and the buff-colored crown, the sweat-stained band. None of it told Ellard what Amos was doing in Yuneetah. Then Ellard had unfolded the drifter's peacoat, smelling the road dust of his travels. Reaching into an inner pocket he had discovered a darned sock that looked like a fat snake, bulging with whatever was stuffed inside. Wary to put his hand in the sock Ellard had sat on the milk crate to upend and shake it out, a collection of objects dropping on the bedroll unfurled at his feet. A hair ribbon, tied into a bow. A Kewpie doll. A toy soldier. The items looked old

and unlikely to belong to Gracie Dodson, as Amos appeared to have
been carrying them for far longer than three days. Ellard had turned
each seeming keepsake over in his hands, thinking dark thoughts,
unable to fathom their meaning.

After taking Amos's belongings out to the trunk of his car he went
to the bluff and helped wrap the excavated bones in canvas. Back at
the courthouse he watched as the professor and his student laid them
out, determined to make sure they were handled with the proper
respect. He had observed with his arms folded as they brushed away
the dirt, as they measured and stood back to consider. After they'd
finally packed up their tools they shook Ellard's hand and went out.
He supposed their business was done. They would go on back to
Knoxville, write up their report about the Deering boy and think
nothing more of him or Yuneetah. Now Ellard lingered in the courtroom standing over the lawyer's table, trying to feel the right way
after all his years of beating the bushes for the Deering child's bones.
It turned out that finding the boy changed little. Wayne Deering
had still lost his son. Looking down at the bones Ellard wished for
some memory of what they were like with skin on them. He had an
image of a child with sandy hair and bowed legs running around his
car when he went down to the hog farm, but that might have been
any of the Deering brood. He remembered them swimming in the
river that ran along the edge of the farm not realizing it could rise
up and kill them as easily as it floated them on their backs in its shal-
lows. Ellard hoped burying the child would bring some measure of
comfort to his father. He didn't know where the surviving Deerings
had ended up, but Wayne would have to be notified.

Thinking of all that needed doing before the day was over Ellard
passed out of the courtroom for the last time, casting one final look
up at the balcony as though someone might be watching, heels scuffing the oak floor that had gone all these months unpolished. The
one lawman around this morning besides Ellard was the Whitehall

County constable, but he and Ellard went way back. They had always come to each other's aid when and however they could. As Ellard went through the lobby on the way to his office he nodded to the constable sitting at the counter behind the box of the shortwave, twisting the knobs and producing static, the dials glowing amber. The constable yawned into his fist, rubbed the back of his neck where his dark hair was clipped close. Ellard thought about telling him to take a break, maybe even to go on home. Yesterday had aged both of them. He could see it in the bags under the constable's eyes and could feel it in his own joints. But he needed what help he could get.

Other than the constable, only Sam Washburn had returned to the courthouse after the events of yesterday afternoon. Ellard had meant to see if Washburn needed medical attention once Amos was subdued and the Dodsons were led away, but the boy had disappeared. Then earlier he had been waiting on the bench in the vestibule when Ellard arrived back at the courthouse with the college men. As Washburn rose to greet Ellard they didn't mention what had happened down in the basement, or the shallow cut under the boy's chin, although Washburn's presence spoke something of his grit. He told Ellard he had met with the director of the TVA first thing this morning. If Gracie was still missing tomorrow, a drawdown would be ordered. Ellard found this concession somewhat hard to believe after how their meeting with Harville had gone but he saw no reason to doubt Washburn's word. He supposed the boy knew better than he did how to deal with his own kind. When Washburn told Ellard he was headed to the Walker farm, Ellard said he would drive out directly to see the Dodsons himself, but he knew they'd be in good hands until he got there. It was his way of thanking Washburn for coming back to Yuneetah when others hadn't. Their eyes locked and Ellard thought they understood each other.

Now Ellard stepped into his office and closed the door behind him, shutting out the static from the radio. He considered all the hours he'd spent in this long room, drafty enough in the winter to wear a coat and hot enough in July to sweat through his shirt because of the tall window overlooking the square. He glanced at the portrait on the wall of his predecessor. Twenty years he'd spent here, and this was the end. He wondered if the man in the picture over the desk would have appreciated more the gravity of this moment. If he would have done better by the town in its last days. Right now Ellard felt as wrung out and empty as the street beyond the window. He had never been more ready to head back up the hollow to his childhood home.

Then out of the corner of his eye he saw Silver Ledford rushing up the sidewalk, looking like the lone survivor of some disaster. Ellard knew she wasn't coming to see him. He would meet her at the door and send her away but for a few seconds he allowed himself to observe her. Before yesterday, he hadn't seen much of her in the last three decades. He would nod if he met her coming out of the store or drove by as she traveled down the road dragging her cotton sack through the pricker bushes. When he was younger he thought about her for days after encountering her. He turned the memory of her over in his mind in the night. When people teased that his apartment was too big for one man or said he needed a wife to cook for him, he grinned and lowered his head. There had been other women. He just hadn't met one since Silver that he wanted to marry. As he grew older he was able to forget about her for long stretches. He would think he was over her until he heard somebody snickering in Joe Dixon's or at McCormick's Cafe as he ate his dinner, the ones who bought whiskey off Silver saying they had seen Amos up on the mountain. After all this time, he couldn't stand to think about her with anybody else. Even now it galled Ellard to know she was here for Amos and not for him.

He was about to move from the window when he saw that Silver wasn't coming by herself. There was a redbone coonhound trailing behind her, its nose to the ground. Ellard frowned, squinting through

the flawed glass panes, trying to make sense of what he was seeing. It
was the Dodsons' dog, there was little question about it. As Silver left
the pavement and started across the lawn it trotted through the grass
at her heels. When she and the dog both disappeared from view of
the window Ellard got moving. He was emerging from his office just
as Silver was bursting into the vestibule, a shaft of sun falling in the
door behind her. The dog halted at the threshold, stood on the top
step looking in at the tile floor. Silver let the heavy door slam behind
her and came farther inside, her feet leaving wet tracks. She tried
to speak but didn't seem to have enough wind. "What is it, Silver?"
Ellard asked, his eyes searching her face.

"It's Gracie," she managed.

Ellard touched her shoulder. "Slow down and get your breath. Tell
me from the start."

"I was up on the ridge and heard the dog barking."

"All right."

"By the time I made it down the mountain Annie Clyde and James
was getting in the car with some government man." Silver took in a
hitching breath. "They had Gracie with them."

"You're saying they found her?"

Silver nodded.

Ellard tried to organize his thoughts, his mind racing with questions. He didn't know which to ask first. Finally he settled on the
most important one. "Is she alive?"

"I think so. They was in a hurry."

"Could you tell what kind of shape she was in?"

"She didn't look well, from what I could make out."

Ellard hesitated, searching Silver's face again. "You don't look too
well either," he said. "Come in here and have a seat." She didn't protest when he took her by the arm and led her through his office door
to a chair in front of his desk, the same one James Dodson had been
sitting in two days ago. She took several minutes to tell it all, in a

fragmented way that Ellard, watching her lips so as not to miss a word, had trouble putting together. She'd been up on the ridge this morning when she heard the clamor. She tried to see off the ledge but couldn't for the trees. The barking was coming from the woods and not the house. She thought the dog must be in a tangle with a coon or a skunk. She stayed where she was until she heard high voices mingled with the yelping. Then she made her way as fast as she could down the rocks, scrambling to reach the farm. But in the woods at the foot of the mountain where a beech tree was fallen she paused to absorb what she saw. The beech's root ball was hacked to chunks, the mud around it ravaged. There was a hole in the ground underneath the tree, a narrow cave or burrow, but she hadn't realized then that Gracie must have been inside it. When she ran out of the pines into the hayfield she found a path trampled through the weeds. She pursued James and Annie Clyde but was too late to catch them. Stopping at the side of the house with a stitch in her side, she saw James lowering himself with Gracie in his arms into the back of the government man's car.

A hush fell over both of them. Ellard went on studying her for a while, the sun reflecting off the white plaster walls into his eyes. It took a minute for him to get it straight in his head, that Amos had never been involved. "What time did you see them?" Ellard asked at last.

"I don't know. I went down the road after the car a piece. I tried to follow their tire tracks but I gave up. I'd say it took me about an hour to make it here walking. I couldn't get a ride."

"What direction was they headed?"

"South. Over into Whitehall County."

"Taking her to the doctor. Sit tight and I'll be back as soon as I know something."

"Wait," she said, before he could leave. "What about Amos?"

Ellard stopped. In the stillness he heard the constable's voice, the crackle of static. "Let me ask you something, Silver. What put you in such a rush to get here? Was it Gracie or Amos?"

Silver looked away. Ellard had never wanted to slap a woman before but his hand itched now to meet with her cheek, to strike some color into it. He could even imagine how the print of his fingers would appear there as stripes. "I reckon I ought to let him go. Just take your word."

"You think I'd lie to you about a thing like this?" she asked.

"I don't know what you'd do for him," Ellard said. But as quick as the old fire flamed up it died out of him. It was suddenly meaningless. It occurred to him that if he and Silver stayed here long enough the flood would wash them out, float them up like the curtain hems and the papers on his desk. In those few seconds he pictured how the shine of the window would look through murky water, lighting Silver's waxen face riven with lines. A clutch of bubbles purling up from the slits of her nostrils like unstrung pearls. Both of them swimming in the coils of her black hair, in the rags of her calico dress. If they didn't move they would both be buried underneath the lake. Whether they moved or not, they would both be forgotten with the rest of Yuneetah. Even Gracie. The dam would stand in memory, but not of their individual lives. Only of a moment in history. Ellard's arm felt like lead as he reached for the doorknob. Then he dropped it when he heard the constable's brisk footsteps approaching, resounding on the tile.

Ellard's eyes remained on Silver as the constable knocked on the door and opened it without waiting to be invited into the office. "A call came in from my boys over at Whitehall County," he said, all of his previous weariness gone. "Gracie Dodson has been found."

"That's what this woman is telling me," Ellard said. "Who reported it to them?"

"I reckon it was Dr. Brock's nurse."

"What did they say about her condition?"

"They didn't have a whole lot of information. Her mama and daddy brung her in. I reckon the doctor has done took them on to the hospital in Clinchfield."

"I better head out there," Ellard said.

"What about your prisoner?" the constable asked.

Silver raised her face to Ellard. A greenfly had entered with her and it buzzed between them. Ellard spoke more to Silver than to the constable. "I don't reckon we can hold him."

"You want me to turn him loose?" the constable asked.

"Naw," Ellard said. "If you will, get on the radio and see what else you can find out."

When the constable left the room Ellard went to his desk, strewn with paperwork from the power company. He opened the right-hand drawer with a key on an iron ring inside, took the key out and placed it on the desktop before Silver. As she stared down at the key he got up and went to the wall behind the door where Amos's peacoat hung from a hook beside his own rain slicker, as though Amos was a guest and not a prisoner. On the floor beside Ellard's rubber boots was the drifter's bedroll. He hefted it under his arm, then took the coat from the hook. He carried them both to Silver, shoving the drifter's things into her lap. "Here. You let him go. I can't hold him, but I can't be the one that turns him loose. I'll let it be on your hands, since you think so well of him." When Silver said nothing Ellard gritted his teeth. "There ain't no telling what he's done before and what he'll do after this. You know that, don't you? You know it and you don't care."

Silver blinked at the key on the desk, then up at Ellard. "Don't be like this," she said.

"I don't know how to be any other way."

"I don't either. That's been our problem, ain't it?"

Ellard glanced out the window and saw the hound sniffing at the tires of his car. Amos was still down there in the bowels of the building. Ellard considered going downstairs to question him further but in the end he had nothing more to say to Amos. As there was nothing more to say to Silver Ledford now. "Should I wait on you in the car?" he asked her.

"No," she said, looking so ill that he thought she might need a doctor herself. "I've got to watch after Gracie's dog. But you come up and tell me how she is as soon as you get back."

"You can stay here and wait for me," Ellard said. "Unless you're going off with him."

"I'll be around, Ellard," Silver said. "Like I always have been." Then she took the key and Amos's possessions to the door, so tall her head nearly touched the frame. Ellard sat on the edge of his desk and looked across at her with the grayed roll of the bindle in her arms, past her shoulder the notice board tacked with papers as flimsy as their lives still seemed to him. He took in her paleness, the dark hair that spilled down her back almost to her waist. He didn't try to close the distance between them as he once did on the riverbank. He had Silver for a summer when he was seventeen and he guessed that would have to do him. But he would think later that letting her go didn't mean she never belonged to him. Nothing could change what was already done. The past at least was permanent. Whatever there was to come for himself and the neighbors he'd served and protected for twenty years, whatever lives and places they moved on to, he had known them in this one. As he'd known Silver Ledford in a way that nobody else ever could. The thought would comfort Ellard some when he'd remember how she turned her back on him with the bindle in her arms. How she left him there as she had done before and went to Amos.

At one o'clock Beulah Kesterson sat in the slat chair she kept beside the front door with her shoes off to let her blisters dry in the sun. Her legs and feet still ached from walking to town and back yesterday.

It was hard to figure how she had traveled ten miles a day with her mother when they were peddling. She lifted her face to the breeze. As high over the valley as she lived, she could smell the river. It made her think about musseling. When her mother was alive they called it toe digging, pulling the shells from the riverbed silt to collect in their pans, taking turns with the good shucking knife. Sometimes they would boil the mussels in a smoke-blacked pot on the shore when they stopped to rest beside the river on their peddling rounds. The best mussel bed they'd found was now on the other side of the dam. It was past dinnertime and Beulah's stomach was empty. She hoped Amos wasn't hungry down at the jail. They had gone musseling together often when he was a child. The lassitude of the work had suited his patient nature. She had a notion to take him a pan of mussels right now, worn out as she felt. Even without her fortune-telling bones, she still had her intuition. She hadn't escaped her inheritance. She supposed the discernment was like her blood, unseen but there inside her, a thing that could die only when she did. If she went to the courthouse Ellard Moody would let her in. She was the one who birthed him. He owed her some respect. She looked down at the bunions on her feet, the weeping blisters, and knew that she had to go in spite of them. She heaved herself from her chair, put on her shoes then went inside to find her musseling pan and her shucking knife.

Leaving the cabin again with an apron tied around her waist she made her careful way down the steps, taking them one at a time, then ambled across the yard in her mannish brogans and set off down the hollow. On the footpath she flushed a baby rabbit out of the briars. It went skittering off into the graveyard, its cottontail flashing between the pickets and disappearing into the grass behind them. Beulah half expected when she turned her head that way to see Clyde and Mary Walker standing at the fence. Beckoning her over to whisper into her ear what had become of the grandchild they would never hold.

She could almost make them out, Mary still slim with the black curls she had kept until the end. Clyde tall and sunburnt. Beulah would have welcomed such a visitation. But there were only sugar maple trees standing against the fence, shedding the last raindrops. Once the graveyard was underwater Beulah wouldn't even be able to see the headstones of her old friends.

As she picked her way down the slope she consoled herself with the thought that after this she wouldn't leave her cabin again for a long time. The blisters on her heels had reopened and her breathing pained her chest. The musseling pan tapped against her aching leg as she limped through the springing grasshoppers down to the track dividing the hollow from the Walker farm. On the way to the road she took care not to twist her ankle, avoiding clods of tire-churned earth and the divots they left, filled with rain. When she glanced at the house and the land it looked vacant. A hawk was circling over the cornfield. A sumac vine with reddening leaves was winding up the fieldstone chimney. The townspeople had given up searching for Gracie Dodson. As the end of this hard decade approached she guessed they dared not hope a little girl declared dead in their minds would be found alive. Beulah couldn't judge her neighbors. These days she knew too well how a person's belief could waver. She looked over her shoulder. There wasn't much of a breeze but she heard a sound carrying across the hayfield, a lonesome creaking. The ropes of Gracie's swing in the apple tree. Annie Clyde and James were gone as sure as the child was, and the dog that used to come out from under the porch wagging his tail to greet Beulah when she went picking strawberries in the field. She had another intuition, more like sadness than a premonition, that none of them would come back to this place. The last holdout had given in. The last farm was abandoned. There was no turning back from the course Yuneetah had been set on. Standing there on Annie Clyde's land Beulah could almost feel the forward motion. She had seen and lived through so much but eighty-five years still seemed short to her. It seemed like just the other day she was out in that smokehouse with Mary, packing pork shoulders in salt. Time was unmerciful. She'd always known it, but today the vacant Walker homestead was her proof.

Beulah went out past the cornfield then paused in the middle of the road with a hand on her hip. The Whitehall County line and the mussel bed past the dam were off to the right but she turned for a moment in the opposite direction, where she could see lake water running off the steps of the bank into the gully. Farther down she could see more water through the scratched lenses of her glasses, part of the roadway washed out. Even farther on than that, beyond the sparkling slough, she believed she saw movement. There was a bobbing head coming around the bend. Her eyesight wasn't what it used to be, but she thought it was a man. Tall and reed thin, black-haired with a bindle on his shoulder. The late summer trees gathered behind him, crowded up against the ditch as if to watch him come. As if to see what Beulah's face would do when she recognized him. Her heart lifted, not only to realize that Ellard had turned her son loose. In that instant it came to her what Amos's appearance must mean. Gracie Dodson had surely been found alive. If she had been drowned, if her bones were broken, Amos would have been blamed. Beulah hadn't wanted to agree with Silver Ledford last night but she knew that it was true.

Amos took his time meeting Beulah and she savored every moment until he reached her. For as long as her son remained obscured behind the afternoon heat rising up from the road and the glare of the sun on her glasses, she could feel relieved. It was only when he closed the distance in front of the Dodsons' cornfield that she was saddened again by his battered face. It looked worse than yesterday. The split cheekbone, the bloody lips. But underneath the bruises he was much like the boy she had found in the woods, even with a missing eye and whiskers. She reached for his coat sleeve, needing to touch him. "They found her," he said.

"I figured as much."

"Your bones told you?"

"No, you told me. If she wasn't found, you wouldn't be standing here. Was she—"

"Alive."

"Praise Jesus," Beulah said. "Is she going to be all right?"

"I thought you'd be able to tell me that." His eye settled on her bare neck where the frayed pouch used to hang She couldn't put anything past him. "Where are they anyway?"

"I got no more use for them," she said.

"I guess you've renounced the old ways. Like the rest of the town."

She waved her hand. "I ain't renounced nothing. I reckon a body can have it both ways."

Amos looked toward the mountain where her cabin was nestled. "How long until they string their power lines up the hollow? Did you divine that before you gave up your bones?"

Beulah looked with him. "I don't know. Might be nice to have me a washing machine. One of them electric stoves." She shook his sleeve, changing the subject. "Did you eat yet?"

Amos glanced at the musseling pan. "You must know the answer to that at least."

"Let's see if we can dig us up some dinner then," she said.

Without another word they turned toward Whitchall County. Walking beside Amos as if nothing had happened was bittersweet. It occurred to Beulah that love was so often a burden. She knew it was the last time she would ever be with her son, whichever one of them departed first. She tried to push off the weight of her sadness and appreciate his silent companionship. If she didn't look at him she could pretend his shoulder was level with hers as they went along, like back in the days when they'd lived together, before he stood two heads taller than her. She could pretend the sound of trickling water was Long Man from some time before and not the power company's lake running off the banks. When a blackbird burst out of the pines and flew off ahead of them toward the dam she tried not to see it as a portent. She tried not to remember droplets seeping up through her tablecloth, flowers magnified in a circle of bones. She thought how confounding it was that this dark man beside her had been the light of her life. She thought how the Lord's ways were mysterious and there was no use in questioning them. She'd learned to accept His unfathomable nature, the same way she had quit trying to understand Amos. But she couldn't quit trying to protect him. She couldn't ever quit praying that her son would outlive her.

They went past where the dam brooded in the woods without looking that way or mentioning its presence, but Beulah was glad when it was behind them. They kept on until they could see the river between the trunks then took the road a piece more before heading down to the water. She carried her pan to the river's edge, searching for the mussel bed she had found with her mother back when she was young. Amos went ahead of her with his hat off to fill like a bowl. When he bent over stiffly Beulah could see his soreness, but he didn't let on. They dug side by side, cold water swirling into Beulah's shoes. Though they had come almost a mile from the dam its flagged tower rose above the distant sycamore and bluff oak trees. When Amos found a large shell with an iridescent blue sheen he dropped it into her pan, still prone to unexpected acts of kindness. After a while, he took out a pocketknife to hunt for pearls. "Mammy said people used to come in droves to go pearling," Beulah told him, taking her own shucking knife from her apron. "These days you can't hardly find any, but back then some man collected two hundred dollars' worth in a week's time. Bought hisself a farm." Amos seemed to listen as she prattled on, talking to hide her mounting unease. She had the same feeling here with him that the vacant Walker house gave her. As relieved as she was in that first moment to see him released from jail, she had to remember the reason she'd turned him in. She knew his mind was moving beneath his stillness. After working a minute longer she looked into his hat. "I believe you got them all."

He smiled. "There's at least two or three left."

"Well," she said. "Let's cook some of these up. Then you better get on down the road."

She thought at first that he was going to ignore her. But finally he responded without looking up from the mussels. "I told you. I'll head out after I've finished my business."

Beulah shifted in the boats of her shoes, reached out of habit for her discarded pouch. "I need you to listen to what I'm telling you for once," she said. "You can't go on doing wrong, Amos. One of these days you'll answer for it."

He pried open a mussel with his knife, plucked out a grain of pearl and slipped it into his pocket. "I have no problem with that," he said. "As long as the same rule applies to everybody."

"This river will always be here. It'll keep on running, no matter how they dam it up."

"I've been all over the country. I've seen how it is. Once the electric power and the factories come around, nobody in this valley will remember what the river gave them."

"You're wrong," she said. "This river's underneath their skin. They won't forget."

"They think they're saved," he said. "But a hundred dams wouldn't fix this mess."

"Well. I've lived a lot longer than you, Amos. Good times always come around again." Beulah paused, standing on the shoals where they had dug when he was a boy without the dam watching them through the trees. "Promise me, son," she said, looking downstream and then into his eye, its white turned crimson. "Promise you won't do nothing else to get yourself hurt."

Amos regarded Beulah, studied her face. His own face was no longer blank. Everything he had seen and done seemed written there. She guessed she had never been certain before then if he loved her back. "I promise," he said. Beulah's breath came ragged but she willed away her tears. They went back to the mussels, working on for a spell in silence besides the running river. Finally she noticed that Amos had cracked open a dripping shell. He stood gazing down into it.

"What is it?" she asked. "Did you cut yourself?" He tipped the big shell to one side, until something that Beulah couldn't see rolled into his palm. She put down her musseling pan and went to him. He held out his hand. There was a good-sized pearl in it, misshapen and gritty. "They laws," she said, as he held it aloft in the sun. Then he turned and offered it to her.

"Here," he said.

Beulah stepped back. "What?"

"Take it."

"Lord, Amos. Have you lost your mind?"

"No, ma'am," he said.

"There ain't no telling how much that's worth. You take it to a druggist somewhere and he'll send it off to New York for you. Why, you could live off of that for a long time."

Amos shook his head. "It's for you."

"I don't need it. You're the one without a home."

He stepped closer. "I want you to have it."

"What for, Amos?"

"Please. Take it."

It occurred to her that since she'd found Amos he had never asked her to do anything. She held out her hand and accepted the pearl. She lifted it to her nose to smell the river that formed it. "See," Beulah said. "I told you things'll get better. I don't need bones to show me that."

It was almost sunset when Amos made his way back downstream to the dam. After Beulah left him at the riverside he lingered over the remains of their cook fire, smoke still rolling from the sodden kin-

dling they'd used. He slouched over the guttering flames prodding
with a stick at the charred mussel shells in a ring of stones until the
shadows of the hemlocks behind him stretched out long on the rocky
shore. Then he put on his hat, hoisted up his bindle and faded into
the trees. He walked through the shade a mile or so until he came out
again on the hillside where only yesterday at dawn he had scouted
the dam and its buildings from the east. He knew he'd be exposed
in the open for several minutes as he emerged from the hardwoods at
the top of the slope and went across the closed highway's pavement,
then skidded down an embankment on the lake side of the dam and
followed the sand a ways before receding again into a peninsula of
evergreens. It took him some time but not much to find the ancient
spruce he was looking for, its roots twisting up from a pile of needles.
There was a hollow near its base and he got on his knees to reach into
the knotty depths. Yesterday morning, after leaving Beulah's shed
with her bolt cropper and a burlap sack, he'd made a stop on the way
to his camp in the clearing.

If the cinder-block hut in the woods along the stone wall marking the boundaries of the watershed had been empty when Amos
broke the padlock he might have left Yuneetah already. But the hut
wasn't empty. There had been enough light when he pushed in the
door. He had stood in the opening with the rain pouring off the cor-
rugated eave above him, running downhill and away from the hut,
built off the ground to keep its contents dry. Against the block walls
he'd found sacks of cement, digging implements, and stacks upon
stacks of rectangular wooden boxes with a maker's label stamped on
their sides. From the cobwebs he deduced that the building hadn't
been entered in weeks, perhaps a month. Amos had stepped inside
the stale shadows and opened the hinged lid of a box on top. Yellow
sticks, cylinders lying end to end. He recognized this brand of plastic explosive from his time blasting tunnels through mountains. The
TVA had set off these charges to loosen tons of rock from the river-

bed. They drilled holes, a hundred or more, then blew them clean with compressed air. They rammed a stick into each hole, pouring sand in and tamping it down. Then they wired the fuses into a central switch. He inspected the sticks to make sure they weren't sweating. Unless dynamite was frozen then thawed or stored in the heat, it wasn't all that unstable. It required a detonator to go off, unlike in the old days when pure nitroglycerin was used for blasting. Amos had carried dynamite by hand many times, working in coal mines and on road crews. But as he filled Beulah's burlap sack with explosives, he transferred them with the same care he'd first learned to take as a powder monkey at a quarry.

Yesterday morning he had made two trips from the cinder-block hut to this hollow spruce he'd discovered along the lakeshore. Then he'd covered his footprints, rearranged the boxes and slung the broken padlock far out across the reservoir where it sank without making much of a splash. Amos assumed the watchman didn't come up the trail along the watershed often. He had found no tracks but his own. Now he hoped the power company hadn't discovered thirty sticks of their dynamite missing, as he eased out what was stashed in the spruce. The burlap sack was damp but the explosives inside were waterproof. Besides the sack, there were two more bundles of dynamite knotted along a length of the detonating cord he'd brought out of Nebraska. He had made a second bundle from his undershirt and a third from a mildewed blanket. He had tied one end of the detonating cord to the head of a railroad spike found lying corroded with rust along the tracks, leaving some of the cord trailing as a fuse. He would drive the spike into the concrete of the dam with a ball-peen hammer he'd stolen from a blacksmith shed. The hammering might draw attention, but by then it would be nearly over. The chain of charges would explode almost in unison after he lit the fuse. In his trouser pocket he kept a small corked glass bottle of wooden matches. He had dipped the match heads in turpentine, which would keep them water resistant for months. But he'd sealed them in the bottle to be certain. The fuse was reinforced as well, coated in olive drab plastic. Even soaked it would detonate, as long as there was a dry end to ignite. Even underwater the wick would burn. Soon after sundown Amos could place the three bundles in one of the two rowboats tied to the dock near the dam if he chose. Though he'd made preparations he hadn't decided to carry out his plan. There was light left in the sky. He would know in the haziness before nightfall, after bats had begun to dive around the dam's tower.

For now, he leaned back against the spruce with the bundles gathered into his lap. His coat scratched and caught on the rough bark as he tried to get comfortable. He was tired after having spent the night before tossing in pain on the jail cell bunk, but he kept alert. He listened for the watchman, thinking because it was Sunday and because of the excitement with the child the dam workers might not appear. But before half an hour had elapsed Amos heard echoing voices and carefully replaced the dynamite bundles in the spruce hollow. Then he padded through the coppery needles to the edge of the evergreens and stood there without breaking cover, observing the watchman's shadow on the sand, the silhouette of his hatted head moving up on the dam's pedestrian sidewalk. When Amos heard calling voices again from somewhere distant he knew there was more than one worker patrolling the site. But as the dark deepened the voices subsided and Amos's mind quieted with them. He went back through the woods underneath the low boughs to the spruce and settled once again to rest against its scratchy bark. He wasn't worried about the watchman. He wasn't worried about the sheriff of Yuneetah finding him again either.

Ellard Moody had been afraid of Amos since they were boys. His face was sheepish even as a child, his timid eyes downcast, always tagging after the Ledford sisters. Amos used to lure Silver Ledford away from Ellard just to watch the other boy's ears turning red. But as often as Amos goaded Ellard into anger, he had never once struck back. Ellard would stand aside and let Amos steal his marbles away from him, his slingshots and nickels, without putting up much of a fight. Now Ellard had given Yuneetah up to the TVA out of the same weakness. Amos had watched unsurprised as his boyhood neighbor grew into the kind of man who took what the government gave him. The kind who licked boots and did as he was told. When Ellard pointed his revolver in the courthouse basement yesterday Amos had seen over the barrel of the gun the knowledge in the sheriff's eyes. Ellard knew he was a failure. Amos could do more for Yuneetah in the next few minutes than Ellard had in twenty years as sheriff. He had traveled this whole country unseen, but that was by choice. He could make thousands look at him if he wanted.

This afternoon Ellard couldn't face Amos long enough to even turn him loose. He'd sent Silver Ledford to do his bidding. She said nothing as she rattled the key in the lock but Amos knew what it meant that she was there. She swung the door open wide and came inside where it was dim although the sun was shining on the rest of Yuneetah. She placed his bindle at his feet and examined his face, made speechless by the state he was in. Amos had no urge to touch Silver as he'd done in the past. But hers was the only companion-ship he missed sometimes on the road. When he saw lava rocks in New Mexico unlike anything they had found in the caves of Yunee-tah. When he saw redwood trees too tall for either of them to have climbed. Silver had aged but he always remembered her as an almost feral child standing at the edge of Beulah's yard staring at him with open curiosity. He remembered her swimming in the river with min-nows flashing, caught in the snare of her hair. He remembered her exploring the abandoned iron mine with him, climbing up the buried grooves of a track to what was once the superintendent's house, the windows broken and the front door gone. Together they had crawled underneath the clustered blooms of an overgrown lilac bush planted at the porch corner, and Silver had asked Amos if they could stay there forever. Hiding out from the ones in town below who considered them nothing.

Silver had been wilder as a girl, before her sister Mary ran off and left her alone. Amos supposed some of what had drawn him to Gracie Dodson that morning in the cornfield was her resemblance to his only friend. The child looked like Mary except through the eyes. There he had seen the curiosity she inherited from her great-aunt Silver. He had seen the Cherokee in her, as he did in her mother. They were remnants, shadows, of those who first lived on this river and gave it a name. Gracie Dodson, one last child occupying the land that was taken from them all, standing in the corn with a drop or two of Indian blood coursing through the threads of her veins. About to be purged by the same government, unaware in her innocence that her birthright was being stolen. Amos usually took something to remember the children he met in his travels but he'd felt compelled to give Gracie Dodson something instead. Now he saw looking through the branches at the lake spreading closer by the hour to the loam she had claimed with the print of her toes that a toy wasn't enough. If the child had been found drowned or not at all Amos might have reached another conclusion. But it came to him now that the act he was about to commit would join them. She wouldn't be told her own story without hearing Amos's. If he taught her something of defiance maybe she wouldn't change. He knew the risk he was taking. As he knew that he couldn't stop the dam builders. They had plans to inundate hundreds of thousands of valley acres. His act was no more than an obstacle to their end result, but he wasn't meant to grow old anyway. If he died blowing up one of their dams, they'd have to admit he had once been alive.

It had become impossible to shift to a more comfortable position against the tree for the ache in his ribs so Amos roused himself. He looked up at the emerging moon, thinking there was enough light to see by and enough dark to hide him. With caution he retrieved the bundles and carried them wrapped in detonating cord back to the edge of the evergreen woods. He waited there for a while longer listening to the reservoir lapping at the sand, until there was no other movement or sound in all of Yuneetah it seemed. When he finally headed on to the shore his boots gritted in a way that reminded him of snow and the winters he'd spent here. His fingers frozen around the axe handle as he chopped Beulah's wood, his face baking in the heat as they roasted chestnuts so that it felt about to crack open. The same way it felt now for a different reason, his bruised bones chafing at his knuckle-split skin. He cradled the bundles in his arms like a newborn as he went, pulling his hat brim down to hide the glint of his eye just in case, although it was filled with blood. His peacoat over his dingy shirt, his trousers and boots so grimy they had ceased to be any color, he moved like smoke toward the dock near the dam.

Amos would have to launch out here in the open and row all the way across to the seam where the concrete met the bluff since there was no shore on the opposite side of the lake, nothing where the poplars and cottonwoods ended but cairns of rubble. He knelt on the dock, so recently built it smelled of raw lumber, glancing up at the dam to be sure the highway was still deserted. He placed the bundles in the well between the rowboat seats, checking to see that the oars were in the oarlocks. That the handle of the ball-peen hammer was tucked in one of his deep coat pockets, though he could feel its ten-pound weight. He lowered himself into the bow of the boat and cut it loose from the tie-off pin with his hunting knife, then eased into the water and rowed out in the shadow of the dam. He drew as close to the concrete wall as he could get, its face on the lake side striated with lines where the reservoir had risen and receded in the rain. The dip of Amos's oars was nearly silent as he went along the stretch of the spillway, closing in on the west abutment wall. When he reached the other end he would lower the explosive charges knotted along their tether into the reservoir where he thought the rock seam was faultiest, maneuvering the rowboat so that the bundles came to rest at intervals along the sloping wall. Then he would hammer in the railroad spike to anchor the explosives where he wanted them. After the fuse was lit he'd row as fast and far as he could, gaining as much distance as possible from the blast. He hoped for enough time to scramble up the bluff and watch as the underwater explosion separated the lake bottom from the dam's foundation, the water retreating then rushing back toward the fractured seam, a torrent of silt and river roaring unleashed through the chasm.

Amos had rowed the boat out to the middle of the spillway, the bluff drawing closer with each stroke, when he heard the sound of movement somewhere behind him. His ears had grown attuned long ago to approaching footsteps, however distant. When he looked over his shoulder he saw the watchman standing on the dock, a tall figure in a hard hat and coveralls. Then the voice that had once come from up on the highway echoed out across the water, shattering the silent calm. "Halt where you are!" From forty yards away Amos couldn't make out the features of the watchman's face but he could see in the last indigo evening light the rifle the man was pointing. Perhaps the power company had discovered their dynamite missing after all. Perhaps they had been watching and waiting for Amos. In one swift motion he switched from the bow to the stern of the boat and began rowing backward toward the west abutment wall, still keeping as close to the dam's spillway as he could manage, counting on the watchman not being skilled enough to shoot a moving target. "You better do what I told you, buddy!" the man shouted after him.

"You don't want to pull that trigger," Amos shouted back. "I've got a boatload of dynamite here." But before the words were out of his mouth he heard the whine of a bullet passing close to his ear, ricocheting off the water between his boat and the dam. He saw another worker running down the grass embankment along the east abut-

ment wall to join the first man on the dock. Amos realized that he
wouldn't make it to where the vulnerable seam met the bluff. Halfway there would have to be close enough. He was reaching into his
trouser pocket for the corked glass bottle of matches when he heard
another report. The next second he felt something like a great fist
striking the left side of his body, fire ripping through his upper arm.
The bottle flew from his hand as he fell backward. His head knocked
against the boat and he caught a glimpse of the dam's tower, its flags
hanging two hundred feet above him. He took a stunned instant to
collect his wits before scrabbling to his knees, the rowboat wobbling
as he dragged up his struck arm. He looked ahead across the water
and saw the two men on the dock, blurred through his tearing eye.
His sleeve was soaked with blood but he felt no pain. Only dizziness.

The men would be rowing out in the other boat. He would have
to think, as hard as it was to concentrate. He reached down between
the seats of his own boat where the bundles of dynamite still rested,
darker than the light wood of the bottom. As he fumbled them up
by the detonating cord another bullet struck him in the chest on
the right, near his shoulder. This time he flailed over the stern and
splashed into the lake. His eye bulged in the swirling murk, his lungs
already grasping to fill. He could see the bottom of the boat growing smaller as his coat, weighted with the ball-peen hammer, sank
him fast. Beside the boat's shadow on the surface of the lake, Amos
noticed his hat bobbing. He had gotten years of use from the hat.
He was seldom without it. Somehow the sight of it drifting away
told him that he was dying. He had to use whatever time there was
left to finish what he'd started. It took an almost inhuman act of will
to wrestle out of his coat while sinking underwater. When he was
finally shed of its weight he battled upward, swimming one-armed.
He broke the surface with a gasp and hauled himself up by the side
of the boat, nearly capsizing it, coughing bitter water. He couldn't
feel the wounds spurting warm blood inside his shirt. Balancing on

the boat's edge, too weak to hoist himself over inside, he reached down into the shallow well and managed with his arms to gather the three tethered bundles of dynamite from between the seats up under his chin. With his left hand he groped around the bottom until he located the bottle he'd dropped when the first bullet struck him. He ground his teeth as he pried at the cork then shook out a turpentine-treated matchstick. When he swiped the match against a patch of fairly dry-looking wood on the bow side seat he had a moment of certainty that it wouldn't flare alight. But with the other boat nearing, rocking the bloody waters with its oars, the match head burst into dancing flame.

As the second rowboat drew within yards of where Amos's own still floated near the middle of the spillway with him clinging to its side, he touched the match to the long fuse trailing from the head of the railroad spike. He held the flame against the detonating cord with the strength draining out of him, sensing the watchman taking aim again.

When the blue flame began to travel down the wick Amos sucked in a breath that he would never exhale. He slipped back into the lake cradling the bundles of dynamite as the watchman's bullet splintered the boat side not an inch above his skull. He had lost the hammer with his coat. He couldn't attach the charges to the dam with the railroad spike. He'd have to sink them with his body, as close to its foundation as he could get before they exploded. He'd have to press the dynamite against the concrete with his chest. He didn't need to swim much. The dam was a yard from the boat. He held out his injured arm until his hand bumped the wall.

Amos's blood flowed out in ribbons as the impounded waters of the river Long Man flowed back into him. But he would drown before he bled to death. He knew the feeling from his veiled memories of being cast into a flood. He kept his eye open for as long as he could to see the dam, his shoulder grazing its concrete as he sank down its length toward the foundation, hugging the first bundle of charges in his numbing arms, the other two tangled in his legs, dangling knotted to the lit detonating cord. The flame went on traveling down the reinforced fuse, harder to drown than a man. Outside the halo of the wick's burning trail the lake was as black as the night outside Beulah's cabin in winter, as cold as the fallen snow. As he curled himself around the dynamite and turned to press it with his bleeding chest against the wall, Amos's last conscious thought was of the promise he was breaking to the woman who had loved him like a mother. Not of bringing down the dam or any of his reasons for trying. His eye was still open when the blast shot a glaring fireball along the wall but he didn't see it. His soul was released into the water a moment before his ashes. His life, begun with a lie, had ended with one.

AUGUST 3, 1936

Outside of Clinchfield Regional Hospital, Sam Washburn sat in his car. The hospital was a brick building shaded by oaks, situated on a rise overlooking the small but industrialized town. It was on the other side of Whitehall County, about forty miles from the Walker farm. Washburn had relocated several families to Clinchfield. He could see the lights of the knitting mill, workers pulling the graveyard shift. Farther off was the mountain he'd come across before sundown, following Dr. Brock's Buick. Nobody would have noticed if Washburn had turned and gone back to Knoxville once he delivered Gracie Dodson to the doctor's office, but it hadn't occurred to him. He wasn't thinking as he rushed toward Whitehall County with a dying child in his backseat. What happened when they arrived was a blur. There were others in the waiting room but the woman at the desk took one look at the child and led them down a hallway. The doctor, old but not doddering, came out to meet them. He took charge right away when Annie Clyde held the child out to him with helpless eyes. Washburn shouldn't have followed them but he felt swept along. When he saw that he was in the way he stepped out to the hall again but stood there looking in at the examining room. Dr. Brock took the child to a white enameled table under a floor lamp. He handed Annie Clyde the soiled suit coat, which she clutched to her breast as if it still held her daughter, then went to his instrument cabinet. When he lifted the child's lids and shined his light into her eyes she stirred and fussed. Washburn raised his hands to his head, looking for his fedora to take off, but it was lost in the hayfield. Then he paced circles until Dr. Brock came out with the child in his arms to tell the receptionist he was driving the family to the hospital.

Washburn might have gone home then, but he needed to know Gracie Dodson was going to live. He needed to know that her mother would be treated. It was on the way across the mountain, when he was alone in the car smelling the dead leaves and dank earth the child had left in his backseat, that reality began to sink in. The whole way he clenched the steering wheel, fearing the doctor's Buick would become a hearse before they got there. His only solace was that the other car kept moving on ahead of him, tires spitting gravel as it sped along the curving dirt road. There hadn't been as much rain in the higher elevations, the worry of getting mired behind them. But the going was treacherous in places anyway. He worried more about rockslides and fallen trees, or that they might turn over and be spilled between the sourwood trunks down a plunging cliffside. As he kept his eyes on the shadow of Annie Clyde through the Buick's back window, he kept reliving the events of the morning. James Dodson carrying his daughter out of the woods. The barking dog running before him and the child as if to herald their coming. Crashing through the hayfield with Annie Clyde, delirious from lack of wind. Handing his coat across the seat, seeing the child lying still in her mother's lap, the clay mud hard to distinguish from blood.

Now he got out of the car and leaned against the hood to have a cigarette before going back inside to ask about the Dodsons. He had spent too much time in this Dodge coupe, a company car, traveling back and forth to Yuneetah. The wear and tear showed in the lit parking lot. The fenders dinged by rocks, the doors scratched by crowding branches. He knew that he had been sitting out here for too long, but he'd grown claustrophobic in the waiting room on the second floor of the hospital, a parlor lined with straight chairs and hard mahogany benches pushed against the damask-papered walls.

The duty nurse had reached over Washburn's head to pull a shade against the glare of the evening sun but it was still too hot. When he realized that he was famished he had left the hospital to find his supper. In a diner on Main Street where the wainscoting was shiny with cooking grease he sat at the counter to have a hamburger and a cup of coffee. Beside him sat a mother and her two children, a baby in overalls and a girl in a flour sack dress climbing on the stools. They looked no different than the people of Yuneetah, but the electric pendant lights hanging over their heads and the number of cars passing outside the plate-glass window, the sign above the silver coffeepot advertising Blatz beer on tap, told Washburn he'd come out of the valley town ringed in mountains and into the rest of the world.

After supper he had gone back up to the second floor and seen the hallway lined with people, the waiting room crowded. At first he didn't understand. Then he recognized one of the men sitting there, Ruble Williams. His was one of the first families relocated. He had gone to work here at the knitting mill. He must have come straight to the hospital after his shift. There was still lint in his hair. Washburn approached Ruble and learned that he was a distant cousin of James Dodson's aunt. She was sitting in the corner with her husband, fanning herself with a magazine. Ruble had heard about the child from them. Looking around Washburn saw more familiar faces. He'd sat in their front rooms and kitchens asking them questions, taking notes about them for his report. They must have arrived by the car and truck load while he was gone, traveling from wherever the dam had scattered them to see proof of a resurrection from the graveyard of their drowning town. Even those who hadn't helped with the search, those unable to bear the prospect of the child's death, had come seeking evidence of her life. "The sheriff was here for a little while," Ruble said, half startling Washburn. "But a deputy came and got him. Sounded like he said something happened to the dam. I ain't the only one heard it." Washburn thought of calling in to the office. He wondered what could have gone wrong, maybe a leak, but in the end found himself too tired to care. There was nowhere to sit so he'd returned to the car.

He had slept for a while behind the wheel. For as long as Gracie Dodson was missing, he hadn't rested. When he did sleep he woke in the middle of the night from dreams of her wandering a wilderness road crying for her mother or forgotten in an orphanage among other unclaimed children. That's why he went back to Yuneetah, even after what had happened at the courthouse. Thinking about it, Washburn felt his tender windpipe. He shouldn't have taken Annie Clyde where the drifter was being held. But he had been invited by James Dodson's aunt to wait in the kitchen. He was drinking coffee at the table when Annie Clyde came limping through the door. After the aunt repeated what some of the searchers told her, that they'd seen Ellard Moody on the road with the drifter in the back of the sheriff's car, Annie Clyde took off on her swelling foot. Washburn couldn't allow her to walk five miles through the rain in her condition. But now he couldn't forget the man in the cell with a pit where an eye should have been. The man's arm had been strong for one so gaunt, his wiry muscle like iron. It made Washburn sick with humiliation to remember. He'd vowed when he left the courthouse that he'd never return to Yuneetah. But he woke up this morning and the first thought he had was of Annie Clyde Dodson standing in her kitchen doorway streaming water, alone in her conviction that her child was alive.

Washburn pulled out his pocket watch and realized it was after midnight on the third of August, the day of the deadline. The day he had been dreading as he sat in his cubicle at the TVA offices staring down at a pile of paperwork and wondering what he was going to do about the Dodson woman. He couldn't have dreamed a month ago where he would end up during this first hour. Sitting in a hospital parking lot in Clinchfield. Finally he tossed the butt of his cigarette into the weeds and crossed the pavement to the building. He took the stairs to the second floor again and saw that the waiting room had cleared besides James Dodson's aunt and uncle. The aunt slept on her husband's shoulder, the uncle's head reclined and his fingers laced across his suit vest. Washburn wanted to ask about the child but didn't disturb them. He was about to look for a nurse when one appeared in the doorway in her peaked hat and starched uniform dress. "Are you Sam Washburn?" she asked. When he nodded she said, "Mrs. Dodson has been asking for you. She's a stubborn one. But it's past visiting hours, so be quick."

She sent him down the hall where the Dodsons had been given a private room. He went with his hands shoved in his pockets to steady them, not taking them out until he reached the door. He rapped lightly. If Annie Clyde asked him in he didn't hear. After a moment of uncertainty he stepped inside. There were two narrow beds in the room, the one nearest the door unoccupied and neatly made with a white blanket, a partition that could be pulled on a metal rod left undrawn. Between the beds James Dodson slept in an armchair with his chin on his breast. The electric lamp above the other bed was switched on, casting an amber circle on that side of the room. Washburn stepped out of the shadows into the light to make himself known. Annie Clyde was lying in the bed near the window, the flowery curtains open although it was dark outside. As he approached he noticed that her eyes were closed. There was a glass of water and a bowl of broth on a tray table across her legs, her bandaged foot elevated on a pillow. Tucked at her side, in the curve of her arm, was the child. Gracie Dodson slept with her lips parted, hugging her mother's waist, her head resting on her mother's thin chest. Washburn imagined it was soothing for her to hear Annie Clyde's heart beating. She had been washed but he saw in the shine of the lamp each tiny fingernail traced with brick red clay, her curls dark against the gauze swathing her head wound. By the bed a stand with a metal hook held a bottle of clear fluid.

Annie Clyde had been bathed herself, dressed in a clean hospital gown. She was propped on the pillows, her hair loose on the linen. Washburn reached again to take off his missing hat as he moved to the bedside. Then his wingtip shoe squeaked on the tile and James Dodson started, straightening in the armchair. Washburn froze in his tracks. "Oh," he said. "I'm sorry. Should I come back later? Tomorrow?"

"That's all right," James Dodson said, getting up. Someone, Washburn supposed his uncle, had loaned him clean clothes. His arms strained at the seams of his shirtsleeves. The two men contemplated each other, neither knowing what to say. James opened his mouth, perhaps to offer some word of gratitude for driving them to the doctor's office yesterday, but Washburn hoped that he wouldn't try. Finally they turned from each other toward the bed where Annie Clyde lay asleep with the child. "You can go ahead and wake my wife up. She's been waiting for you," James Dodson said. His eyes lingered a moment longer on his daughter, probably making sure she still breathed. "I believe I'll step out and see if I can find a cup of coffee. Can I bring you some?"

"No, thank you," Washburn said. "I won't stay long."

After James Dodson left the room, Washburn went around the bed. There was no other armchair near the window but he would have been uncomfortable sitting down anyway. He felt stiff, as if they were in church and not a hospital room. When he put his hand on the iron bed rail Annie Clyde opened her eyes. She smiled some when she saw him. Washburn had known that her face must hold expressions other than the fierceness she'd turned on him, but it took him aback nonetheless. She was pale and emaciated but he could still see in her the intimidating woman he'd met with a Winchester rifle propped in her reach. If she had seemed for a second to be made of water that first time Washburn saw her, this time she seemed made of light.

"Mr. Washburn," Annie Clyde said. "I'm glad you're still here."

"I had to see your daughter," he said, tearing his eyes away from her to look at the child. Maybe he had wanted more than believed Gracie Dodson to be alive but here she was, given back to her mother. It was a memory he would turn to in times of doubt, the two of them lying joined almost like one person. It would become his faith, that such things could and did happen.

"She's doing better," Annie Clyde said. "She's been trying to get up and see out the window." She paused, stroking the child's curls above the bandage. "The nurse offered to bring a crib in here but I told them I'd just keep her in the bed with me. I couldn't let go of her."

Washburn cleared his throat, feeling hoarse. "I'll bet they couldn't have made you."

Annie Clyde looked back up into Washburn's eyes, her smile still there but altered, tempered. "She won't even remember this. But I don't know when I'll ever get over it."

"Me, either," Washburn said. Then he had to turn his head away. He saw himself and the Dodsons reflected in the window glass and felt so out of place there that he knew he ought to be going. He stared through his reflection at the twinkling town, the streets two stories below overhung with power lines. No wonder the child wanted to look out. She had never seen electricity. That was another thing she wouldn't remember from her first three years. How black the night could get in Yuneetah, especially in winter, when he'd stayed too late after supper with one of the families. Annie Clyde wasn't made for electric light, despite how the lamp glow lit up her face. She might never get used to it. But her daughter would know nothing else.

Washburn was about to excuse himself from the room when he felt a feathery touch, a plucking at his finger on the bed rail. He turned from the window to see that the child's frail hand, the one with the tube attached and feeding water into her veins, had moved on top of his own. She was awake now, her head still lying on her mother's heart, her eye open under the bandage, glassy and peaked but also curious. Annie Clyde laughed a little. "She likes your ring."

Washburn looked down at it, the topaz stone gleaming, the band engraved with the year of his graduation from college. Nineteen thirty-three, the same year the child was born. Washburn thought of his father, who once came out with a lantern to save him from a flood. When he was small he used to be drawn to the glimmer of his father's wedding band. "Watch," Washburn said. He tugged off the class ring and spun it on the tray table across Annie Clyde's legs, a golden blur, until it wobbled to a stop and fell still with a clatter. The child watched as if witnessing a magic trick. After a moment Washburn took the ring from the tray and slipped it into the child's warm hand. "She can keep it," he told Annie Clyde.

"No, no," Annie Clyde said. "That's not necessary."

"I want you to have it," he said. "For her to have it, I mean."

Annie Clyde studied Washburn. "She can't thank you herself, so I'll have to."

This time Washburn held Annie Clyde's gaze. He wanted to remember the alignment of her features. He wanted to remember how it had felt when she leaned on him, her heat branding his arm. He would never see her again, but he might never stop thinking about her. What she had done to him was hard to sort out. When he returned from their first meeting he'd gone up to his room over the coffeehouse and thrown open the windows to let in the noise of the city, trying to shake the dust of Yuneetah off his shoes. But her presence had clung to him as if she'd followed him home. Something had shifted in him as he stood on Annie Clyde Dodson's porch, though he didn't know it a month ago. He went there to convince her to leave and somehow she convinced him instead. The removals were forcible evictions no matter how politely the TVA was going about them. He hadn't really seen the people of Yuneetah, had concentrated more on his notes about them, until Annie Clyde made him look at her. He hadn't listened to those he thought he was helping until she made him hear. Now he didn't know what he thought anymore. Maybe the chief was right. He was too young for a job this big. "I'd better let you sleep, Mrs. Dodson," he said.

But when he started away she stopped him. "Wait, Mr. Washburn," she said. "Your coat."

Annie Clyde glanced to the table by the bed and Washburn saw his suit coat folded there. When he picked it up dried clots of dirt pattered to the floor. "I'm afraid it's ruined," she said.

Washburn looked down at the coat, drew it to his stomach. "No," he said, his voice tight. "It's not." He hesitated then crossed the room and went out, shutting the door softly behind him.

Washburn's shoes squeaked again on the tiles as he passed other doors closed or ajar to show glimpses of convalescing patients inside, one man with his leg in a pulley. He nodded to a woman shuffling along in a robe and slippers, holding to the rail on the wall. When he went by the waiting room, having almost made it to the stairwell at the end of the hall, a short man in suspenders came out holding a stenographer's pad and a pencil. "Sam Washburn?" he asked.

Washburn thought of lying, but it wasn't in him. "Yes."

"I'm with the *Knoxville News Sentinel*," the man said. "Do you have a minute to talk?"

"It's after midnight," Washburn said. "I doubt you'll be making your deadline."

The man rubbed at his eye with the knuckle of the hand holding the pencil. It looked red and irritated. "I've been all over the place tonight, trying to find somebody that knows what's going on in Yuneetah," he said. "The sheriff has all of the roads into town blocked off."

Washburn looked over the shorter man's head toward the stairwell, wanting to get away. "I've been here with the family all night. I haven't been through Yuneetah since this morning."

"Do you know if the explosion at the dam and the missing child are related in any way?"

Washburn frowned at the reporter. "What happened to the dam?"

"Somebody blew a hole in it, is what happened. Aren't you with the TVA?"

Washburn blinked at him, trying to picture the structure as he'd last seen it when he visited the site, wearing a hard hat as he stood on the riverbank. Trying to imagine what must be going on at the offices where he'd spent much of the last two years. It all seemed distant. "I don't know anything about the dam," Washburn said. He passed a hand over his unshaved face. "But I can tell you about the child. Her name is Mary Grace Dodson. They call her Gracie." He paused, watching the reporter scribble on his pad. "Every newspaper in the country will be wanting to know her name," he said. "You'd do well to get it right." Then Washburn took his coat on down the hall, his blue eyes focused straight ahead.

JULY 31, 1937

S he'd seen the explosion from the ridge last summer. She had gone back up there from the courthouse unable to face the shack where she once lived with Mary. On that lonesome evening Silver would have taken even the company of her grandmother. But there was only her niece's dog. He lay panting beside her on the ledge where she sat with her knees gathered up when the blast came not long after sundown, a flash then a thunderclap that she felt in her chest. She leapt to her feet and the dog began to bark. Near the bottom of the spillway slant she saw a plume spouting, then a sooty billow charging out into the river and the trees on both shores. Behind that gush of smoke and silt the impounded waters came crashing. Silver could hear the rending sounds of what the unleashed river took with it, churning out of its banks around the bend, roiling with saplings and rubble. Then from the gorge a cloud rose against the evening sky, hiding the site and the bluffs from view. In the aftermath of all that there came an ominous silence. When the cloud settled in the tops of the trees Silver saw that the blast had made its own wind through the pass, blowing leaves and wisps of smoke as darkness claimed the valley again. She saw as well from her perch on the limestone ledge, with her limbs locked and her eyes staring out of their sockets, that the two-hundred-foot concrete wall of the dam was still standing.

The weather this July had been different than last. There was a drought instead of rain. Silver's cornstalks were husks, her cucumbers shriveled. Her green beans never came up at all. The withered leaves of the trees topping the bluffs were tattered and bug-bitten since the locusts and beetles had been driven up from the valley to higher ground. As parched as the land was on the mountain, below it was all covered with water. Silver had gone to the market a week after the blast and bought a newspaper. She'd traded mink hides for coffee and had a nickel left over. She could decipher enough to understand. Maybe one of the charges had failed to detonate, or Amos hadn't placed them right. There had been a crack made, a leak spraying lake water over into the river, swelling it out of its banks. There was damage done but not enough to derail the power company for long. Silver had wanted to see the crack up close but while the repair was under way nobody was allowed within a mile of the site. The freight trucks returned, the calling men on scaffolds, the clang of machinery. When the grit settled again for the last time the lake went on spreading. Now at dusk down there at the dam the lights came on. She could see them shining out of the charred and broken treetops with their own cold beauty to rival the stars and the moon.

She didn't want to think Amos died for nothing. Maybe he was sending a message to those who thought they owned everything. Or to the people of Yuneetah who always turned their heads. They couldn't look away from him now. The story of the man who blew a hole in the dam and the little girl resurrected from the ground made the newspapers not just in Knoxville but all over the country. Amos hadn't meant to bring the wall down. He had only wanted to be heard.

Amos had left behind no body and so it was easy for Silver to imagine him going on out there somewhere, as he had always gone on. But no. He and Mary, the two people that had known her best, both were dead. The dog was her only companion. He didn't hold it against her that she'd kept him penned up in the shed last summer. He hadn't left her side since he followed her from the Walker farm to the courthouse after watching the government man drive off with his owners.

```
CANYON WAY BOOKSTORE
07/18/16   01:56   E      0      3022

   READ TO YOURSELF! -- READ TO A CHILD!
           RETURNS ACCEPTED  FOR
STORE CREDIT ONLY-NO CASH/CREDIT REFUNDS




CANYON WAY BOOKSTORE
07/18/16   02:12   E      0      3022
   1@  16.00 9780312150600   $     16.00
           BEHIND THE SCENE
   1@  15.95 9780307476876   $     15.95
           LONG MAN  */R
SUBTOTAL         0000105011   $     31.95
TOTAL                         $     31.95
TENDER Cash                   $     31.95
/------------------------------------\
|      BOOK CLUB AWARD STATUS        |
|      10 UNITS   $  177.77          |
\------------------------------------/

   READ TO YOURSELF! -- READ TO A CHILD!
           RETURNS ACCEPTED  FOR
STORE CREDIT ONLY-NO CASH/CREDIT REFUNDS
```

It had taken Silver a while to get used to him and his needs, nosing at her hands to be petted. She'd resisted at first but finally allowed him to sniff and then to lick her fingers. Soon she'd begun to stroke his head, to study his lively brown eyes. She had come to depend on his presence. She used her voice more often with the dog around, talking and singing to him while she worked up at the still. She was supposed to keep him only until the Dodsons got settled somewhere. Now she hoped if they ever came back it would be to visit and not to take him.

Other than the dog, Silver had the mountain to herself. For a year she'd kept away from Beulah Kesterson, unable to bear her grief. She hadn't visited the cabin but she saw Beulah once. Silver was pulling weeds from around Mary's headstone last fall when Beulah came up the hollow footpath leading a nanny goat with a bell around its neck. Silver figured she'd bought it to have milk through winter. She stood at the graveyard gate and watched Beulah pass but in the end she didn't call out. Beulah's eyes were on her feet, her hair unbraided and unwashed. Losing Amos had nearly done her in. But it was a favorable sign, that Beulah seemed prepared to survive.

Silver hadn't spoken to Ellard Moody either since the day Gracie was found, the day she'd turned Amos loose. But she knew Ellard had moved back into the frame house where he used to live with his parents. He'd been improving the place. Curtains had gone up in the windows. The lot was mown, humped with piles of milkweed-fluffed grasses. She had walked down to see it last September, taking a shortcut through the blackberry canes, stopping at the edge of the woods when she saw smoke threading up from the chimney. She'd figured Ellard was inside cooking his supper. There were a few banty hens scratching in the dirt around Ellard's porch and she wondered if he had fixed up the coop where they once lay together. She'd seen his flannel shirt hanging on the clothesline and wondered what he would do if she took it down and carried it in to him. One day Silver thought she might approach the door and knock. Or maybe she never would. Ellard could have come up the mountain to see her anytime in all of these decades.

Not too long afterward Silver and the dog had set out elsewhere. She'd seen James Dodson at the end of August, when he came back to the Walker farm for the rest of their belongings, before the water had washed out the main road in from Whitehall County. He told her where he and Annie Clyde and Gracie were moving, the name of the road they would live on. He said Ellard had found them a farm about twenty miles from Yuneetah, a community somewhere between Whitehall County and Clinchfield called Caney Fork. It seemed Ellard had a first cousin who'd decided to sell his fifteen acres and take up coal mining in West Virginia. When James told Silver the Dodsons were staying in the valley after all, he'd looked resigned. There wasn't much light in his eyes. Even his hair didn't seem as bright. He'd given up the chance to have a different life with his wife and child in a northern city. But at least he still had them.

Last October Silver had traveled out to that farm in Caney Fork Ellard had found for the Dodsons. She'd told her niece that she didn't think she could look her in the face again. She had believed her own words when she said them. She hadn't even gone to the hospital where she knew Gracie was recovering. But as the weeks passed with both Amos and Mary dead all Silver could think about was Annie Clyde and Gracie, alive only twenty miles south of Yuneetah. She had to see them at least once more. She and the dog had made it most of ten miles on foot, then the other ten a friendly man stopped to let them ride in the back of his Willys truck. Something she would never have done a year ago. All things changed it seemed, even Silver.

On the road to the house crimson leaves fluttered around her. The fields were flaxen with rolled hay. There was enough frost in the air to wear her shawl. She stopped at the post fence around the lot when she saw the name on the mailbox, as the dog went on through the open gate. The house was smaller than their old one but the paint was fresh, shutters the same color as the rusty roof. Leaves littered its peak and drifted around the chimney, swaying down from a hackberry tree. Through a front window she saw a lightbulb burning. Then she was caught off guard when Annie Clyde came around the side of the house with Gracie, the child lugging a bucket of water. Annie Clyde halted at the porch corner, her smile faltering. With her eyes on Silver she took the bucket as the dog ran to lick the child's face. If Gracie had any scars outside or in, Silver couldn't see them from the road. She let out a breath she'd been holding for months it seemed when she heard Gracie laughing. She braced herself before passing through the gate and across the yard. Annie Clyde watched Silver come to the side of the porch, her expression hard to read. "Hey, Silver," she said. "Did you walk all the way out here?" Silver knew then that Annie Clyde would pretend to have forgotten their conversation that night in Mary's bedroom. They would both pretend. Silver could have wept. "Not all the way," she said.

Annie Clyde gave Silver a drink of water from the bucket and once she'd drained the dipper they went out to see the lay of the land. Gracie went with them but didn't acknowledge Silver. She might have remembered Silver taking her dog, or she might have grown more shy of strangers. She had gotten bigger in the short time since Silver saw her last. Her legs were too long for her dress. Her hair was longer, too, dark curls piled on her shoulders like Annie Clyde's. But she must have still been a handful for her mother. There were scrapes on her shins, dirt on her knees, as if she'd been exploring her new place. The plot was flatter than what the Dodsons had farmed in Yuneetah, sloping gently behind the house to a stream that trickled through a tract of bur oaks separating their property from a neighbor's. Annie Clyde showed off her garden and the field where she was thinking of growing tobacco. She could farm fifteen acres by herself while James worked at the steam plant that had opened up on the river in Whitehall County. Even as she spoke to Silver of these things her hazel eyes followed the child, letting Gracie roam but keeping track of her. When they got to the stream Gracie crouched, wetting her shoes and the seat of her bloomers, where the edge of the bank shone yellowish with mica like the shoals of the river. Gracie picked up a piece of the fool's gold that always reminded Silver of her mother and of playing in the water with Mary. "I found this," she said, holding it up to shimmer in the sun.

"Me and your granny had a jar full of that," Silver said. "You didn't know her."

Silver glanced over then and caught Annie Clyde's attention. They didn't say it but Silver knew they were both thinking about that February night they'd sat up together watching the person they both loved most in the world pass out of it. After a while they started back to the house without speaking, the dog leaping alongside Gracie, chasing the stick she held high over her head. When they got to the porch Silver and Annie Clyde sat down on the steps as the child and the dog went off romping. Silver looked out across the yard toward the road and the loblolly pines on the other side, these not hiding Long Man behind them. A panel truck passed by and the driver raised his hand to Annie Clyde. Silver could see sitting close to her niece on the porch that her eyes had dimmed somewhat, like her husband's. But she had put on weight and there was no way to tell that her foot was ever afflicted. Silver noticed, too, the small hole in the toe of one of the girl's shoes. The fraying hem of her shift. Electricity couldn't put right everything wrong in this valley. Silver could have told the Dodsons that much if they'd asked her opinion. They would still struggle, but she guessed they'd make it together. Not alone, like her. Silver bit her lip, reluctant to say why she'd come, but considering how devoted the dog and the child remained to each other she had no choice. "I figured she'd be missing Rusty by now," Silver told Annie Clyde. Hearing his name, the dog left Gracie and loped over to Silver wagging his tail, nudging his nose into her lap. Silver took his head in her hands and scratched his ears.

After a moment Annie Clyde said, "Maybe you can keep him."

Silver's fingers stopped scratching. "What about Gracie?"

Annie Clyde looked at her daughter in the yard, plucking butter-cups from the browning grass. "She'll have some company," Annie Clyde said. She took Silver's hand and placed it on the warmth of her belly. "I'm not far along, but I can tell."

Silver left soon after that, unable to think or know how to feel about what Annie Clyde had told her. About this coming baby whose voice she wouldn't hear drifting up to her from the farm. A child she might never lay eyes on. Now that she was satisfied her kin were all right she wouldn't have cause to travel again. She'd go back up the mountain and live out her days, content to see no more of the country-side than what was visible from the ridge. It was late October and dark fell early. As she walked back along the dusty roads meander-ing out of Caney Fork lights came on in the houses. There was one made of river rock set closer to the path and Silver peered into its window when she stopped to dig a pebble out of her shoe. Through the parted curtains she saw a framed portrait of Franklin Roosevelt hanging over a mantelpiece. She wondered if this family had come from Yuneetah, forced off their land like the Dodsons. Silver hadn't seen James that afternoon. He was gone to work at the steam plant. But she imagined he might hang up such a picture if his wife would allow it. Maybe one of these days Annie Clyde would be willing to let him. Once Silver had dumped out the pebble jabbing her foot sole, she went on. The dog ranged ahead or lagged behind, sniffing the corpse of a mole or snapping at the gypsy moths that fluttered up from the weedy ditches. But he always came back to her side.

That autumn Silver and the dog watched from the ridge overlook-ing the valley as the water came to drown her niece's farm. It felt to Silver as though somebody ought to bear witness. She and Rusty were the only ones who saw it come. It advanced over the fields laid out in patches of green from pale to the near black of the hemlocks, crossing abandoned property lines marked off with stone or rail fences. It moved in falls and fingers and ponds giving back the sun, pouring into the basin between the bluffs topped with pines. Each evening it drew a little closer, until it sampled the crumbles of soil between the corn rows and the long grasses of the yard. It went sucking lead from the painted porch steps and sliding underneath where the dog used to pant in the cool dirt. Stripping off scales of peeling clapboard as it rose up the outer walls onto the porch where a pair of boots were left. These the current lifted, laces floating among the white specks of the snowball bushes as it entered through the cracked front door. Stealing inside like an intruder with a whine of corroded hinges. Swirling over the threshold and washing into the front room across the floorboards smudged by decades of brogans hauling eggs in from the coop and buckets from the spring. Lapping over the ashy hearth of the fireplace and up the chimney. Seeping into the wallpaper and flooding the stairs, trailing the banisters with strands of algae. Overflowing the upper room of the house where one had died and another was born, carp swimming between the maple bedposts. Streaming out the kitchen door and across the back lot past the shading elm, rushing in to fill the barn stalls. Leaking into the knotholes of the smokehouse boards, trickling through the hayfield weeds to climb the bark of the apple tree with a few last fruits clinging to its limbs. Until the still and fathomless depths of the lake covered all forty of the Walker farm's acres. Until there was nothing left to see but miles and miles of blue.

Acknowledgments

Much appreciation to Robin Desser, Leigh Feldman, Stephanie Perryman, Terri Beth Miller, Sara Sparkes Hill, Carl Greene, Silas House, Jill McCorkle and Joe Schuster. Special thanks to my beloveds, Adam, Emma and Taylor Greene.